SENTIENT BEING

To my friends—
This one is for you.

"Out beyond ideas of wrongdoing and
rightdoing there is a field.
I'll meet you there."
-Rumi

Part One:

Separation

and

Captivity

Chapter One

Bray

June 2040

Reality sank in. Bray Hoffman's entire life was turned upside down in two months' time. And clearly not for the better.

Bray lay on her side, staring at the wall across from her. Her twin-sized bed was about as hard as packed earth. It smelled of stale cigarettes and something unbearably sweet. The pillow was like a stranger she wished she didn't have to get to know. And though she stared at the wall, its concrete bricks the color of eggshells, it wasn't the wall she was watching.

Bray's mind carried her backwards, to the events of the last week, and held there. Her thoughts fixated on the plan she'd carried out, along with her friends Kage and Elliott, to link U.S. citizens to the sensations experienced by individual cows headed to slaughter. They set up the link via the citizens' 4-D Embedicare implants. Embedicare had created a microscopic computer chip that could be surgically inserted into a user's forearm. The chip used radio-frequency identification, or RFID, to pick up Embedicare satellite signals in order to alert the user of important notifications such as criminal activity. In addition, users had the option to purchase advanced 4-D models that set off shocks and various sensations in the embedded implant, giving the user sensory experiences when watching the news, television or films. With the help of Elliott, who had experience hacking corporate databases, Bray broke into Embedicare's national system and controlled it, all with the power of her mind, and linking people—those using the Embedicare 4-D implants—to the terrified cows. The plan had worked, creating awareness of the horrors of factory farming in particular and the slaughtering of animals for food in general. Bray learned later, though, that they had caused thousands of people throughout the nation to panic, succumb to fear, and in some cases, end up in the hospital. Miraculously no one was killed or severely harmed in the process, but people feared terrorism, and this fear shook the nation for days. For all she knew, the country was still bouncing back from what was now being referred to as "the Embedicare takeover."

A buzzer shocked her out of her mental processing. That meant it was 6 a.m., time to wake up. She knew this because yesterday, when she was admitted to this state prison somewhere in Arizona, they'd given her an entire orientation to her rights as a prisoner, her schedule, an ID badge, a uniform, and assigned her to a unit where she would remain for an unknown amount of time.

Bray sat up, unwillingly, and stared at the cell door. It was steel and encased in that drab eggshell color. All the walls were the same. The narrow, six-by-eight-foot space was equipped with the bed, a chair and desk small enough for a child, and a window that looked out at sky and land.

The sun had already started its rise. It was far on the other side of the prison, but as Bray came to her feet, she saw how its light rested along miles and miles of empty desert beyond her window.

There was nothing out there.

Bray made her bed as she had been instructed to do. She turned and stood beside it, facing the wall. A mild scent of urine emanated from the toilet that popped out from the far wall, across from the bed. She stared at it. It gave her goosebumps, the way it was exposed, with no enclosure. It made her feel unsafe.

The cell door clicked open. A guard entered. Six feet tall, clean-shaven, dark buzz cut. His uniform was completely black, reminiscent of those worn by S-Corp security guards. Bray would know. Her mother, the woman responsible for locking her away in here, was one of S-Corp's regional presidents. S-Corp, short for Sustainability Corporation, was the multi-trillion-dollar company that controlled the nation's food and water supply.

Her mother. Bray recalled the night before, telling her mother they were estranged as far as Bray was concerned. Her mother had said nothing in response. Nothing.

"Did you hear me?" the guard asked.

Bray looked up at him. His name badge read *Steve*.

"Sorry, what was that?"

"Make sure you check the bulletin board. Your interview is this morning."

The guard proceeded to check her cell, as the guards were instructed to do every morning at wake time, and then left.

Bray exhaled. She sat back down on the bed. The khaki shirt they'd given her made her back itch. She scratched her back, then turned and noticed the cell door was still open. She had no idea what prison was really like, but she assumed she'd be locked in a cell except for meal time or recreation.

She rose to her feet, found her pair of shoes and socks sitting at the end of the bed. Pulling them on, she walked out into the hall. It didn't seem as confining as she'd remembered it from the night before. Maybe because it was daylight? The walls were charcoal gray. Along the ceiling, the fluorescent lighting made her sick to her stomach.

Female prisoners began forming a single line along the wall. Bray followed suit, got in between two of the women. The one standing behind her, a thin, middle-aged woman with pale blue eyes, nodded and offered a smile that implied to Bray that she felt sorry for the girl. As Bray watched the prisoners exit their cells, about thirty of them in this unit, Bray was not surprised to see she was the only minor.

The cafeteria was one vast, open room, nearly the size of a gymnasium. There were more tables than she could count, all round with stainless-steel tops and stools bolted into the linoleum floor. Along the far wall, a series of barred windows barely let in the daylight. Food sat in vats beneath a glass shield, like a buffet, and behind it, prisoners wearing hair nets divided out portions onto plates and handed the plates off to prisoners who stood in line. On either side and adjacent to the buffet were smaller bars, one hot, one cold, containing side items such as toast, hash browns and fruit.

Bray collected a tray of food from the main line and sat down among fifty or so other prisoners. She avoided eye contact with those around her. She did not wish to be seen or heard or spoken to.

Admittedly, she was afraid.

She stared at her tray. The food consisted of scrambled eggs, oatmeal and a cup of milk one of the kitchen staff made her take.

No thanks, she thought.

Bray had selected a bowl of fruit from the cold bar, and this would be her breakfast. Her stomach was empty and absent of appetite. She made herself eat the cut-up bananas, strawberries and melon. She wondered where it came from. All S-Corp lab-grown food, she figured.

It didn't take long before prisoners began exiting. They all had jobs, and Bray would be required to work, too. She figured today's interview, which was scheduled right after breakfast, would be about that.

The temperature in the prison remained consistently cool. Bray did not like it. The shirt they'd given her was short-sleeved and not enough to comfort her from the air that pushed out through vents in the walls. Along her left arm, the sleeve of her shirt rubbed up against her forearm while she sat. The shirt was a little too big for her, but it was the smallest they had.

As the edge of the sleeve rubbed along her skin, her forearm began to itch. Having finished her fruit, she dropped her fork and began scratching her arm. She looked down at it, rubbing the area where, only days ago, she had willingly injected herself with an Embedicare 4-D implant as part of her attempt—working with Kage and Elliott—to bring down S-Corp.

The area around the implant began to warm.

And then it began to vibrate.

"Shit," Bray whispered.

Bray slid both arms under the table and

continued to watch as prisoners exited the cafeteria. She had no idea if these prisoners also had implants, but she didn't want to draw attention to herself. She glanced up at the clock above the exit. It showed 6:45 a.m. She had fifteen minutes to get to her interview in the Health Services Department, and she had no clue where that was.

Her arm vibrated again. The vibration rolled through her bloodstream, up her arm, into her shoulder. It hurt.

Then she began hearing voices.

Chapter Two

Bray

"You're late."

Bray stood at the door of an office in the Health Services Department, which she found only by the help of one of the unit staff. Sitting at a desk facing the door was an older man, perhaps in his fifties, wearing square black glasses. His dark hair waved back into curls behind his ears. He had a goatee and, along his cheeks, a five o'clock shadow, and Bray saw a Bluetooth device in his ear. He was not smiling. As a matter of fact, his face was expressionless. Had it not been for the navy-blue button-up t-shirt with what appeared to be pink flowers plastered all over it, Bray would've thought him to be a stiff. And maybe he was.

"Sorry. I'm still finding my way around," she replied, remaining at the door.

"Understandable. Try to be on time. They'll ding you for it moving forward," he said, glancing up at her. "Have a seat."

Bray stepped into the office. She stood on a light-blue rug that covered much of the tile floor and stopped a foot from the wall where bookshelves held stacks of books on psychology, mental illness and the like.

So it was that kind of interview.

"My name is Jacob Stalzky," the man said, standing up. He picked up the laptop and came around the deep wood desk, its surface empty save for one ballpoint pen and a notepad. "I'm the unit psychiatrist."

Jacob set the laptop down on one of the chairs. Passing Bray, he closed the door, turned and plopped down into one of two chocolate-colored lounge chairs, facing her.

"Come have a seat," he said, waving her over.

Bray shrugged, sat down across from him. He was a bulky man with broad shoulders. His eyes, as she looked at them more closely, were a soft hazel. If she weren't a lesbian, she might've found him attractive for an old guy.

"We do interviews for all the new people. It's a chance for us to talk, to see how I can help you," Jacob began.

A series of thoughts ran through Bray's mind. *It's going to happen again. . .I just know it. . .*

Bray recognized the voice in her head immediately.

It was a woman by the name of Dawn Harpender, one of the hundreds of citizens Bray had connected to during the Embedicare takeover. Bray had linked Dawn to a cow on its way to slaughter so Dawn could experience the animal's terror. Now Bray was hearing Dawn's thoughts, and what was more. . .a wave of fear jolted her. That was *Dawn's* fear.

"Bray?" Jacob's voice, deep and monotone, brought Bray back to the room. "Are you here with me?"

That was an odd question.

"Yes," she replied, clearing her throat.

"I was asking how things have been, since you arrived."

"Fine," she answered quickly. Her main interest was in these voices she was hearing in the back of her mind.

"I want to ask some questions. That

okay?"

"Sure." She'd been interviewed by enough psychiatrists to know the drill. She'd have to answer in such a way as to show she was of stable and clear mind, so they wouldn't place her back on medication.

Maybe we should leave. . .move down to Mexico. Probably safer there than in the U.S.

Mateo Perez. The name floated through her memory with ease. Bray was astonished. How clearly she could hear the voices of the people whose minds she had touched. Had that only been five days ago? Now the implant warmed her arm again and the warmth moved up into her shoulder and down into her chest. A wave of nausea swept through her. She felt sweaty.

"Are you okay?" Jacob asked.

"They put me in prison. How would I be okay?" Bray asked, defenses up.

"Of course. Let's get you some water," Jacob replied. He stared at her while lifting a finger to his ear, pressing into the Bluetooth.

"This is Jacob. Can you please bring a cup of water? I'm in here with Bray Hoffman."

Jacob clicked the Bluetooth again.

"I've been looking through your file," he said. "Looks like you've had quite the history in and out of psychiatric wards. . .since you were a kid."

"Yes," Bray said, trying to focus. Trying to keep the voices at bay.

*I need to talk to Emerson. What if he doesn't want to talk? I just want to see him again. . .*Somehow Bray knew this was Elisha Andrews.

How many was she linked to, Bray wondered, panic growing. This had never happened before. In the past she had only been able to link with animals and only one at a time, never a human. But that was without the implant. She glanced down at her arm, then up at Jacob. His eyes were on her. She crossed her arms to hide the implant.

"And you escaped Denver Health about two months ago?" Jacob added, glancing down at the laptop screen. "At some point I'd love to talk more about this. . .this Embedicare takeover you were a part of."

"Do we really have to talk about my past?" Bray asked. She didn't want to think about all the times her parents placed her in the hospital when she refused to take her medication. And she especially didn't want to talk about the takeover. Not with this guy, someone she knew would never believe her.

"The past helps inform the present," he replied. "Besides, I want to understand what happened. I'm here to help."

"You're here to help, or you're here to place me on meds?"

Suddenly there was a knock. Jacob shifted in his chair.

"Come in," he said.

A guard delivered a clear glass of water.

Bray drank the water, found she was a bit parched, after all. It did help ease her stomach.

"I get the impression you don't think you need medication," Jacob replied.

"I do not," she said simply.

They're freaking out for the wrong reasons. . .That was Tim Saffi. A guy who. . .wasn't concerned about terrorism so much as he was. . . climate change. How did she know these things? About other people? Complete strangers?

The room began to spin. Bray's eyes

followed the spinning, up along the shelves behind Jacob, where plants hung from the tops of the shelves, draping downward toward the floor. Then over to a tall, clouded window that let in natural light without providing any clue as to what was outside. A muffled sound jumped into her ears, then escaped. Bray's body felt both cold and sweaty. The implant pulsed in her arm, rather painfully.

"Bray? You with me?" Jacob's voice came through, but barely.

"What's that?" Bray asked.

"I was asking about your symptoms. Looks like the chart your previous psychiatrist sent over has you marked for hearing voices, hallucinations? Can you tell me more?"

"What's-" Bray started. She meant to say: "What's the point?" but instead, when her mouth opened, nausea stormed up into her throat so strongly that she had no choice but to bend over and expel vomit onto Jacob's nice rug.

Chapter Three

Bertan

Bertan Duarte sat alone among a sea of strangers and they should not have been strangers. They were all undocumented, like himself. All of them had brown skin, black skin. They were mothers, children, fathers, men.

Bertan deserved this. Hundreds of hours spent knocking cows in an S-Corp slaughterhouse—placing that knock gun between their eyes and knocking them unconscious to prepare them for slaughter—coupled with the years of violence he committed prior to that, it had all led him here.

A buzzer went off. Across from the bench on which he sat, a group of men huddled on another bench and stared up at the ceiling. Behind them, rows and rows of people, all from Latin America, Bertan surmised, awaited a similar fate.

Voices bounced in and out of his ears, too many to count. All in Spanish: what is happening, when are we getting out of here, where are we? More questions than answers. Bertan made every effort to keep his mind and his body in the same place. He did this by counting the people in the detention facility. Not the guards, who stood along the walls and watched as if this was some circus, but the imprisoned. Thirty in his square encasement alone. Then another fifty in the next group. Some were hard to count, given that the children and women were lying atop aluminum blankets on the floor, women holding children, rocking back and forth. Bertan knew the smell of fear, and he smelled it here.

Another buzz. The men around him stood. Bertan did the same. A pair of guards approached the fence and unlocked the entrance. Bertan remained at the very back of the crowd, watching as the guards began cuffing the men at their wrists and ankles, the women at their wrists, and leaving the children untouched.

Bertan gulped. He counted his breathing, a technique his friend Ruben had taught him. A guard approached, wearing a black uniform with a bullet-proof vest and the I.C.E insignia—a white circle with a blue eagle in the center and the words "U.S. Department of Homeland Security"—posted on his upper arm.

"Hands," the guard said.

Bertan held out his hands, allowing the guard to cuff his wrists. He watched the crowd as guards slowly corralled everyone out of the center in a single line. The guard cuffed his ankles, a two-foot chain linking his wrists with his ankles. He had to drop his hands to prevent himself from tripping.

"Let's move," the guard said, stepping to the side. Bertan got in line.

They shuffled out, emptying the cage in which they had waited, Bertan feeling an odd sense of familiarity. He'd experienced this before, only then he had not been the one corralled.

Chapter Four

Bray

When morning came, Bray was lying in a hospital bed. The sound of nearby beeping brought her slowly into waking. Groggy, she gradually opened her eyes. Everything was blurry. She blinked a few times until the room came into view. Last she remembered, she threw up in the psychiatrist's office. Lifting her head slightly, she looked around for staff. A strong scent of chemicals mixed with body odor inflamed her nostrils.

The room felt closed in, not that this surprised her. She was in prison, after all. The room was narrow, and at the other end she could see a set of double doors. Between her and the doors lay an array of hospital beds, some empty, some holding prisoners who were asleep or reading. Beside each bed was a table covered in medicine bottles, cups and garbage. Bray glanced over and saw the table beside her bed was empty.

No curtains or walls separated the prisoners from one another. No privacy. She cringed at this. She shifted in bed, remaining lying down, and looked in the opposite direction, away from the doors. She saw a sectioned-off space with a desk and a laptop. Bray could see a nurse speaking with the psychiatrist. They both glanced her direction. Bray quickly closed her eyes. She didn't want to be bothered or prodded. Maybe if they thought she was asleep, they'd leave. Why had she thrown up, and why had she been hearing so many voices? Since she'd awoken, the voices had remained mute.

Her eyes kept closed, Bray heard footsteps coming toward the bed. She recognized the voice of the psychiatrist, Jacob. The nurse's voice was rough, unappealing.

They continued talking.

"Did you find anything else?" Jacob asked.

"Nope. Just dehydrated, that's all. Blood work is good. She must've come down with a 24-hour bug," the nurse replied.

Bray continued to lie there, feigning sleep. She gathered they'd taken her blood the night prior. This explained the bandage she could feel covering the inner elbow of her right arm. There was a brief pause in their conversation. Bray listened attentively, waiting for them to walk away.

"I just don't understand why they'd place her in this prison," Jacob said. "She's just a minor."

"Yeah, but she's also a terrorist."

"I don't know," Jacob said, his voice trailing off and then coming back. "Seems to me she would be better served in a mental health facility. Not here."

Another pause. Bray didn't like the sound of that pause. But if they did transfer her to a facility with less security, maybe she could escape like she had in Denver.

"Be careful, doctor," the nurse replied. "Remember the last time you had too much compassion for a prisoner?"

Intrigued, Bray did all she could to keep her eyes closed, to pretend she was asleep and not listening.

"Is there such a thing?" Jacob asked.

"I never forget these are

prisoners. . .criminals," the nurse
replied.

"They're also humans."

Bray heard Jacob exhale. She felt his
energy near her bed. She felt the nurse's
energy too, but it wasn't the nurse she was
curious about.

"I need to complete my
evaluation. . .before we can put her on
meds," Jacob spoke. "Let me know when she's
awake and stable. I'll come back and finish
it here."

With that, Bray listened as they moved
away. She lay there, opened her eyes, and
stared blankly at the ceiling. The voices
in her head returned. They were the same
voices as before: civilians processing what
happened after the Embedicare takeover.
They sounded like voices, but they felt
more like racing thoughts, and Bray
gathered that the country remained under a
terror threat and people were not permitted
to leave their homes, unless they were city
or government employees or "essential
workers."

Bray continued to listen, this time more
astutely, less fearfully. She wanted to
learn all she could about what was
happening before they placed her on a
medication, which she was certain they
would do.

#

That afternoon, Jacob returned to
interview Bray. Best to get it over with,
she knew. She didn't like being stuck in
this bed, unable to walk around. Her cell
wasn't much, but at least there she could
be alone.

"Feeling better?" Jacob asked. He sat in
a metal chair beside her table, where the
nurse had left a cup of water and a banana.
Bray had finished the cup of water and had

yet to touch the fruit. She still didn't feel much like eating.

"Yes," she replied. The bed had been adjusted so she could sit up, the pillow supporting her head. From this angle she noticed restraints on either side of the bed, and she was grateful for the freedom of her hands.

"I'd like to finish our interview. That okay?"

"Do I have a choice?" Bray asked, her mouth dry.

"No," Jacob snickered.

Past Jacob's head, a prisoner was being assisted out of bed by two nurses. She was bald. The skin of her arms was wrinkled and covered in tattoos. As she came up to sit, her gown revealed the upper part of her back where a tattoo read ALWAYS VEE. Bray wondered what the "Vee" stood for.

"Let me start by asking you about your symptoms," Jacob said, holding a pad of yellow paper, pen in hand.

Bray's eyes gravitated back to him, away from the elderly prisoner who was gently being moved into a wheelchair. How they could justify keeping such old people in prisons, she did not know.

"In the last twenty-four hours, have you had any hallucinations?"

"No," Bray replied quickly. She found this to be trite.

"Hearing any voices?"

Bray shot a glance at Jacob. If only he knew. If only he could really get inside her head, understand that the people in her head were more than voices. The citizens she listened to were legitimate, frightened people. Men, women, some young, all older than her, with lives and families and partners. Most of them expressed how they'd nearly lost their lives in the chaos, confused as to why Embedicare would force them to endure the slaughter of cows. Puzzled by what seemed so random. Their thoughts bounced back and forth from memories of the slaughter to a barrage of concerns about S-Corp. Had the eco-terrorists been telling the truth all along?

Oh. . .if Jacob only knew.

"No," she said finally. "No voices."

"Hmm." He nodded, jotted something down on his notepad. "Can I ask you about the Embedicare takeover?"

"Sure, but you won't believe anything I have to say about it."

"You don't think so?"

"Nope," Bray replied simply.

"Why's that?"

"No one in the medical community has ever believed me."

Jacob made another note.

"What have they said?" he asked. He leaned back in the chair, crossed his legs as if he were at a social gathering.

"You know what they've said. You've read my file."

"That you have schizophrenia?"

Bray nodded.

"And you disagree," he said, almost as a question, but it came off as a statement.

"I do."

Another note. Every time he marked something on his notepad, it was a mark against her. There was no winning in these games.

"Tell me what happened with the takeover. Your side of the story," he said, changing the subject.

"What do you want to know?" she asked, shrugging. She didn't much want to talk about what had happened. She was still trying to sort through it herself.

"What made you decide to do it?"

"Do what?"

Jacob's chest rose and fell. She sensed he was getting frustrated.

"The video."

"I wanted the country to know the truth."

"That S-Corp lied?"

"Yes."

Jacob uncrossed his legs. He leaned forward, scribbling more on the notepad.

"I saw the video. How were you able to make it, and then upload it onto Embedicare's system like that?"

"This sounds like an interrogation," Bray said.

Suddenly a voice bounced into her mind, more prominent than the others, which had quelled to insignificant whispers during her conversation with the psychiatrist. The thought she heard now was from Tim, something about how he was beginning to think Bray Hoffman was right. . .that there was no "terrorist attack." She found herself fixating on it as it repeated in her mind. It was the first time she'd heard someone express support for what she and Kage and Elliott had done.

"Sorry," Jacob replied. "Believe it or not, this does help me understand."

"What do you want to understand?" Bray snapped. She'd been alert long enough for her empty stomach to begin growling. That banana waited for her on the bedside table, but she didn't want to eat while sitting here with Jacob. She wanted to eat alone.

"I'm trying to sort out your current symptoms. . .so I can determine how much dosage you need."

"You mean medication?" she asked, unsurprised.

"Yes."

Bray didn't know what to say. Tim's voice in her mind continued: *I don't even feel like I can talk to anyone about this. . .people are going to think I'm crazy if I tell them this wasn't some terrorist attack.*

"Your blood work came back and it's all good. You haven't been on meds for, what? About a month or longer?"

"Sounds about right," Bray said, though she was lying. It had been longer than that. When she'd been in Denver Health's youth psychiatric unit, she was able to purge the pills they gave her, and then she had escaped.

"And since then, you escaped Denver Health, went on the run with this. . .what was his name?"

"Elliott. He was my friend." Bray's eyes turned down. How she missed her friends, not just Elliott but also the ones she had lived with in Meeteetse. If only she could hear their thoughts now, to know they were okay.

"Was?" Jacob asked, pulling her back to the present.

Bray did not reply, and she didn't feel she had to. What would they do to her if she didn't complete the interview that was any worse than what they'd already done?

"Right, sore subject, I gather. We can talk about that another time," Jacob said. "As I was saying. . .you ran off with Elliott, were somehow able to get past the border from Colorado into Wyoming, and if I remember from your file, a Marshal was killed after an encounter with subjects matching your description and Elliott's, and then you somehow just. . .disappeared off the grid. Next thing we know, you're doing this video and then the whole nation goes dark."

"What are you trying to say?" Bray asked, her back tense.

"Nothing at all. Just want to know if I have that right, or if you want to add anything I might be missing."

Bray took a deep breath. She looked closely at Jacob, his eyes currently darker beneath lackluster overhead lighting. What was it going to matter, if she lied or told him the truth? He would not believe one or the other more fully, so why not tell him what really happened?

"I escaped Denver Health because I was wrongly diagnosed, and my parents refused to listen to me. Elliott was my only friend at that time, and he agreed to take me with him up north, to get out of the state, so we went together. We got stopped at the border. A band of wild horses came running through the area, and we happened to break free from the Marshals there. I knew that if I went back home, my parents would put me in the hospital again. Do you know what that's like? Have you ever been locked up?"

Jacob shook his head.

"I'll tell you this: I've been locked up more times than I haven't, and I am only seventeen. And now my mother put me in here, in prison!" Bray stopped, mostly for effect, but also because she noticed Jacob's eyes, the way they rose and his eyebrows lifted above his glasses, indicating surprise.

"That's right," she continued. "My mom brought me to this prison. You know who she is, that she's the western regional president of S-Corp?"

"I saw her name in your file, but it didn't ring a bell."

"How would you feel if your own parents kept you locked away all your life? So yes, I ran. I ran as far as I could, and Elliott

was gracious enough to help me. That
Marshal was killed by rabid dogs. And they
came after us, too, and bit Elliott's arm,
nearly killed him." Bray paused. "The more
I talk, the more I realize. . .everything I
say is just going to sound like magical
thinking to you. Don't think I haven't
learned about schizophrenia. I know what it
is, and I don't have it."

Heated, Bray sat back, slightly shaken
but poised to defend herself further if she
had to.

"I am sorry that happened to you. Sounds
like you're very upset with your parents.
And yes, I would be upset, too. I've never
experienced what you have, and I can't
imagine what it might be like. I have
compassion for that, truly, I do."

Bray met eyes with Jacob. She could see
a sheen in them. He blinked, turned and
looked at the wall, then turned back.

"I can see that you're upset. I think I
have the information I need, so I'll leave
you be, for now."

Jacob stood up. He turned and looked
down at her, standing there beside her bed,
watching her face as if this were the first
time he'd ever seen her, and he spoke under
his breath.

"When I saw that video. . .that one of
the cows going through slaughter. . . it
moved something in me. It got me
thinking. . .is this how my clients feel,
when they have these deep inner lives that
are nothing like my own, when they try to
get me to see and I just can't?" Jacob
said, his eyes staring wildly down at
Bray's face, as if he wasn't in the room
but somewhere else. "I don't know how you
did it, whether you acted with a group of
terrorists or not, but whatever the truth
is, I have a duty to protect you in some

way, even if it's in a way you can't agree
with. And that's what I intend to do. Rest
well, Bray."

Jacob dropped his hands to his sides,
turned, and walked away. Bray sat in her
bed, watching as he made his way through
the room and out the double doors.

Chapter Five

Bertan

After they exited the detention facility, Bertan and a group of men were placed on a bus. Outside, the land lay flat and empty. No hope. No promise. Miles upon miles of dead ground where grass once grew. A road led to the north or south, and who knew which direction Bertan was headed.

A pair of additional busses remained behind, with the families and children placed inside. Bertan gathered they were being sent somewhere else. According to the men on the bus, Bertan was headed to prison.

As the bus shook along a battered, rural road, it passed miles of untamed, cruel land of white, blinding sun that hurled its rays onto and into the bus, against the faces and backs of the men. One in particular, wearing a black t-shirt, reminded Bertan of his friend Ruben. The man sat a few rows ahead. Bertan stared at the back of the man's neck, full of sweat that trailed down and moistened the shirt. An image flashed through his mind of the last time he'd seen Ruben: unconscious in a slaughterhouse utility closet, the same closet Bertan was thrown into after he was knocked out by some unknown S-Corp security personnel. Bertan had agreed to assist Ruben with a plan that was supposed to bring down S-Corp. A plan involving the mysterious seventeen-year-old girl, Bray. . .was that her name? The girl who said she could communicate with animals, like ESP or something. Bertan didn't believe it, but Ruben seemed to, and he respected Ruben. Not to mention Bertan needed S-Corp gone. They'd been linked to a sister corporation, Medina, for whom Bertan had worked in Honduras. He'd committed atrocities on behalf of Medina, destroying the lives of campesinos, Honduran farmers whose land Medina wanted for its own profit. The only way he'd been able to escape Medina was to escape Honduras, to come to the U.S. for a "better" life.

So much for "better."

But now, as he sat on the bus, he had nothing more to do than fixate on Ruben, on what had happened as they tried to carry out their plan. What had gone wrong? To end up in a utility closet beside his closest friend, who was beaten and battered so severely, sweat dripping from his head down into the duct tape covering his mouth, that Bertan hardly recognized him. To end up here, on his way to prison.

The afternoon sun gradually dipped toward the horizon. Before total darkness, they came upon a fenced-in piece of land. The fence seemed to form a perfect square around a group of flat-top, discrete buildings, at least ten of them. The buildings reminded Bertan of the two S-Corp beef processing facilities where he'd worked. He had to remind himself that he was not headed to a slaughterhouse. This place would be much worse.

Bertan clenched his jaw. The wrist cuffs dug into his skin, hot from the humidity and lack of air on the bus. The bus turned off the road and onto a drive toward the enclosure. A ten-foot-high gate rolled open. As the bus pulled in, Bertan turned and watched the gate close slowly behind them.

A familiar feeling clouded into his body, from his head down into his abdomen. The images of guns and guards and fences spun around in his mind, which grew darker by the moment. He was beginning to feel himself dissociating, a word Ruben had taught him. Ruben. . .a plant manager by day and undercover activist by night, who'd helped Bertan because he believed Bertan had post-traumatic stress disorder.

Everyone was hurried off the bus. The men shuffled into the building. One by one, they were processed. Those who waited, Bertan included, sat in a large holding room, their wrists and ankles bound by metal. No one spoke.

Eventually, Bertan's time came. He was gathered by two guards who guided him out of the holding room and into a narrow, dark hallway. Cold emanated from the concrete walls. Bertan sensed they were underground, with no windows in sight. He was pulled down the hallway, past closed doors that contained things he'd never see. Around a corner, the guards led him to a small room.

Inside, he was turned to stand facing the two guards. Before him, a table held an olive-green uniform. One of the guards stepped up and removed Bertan's ankle cuffs and handcuffs.

"Undress," the guard commanded. He was six feet tall, towering over Bertan like a bad dream.

Bertan looked up at him. Was he to undress with these two men watching? He'd never been to prison so how was he to know?

The guard raised his voice. "Undress!"

Bertan did what he was told. His hands shaking, he pulled off his boots and unzipped his beige trousers, letting them fall to his ankles. His underwear revealed, Bertan felt eyes all over him. The room seemed to shrink. The walls looked down at him with nothing to say. His skin felt as though it were peeling off.

The faster he moved, the sooner he could get this over with. So he kicked the pants away from his feet. He unbuttoned his teal shirt and pulled it off. He let it fall onto the pants, together a remnant of someone he once knew: Ruben. The man from whom he'd stolen this suit. A man he'd lied to.

"Put on the uniform," the guard said, nodding at the green clothing on the table.

Bertan picked it up, felt the harsh fabric in his hands.

"Don't I get a phone call or something?" he asked, his legs and arms beginning to develop goosebumps. The temperature in the room was freezing.

"Maybe later. Right now, put on the uniform."

Bertan exhaled. He held up the uniform and let it unravel, a one-piece that, when he slid his legs into it, scratched against his skin and made him itch. He pulled it up to his chest, slid his arms into the sleeves, and zipped it from waist to neck.

"We'll take that," the guard said, pointing at the chain around Bertan's neck. Bertan reached for it. He'd forgotten it was there. He touched the clay thumbprint piece his daughter, Gabriella, had made for him. It was the size of a penny and held an indent he'd rubbed so many times a hole had developed in the center.

"My daughter gave me this," he said, squeezing it.

"You can't have jewelry in here. We'll keep it with your belongings," the guard replied, reaching toward Bertan's neck.

Bertan considered resisting their request. But he promised himself he would

not intentionally become violent. It was a
secret promise to Gabriella, and to his
wife, Carmen.

"Hand it over." The guard waved.

Bertan unlatched the chain and held it
out in his hand. Longingly he stared at it,
his eyes memorizing it while they still had
the chance, that memory of Gabriella when
she was two years old, how it felt to hold
her against his chest while he helped her
press her tiny thumb into the piece of
clay.

Bertan watched helplessly as the guard
dropped the chain into a clear plastic bag
and then brought out a larger, translucent
bag for all of Bertan's belongings.

Slowly, he was being ripped of his
identity.

#

Suddenly, the door clicked open. Another
guard peeked in.

The two guards in the room turned in
unison.

"They want to see him. . .upstairs," the
guard whispered from the door.

"What? Why?" asked the guard holding
Bertan's bag of belongings.

Bertan stood there examining the
situation.

"Just bring him up, will you?"

The door clicked shut.

The guards glanced at one another.
Without a word, they cuffed him again,
wrists and ankles.

"You bring him up. I'll take care of his
belongings," one guard said to the other.
He opened the door and Bertan watched as
the man disappeared with the last of his
things.

The guard led Bertan down the hall to a
flight of metal stairs. Together they
climbed, chains clanking against the steps,

the guard holding him by his handcuffs.

At the top level of the prison, a set of windows glanced down at Bertan from their position near the ceiling ten feet above. His head turned for the sun but his body was pulled further down a hallway darkened by lack of light. Any light that fell from the high ceiling was lost by the time it reached the tile floor.

A heavy set of doors poured open into the warden's office. There a desk stood a few feet from the back wall, a man sitting behind it. A light cowered in from half-open curtains. Bookshelves ran along the opposite wall. The room felt open and smelled of must.

The guard led Bertan to one of the chairs, and Bertan sat down. He got the impression that a private meeting with the prison warden wasn't typical. It made him nervous.

The guard left, closing the doors behind him. Bertan stared at the warden, who sat in a chair clearly too large for his body. The warden looked to be no more than five feet eight, with a balding scalp and thick glasses revealing beady, dark eyes. He was thin, almost. . .frail. Not at all what Bertan pictured a prison warden to look like.

Behind the warden, the wall stood covered in framed photos. Bertan's eyes scanned them, for he immediately recognized the trees in the photos. These were oil palms, trees he most associated with his home in Honduras.

The warden swiveled slightly in his chair and glanced up at the photos.

"Ah, yes. The photos. See something familiar?" the warden asked.

"Those trees," Bertan replied, lifting his cuffed hands and pointing. "That looks like Honduras."

"That's because it is." The warden turned back to Bertan, grinning.

Bertan squinted at one of the photos. In it stood two young men, perhaps in their twenties, wearing shorts and plain t-shirts. A faded blue sky hid behind them, along with a distant grove of trees grown for palm oil.

"What were you doing there?" Bertan asked, relaxing slightly.

"Just a work trip. I spent some time there as an intern while I was in school for criminal justice." The warden opened his mouth as if to say more, then stopped himself. He readjusted himself behind the desk, leaning forward.

"Honduras is a beautiful country. I imagine you must miss it."

"I do," Bertan replied, cautious. He was speaking with the warden, he reminded himself.

"You have family there?"

"I'm sure you can find that out for yourself."

"Yes, that's true." The warden leaned back in his chair, looked Bertan in the eye.

"I have a proposition for you, Mr. Duarte."

"What's that?" Bertan asked.

"I am aware of your charges. . .what you were brought in for. That Embedicare takeover was quite the stunt. Could've harmed thousands of lives, if not worse."

Bertan did not respond. He sat still, clenching his fists. His shoulders tightened. He'd been in situations where he'd had to make deals with evil men, to keep his own life. This was beginning to feel like that.

"I'll come right out with it: you give

us the names and locations of the terrorists you helped, and we can see about decreasing your time here. Let you get out early. . .get home to your family."

Bertan snickered. The expression on the warden's face was plain, flat, like a hot lake in summer. Bertan kept his composure and stared at the warden for some time before the warden finally spoke.

"If you need some time to think about it, I'll give you two days. After that, I rescind my offer."

"No, thank you." The words slipped right out of Bertan's mouth. He raised his eyebrows, surprising himself, but he had no desire to take them back. He hardly remembered the names of the activists he and Ruben had worked with, other than Bray, and he certainly didn't know their locations. They had worked from an abandoned trailer in Idaho. He knew the activists didn't live there. And even if he had known where to find them now, he wasn't about to rat people out. That was his first lesson in crime years ago when he'd worked for Medina: never, ever give away your people. Even if it meant death.

"You sure about that?" the warden asked, leaning forward, his arms on his desk.

"Yes, sir."

The warden stared at him, apparently surprised. A moment later, he picked up the phone and requested the guard.

Bertan heard the doors open behind him.

"Take him on down to processing," the warden said, turning away.

A sudden chill fell over the room. Gooseflesh ran up Bertan's arms. He shivered. The guard called to him from the doorway.

"Let's go, inmate."

Bertan let out an exhale and stood.

Angered by the warden's proposition, the way he'd tempted Bertan with freedom in exchange for the names of people Bertan believed were in the right, it took everything he had to stop himself from stepping over and punching the man in the face.

The warden, facing the window, did not move even as the guard shuffled Bertan out of the office. Gradually, the guard led Bertan back down to the bottom level where processing began. As his body sank down into the prison, so too did his mind begin to struggle with staying present, holding strong to the images of those oil palms in the photos. His home. His history. Bertan's mind descended further into the past.

Chapter Six

Bray

Within the Health Services Department, a series of doors along the far wall led to private examination rooms. Bray sat in one of those rooms after having received IV fluids for the past six hours. Apparently she'd been dehydrated, and why would that surprise her? As she stood alone in the room, awaiting the nurse, she reflected back over the past week. When was the last time she'd had water? An actual meal? With Elliott and Kage, before they hacked into Embedicare? Sounded about right. Those days felt like lifetimes ago. She felt a sudden sadness. Those days were gone.

In the exam room, it felt as though minutes kept dropping, like the rain she used to listen to as it fell against the roof of the house she had shared until recently with a group of animal rights activists in Meeteetse, Wyoming. She was reminded, too, of her time spent in the psych ward back in her hometown of Denver. How the time there would not move at all, but hung, suspended in the air where nothing could reach it. A breath held, a fear of waiting for what would come next.

Bray had experienced a taste of freedom in Meeteetse. Enough to truly understand the level of confinement she was up against now within these walls.

Then, the door clicked open. Bray turned. A woman in blue scrubs entered. She was petite, broad shouldered, with blonde hair up in a ponytail. Behind her, a guard followed, shut the door and remained beside it, his eyes focusing ahead at the wall opposite.

"Hi," the woman said, approaching Bray with a smile that felt inappropriate for the setting they were in. "You want to have a seat on the table?"

"What's this about?" Bray asked, crossing her arms and remaining where she sat.

The nurse walked over to a set of cabinets suspended above a metal table. She searched a top shelf, bringing out a box of latex gloves, then slid a pair on over her hands.

"You're getting your first injection," the nurse replied, her back turned to Bray. "It lasts three months, so you won't have to do this again until September."

Bray refrained from replying. She had known this was coming, but it still shocked her. She had managed to avoid an injection medication back in April by escaping the psych ward, but there was no escaping this time.

Bray's parents had long believed she was mentally ill, all because she told them when she was a child that she could communicate with animals. And so began years of doctor visits, medications she'd refused to take, and long stays in teen psychiatric units. Her mother wanted her placed on an injection back then. To Bray, this was her mother's way of controlling something she refused to take the time to understand. All while her father stood idly by and let it happen.

But Bray—only a mature seventeen years of age—could not stand by and let this happen to her. She would do what she could to fight it.

"Injection for what?" she asked, hoping

at least to delay the process.

"I think you know," the nurse replied. She opened a package to reveal a syringe full of clear liquid.

"Enlighten me," Bray replied, standing in the middle of the room.

The nurse turned and leaned against the counter.

"My understanding is that you have a diagnosis of schizophrenia. An entire history of being in and out of psych wards, in fact."

"Is that what the psychiatrist said?" Bray asked in defiance.

"Yes." The nurse stepped away from the counter and approached Bray. "Will you please have a seat so I can give you the injection? It'll only take a second and you can be on your way."

"On my way?" Bray asked. "On my way to where? I'm in prison. I'm only seventeen. What am I even doing in here with all these adults?"

"That's none of my business."

"I'm not moving," Bray replied. "Because I don't have schizophrenia and I don't need an injection." She stomped her foot.

The nurse's gaze shifted toward the guard. The guard made eye contact with the nurse, and then with Bray.

"If you won't sit down, I'll have to force you. Don't make me do that," he said.

"I can't make you do anything," Bray replied.

The guard let out a loud exhale. He stepped up and grabbed Bray by both arms. With ease, he lifted her a few inches off the ground. Bray's heart raced, but she didn't feel herself in any real danger. She froze as he carried her over to the exam table and set her on it. He walked around to one side and pressed his hands down onto her shoulders.

Bray watched helplessly, the weight of the guard's hands bearing down on her in a way that made it impossible for her to move, as the nurse turned to her and lifted up the sleeve covering her arm. Everything in Bray screamed at her to make a run for the door. The nurse brought the needle closer to her exposed skin. The door was too far away. She couldn't make a run for it this time.

Bray felt a sudden sting. Her muscles tightened. The nurse pushed the syringe. Bray was swamped by a feeling of powerlessness, reliving all those times she'd lost the battles she fought. It was not just a liquid they had forced on her. Not just a medication for an illness she didn't have. It was the sudden memory of years and years of being ignored, of being dismissed and then, after getting so close to saving all that meant something to her, losing it again. The needle brought back her mother's cruelty. Her father's avoidance. Her own dismissal of one grim reality: perhaps she wasn't so capable of changing the world, after all.

Chapter Seven

Bertan

Some time ago, perhaps a week, perhaps longer, Bertan had had a sobering conversation with Ruben. Bertan had been working a new security job at a new S-Corp facility, a job Ruben arranged in order to get Bertan away from the violent world of knocking beefs where he'd been for ten years. Bertan confessed to Ruben that he had felt himself "slipping," losing track of time, ending up in places without knowing how he'd gotten there. Ruben had shown him a video of himself tampering with the facility's cooling unit, which he hadn't remembered doing. The only thing Bertan recalled now about those days was that he was actively trying to sabotage S-Corp. He believed that if he could destroy the corporation from the inside out, he could force Medina to shut down, and then he could safely return home to his wife and child in Honduras. Looking back at it now, he could see how outlandish his thinking had been. But what he continued to find disturbing-something he had little understanding of-was Ruben's explanation for Bertan's patterns of forgetfulness. Ruben told him he feared it was some kind of "dissociate fugue."

Not long after that talk with Ruben, Bertan decided it best to keep distance from his friend. To keep his fugue hidden from Ruben and from the world, because maybe it could still help him end S-Corp.

He couldn't have been more wrong. Now, as the guards moved him from one room to the next. . .fingerprints here. . .policies and procedures there. . .it was fair to say he was beginning to lose himself.

"Hey!" A voice leapt into his awareness. "Do you understand what I just read to you?"

Bertan had been sitting in a metal chair, in front of a metal table. On the other side of the table, a man in a white pullover shirt held a tablet in his hands. Behind him, a guard stood beside the door. Bertan was inside an interrogation room. Walls painted charcoal, no windows, and a dull, flickering light above.

"What?" Bertan asked.

"Do you understand what was read to you? Have any questions?" He was a heavy-set, bearded white man with deep circles beneath his eyes.

Bertan hadn't heard any of it. His mind had been somewhere in the past.

"I'm sorry, could you repeat it? My English is. . .so-so," Bertan lied.

The man shook his head, stiffened, and continued. Bertan tried to focus. Something about rules in the prison. . .no visitors, no phone calls, do this or do that and be subjected to isolation. He tried to pay attention, but between the man's sentences, his mind continued to drift back into places he hadn't visited since working for Medina, since the days he was back home.

When the man finished, he set the tablet on the table, slid it over to Bertan.

"Sign here."

Bertan lifted his hand, burdened by chains and cuffs, and used his fingernail to sign his name to the document.

The man got up and left the room, and the guard stepped over to Bertan, lifted him to standing. Bertan kept his mouth shut, allowing himself to be led out into the hall, where the guard guided him

through the very next door. The walls in
this room were brighter, a silver ash.
Across from the door sat a rectangular
table, perpendicular, where a man sat
clicking a mouse, staring into two laptop
screens.

The guard led Bertan over and had him
stand against the wall, then he pulled back
and remained in the nearest corner. Bertan
faced the table. All he could see were the
laptops and a floor-to-ceiling protective
sheet of plexiglass, which stood between
him and the table.

"Please state your name for the record,"
a voice called from behind the set of
laptops. Bertan made out the face of a
brown-skinned man, perhaps the same age as
him, maybe younger by the lack of wrinkles
on his face and pain in his eyes.

"Name please," the man called again.

Bertan shook his head, tried to recall.
He glanced down at his body. What was
this. . .bland, one-piece outfit he was
wearing? And where had they brought him to?
All day he'd been carried from hallway to
hallway, from one nondescript room to
another, and now he was so mixed up, he
could barely hold on to what was happening.

This was how it would begin, every time.
Forgetting his name. Dissociating from his
body.

Before he knew it, the guard had
approached and was looking down into his
face.

"Something wrong?" the guard asked, his
voice strained.

"I-I. . .don't feel well," Bertan said.
It was the only thing he could come up
with.

"Just give your name and we can get you
to your cell."

Bertan nodded. He felt a tightness in

his chest, like something had come to sit and rest upon his ribs and heart. Something hard and angry. Something that didn't want to give his name, shouldn't have to give his name.

His jaw clenched.

He closed his eyes. He tried to focus. There was a name he knew he was supposed to say, and a name he was becoming in this moment. Both names were him, and they were different.

"Bertan," he said under his breath. "Duarte."

But he had wanted to say something different.

"Look into the camera please," the man said.

The guard pulled back, returned to his place in the corner.

Ten feet away, there was a black, finger-sized apparatus clipped to the top of one laptop. A lens peered at him like a black eye. Bertan stared back at it. He did not blink. He did not smile. There was a click. He swore he saw the eye blink.

And then everything flipped, not upside down so much as right side up. Suddenly, he was seeing the world through a more accurate lens. The lens of a man who didn't know how he got here, but didn't feel all that surprised. Men like him often ended up in prison.

The guard approached him. He watched the guard's hand lift toward his shoulder.

If this man thinks he's going to put his hand on me, he's got another thing coming.

The guard's palm came closer. In an instant, Bertan raised his cuffed hand and, with all his arm's strength, grabbed the guard's fingers and squeezed them into a tight lock, twisting the wrist so swiftly and firmly it made a snap.

"Don't you dare touch me," Bertan hissed.

The man behind the laptops leapt from his seat and went for the door. Bertan was still immersed in eye contact with the guard beside him. The guard had already pulled a taser with his free hand and stuck it into Bertan's side.

Bertan let out a scream.

A second guard was now in the room. Where did he come from? The two guards came at Bertan, twisting his arms tight around his back and bringing him down to the floor. He couldn't fight them off. The pain of the taser lanced through his flesh and into his bone, striking him with a burning sensation in his lower back.

Together they held him down and then yanked him up to his knees.

"You're going to segregation, buddy," the guard with the injured wrist said. "We'll have someone bring you your ID."

The ID card wasn't going to matter. The man who'd had his photo taken was not the man they had brought into this room. The man being pulled up by his elbows and forced out into the hallway called himself by another name. He was Oscar Reyes Mejia, and he was a Medina henchman.

Chapter Eight

Oscar

They transferred him between buildings. When he was briefly outside, he passed between ten-foot-tall fences on either side, a white sky glancing down, unamused. Oscar smiled as the fences, their barbed wire coiling at the top, reminded him of his younger days. Days in his twenties when he'd harass campesinos whose land lay confined inside the fences. They'd do all they could to protect their land from Medina's far-sweeping hand, but the campesinos were farmers, not violent by nature. Not like Oscar, who'd stand outside their fences at night, waiting, watching as the ocean winds had their way with the palm trees, pushing them down. He loved watching how the palm trees bent, nearly to the ground, but never broke.

He saw no palm trees here. In the brief moments it took to move from one building to the next, Oscar was introduced to the external layout of the prison, and to the desert beyond.

One of the two guards who walked with him stepped ahead to a panel beside a door and entered a series of numbers, followed by a fingerprint. The steel door clicked open. They entered a hallway with dim overhead lighting that revealed charcoal walls. A hundred feet away, the hallway ended at a stairwell.

A few feet down the hall, the guard approached a door, unlocked it, and led Oscar inside. The second guard remained by the door, taser ready, his body turned and facing Oscar. Meanwhile, the injured guard removed Oscar's handcuffs. Oscar observed the room. One window facing out at the fences. Too small to fit through, and covered in metal mesh. Concrete, everywhere. Tile flooring. One table bolted into the floor. A different uniform on the table.

The injured guard bent down and unlocked Oscar's ankle cuffs. Oscar considered kicking the man in the face, but the room held a humid, stale, stuck feeling, like the sensation of tension against a trigger right before a kill. Oscar didn't need to do anything physical just yet. The tension was enough.

"Undress and put these on," the guard said. He grabbed the pair of orange pants and the t-shirt and tossed them on the floor. They landed beside Oscar's boot.

"Humph," Oscar chuckled. He would not.

"Every time you disobey, we add another day to your time in the hole. That what you want?"

Oscar stared at the guard. . .and he did not stop staring. He stood there, mouth shut. Eyes narrowed. Little did they know he lived much of his life in the dark. Attacks on campesinos always happened at night.

"Two days just turned to three, congratulations. Now put them on," the guard ordered.

Oscar obliged. He smiled at the guard, winked at him, then bent down and yanked off the prison-issued canvas shoes. He let them drop to the floor.

"Come on, 562. We can stand here all night with you, but we'll just add on more time. Three days into four. . ."

"Four days into ten," the guard by the

door chimed in.

Oscar unzipped the ugly, green uniform he'd been wearing and let it drop to the floor. He continued eying the closest guard as he pulled the pants on over his underwear. Held his gaze, giving the man a wink as he slid the t-shirt on over his tattoo-covered chest. The shoes he slid back into with his toes. When he stood up, he gave the injured guard a look of disdain.

"What did you call me?" he snarled.

"Five, six, two. That's your number. You don't get a name in here," the guard replied. He quickly cuffed Oscar by the wrists and ankles in the same position as before, where lines were beginning to form on his skin.

Without discussion, the guard by the door held onto his taser like a kid to his teddy bear. He opened the door. One of the guards shoved Oscar down the hall and into the stairwell. They walked him down the stairs. A gasp of air blew out from the ventilation system above, and Oscar shivered. This place was far too cold for him. The smells of pure iron and metal, of industrial things, thrust his memory into another time and place, somewhere more recent than the campesinos, and he couldn't quite place it.

Another hallway. Approaching a cell at the far end, in the corner, they stopped. One of the guards removed Oscar's ankle cuffs. He thought again to kick the guard. He could use the chain of his handcuffs to strangle them both, get the hell out of here. But if he was going to escape prison— and a prison he was pretty sure was in the U.S.—he'd need a plan. His only indication of the location was the moment he had spent outside. Instead of lush forest and the

familiar jungle climate of his homeland, he
had seen miles of desert. How he ended up
here was a deeper quandary for another
time, but he was willing to bet Medina
would get him out.

One of the guards unlocked and pulled
open the cell door. The second guard led
Oscar into the cell, turned his body so he
was facing the cell door, then stepped
back. Oscar stood there, feeling suspended,
a smile on his face, as the guard shut the
door. A second later, a slot in the center
of the door screeched open.

"Hands!" the guard yelled.

Oscar slid his hands through the slot.
His handcuffs were removed. He turned to
face the tiny room, loosening his arms by
his sides. The tray slot jolted shut. He
flinched. He blinked several times, and
suddenly. . .he was Bertan.

Chapter Nine

Bertan

The cell light shut off. Darkness encompassed everything. No window and therefore, no light. Bertan had been standing there, in orange pants and white t-shirt-he would have sworn he'd been wearing a green jumpsuit. He remained frozen until his eyes adjusted.

Up against the wall was a single twin-size bed. The mattress was covered with a blanket. There was a pillow. Bertan slowly stepped over and touched the blanket. It felt like sandpaper. He pressed his fingers into the mattress. It was firm. The pillow, too soft for his liking. But there were far worse things in this moment. Like the screaming from next door and above. The sound of shuffling feet. Someone in another cell kicking at something. Distasteful country music blaring from outside.

Bertan could not sleep in a place like this, not that sleep ever came natural to him. He was wired, but not surprised. The fugue had indeed returned. The last thing he remembered was having his photo taken. Now, he sat down on the cold, concrete floor. He assumed this was his cell, but it was so. . .naked. Was this how it would be? Nothing but a bed, a toilet, and a sink? Not even a window?

He turned to lie on his back. Reaching for his neck chain, he realized it was gone. They'd taken it, along with everything else. He had nothing left. No family. No Ruben. Not even the familiarity of his security job at the S-Corp facility.

He'd take that over this right about now.
At least then, he had the perception that
he was somewhat free.

Closing his eyes, he pretended. He felt
the floor beneath him, pretended it was the
throbbing, life-giving and bloodstained
earth of his home in Honduras. His stomach
rose and fell. Ruben had told him to keep
close to the six senses, as a way to remain
present. So he tried. His hands stroked the
floor, but it did not help. Instead, it
calmed him to imagine himself back home,
with Carmen, with Gabriella. He turned his
head to the side to imagine his wife
sleeping beside him in bed, how she always
slept in a fetal position. On nights when
he could not fall asleep, he'd turn toward
her and wrap his arm over her body, feeling
her warmth, feeling her nestle into his
chest. It was only then that he could find
some brief solace.

Eventually, Bertan did manage to fall
asleep. Somewhere along the way, his ears
picked up the sound of distant gunshots.

Blat, blat! Then a pause. Then. . .*blat,
blat, blat, blat!*

Bertan sat up. His heart racing, he
looked around and saw nothing. Heard
nothing. He remained still. . .waiting.

Then came a series of shots from a
machine gun. Bertan froze. His eyes
watered.

They were coming for him.

Medina had found him, and they were
coming. When he'd escaped to the U.S., he'd
left unfinished business. The only way he
could escape was to betray them, to abandon
them, and Medina did not take kindly to
such things.

The gunshots grew louder, closer.

Bertan shuffled backwards across the
floor of his cell, farther from the door,

until his back hit the wall. There was nowhere else to go. He was stuck. Nothing would save him in here.

A trill of a noise rolled into the hallway. Any second they'd blow down the door. And enter. What could he use to protect himself? He pulled the mattress off the bed frame. The sheet and blanket dropped to the floor. He shielded himself with the mattress, both laughing and crying at the hilarity in using a flimsy mattress to protect himself from gunshots. A shitty, fucking mattress.

The shots came and came and came. For a moment Bertan looked up to the ceiling, as if calling for God would somehow save him. As he stared into the black emptiness above him, for the first time in his life he considered maybe there wasn't a God. What if, in this terrifying moment when he thought to call out, there was nothing to call to? His cries would not be heard.

The sound of a click jolted him up onto his feet. He ran the mattress at the door, pushing fabric up against steel as if it would somehow stop them from entering.

Panicked, eyes wide, he stepped back and prepared himself. The darkness was part of it, a heavy enemy trying to drag him down. He began punching at it, feeling pain in his knuckles, his fingers. A sensation of warmth oozed from his hands. He continued to strike the darkness. A feeling of pain mixed with anger quickly turned to constructive violence. The kind of violence that made him feel he was in control. That he had power over whether he lived or died in this moment.

Bertan was spun around the room. Or maybe the room was spinning around him. The gunshot sounds dissipated, replaced with the sound of his own heavy breathing, and a loud scream inside his mind.

"Fuck you, you mother fuckers!" he yelled and spat into the darkness.

He dropped to the ground. He pounded his fists against the metal bed frame ferociously, arms rising all the way up into the depths of darkness, then swinging down with every ounce of power and anger he had left. And he had a lot.

Abruptly, an uncompromising light popped on.

He froze.

Heaving, he took stock of his surroundings. Four walls. One with blood on it. A mattress up against the door. Trying to catch his breath, Bertan turned his head slowly downward. Flipping his hands over, he saw that his knuckles were bloody. He brought his hands into his stomach, holding them, feeling the pain for the first time. Adrenaline wore off, replaced with stinging and throbbing and shaking. He pulled off his t-shirt and wrapped his hands into it, a makeshift bandage.

He ran over to the door, kicked the mattress away. Lifting his arms up, he began hitting the door with his wrapped hands.

"Help!" Bertan yelled. "I'm bleeding!"

The tray slot screeched open. Bertan stood back, bent over and looked out. His breath was heavy. Sweat rolled down his face. He met the eyes of a guard, one he didn't recognize.

"What is it. . .562?" The guard's voice was southern in accent, but gruff.

"My wrists are bleeding!"

The guard rolled his eyes. The tray slot shut. Bertan shuddered.

A second later, the cell door opened. The guard noticed the mattress on the floor. His eyes shifted over to the bed frame, the blood on the wall.

Blocking the door, the guard placed his hands on his hips.

"Geez!" he said. He leaned his head toward the hallway and called out. "We got another one!"

A second guard appeared. Another white man Bertan had not seen before. Bertan began to fear he wasn't going to get the help he needed.

The guard with the southern accent cuffed Bertan's feet. Together, the two guards grabbed Bertan by either arm and walked him out of the cell. For the first time, Bertan saw where he was: a unit of cells with thick, gray doors and loud voices and a scent that reminded him of an S-Corp slaughterhouse kill floor. He felt he might puke, light-headed and shaky as they carried him up a flight of stairs and into a room.

There, they set him in a chair and told him to wait.

The southern guard disappeared outside while the other remained blocking the door, arms crossed. Bertan's vision blurred. He glanced down at the shirt around his hands. It was collecting blood, turning from white to red.

A knock came at the door. The guard stepped aside, opened it. A man dressed in gray scrubs entered the room, in his hands a first aid kit. He was of shorter stature with a paunch belly and a wry smile.

"What'd you do to yourself?" the nurse asked, kneeling down in front of Bertan.

"I-I don't remember." Bertan was unable to think clearly.

"Let me take a look."

The nurse unraveled the t-shirt slowly, carefully. Bertan kept his hands held out as the nurse's gloved hands pinched the shirt, then dropped it into a nearby basket.

The brown skin of Bertan's wrists flapped open in places, exposing raw flesh and blood.

"Oh my," the nurse commented, holding Bertan's hands palm up while he examined the skin. "You don't need stitches, so that's good."

The nurse opened the first aid kid and pulled out a bottle of hydrogen peroxide and a packet of wipes.

"This is gonna sting," he said. He looked up at Bertan. Bertan nodded, his head beginning to spin.

The nurse began treating the wounds, two on one hand, three on the other. The burning sensation seeped into the cuts. Bertan cringed, nearly pulled away, but allowed the man to do his work. There was something in the way the nurse's hands held him, something soft and forgiving. Something Bertan was not accustomed to.

The nurse covered his wrists with ointment and wrapped them in gauze.

"That should do it." The nurse stood up with the first aid kit in hand. He addressed the guard. "You may want to have him seen by psych, though."

The guard did not reply. He opened the door, motioned for the nurse to leave.

The guard approached Bertan with handcuffs. Bertan tried to resist but didn't have enough energy. His wrists throbbed and his stomach began to growl. The guard slapped the cuffs around his wrists, grabbed his arm and pulled him up. He walked Bertan back to his cell, where the southern guard was still standing.

When he arrived before the cell, the light from inside blared out at him, so

much brighter than the hallway. He no
longer had a shirt, and the air blasting
from the vents landed on his bare skin,
goosebumps developing along his back and
arms.

"Can I have another shirt?" he asked.

"We'll bring one with your food. Now get
inside."

Bertan entered the cell. The door
slammed shut. He startled.

"Hands!" the guard yelled.

Bertan turned and looked at the closed
door. He had no idea what the guard meant.
His hands were cuffed.

"I said, hands, inmate!"

The door's tray slot was open. Bertan
stepped up, peeped out. He could only see
the guard's waist.

"You keep delaying and we can delay your
time down here another day."

"What do you mean. . .down here?" he
asked, confused.

The guard chuckled. He leaned down and
looked in through the slot at Bertan.

"Hands, now!" the guard said, motioning
through the slot with his fingers.

Finally, Bertan understood. He lifted
his hands to the slot, pushing them
through. His breath held, he feared what
the guard would do to his healing wrists.
He felt the cuffs removed, a weight lifted.
He pulled his hands back inside, and the
slot was shut.

"Where am I?" he yelled at the door.

"Don't be an idiot," the guard's voice
yelled back. "You know you're in the hole."
Footsteps, away.

The hole? Did he mean. . .solitary? Why
would he be in. . .wait. He must've done
something while he was in another episode
of fugue. Something that put him in
solitary. Dizzy, Bertan went over to the

mattress, still on the floor, and lay down on his side. He closed his eyes. He thought of Carmen again, of something safe.
Yes. . .how she'd lie in fetal position while she slept. He mimicked her position, raising his knees to his chest and crossing his arms to protect his wrists.

There he lay for three days.

Chapter Ten

Kage

No one slept that first night after S-Corp discovered their home in Meeteetse. After S-Corp murdered one of Kage's closest friends, Ethan, a man who'd become like a grandfather to him. After Bray turned herself in and S-Corp security took her away. Kage and his five remaining housemates had no choice but to flee the home Ethan had built, the place destined to be a sanctuary for animals yet turned harshly into a place of sorrow.

Now it was morning of the third day. Kage slouched beside the kitchen window of Elliott Bansfield's apartment in Red Lodge, Montana, the only place he and his friends could seek safety because, as Elliott had once explained, the town remained completely off-grid.

The blinds were drawn to keep him and the others hidden. Every few moments he'd slip his fingers through the slats, pull them down an inch and peek at the street, waiting for S-Corp to show up in their black SUVs. But so far, they hadn't. The street remained empty, save for the occasional passing of people, one here, two there. The concrete street was cracked in places and free of cars. Down a few blocks, western commercial-style buildings sat cramped together. A subtle, orange light gazed upon the buildings as the sun rose out beyond the Beartooth Mountains.

The kitchen light flipped on. Kage turned, looked past Trevor, who'd been sitting at the kitchen table. Elliott had entered the dining area where a wooden

table and four chairs sat empty. Elliott
was Bray's closest friend, a Black guy in
his early twenties with short dreadlocks
and the muscles of a pro athlete. He nodded
to Kage. Kage nodded back. Elliott opened
the refrigerator. He poured a glass of
milk, stood there, and drank. Kage wondered
how Elliott could drink cows' milk after
all that had happened, even if he wasn't a
vegan.

Only days ago, Kage and Elliott had
sat with Bray in a trailer on some
abandoned property in Idaho while Elliott
hacked Embedicare with his IT skills. This
enabled Bray to use an implant to link the
minds of citizens to those of cows inside
an S-Corp slaughterhouse. Both Elliott and
Kage had witnessed much of the slaughter
via Elliott's laptop.

If Elliott could still drink milk
after all that, then what could Kage do
about it? After what he'd just lost, first
Ethan and then Bray, he found he didn't
much care. Elliott was a decent guy, after
all, and Kage wasn't interested in
proselytizing today.

Kage's interest remained singular:
making sure everyone remained safe and
hidden, that S-Corp hadn't followed them
here.

With him in Elliott's one-bedroom
apartment were Trevor, Emily, Virgil,
Dennis and Lana. Emily, Virgil and Dennis
currently sat on the deep brown couch in
the center of the spacious living room.
Kage turned and saw Lana standing at one of
the two living room windows. Lana had been
looking his way. His eyes met hers. Her
eyes welled up. She tried smiling at him.
He wanted to go over to her, but the path
to get to her was too much for him to
travel. Too much had happened since he

first met her a few months back. She was an activist with her own team of people who were determined to bring S-Corp down. But because of some idiotic mistakes Kage had made, Lana's entire team was compromised, and they had since disappeared. It had been Kage's selfish desire to find out what happened to his missing parents-who he believed were taken by S-Corp-that led to both him and Lana being caught by S-Corp security. If Kage hadn't gotten them free with a little bit of luck and ingenuity, they'd both be disappeared. Perhaps incarcerated like Bray. All because this country was no longer safe for activists. S-Corp and the government had made sure of that.

He began to sweat, feeling the moisture cool his skin with discomfort, feeling Lana as if she were reading his feelings. Exposed. The air in the apartment was stifling. The lack of moving air was something Kage already missed about his home in Meeteetse.

"There's some fruit in the fridge," Elliott said, breaking the silence in the apartment. He carried his glass of milk over to a rectangular, glass desk that rested against the wall in the living room, parallel to the couch. He sat down in his swivel chair, leaned back, and stretched. He was still wearing the same clothes he'd had on for days, as was everyone else. This left the place smelling a bit dank. Everyone needed showers, though it seemed no one wanted to, or no one could move. There was a sense of pause in the air, of shock and fear. As if another person moved, S-Corp would come pounding the door open.

At least, that was how Kage felt. Maybe he was projecting it onto the rest of the room, but he couldn't help wondering what everyone else was feeling, an invisible tension hanging in the air. Emily had already cried twice during the night, Virgil comforting her from his place beside her on the couch. Virgil was a Cheyenne person, quiet, pensive, wise. Deeply spiritual, he didn't see eye to eye with Kage on much yet they'd never had a disagreement. Virgil was not one to argue.

Trevor, Kage's uncle, had paced so much he could've worn a path on the hardwood floors with his sneakers. Occasionally he would stop, his shoulder-length black hair slightly disheveled, and glance at Kage with those cobalt eyes. All Kage could do was look away.

Elliott's bedroom, accessed via a hallway with barren walls, remained empty. Elliott had offered it to anyone who wanted it, but all six of the newcomers remained within sight of one another, Kage the furthest away. He'd spent hours sitting at the kitchen table, biting his cuticles, standing up and glancing out the window, and repeating the sequence with no new results.

Most of the night, he'd forgotten to breathe.

"So. . ." Dennis finally spoke. He leaned forward on the couch, looked toward Elliott. "How many people are here, in Red Lodge?"

Elliott swiveled to face Dennis, setting the cup of milk down on a piece of paper beside his keyboard. He picked up a toy T-rex and began fidgeting with it.

"About seventy, I think."

Dennis was always inquisitive. An engineer by trade, he made decisions by logic alone. During the twelve years Kage had come to know the man, he'd not once seen Dennis show emotion. Not that Kage was much for emotion himself, but he rarely hesitated to react in anger if the situation called for it. Dennis, though, was stoic, reserved, knowledgeable.

"And you've been here for how long?" Dennis continued.

"About a month or so."

"And you're sure it's safe?"

Kage, intrigued by the conversation, moved away from the window. He and Bray had asked Elliott similar questions back when they first visited him here, when they had come to ask for his help. Kage stood at the edge of the dining room where his boots stopped at the start of the rug. His eyes bounced back and forth between the two as Dennis questioned and Elliott answered.

"Yep. I work for the Red Lodge security department. I'm helping expand their wall of protection another ten miles beyond the perimeter of the town."

"Wall of protection?" Trevor asked. He paused his pacing and stood beside Lana. He was frowning, and his eyes appeared heavy and tired.

A smooth light edged into the room from the window where Lana had rolled the shades open slightly. As a result, Kage noticed that her hazel-green eyes took on a pear-like color, more so since she'd been crying.

"It's IT speak," Elliott replied, tossing the T-rex toy up into the air, then catching it. "It basically means we have an area that's protected from drones and any other government-issued surveillance. They have no idea we're here."

Dennis nodded, staring down at the rug for a moment.

"I saw solar panels on some of the rooftops on the way in," Dennis continued.

"I assume everything is solar powered?"

"And hydroelectric," Elliott replied.

"What about food?"

"Just like what you all did in Meeteetse, we also grow all our own food. We have. . ." Elliott paused and cleared his throat. "We have animals for milk and eggs."

Kage crossed his arms. He opened his mouth to speak, then stopped himself. Unlike their home in Meeteetse, this was not a vegan commune, after all. Why was he surprised at their use of animals? For the past twelve years, since he was sixteen, Kage had lived with Trevor, Emily, Virgil, Dennis and the recently deceased Ethan, all vegans who'd attempted to end factory farming in the twenty-twenties. They'd swiftly been threatened by the government and forced into hiding.

"Please tell me they at least don't slaughter the animals. . .for food?" Emily asked. Dark rings were beginning to develop beneath her eyes. She was of similar age to Trevor and Dennis, mid-forties, and she had shiny, long dark hair. Her toothpick-like physique made her appear easily breakable, but Kage knew better.

"Everyone here is vegetarian. Not my favorite thing, but I make do. It's worth it to be in a place where I know I'm safe, and I can live as I please," Elliott said, squeezing the T-Rex toy in his hands.

Trevor left Lana's side and went to peer out the second living room window.

"Who runs the place?" Trevor asked.

"Rebekah and Chad Saler. Husband-and-wife team. Which reminds me," Elliott replied, "you'll all need to complete interviews. . .if you want to stay."

Kage's ears perked up. He didn't like the sound of that any more than the sound of animals being used for milk and eggs.

"Interviews?" he asked, releasing his arms and glancing down at Elliott.

"Everyone has to. I did one. They just meet with you, individually. . .ask some questions about where you came from, why you're here. And what you can contribute so they can put you to work. I doubt they'd turn you away, especially when they hear about your activism and how S-Corp is after you. They are very anti-S-Corp here."

Kage said nothing. He found he was too tired to disagree or even speak. He didn't want to do any interview. What he wanted was to find Bray, and to finish what she started: exposing S-Corp to the public.

Chapter Eleven

Bray

Bray slept. She did not hear the 6 a.m. bell. Her dreams were vivid and non-stop. In this most recent one she was sitting in Emily's room back in Meeteetse. Emily had picked up a singing bowl, hit the side of it with a mallet and began circling the bowl with the mallet for what felt like ages. She brought the bowl closer and closer to Bray's face, until it was less than an inch from her eyes.

There was a sudden clack. Commotion, followed by more clacking, entered her cell from the hallway.

"Up, up, up!" yelled one of the guards.

Bray's eyes opened. The room slowly came into focus. An eggshell wall. A desk with a chair. She was not in Emily's room. She was not in Meeteetse.

"Come on, you're late," the guard said, standing above her bed.

Bray moved to sit up, but her head felt as though it weighed a hundred pounds. It hung down toward the bed as she used her hands to push herself up to sitting. For a moment she was light-headed. She held the sides of her head as if that would get the spinning to cease.

"Something wrong?" the guard asked.

Bray slowly looked up at him. It was Steve. He was assigned to this unit, so Bray had become familiar with him. He wasn't as mean as she'd expect a prison guard to be, but he was not kind. He was. . .indifferent.

"I'm just. . .really dizzy," Bray

replied.

Steve stood there, looking down at her.

"You've got to make your bed and get to breakfast," he said. "I'll have to give you a strike for this."

Strikes were given to prisoners when they did not obey the rules. Anything from being late for morning call to attacking a guard warranted strikes. One strike for being late, more for refusing to go to work, etc. So many strikes and a prisoner would be reprimanded. . .and sent to solitary confinement.

Ten strikes, you're out, Bray thought.

Her head stopped spinning.

"Okay," she said, and came to stand. It took another moment for her head to adjust to the movement. She began making her bed.

Another bell rang. That meant it was time to line up and get to breakfast.

"Fix the bed later," Steve said, stepping to one side and making space for Bray to exit the cell. "Go get in line."

Bray did as she was instructed. In the hallway, there were fifteen prisoners standing in a single line, waiting. Bray immediately combed her fingers through her shoulder-length hair, fearing she looked awful, and got in line behind the last prisoner. She placed her hand against the wall, steadying herself while the light-headedness continued. Her sleeve gave way to a bandage on her upper arm.

The injection. She'd nearly forgotten. She was medicated. That was why she was so groggy. Bray had always been sensitive to medications. The smallest dosage of children's nausea medicine would lead to a day of sleep. So it was no surprise to her now that she'd slept through the morning alarm, even considering how sensitive she usually was to sound.

Another buzzer went off. Up ahead, a set of doors rolled open. Two guards stood on either side of the doors. The prisoners started down the hallway toward the cafeteria. Bray followed carefully, making sure not to reveal how much her body wished to return to sleep.

Entering the cafeteria, she gazed at the hot bar beneath the windows. Beside it, the salad bar with fruit. The kitchen and its staff, all prisoners, worked busily behind a long buffet, handing plates to the prisoners as they stood in line with trays.

Bray needed to eat something, but she was not going to eat their animal food. Of course, most of this food wasn't real. The fruit, yes. Anything that could be imported from other countries, was. But everything else, such as the oats in the sloppy oatmeal on the hot bar, was grown in labs-- beneath the ground--by S-Corp. All because of the fertilizer disaster in 2027. All because of S-Corp. This made her think of her mother, and did little for her appetite.

She grabbed a glass of water, a banana and two pieces of dry toast. Fumbling with her tray, she stopped beside the hot bar, adjusted her tray, and turned for the tables.

There were prisoners everywhere. Too many for her comfort. She walked over to the nearest table and sat down on the cold, metal stool. Everything felt so sterile, so mechanic. It gave her goosebumps.

Two women came and sat on either side of her. Their trays were full of steaming foods: oatmeal, sausages, scrambled eggs. Bray felt woozy enough from the meds. Now she thought she might puke. She turned her head down to her tray and began chewing on the toast.

"You're Bray, right?" asked the woman to her left. She was Black, with curly hair and wide, vast dark eyes.

Bray swallowed the bite of toast, felt its substance crawl down her throat and into her empty belly. It was quite soothing. She turned to the young woman, surprised.

"How did you know?" she asked. Her eyes wished to close. It took considerable effort to keep them open, to stay engaged.

"We saw you. . .on the news," the woman replied. She began eating the scrambled eggs.

Bray felt her eyes closing. Facing the tray of food, she stared at it while telling herself to stay awake. The woman's words barely registered in her mind. . .something about the news?

"The news?" she asked.

"Yeah!" The woman let out a laugh. "What you did was inspiring."

Bray's eyes closed again. She swore she heard the woman say inspiring. Did she hear that right? Or was she also losing some of her mind with these meds? She'd already lost the ability to hear the voices that had so easily come to her the day before.

"Hey, you okay?" asked the woman.

Bray's head began to droop. She felt something soft on her back. Maybe a hand? She took a deep breath, a relaxing exhale. She wanted to sleep. Was that too much to ask? To go lie down and just be alone? To sleep off all the years of being discounted and drugged?

She could not keep her eyes open one more second. No, it felt better to close them. To stop fighting. Emily had said not to resist things, hadn't she, once? To allow things to be as they were?

Yes, let's do that.

Bray's head dropped forward. Something pressed gently into her chest, her upper back. Someone helped her up. There were voices, but they sounded like they were under water. It amused Bray and she chuckled.

Suddenly Bray felt herself pulled up, up. Then dropped, plopped. Plopped like a pillow. Could pillows plop? She didn't know. What was happening? Everything so dark. So delicious and sweet, sleep would be. Yes, sweet sleep.

A lift again, this time with more force. Carried. Like on a cloud. Drifting. Felt so good. Head dropped, submitting. To deep sleep. To being carried somewhere. Now darker. Now down. Down some more. Clicking. Clacking. Turning. Shifting. Down. Stopped. Unmoving. Still. Asleep. Asleep for good.

Chapter Twelve

Cole

The city of Denver remained in lockdown. Five days had passed since the Embedicare takeover. It was morning and the streets were dead. Cole Hoffman stood at the double doors to his patio and glared downward to ground level. A Marshal vehicle passed by from time to time. A thick silence slid in through the windows, quite a contrast to the usual bustle of morning rush hour below. Across the way, a similar high-rise gazed back at him, its tinted windows hiding anyone inside. He liked to believe there were people there, too, looking out and watching from the safety of their homes.

It was altogether eerie. His skin crawled.

Backing away, Cole turned toward the two white couches in his living room, and to the flat-screen, smart television that hung on the wall opposite him.

"Turn on the TV, please," he said.

The television blinked on. The channel was always set to a media news station. It was hard to explain why, but for Cole, listening to the voices of newscasters had once made him feel less alone. Like there were people in the room with him. Now, even though the subject matter was dire, as a U.S. Senator he listened to it with an air of detachment. News had been bought out and controlled long ago. It was more entertainment than anything else.

But today it was not that. Today the only way he could learn of his daughter's whereabouts was via the news. This made him sick. And he knew exactly who was at fault. His wife, Dianna.

One day after the takeover, he found out Bray had been taken into custody. What was missing was any form of video confirmation of her whereabouts. The news showed a brief, five-second video of his daughter in handcuffs, her eyes puffy and dark underneath as if she'd been through torture of some kind, and that was all. He'd been given no other information. No calls from Dianna. The media hadn't reached out to him for a quote. It was odd, since he was a public figure. . .but he knew what they were doing. They were planning to keep him out of the loop because they knew, Dianna knew, that if anyone officially notified him, he'd try to find Bray.

During these five days in lockdown, Cole had attempted to reach Dianna, to reach anyone who would know something about Bray, and he'd gotten nowhere.

His eyes focused on the TV screen as the newscasters spoke: "We've entered the fifth day of a national lockdown. With no clear indication from the government as to when the lockdown may be lifted, we turn to Allie Howard, who comes to us live from Denver Health."

The screen switched to a view of a young woman standing outside the main entrance to the Denver hospital. The sun was rising behind the building, providing an orange tint to the sky above.

"We are here at Denver Health, where hospital beds remain at capacity. . ."

Cole listened, but only half-so. His mind was divided between concerns for the hundreds of people throughout the country impacted by the takeover, and concern for his daughter. She had helped orchestrate the entire situation, and that would take more days for him to wrap his mind around. He just could not believe it. Hospitals at capacity due to panic attacks, mild heart attacks, people having passed out in the streets after his own daughter (and, he suspected, her friend Elliott) had somehow hacked Embedicare's system to reveal truths about S-Corp to the entire nation. Not only that, they had somehow linked the minds of citizens wearing 4-D implants to the moment-by-moment experience of cows who were going through slaughter.

And Cole was one of those who had shared that horrifying experience.

"We continue to hear reports of multiple cases of people experiencing first-hand the slaughter of these cows. . .cows that we are now finding out were a part of some secret, illegal testing that S-Corp was doing, but S-Corp has yet to provide comment or further details. . ." the newscaster continued.

While everyone else wanted to know what the hell had happened, all Cole wanted was to know was where the hell they'd taken his seventeen-year-old daughter.

Snapping out of his trancelike state, Cole turned off the television. He needed to focus. He needed to find Bray. For so long he had been absent in her life. He hadn't been a good father to her, and he felt guilty.

Ever since he filed for divorce a month ago, the communication between him and Dianna had come to a halt. Ever since Bray revealed herself in a video that spanned every television screen and Embedicare screen throughout the nation, when Bray announced she was the daughter of Dianna Hoffman, regional president of S-Corp, when she exposed evidence of S-Corp's corrupt practices—things Cole didn't even know himself—Dianna had not spoken to him. She ignored him every time he reached out to her. That was how she had always operated in their marriage; she communicated or chose not to communicate, whichever served her, in order to get her way.

And he'd allowed it.

Suddenly much of this was feeling like his fault. The way he'd left himself out of Bray's childhood while pursuing his political career. Things might be different had he paid attention to his daughter.

Cole shuddered.

When he considered how he might track down Bray, only one person came to mind. An old friend, one who helped him find her after she escaped Denver Health several weeks ago. If it wasn't for Thom, he never would have found Bray out in supposedly-deserted Wyoming. He never would've had the chance to help her protect those dying sows she'd saved from a transport truck. Cole still wasn't sure he could believe everything she said about communicating with animals, but she was his daughter, and he could at least support her. So when she gave him the chance to help, when she asked him to protect the sows she'd saved, he was on it. For once he didn't have to believe her in order to help her in the way she wanted. As hard as it was to accept, his daughter was growing up. Less than a year and she'd be an adult. Soon he'd have to start treating her like one. And that started with finding her and giving her a fighting chance to live a fair life.

Cole sat down at the table and made the call. Thom answered before the phone rang.

"Hey man. I'm glad to hear from you," Thom said. "How are you?"

"I don't even know," Cole replied honestly. His feelings were everywhere and nowhere all at once.

"I heard about Bray. What's going on?"

"A whole lot of crap I can't even go into right now." Cole's eyes meandered down to the pen on the table. He picked it up and squeezed it.

"I can't imagine. I'm beyond perplexed myself. All my employees are afraid to leave their homes. It's like the pandemic all over again, but worse."

Cole listened. He wondered what else people in this country were thinking. Bray and her friends-whomever else she was working with-had really made a mess of things. He feared what she may have gotten involved with, feared for her life.

"You there, buddy?" Thom asked.

"Yeah, sorry," Cole replied, coming back to the present. "I need your help again."

"What do you need?"

"You probably saw that Bray was taken into custody."

"I did," Thom replied plainly.

"Can you find out where they took her?"

"You mean. . .you don't know?"

"Dianna's keeping me in the dark. So is her office. And Marshals seem to know nothing."

"Marshals are worthless," Thom replied, laughing.

Cole turned and glanced outside. Beyond the high-rise buildings of downtown Denver, the Rockies rose and fell and circled the city. They were a formidable presence in this state, in Cole's life. A place far away he could go to escape. A heavy, still, grand constant in his life. A mountain could reveal the depths of a person's fears in one breadth. He was always struck by how they sustained themselves despite what went

on around them. In the mountains, very
little changed. They could be relied upon.
He wanted to be that for Bray.

"So can you help?" he asked.

"I'll try. With the shelter-in-place
order, that slows things down, with all my
people working from home. I don't even
think they're in the right frame of mind to
work. Not sure anyone is. But I'll pull all
the resources I can. You have any idea
where she could've been taken?"

"No clue," Cole said. Maybe he wasn't in
the right frame of mind, either.

"Can you at least tell me what state she
might've been in when she was caught? Or
when you last saw her? I need somewhere to
start."

"Wyoming," Cole said at once.

"Ah, yes. I remember now. She went there
after escaping the hospital," Thom said.
"Give us a few weeks or so."

"Thank you so much. You don't know what
this means." Cole exhaled.

"I've got kids, too. I get it," Thom
replied. "I'll be in touch soon."

Cole ended the call. His mind growing
heavy and tired, he lowered his head until
it landed softly on the table.

Then, he proceeded to cry.

Chapter Thirteen

Dianna

Dianna Hoffman sat at her desk in the S-Corp West office building. It was morning and already she could hear the protestors below her windows. They'd gathered first thing, before dawn, and waited for staff to enter the building. She was sure they were waiting for her, but Dianna had holed herself in her office since she'd returned from Arizona three days ago.

This was Day Three of protests. On Day One, Dianna had counted more than fifty people down below her floor-to-ceiling windows. The Marshals came out each day and arrested more and more of them.

You'd think they'd get the point, she thought, shaking her head.

She had shut off her Embedicare implant with the use of an app on her phone. The news alerts and constant interruptions were too much. Not to mention the bombardment of calls and texts she'd received. All work-related, none personal.

But she couldn't ignore her emails. She was currently staring at one from Michael Brisbon, her boss, the CEO of S-Corp:

YOU'VE GOT A LOT OF EXPLAINING TO DO. WE'RE TAKING ALL THE HEAT FOR WHAT APPEAR TO BE YOUR MISTAKES. YES? FUNDING TEST PROJECTS BEHIND MY BACK, TO SAY THE LEAST. AND YOUR DAUGHTER? HOW ON EARTH SHE GOT THE INFO SHE GOT?
AS SOON AS I GET SOME TIME TO BREATHE, I'LL SCHEDULE A MEETING.

WE'VE GOT SOME THINGS TO DISCUSS.

"Great," Dianna whispered. She read the email five times, at least. She suspected Michael thought she was somehow in on Bray's plan. Was that it? Was it not enough that she'd placed her own daughter in prison for the sake of S-Corp-and the rest of the nation?

Her skin crawled with gooseflesh as she recalled the last thing Bray said to her:

"When I was a child, my mom and I used to have fun. I remember how she always took me to the library so I could pick out books to read. I used to love reading with her. I'm not sure where she went, but she's not here anymore. . .If you decide to leave me in here, then you'd better say goodbye now because I am never speaking to you again."

When Bray was a child, Dianna seemed to have more time. Her evenings were free. As Bray's mental health worsened, Dianna stayed home to keep an eye on her. At night before bed, as Bray was beginning to grow drowsy from medication, they'd sit together and read stories in Bray's bed. Always stories about animals. Bray loved animals.

Bray was so intelligent. She picked up on reading faster than other children her age. She excelled in school, but as she developed schizophrenia, parenting her became harder the older she got. Eventually, Dianna started busying herself with work.

Truth be told, she'd given up. She wasn't equipped to care for a child with a mental illness. Thus the years in and out of the psych ward whenever Bray stopped taking her medications. It was a frustrating time, and times only got more and more frustrating the older Bray got. And now this. Her daughter, a known eco-terrorist. What other choice did she have than to put her daughter away? How else could she keep the country safe?

Dianna leaned toward the laptop screen. She clicked REPLY to Michael's email:

YES, BRAY IS MY DAUGHTER. I HAD NO IDEA BUT AS YOU SAID, I AM HAPPY TO PROVIDE DETAILS ONCE WE MEET. LET ME KNOW WHAT ELSE I CAN DO TO HELP MITIGATE.

Dianna hit send.

She checked her messages for something from Carl, the S-Corp Midwest President, with whom she'd been having a sexual relationship. He'd convinced her to use S-Corp funds for one of his pet projects, genetic testing on animals for the purpose of solving the nation's shortage of organs for transplants. Ever since the Embedicare takeover, Carl had ghosted her, and she had no idea why. She'd texted him again last night, but still, no reply.

She swiveled around and faced the windows. The sound of Marshal sirens whirred into the parking lot. She didn't have to get up to look. She knew they were arriving to arrest more protestors. What she noticed were the mountains out past the city. From here they were shaped more like hills, their snowy tops barely noticeable due to cloud cover. Beyond those mountains, miles and miles south, her daughter sat in a prison cell.

Dianna gulped.

She had to keep telling herself she'd made the right call. The nation's safety had depended on it, and when it came to doing the right thing, blood was not thicker than water.

Chapter Fourteen

Kage

The next day, Kage was instructed to meet the Red Lodge community cofounders, Rebekah and Chad Saler, at the Lions Club Park. Located on five acres of land, the park held a number of the community's vegetable gardens, which Kage now passed as he walked along Villard Avenue toward a white gazebo with a brown roof. As he passed the gazebo, Trevor waved to him from where he was sitting with a group of community members. Kage waved back. How ironic it felt to watch people gardening, using the soil as if S-Corp had never caused the fertilizer disaster back in 2027, the one that led to the deaths of thousands of citizens. The one S-Corp covered up with the help of the government, saying it had been a "terrorist attack." Seeing these vegetable gardens made Kage think of the garden he'd tended back home in Meeteetse. An ache fell onto his heart. How he missed his home.

He felt out of place here. Only days ago he was running for his life, and now he was in this unfamiliar commune, about to meet with two strangers for some kind of interview. He shivered. There beside the gazebo sat a single picnic table. Two people, a man and a woman, sat side by side. Kage stopped beside them.

Kage didn't particularly want to sit down to any interview with people he'd never met, even if they had created this inspiring commune as a way to resist the restrictions-against gardening, for one-currently imposed by the government. He wanted to get on with finding Bray, and he had no idea how. But, he was here. If he wanted to stay in Red Lodge, he needed to talk with these people. Might as well keep himself busy until he could figure out his next steps.

"Kage, nice to meet you," said the man, standing up from the bench and offering a handshake. "I'm Chad."

Chad met Kage in height. His hair was well kept, closely shaven on the sides with a thicket of wavy, white-and-gray mixed locks that hung over one side and down an inch. His full beard matched the color of his hair, and his eyes were a faded brown. His skin was leather and parched, a deep red indicating he'd spent plenty of time in the sun.

Kage shook the man's hand, nodded, and sat down. He glanced across at the woman, and she was quite stunning. Shiny blonde hair strung down to her shoulders, pulled back behind one ear. She smiled at Kage, and when she did, crow's feet appeared along the corners of her eyes, vibrant and small and blue. She had a strong, straight nose and delicate lips. She appeared aged in a refined way. As though age had treated her well.

"Hi," she said. "I'm Rebekah."

"Hello," Kage said back, trying to hide his instant attraction for her.

The couple looked at Kage from across the park bench, smiling with an openness he seldom saw in others.

"We won't keep you long, just had a few questions," Rebekah said.

"Ask away."

"You came here with Trevor, Emily and that group, right?" Rebekah asked. Kage was distracted. Out of the corner of his eyes he saw people working in the garden, pulling weeds, pushing a wheelbarrow full of fresh manure, which he could smell from here. He got the sudden realization the manure was from the cows they used for milk. The smell certainly confirmed it. This made his stomach turn.

"Yes. Trevor is my uncle."

"And how do you know Elliott?" Chad asked.

Eek. That wasn't a straightforward question. Was he to tell them the truth here? Did they know about the Embedicare takeover and Elliott's role in it? Should he tell them he, too, had assisted in what the nation was labeling a "terrorist attack?" Would they understand, even if they weren't animal activists, what had to be done? He reminded himself of what Elliott had said, that they were "anti-S-Corp," so he proceeded.

"We have a mutual friend. . .Bray Hoffman. Maybe the others told you about her?"

"She's the empath, right?" Rebekah asked, leaning her elbow on the table.

Relieved that someone else had mentioned Bray, Kage continued.

"Yes. I lived in Meeteetse with the others. Bray stayed with us for a few weeks and we became pretty close," he said. Memories flooded his mind, the time he and Bray spent together, how she'd help him wash dishes and they'd fool around like siblings. In all his twenty-eight years, and despite their age difference, Bray was the closest he'd come to having a best friend.

"Anyway, she came up with this idea to show citizens what happens to cows when they go to slaughter, essentially." Kage stopped. He didn't wish to go into details.

"We worked together and came up with an additional idea to expose S-Corp's secrets to the nation."

Kage watched Chad's eyes light up. Chad nodded, scratching at his beard. Kage waited for a reply, but got none. He continued.

"With Elliott's help, we created an encrypted website where we uploaded a video of Bray talking about S-Corp's deceptions, along with a manuscript my father had written. He was an animal activist. He. . .disappeared," Kage's voice trailed off. There was so much to say, so much that had led to him knowing Elliott. He had to stop himself before he said too much.

"We may not be activists here like you are," Chad said, "but we can appreciate the importance of informing the public of S-Corp's corrupt practices. You did the right thing."

Kage wasn't expecting that, but maybe he should not have been surprised.

"Well, that's how I know Elliott."

"Got it. And are you planning to continue this. . .crusade against S-Corp?" Rebekah asked, her eyes narrowing. "Because here at Red Lodge, we live in peace. We don't interact with the outside world. We believe that inaction is action. A kind of. . .resistance, if you will, to the unreasonable standards of western capitalism."

Kage's eyes dropped to the table. There was a time, months ago, when he'd left Meeteetse to go find out about his missing parents. Back then he couldn't handle living in hiding. He'd done it for twelve years too long. He doubted he could allow much time to go by now without searching for Bray.

"That's a good question," Kage

responded. "I don't know, to be honest with you. Activism is in my blood, my bones. I can't live in a society where I have to hide to be myself. I'm not someone who can have full awareness of what happens to animals and do nothing about it. Do nothing about the climate and the way S-Corp is manipulating our scarce water resources. Plus, we don't know where Bray is. I have to find her. If that means you want me to leave, then I guess I'll have to leave."

Rebekah and Chad looked at one another, then back to Kage.

"Where would you go?" Rebekah asked, frowning.

"I have no idea. This country sees me as an eco-terrorist." Kage let his mind run through the scenarios. Getting caught, going to prison. Or worse. Wherever they'd taken Bray, perhaps he'd end up there, too. Then he'd be of no help to anyone. He used to believe he could fight his way out of anything, but he had he learned the hard way how far the hand of S-Corp reached and how powerful they were.

Rebekah met eyes with Kage. She rested her hands on the table, held them together.

"I'm not sure if Elliott told you about our son, Devon?"

Kage shook his head.

"He was seventeen when the fertilizer disaster reached us. We were living in Washington. Devon got sick. . . ." Rebekah's voice faded.

Kage glanced over at Chad. His eyes had grown weary. Rebekah reached over and took his hand. Kage took a deep breath, knowing full well what they were about to say next.

"It all happened so fast, how he died. He would be about your age, if he'd have lived," Rebekah said, her voice dropping to a deeper tone. "It was completely unjust, what happened. And we have no doubt it was S-Corp, despite what the government has said." Rebekah paused. "You can stay, but no trouble, got it? Don't bring it in here. If you have contact with the outside world, do it only for the purpose of stopping S-Corp. We'll turn a blind eye, so to speak. But only for our son. As soon as we see one inkling of your activities causing harm to our community, we won't hesitate to ask you to leave."

"Understood," Kage replied, nodding. He felt a sudden respect for these people, for their loss. It seemed everyone had lost something, and his connection to these losses was becoming more evident the bigger his world became.

"One last question," Chad said, suddenly grinning. "Are you afraid of heights?"

Kage thought of the time he'd been stranded in Cheyenne after being caught by Marshals, how he climbed to the top of a parking garage and jumped from the roof onto a flying volocopter.

"No."

"We've got a job for you," Rebekah said, visibly exhaling. "You'll be helping us fortify roofs. It's for our wildfire prevention program."

Kage's eyebrows lifted. He was impressed. If his priorities weren't already set on finding Bray and continuing to expose S-Corp, it was possible he could see himself living here.

#

Kage followed Chad three blocks south and across a patch of sun-parched grass, through a thicket of Douglas fir trees, to a pair of apartment buildings. The sign by the road read: MOUNTAIN VIEW APARTMENTS.

From where he stood, out to the north he could see foothills of the Beartooth Mountains. Scattered along the flat terrain closer to him were more apartment buildings and houses.

Chad entered one of the apartment buildings through a glass door, held it open for Kage. They climbed a flight of stairs to the second floor. Kage listened for televisions or music but heard nothing.

"People live here?" he asked.

"Yep. They're probably all out working, but both buildings are at capacity," Chad replied. He walked to the far end of the hall where a pull-down step ladder led up into an attic of some kind. Chad stepped up and into the attic, motioning for Kage to join him.

In the attic, ladders, buckets and paint supplies huddled in a far corner. Along the opposite side were what appeared to be neatly stacked piles of roofing materials and sheets of metal.

The attic ceiling pointed upward at an angle. It was dark in the attic, save for the sunlight that shone in through an open window, where Chad's body was half in, half out, his legs sliding through until Kage watched him disappear onto the roof.

"I guess I'm going out there," Kage said to himself. He took a deep breath and proceeded over to the window. Popping his head out, he got a whiff of a downwind scent of the Douglas fir. It was sweet. . .almost citrusy. Kage led with one leg, sat himself on the window ledge, lifted his hand up to hold onto the window's frame, and looked down. From here the roof slanted downward at a forty-degree angle, stopping at a gutter. Beyond that he could see down to a concrete parking lot.

Kage may not have been afraid of

heights, but he still didn't want to fall. His heart raced more than he expected, but he swallowed his hurried breaths and pulled himself over the window ledge, carefully bent toward the roof, using it for leverage as he crawled halfway to the top where Chad was sitting.

From here, he saw the mountains again, more hills than points, covered in a blackish-green. Miles and miles of pine trees blanketed the foothills in darkness. The land was expansive, spreading in fields of dying grasses, then arriving at the houses and community that made up Red Lodge. The faint sound of a cow mooing caught Kage's ears. He turned toward the downtown area, saw a pair of beige barns in the distance. He couldn't see animals from here, but he sensed that was where they were.

Kage grew uneasy at the thought of the cows being held captive in those barns. He clenched his fists, then let them relax. Only days ago he'd sat beside Bray in Idaho while she somehow used what she referred to as her "gift"—her ability to link with animals and experience their pain-to expose the nation to the horrors of slaughtering cows. Those particular cows, due to secret testing engineered by S-Corp, had gained human-like consciousness. S-Corp made sure they were sent to slaughter as a cover-up of the company's illegal practices, but not before Bray was able to inform the public.

"That's where we keep the animals," Chad said, nodding in the direction of the barns. "I assume you're not a fan."

"No, I'm not. Why use the animals when you can easily go without?"

"It's not that simple. And we're not here to discuss ethics and morals. Let me show you to your work."

Chad stood up on the roof. Kage stood too, slipped and caught himself, his hand falling toward the roof. The coarse material of the shingles was easy to grasp, and he managed to get himself up to the top. Along the other side, three people worked, two men, one woman, pulling away shingles and revealing an additional barrier of some kind, gray in color.

"We're replacing these asphalt shingles with metal roofing," Chad said.

"How are you paying for all this?" Kage asked, surprised. "I mean. . .someone must have some bank."

Chad smiled.

"Sorry, I don't mean to offend," Kage said.

"It's okay. You're not the first person to ask. Rebekah and I have been very blessed, as have many of the members of this commune. We do what's called income-sharing. One pot of funds that everyone is free to add to, free to take from. Anyone who wants to take more than a hundred dollars needs to get approval, but it's a system largely based on trust. We put money in for the benefit of the community, not for any one individual. The community voted for the funds to go toward climate change preparations, to keep Red Lodge thriving on into the future."

"And what happens when the funds run out?"

Chad smiled again. The afternoon sun strengthened just above Kage's shoulder. Chad winced at the brightness, brought his hand up over his eyebrows, and looked to Kage.

"That's for another time. Stay awhile, work and do your part. Then maybe you can ask more questions."

Kage nodded. Chad walked down the roof

to the edge, stood beside the other
workers. The two men, both much older than
Chad, with reddened necks and faces,
weathered skin, one balding and the other
with white hair, were wearing orange body
harnesses that strapped over their
shoulders, around their waists, and
connected to a rope that disappeared
somewhere Kage could not see. The woman,
perhaps the same age as Emily, also
darkened by sun exposure, was wearing a
similar harness, but without shoulder
straps.

"Come on down, let me show you," Chad
said, waving to Kage. He bent down and
picked up an extra harness.

Kage did not have the confidence Chad
did. It would take some time for him to get
used to being up here, but he figured it
wasn't a bad skill to learn, roofing. It
wasn't a bad thing that he was here, it
just wasn't where he felt he was supposed
to be. Animals were being used here, and
that rankled him. He wondered if there were
other vegans here, beyond his own crew. He
made his way to Chad, grabbed the harness,
and slid it on over his jeans. Chad
assisted him in tightening it and then used
a carabiner to lock Kage into the
connecting rope.

"If you fall, you won't fall far," Chad
said, winking.

"Right," Kage replied, exhaling. The
closer he got to the edge of the roof, the
more his legs shook.

Chad showed him the procedure for
removing shingles. There was a system.
Moving from the back of the building to the
front, the woman used a tool that looked
like a cross between a shovel and a duck's
foot to scrape beneath the shingles,
pulling them away from their staples.

Kage's job was to lift those shingles and stack them in a pile. The bald man would grab the pile and walk it over to the white-haired man, hand them over, and the white-haired man would disappear over the other side, dropping the shingles into a pile on the ground.

They worked like this for the remainder of the afternoon.

#

Kage's roofing job ended right before sundown, which was at 9 p.m. As he made his way back to Elliott's apartment, his legs were wobbly and tired. He had to stop and rest every now and then, feeling the temperature slowly dropping as the sky transitioned into a crisp lavender and the sun huddled over the foothills of the Beartooth Mountains.

For a moment Kage lost track of where he was. He didn't have a map and was hardly acclimated to the community. He found his way back to the Lions Club and sat down at the picnic table where he first met Chad and Rebekah. The garden was empty. Everyone had left. Perhaps that meant Trevor was back at the apartment with the others. Kage had a sudden hankering to get back there as soon as possible, his chest feeling uneasy in this new environment. It took a bit of effort to remind himself over and over that he wasn't in Meeteetse anymore. That this was Red Lodge.

Eventually, he found familiar streets. It was nearly dark, with lights popping on in homes as he passed them. He could see through windows, people gathering for meals. It occurred to him he saw no children. That everyone was older. At least, older than him.

Entering the apartment building, he shook off some of his tiredness as he neared Elliott's door. He heard a variety of voices, and he smiled.

Inside, warm lighting welcomed him to a lively atmosphere. Livelier than when they'd arrived, than when they'd left Meeteetse. For the first time in weeks, perhaps, people were smiling.

"There he is," Dennis said, standing over by the desk. "Now we can eat."

Kage pulled off his boots, rubbed his sore feet. A stench of ash and wood rose from his body, but with food ready on the dining room table, a shower would have to wait.

The dining room chairs had been moved into the living room, creating a makeshift circle with the couch, and Elliott's gaming chair was turned so that it could also be used during the meal.

So this was their new life, was it? Meals together, working apart? What else would change, Kage wondered, before the week was out?

Everyone grabbed plates of food. Steaming sweet potatoes, salad, a large quantity of root vegetables. It smelled of earth and dirt, the things that reminded him of Meeteetse. Kage's eyes welled for a moment.

"You okay?" Emily asked. She was standing beside him as they both gathered food. Dennis, Trevor and Virgil had already taken theirs into the living room and sat down. Lana was filling a cup with water from a glass container.

"Yeah," Kage replied. "Just reminds me of home, is all."

Emily nodded, turned, and sat on the couch. Kage was parched. He went over to Lana, smiled at her. It was good to see her face after an afternoon of hard labor, something he had not been expecting to do today.

"What'd they have you doing?" Lana asked, handing him a cup from a group of them on the counter.

"Roofing," he said simply. Lana finished filling her cup and stepped away, toward the couch. He poured himself a cup of the room-temperature water, drank it down immediately. He poured a second.

Kage took the last empty seat, a dining chair beside the couch. He set his cup down on the floor and looked around at everyone.

"What a day," Trevor said, from his place across the room. Kage looked to him and thought of Chad, how the man wouldn't answer some of his questions. It reminded him of Trevor. The way Trevor led the commune, how guarded he had been when they lived in Meeteetse. Kage was starting to see that perhaps his uncle had his reasons.

"Where'd they assign everyone?" Elliott asked. He was leaning forward in the gaming chair. He stabbed at a piece of sweet potato and slid it into his mouth, chewing as if he hadn't eaten all day.

"They've got me in the garden," Trevor said.

"I'm helping with food storage and safety for the community," Virgil offered. He was sitting back on the couch, eating slowly. It was fitting for him to be helping with the food. He had always been the best cook in the house, and, when he was young, a sous chef in a vegan restaurant in Cheyenne.

Dennis had been assigned to the hydroelectricity program, which was also fitting. With a background in engineering, he was the one who'd developed their water system back in Meeteetse.

"I know this will be a shocker to everyone," Emily said, setting down the cup of water she'd taken a drink from. "But I'll be teaching yoga and meditation classes."

"I bet you're looking forward to that," Virgil replied.

"I am." She nodded, then looked away as if forlorn, almost. Kage wondered if she was thinking about Bray, an apt student of meditation in Meeteetse.

Lana had been assigned an administration position, something about helping with communal meetings and mediation. Again, appropriate. Lana was a lawyer by trade. The Red Lodge cofounders knew how to position people based on their strengths.

"And you, Kage?" Dennis asked.

"Roofing." Kage shrugged. Aside from gardening and working on cars, which he had failed to mention and did not seem to be needed around here, he had no other work experience.

"You're young and fit. Better you than me," Trevor responded.

The room went quiet. People gradually finished eating. Kage showered, and when he stepped back into the living room, he was given pause.

Everyone was putting on their shoes.

"Where we going?" he asked, though he had no energy to go anywhere. He wanted to lie down and sleep. He was expected to return to the Mountain View Apartments tomorrow at 7 a.m. Today he'd roofed on and off for six hours. He'd be doing nearly double that the next day.

Trevor turned from his place beside the door and looked at Kage. His blue eyes were both expectant and wide, hope mixed with concern.

"We've been divided up and given places to stay," Trevor explained.

"Oh," Kage said, slumping. He didn't

know why he'd assumed everyone would be staying in this one-bedroom apartment. It was Elliott's home, after all. But he was so accustomed to living under the same roof with this group of people that the information came to him as a surprise. And one he wasn't sure he quite liked.

"They didn't ask you if you wanted to move?" Lana asked. She was sitting on the couch, sliding on a pair of slip-on shoes.

"No." Kage had no other words. He was flummoxed.

"Emily and I'll be six blocks down, at the Red Lodge Apartments," Lana said, standing up.

"And Virgil, Dennis and I will be right next door," Trevor said, pointing.

"You can stay here for now, if you want," Elliott said. He was sitting in his usual seat at his desk.

Kage considered it. Having been given the choice, he surprised himself by realizing Elliott would be the best person, out of them all, for him to stay with. Elliott wasn't an animal rights person, but there was something about him. Something easy. . .accepting. Not that the others weren't, but Kage hadn't exactly been on the same page with Trevor since they'd been forced to flee Meeteetse. Trevor had not supported Bray's plan to expose S-Corp's secrets to the nation. He'd said they risked certain backlash, if not worse. And Kage had never much liked Dennis. He felt even less comfortable with the idea of staying with two women, one of whom he was madly in love with, and who he suspected didn't feel the same for him.

"That would be great," Kage said to Elliott. Perhaps this would give him the space he needed to feel out what to do about Bray, and maybe Elliott would want to help him.

Chapter Fifteen

Bray

Bray slept. At some point, a clicking sound entered her mind, followed by clip-claps. They were footsteps, but to her drowsy mind, clip-claps seemed more accurate. She even smiled and whispered: "clip clap," and let out a laugh. This was followed by Guard Steve's comment:

"Yes, clip-clap, clip-clap. Tha-weens-you-wee-to-wet-what."

Indiscernible.

Bray felt heavy, her body like concrete. Guard Steve attempted to lift her from the bed, and she tried to stand. Her feet gave way to a dropping motion followed by a sudden pause in air. She allowed herself to fall backward on the bed until the back of her head touched the wall.

The meds had taken her to a place where all she wanted was to sleep. Her legs were lifted, she was turned, and she was lying down again. Her eyes had been mostly closed this entire time, opening only once while Steve had her lifted from the floor. What she saw was nothing more than blurry clouds.

Time passed. The next clip-clap sound produced a tray of food set quietly on the floor. Bray turned in bed, opened her eyes. Slightly less groggy, she could tell that the cell had gone several shades darker as night approached. She looked at the tray of food, waited for her eyes to clear enough to see details.

A cup of water. She picked it up, her hand shaking. She brought it up to her mouth, opened, tipped the cup. The water fell over her chin, down the bed, onto the tray.

"Dang it," she whispered.

The cup dropped to the floor, empty.

She looked at the plate. A single hot dog, no bun. Over-boiled. Mashed potatoes, a plop of butter in the center. A steaming heap of spinach. She could eat that, she supposed, but her stomach felt so separated from her body, why bother. Instead, she insisted on refuting.

"Not vegan!" she raised her voice to no one in particular.

Within seconds, she was out again.

#

Bray had no idea how long it took for the drowsiness to ease up, but one day she opened her eyes and looked up at the ceiling. Her eyes blinked and she found she could see more clearly. She sat up, felt light-headed and lay back down. She hadn't eaten in who knew how long, so light-headedness was no surprise. Glancing around at the walls, she exhaled in defeat.

"Still here," she whispered.

The cell door opened. In walked Guard Steve. Slowly sitting up, Bray looked at him.

"You look awake for once," he said, bending down to her with a cup of water in hand. Light had entered through the window, dropping glances on the tile floor.

"How long was I out?" Bray asked.

"Two days. Now drink some water. You're probably dehydrated." He handed her the cup.

Bray took the water, tepid, no ice, and slowly drank the entire cupful. She looked at the floor and noticed the tray of food had disappeared.

"Lunch time's in five minutes," Steve said. "Think you can stand up?"

"I think so, but do I have to go? I'm not going to eat."

"Rules are rules," he replied. "The only reason we allowed this much was because your psychiatrist approved your days of rest, to give you time to adjust to your meds."

Bray nodded, frustrated, and handed back the cup. Steve turned for the door.

Bray stood. Her body still felt heavy. Walking over to the door felt like walking against a current. She could do it, but it took effort. She hadn't showered in a few days and she could smell herself, but she found she didn't mind. What she wanted was to finish this lunch and return to bed.

Out in the hall, Bray lined up with the other prisoners. Her head spun. She closed her eyes, woozy.

"You look like you're struggling," someone said from behind.

Bray turned to see the same young Black woman she'd sat with at breakfast a few days ago.

"Yeah," she replied. She didn't want anyone knowing she was placed on a medication for schizophrenia.

Ten prisoners ahead of her, two behind. A buzzer went off. The line moved. Bray wobbled forward, using her hand to gently graze the wall for support, hoping it would not reveal to others how much she was struggling.

They turned the corner toward the cafeteria. The floor was slippery beneath her prison-issued slip-ons, and one of her feet slid out from under her. She stumbled. The Black woman grabbed onto her upper arm, pulled her back in line.

"You need help," the woman whispered. "It's okay. I got you."

Bray allowed the woman to walk her into

the cafeteria. She was not expecting the compassion. Other prisoners noticed, but when they looked back at her, it was with half-smiles, gentle or sympathetic eyes. And then they returned to getting their meals.

What kind of prison was this?

"Want me to get you some food?"

"I'm not eating," Bray said. The words came out slowly, but with accuracy. At least she could speak and understand others at this point.

"Let me get you something. Fruit? A drink?"

"That's fine," Bray replied. She steadied herself over to the nearest table and sat down alone. Everyone else was in line or at the hot bar. The room filled with commotion, but none of it seemed remotely concerning. She had an assumption that prisoners would be violent, or at least scary and intimidating. But as she sat and watched them, they seemed as average as any human. They seemed unlike anyone who would commit a crime. Bray noticed she was judging.

The Black woman approached Bray's table and sat down with a tray of food. She picked up a bowl of mixed fruit and a fork and set them in front of Bray. Bray nodded politely but didn't speak. The longer she was out of bed, the more the tiredness was returning.

"What's wrong, not feeling well?" the woman asked. The table remained empty of other prisoners.

Bray wasn't interested in divulging to someone she didn't know. Not yet.

"Yeah, just adjusting to this place," she responded.

"It can get depressing. I found it helps to talk to the other prisoners, make friends," the woman said, working through a bowl of oatmeal. "My name is Tori, by the way."

Bray smiled over at Tori and turned away. Dizziness loomed again. She looked at the fruit in front of her, waiting for the dizzy spell to pass. She thought of Meeteetse, the elaborate meals. Were her friends still there, eating without her? What had happened to them? How could she ever find out, when this place wouldn't allow her any communication with the outside world? And while medicated so heavily she couldn't even stay awake long enough to try to connect telepathically to animals, something she'd been able to do since childhood. Perhaps she should be glad. It would probably be worse to hear animals suffering beyond these walls and know she couldn't do a thing about it.

This filled her with hopelessness.

Three prisoners came and filled the remaining seats at the round table. They began chatting with Tori. This was fine with Bray. She wished to disappear, in a sense. Into her own mind, if not literally.

"Bray," Tori said. "I want you to meet one of my friends here, Valerie."

Bray had barely been paying attention. She'd quickly eaten the fruit, the pieces cold and unripe when she bit into them. Not pleasant. Two strawberries, a gathering of blueberries, and two pieces of cantaloupe, which she never much liked. She was still daydreaming about breakfasts in Meeteetse.

"What? Sorry," Bray replied.

"This is Valerie," Tori said, giggling. "She'd be another good friend for you, I think."

Bray wasn't so sure. She'd never found it easy to keep friends, so she was not sold on the idea of making new ones. She just wanted to get herself out of here.

But she gave Valerie a nod, for pleasantries. She took in Valerie's choppy, blonde hair that strung down to her shoulders. Wrinkles circled her heavy-set brown eyes. Her eyebrows were prominent, yet soft. Bray suspected the woman was somewhere around her mother's age. What would someone like Valerie have done to end up in a place like this?

The meal bell rang. Time for prisoners to return to their jobs. Bray was not assigned to one yet and didn't exactly feel eager for that to change. She had no afternoon schedule, as far as she knew.

Everyone cleared their trays and returned them to the kitchen, separating off into the direction of their assigned tasks. Bray's head felt heavy, slightly dizzy. She waited for the room to clear as much as it could before the guards waved her out. She returned to the hallway, grazing the wall with the side of her arm to keep herself vertical, and made her way back to her cell.

In this way, a week passed.

Chapter Sixteen

Oscar

Bertan was placed in a new cell. Above ground by one floor. When he entered, the guards removed his cuffs. The door clanked shut. A bunk bed was set into the wall, made of off-white painted metal with thin, twin-size mattresses. A three-foot-by-three-foot window stood across from him, revealing a day that had already gone by. Barely he could make out the ten-foot fences, circles of barbed wire running along the top.

Sitting on the bottom bunk was another prisoner. Bertan was shocked when he noticed the man. Clean-shaven, youthful. Couldn't be older than twenty-five, his hair slicked back and his eyes dug down into a book in his lap. The man glanced up from his book, nodded, and said nothing. He returned to reading.

Feet away from the prisoner, Bertan registered a toilet, sink, and a stainless-steel shelving unit bolted into the wall. On the shelf, a toothbrush, cup, toothpaste and a half-used bar of soap.

This was not a space fit for two grown men. Bertan remained by the door, motionless. Afraid to move an inch. He thought that maybe if he didn't move, this place would not become real.

"Top bunk is yours," the man said in a thick accent. Bertan thought it to be Mexican.

Bertan would not budge. The narrow walls felt close to the skin. He stared out the window, disbelieving.

"You just going to stand there?" The man chuckled. He shut his book, placed it beside him on the bed. When he looked at Bertan, his eyes were curious, open, kind.

"Hablas inglés?" the man asked.

"Sí," Bertan replied, finally making eye contact.

"You must be new."

Bertan nodded.

"De dónde estás?"

"Honduras," Bertan said, feeling the tightness in his chest ease up.

"I'm from Chihuahua. Name is Daniel," the man said, coming to stand. He matched Bertan in height, but weighed next to nothing. "I'm not going to hurt you. We're all in here for the same reasons."

"What reason is that?" The last time Bertan chose to trust someone, he had hurt them. Probably best not to make friends in here.

"Being in the country illegally, yes?"

"Right," Bertan replied. No one needed to know the truth that he was in here because of his part in the Embedicare takeover. He had been their man inside the slaughterhouse, the one who provided information about the schedule and arrival of cows being trucked in from S-Corp.'s illegal lab.

He wished he were alone in the cell. He didn't want to enter into anyone's trajectory anymore. He was destitute, a number placed on his back, just a beef in the processing plant. He figured one day he'd be processed out of here, deported back to Honduras. How long that would be, he did not know, but if he could just hold on and keep to himself, he'd be home someday.

The room began to feel oddly far away

even though he was standing in it. Daniel said something. Bertan looked at him, his mind not registering, then looked away. His eyes trailed out the window, where the last bit of sun etched along the lonely horizon, then a shade of deep blue-black hit the window and muted it. Bertan was entranced by this.

"You hear me, man?" Daniel asked.

Yes, Bertan did hear him, but his mind began to slip outside where the darkness was. Something about it appealed to him.

"I'm going to lie down," Bertan said, climbing up onto his bunk. He lay on his stomach, facing the window. He grabbed the pillow from beneath the rough blanket and squeezed it in half, pressing his chin into it for support. He continued staring out the window. Perhaps if he looked closely enough, he'd see stars.

His eyes grew heavy. The sound of whirring hissed from a vent above the cell door. Gradually, Bertan nodded off. Lights went out.

When outside in the dark, with no moon or stars or light for guidance, it was easy to get lost, and to get lost for hours, if not forever. In these times, someone like Oscar became the darkness. He melded with it, accepted it as a part of himself. One had to do the same in a place like this.

He'd been locked up before. Willingly. He was twenty and had just begun his work with Medina. They took him away from his home, to an undisclosed location along the Rio Aguán. He was locked in a concrete shack for days, his wrists tied behind him and his eyes blindfolded.

There were voices. Screams by grown men crying to be let out. Scratching sounds. A chuckle.

Oscar grew confused. He hadn't

remembered any screams. He was out there in the jungle, left alone. Guards entered intermittently, hand-feeding him cold rice and black beans, laughing and spitting on him.

Something strange happened with time. In complete absence of light, only darkness peering in from the window, he could not tell if his eyes were open or closed. This wasn't the shack they'd locked him in. He lifted his hands to his face. They were not tied. He touched his eyes with his fingers. They were open. Sweat dampened his hair. Had the jungle been a nightmare?

Oscar turned and stared up at the ceiling. His heart beat into his ribs. Clanking and thumping, methodically, from somewhere outside the cell. *Cell?*

Yes, he remembered now. They'd moved him, once he survived his initiation in the jungle. That was what it was, wasn't it?

They moved him to a facility but he had no idea where. He'd been locked in a windowless van and driven there. It had taken hours. And when he arrived, blindfolded again, he was dragged into a room and placed in a chair.

Oscar sat up in bed. When the blindfold came off, he was staring at a black screen. His hands and legs were strapped to the chair.

He blinked. The flashback disappeared. He narrowed his eyes, leaned forward. There was nothing but darkness, but each time his eyes blinked, he swore he saw something. . .else. Him starving for days. A light coming on and staying on for what felt like years. A burning sensation in his eyeballs. Him standing out in the rain of summer, holding an assault rifle. Aiming at a dummy, tasked with shooting until he got it in the head.

A harsh noise evaded his concentration. Several voices all at once, then laughter. Silence for ten seconds, then a barrage of music with a woman's voice. A woman? There were no women where he was kept. Only other men his age, being. . .what? Trained? Oscar shook his head. It began to ache. He dropped it into his hands and shivered in anguish. He let out a wail.

"Shh, man. Trying to sleep."

What the fuck? Who was that? Oscar glanced up. He looked around in the darkness. Grabbing onto the edge of the bunk, his hand squeezing cold metal, he realized there was a man sleeping below him.

"*This is your first task*," a voice called. He could not see the source. Never could he see who was in control. He guessed that was the point.

"*You can shoot a dummy. . .but can you kill a man?*"

Oscar's eyes shot around the room. The voice. . .was it coming from the vent? From some speaker he could not see?

He leapt from the top bunk down to the floor, crouched, and waited. There beside him, movement. He turned toward it. There was a body beneath a blanket, asleep.

"*Kill him, and we will let you go home and see your family.*"

He needed no more convincing than that.

Silently, Oscar pulled the blanket down from his top bunk. He held it in his fists while the bottom of it dropped to rest at his feet. Hanging it in midair, he approached the body. The man was lying on his side, facing away from Oscar. Oscar crept closer. The man's body rose and fell beneath the blanket. Oscar felt the vast difference between shooting a lifeless dummy and squeezing the life out of a someone.

Or shooting a beef.

Wait. . .

Oscar paused. His shoulders dropped. Where did that thought come from? Shooting a beef? He shrugged. The sooner he did this, the sooner he could get out. Go home.

Oscar placed the blanket over the man's head. In one sudden move, he had his hands pressed hard into the mattress on either side of the man, pressing the blanket tightly against his face. The man attempted to lift himself up, screaming for air. Oscar grabbed him around the neck, wrapping the blanket around his head and covering him with it. Oscar pulled until the man's body fell out of the bed and onto the floor. The man flailed, grasping the air with his hands. Oscar began to laugh.

Oscar positioned his head over one of the man's shoulders, looking downward, his forearm pressed into the man's throat.

Without warning, he felt a blade rip into his upper arm. Oscar screamed and fell backward. Turning, eyes wide and forearms trembling, he noticed the knife sticking out of his upper arm.

"Fuck!" He spat. He yanked the knife out, and a gush of blood bubbled out from the wound, streaming down his arm.

The man stood up and ran to the door, banging frantically.

"Help! He's trying to kill me!" the man yelled.

Oscar fell over onto his side. He reached for the blanket, wrapped it around his arm. The blood loss was swift, even with the wound covered. He fell dizzy. His head dropped to the concrete floor. His eyes slammed shut, and he was gone.

When he woke, he was in solitary, again. His arm was bandaged. He lay there

against the wall, tired, huffing. Breaking
into sweats. It would be a week before he
encountered another living being.

Chapter Seventeen

Bray

"You seem to be feeling better," Tori commented. She sat across from Bray at a table in the cafeteria. It was breakfast time again. Outside the barred windows, an increasing sun bore down on the prison walls, shooting blots of light onto the floor and tables, into the eyes of prisoners. There had been more sun than not. Bray was beginning to wonder if it ever rained anymore.

"I'm getting there," Bray replied. She glanced down at her tray. She sighed. Eating bananas and toast everyday was not exactly enticing.

"How long has it been?" Valerie asked. She was sitting beside Bray, her hair up in a ponytail.

"A week."

There was one other woman at the table. Her name was Anna and she was in her fifties. Her face was lined with scarring that was quite rough in appearance as though she'd been left out in the sun and had dried like a prune.

Bray did not know Anna as well. She'd sat with Valerie and Tori at every meal. Bray had taken a liking to both of them.

Valerie was chewing away at scrambled eggs, which were still steaming. She had a kind of smile that reminded Bray of Emily. A smile that said she knew things without ever having to say that she knew them.

"You're not eating," Anna commented.

Bray met eyes with Anna. Anna's lips twisted to one side, the deep lines around her mouth growing deeper. Her eyes were hollowed out, dark, like dots of coal.

"I eat," Bray huffed. She was tired of people commenting on her eating choices. She'd lost weight, but the feeling of lightness appealed to her. She'd never been one to care about her weight or how she looked, and although she felt tired and run down, she was also beginning to feel slightly more clear-headed.

"You had a banana," Anna said. "That's not eating."

"Lay off her, will you?" Tori replied, shooting a glance at Anna.

Anna shrugged. "We all know what happened when we decided not to eat."

Bray's ears lifted. What was this. . .about them deciding not to eat? "What happened?" she asked. Her plate was empty. Her stomach, just the same.

"Years ago," Valerie said. "We went on a hunger strike. Many of us were vegans too, once."

A clanking of plates and silverware from the kitchen hit against Bray's ears. The prisoners at other tables were talking loudly. It was hard to tell if she'd heard Valerie clearly.

"Really?"

"Yep. We tried, and they put us all in solitary," Valerie said, swallowing the last of the eggs. Bray turned her eyes away from Valerie's plate. The sight made her think of Alice, the sow she had connected with as a child, and Rhea, the cow she had tried to save from slaughter only a week ago.

"They left us down there until we broke," Anna added, her eyes drifting away from the table and toward the windows behind Bray.

They had been. . .vegans? That seemed impossible. In today's society, finding another vegan was about as challenging as getting herself away from forced medications. She was beginning to wonder about this place, what everyone was in for. A week had gone by and she hadn't seen or heard of one act of violence by the prisoners. If it weren't for the guards and cells, she might've thought they were at some community center.

Tori shot a look at Bray.

"You, too?" Bray asked her.

Tori nodded. She leaned forward, and spoke.

"I tried to stay vegan when I first arrived here. I refused everything. I told them no food at all until they got me vegan food. I even refused water."

"Oh!" Bray said, shocked.

"They threatened me with solitary. That's when I met Valerie," she said, nodding in Valerie's direction. Her eyes grew wide, staring down at the table. "Val told me what happened to her, and. . .I decided it wasn't worth it. I started eating, too."

"How?" Bray asked, not that she was going to try. She didn't care if they placed her in solitary. She'd spent plenty of her life alone as it was, and she had been plenty isolated in the psych wards, so how would solitary be any different?

"I dissociate," Tori replied, sitting up and shrugging. "I'll go vegan again when I get out of this place."

"Ha!" Anna laughed. "We're never getting out of this place, honey."

Anna grabbed her tray, stood up, and marched up to the buffet line.

Bray sat in deep thought. If there were that many vegans in this prison, and they appeared tame, she wondered what had landed them here.

"Why are you all in here?" she blurted

out. "Everyone seems so-"

"Not what you expected?" Valerie interrupted.

"Yeah."

Valerie exchanged a glance with Tori.

"We're in here for the same reason as you," Valerie said.

"What?" Bray asked. Had she heard right? They could not possibly have done what she had.

"My friends and I-"

The buzzer sounded before Tori could finish. Bray startled in her seat.

Valerie and Tori stood up. Bray did the same. In the commotion of prisoners disposing of their morning leftovers and empty trays, Bray struggled to keep up. Her legs felt heavy, and she knew they would until afternoon, when a brief three-hour window would provide her with the most energy she'd have all day.

Tori appeared through a group of prisoners that had gathered by the cafeteria doors, lining up to move on to the next part of the day. That was how time passed here, from one structured activity to the next. Most went to work, but Bray had not yet been assigned a job. She stared at the prisoners, noticing how their bodies moved with such lack of motivation. No drive. No ambition. Just get from here to there. No meaning or purpose. These people in here, she was starting to see, were the zombie apocalypse of the world.

"Meet me in the library this afternoon. I'll tell you more."

"Library?" Bray asked.

"You don't know about the library?" Tori asked, hands on hips.

Bray thought back. The past week remained a cluster of cloud and fog in her brain. She remembered sitting in offices, certain conversations, ending up in Health Services.

"Gotta go," Tori said, glancing up at the clock. "Just meet me there at two."

Bray watched her exit the cafeteria. Bray started for her cell, hearing the cafeteria doors click shut behind her. The hallway was cold, keeping her alert as she meandered past a number of cells before landing at the bulletin board. On it were various lists of names, prisoners due for physicals, various appointments, and activities they could sign up for. A map hung on one side, showing a diagram of the unit.

"Library," she whispered, reaching up and touching its place on the unit map.

For the first time since she'd arrived, Bray found herself smiling.

#

The library was located on the opposite end of the unit, past the showers and along the same hallway as the unit staff offices. As Bray made her way there, she saw a pair of guards eating fast food at a desk in the hallway and watching prisoners as they passed. It helped that the word LIBRARY was printed on the outside of the gray painted door. Through the door's glass window, she could see into the room, and she was impressed. It looked like an actual library.

When she opened the door, a scent of mildew hit her nose. She entered. Ceiling lights provided decent lighting, looking down along a glossy, tile floor. The center of the room was lined with square tables, four chairs to each. A handful of prisoners sat and read magazines.

Four-foot-high shelving lined the walls on either side and traveled the length of the room, which Bray guessed was about the size of the cafeteria, only more narrow. They contained a multitude of books. Bray walked along them, running her hand over the shelves, touching the spines of so many books. She stopped and pulled out a random book from a fiction shelf and opened it. She touched the pages, turned them, felt a yearning for a dream she had yet to fulfill and often forgot about. She'd always wanted to be a writer, yet she didn't feel she would ever get there.

A checkout desk sat perpendicular to the shelves. Behind it, a pair of floor-to-ceiling shelves stood brooding over the place, watching in resignation, as prisoners pulled books from their stately frames.

Over at the far end of the library, Tori stood holding two books and was perusing the shelves for a third. Bray smiled. She walked over and stopped beside Tori, glancing at the shelf.

"You found it," Tori said, not looking away from the current events section.

"I can't believe they have so many books," Bray replied, her head turning in all directions, taking it all in.

"Want a tour?"

Bray nodded.

"Well, this here is the current events section. I found a couple books on white supremacy that I need to get into."

"Seems like a heavy topic for a place like this," Bray replied. "Though I know it's necessary."

"Exactly. Good to study the past so we can prepare for the future."

Bray nodded.

"What about you? What are you looking for?"

"I like fiction," Bray said.

"That's over here." Tori pointed, walking with Bray toward the front entrance, where Bray had been a moment ago. "Anything in particular you're looking for?"

Bray thought. She hadn't done any reading since she'd been in the psych ward back in Denver. It was challenging to stay focused whenever she was placed on medications. Not much different from how she felt today, groggy and heavy-headed. In Denver, when she'd opened a book to read in bed, within minutes she'd be asleep. Or she would sit in silence, book on her lap, communicating with Alice telepathically. Sometimes she would tell Alice about a book she was reading.

"Let me show you the rest of the place," Tori said, bringing Bray back to present.

Bray followed Tori to the back of the library, around a set of floor-to-ceiling shelves, featuring displays of old periodicals and books no longer in print. The displays stood in the center of the room, and circling them were three more tables.

Tori walked over to one of the farthest tables, set her books down, and took the chair across from Bray. Bray sat down beside a bookshelf labeled SPIRITUALITY. Her eyes began scanning the section of books until Tori spoke, ending her distraction and pulling her back to the table.

"As I was saying earlier," Tori began, "I had some friends. . .they're in here somewhere but in another unit, so I don't get to see them."

"That must be hard." Bray thought about her own friends—Elliott and, of course, the group in Meeteetse—and whether she'd ever get to talk to them again. There were so many unknowns after the fallout of the Embedicare takeover. What had happened in Meeteetse after she turned herself in to her own mother so her friends could remain in hiding? Did they get away? Or were they in prison somewhere and she would never know? And what about that Honduran man. . .Bertan, who had given them the information they needed to set the takeover in motion at just the right time? What had happened to him and his work friend, whose name Bray was embarrassed to realize she could not remember.

Tori interrupted her thoughts. "We had a hideout in the mountains. We were doing some animal activism work, to try to build up a case against S-Corp." Tori's voice was low, although there were no guards in the room, which Bray also found interesting. "But they found us. . ."

Tori's voice trailed off as Bray relived a memory. She'd read through the manuscript Kage's father had written years ago. Kage still had a copy. It had gone into grave detail on the experiences of animal activists who'd risked their lives to save animals from testing sites and factory farms. The activists' lives were threatened, and some of them were placed in prison.

Bray's eyes drifted away, caught by the series of books along the shelf of the spirituality section. Here she noticed a number of Bibles, various versions. Two books on Hinduism, a couple more on Buddhism.

"Grab them, if you want," Tori said. "You're allowed to take out three books at a time, for three weeks."

Bray stood up and bent toward the shelf. She pulled out a book on Buddhism,

set it down on the table. She turned back
to Tori.

"You can finish your story, I'm
listening," she said.

"There isn't much else to say. They
caught us in our hideout, took all of our
evidence, and transferred us here."

"No court or anything?" Bray asked,
trying to sound like she knew something
about due process, but she didn't. She
assumed that was about to change for her.

She continued scanning the bookshelf.
Her eyes stopped on a book about
meditation, something she'd never heard of
before she spent time with Emily in
Meeteetse. . .

"Nope. They still haven't given me a
court date. Val hasn't received one, and
she's been in here over ten years."

Bray shot up. She turned and looked at
Tori. Tori raised her eyebrows, nodding
slowly. Bray was appalled to discover that
people could end up in prison without due
process, and left here with no way to
communicate with the outside world.

"How long have you been in?" Bray
asked.

"Two months."

Two months, Bray thought. She looked
more closely at the meditation book.
Transcendental Meditation. Something she'd
never heard of before. But two
months. . .that sounded familiar. The
phrase itched at the instinct in her, the
part of her that knew what it knew, beyond
her own understanding. The part that could
communicate with animals.

Bray grabbed the book and sat back down
at the table, setting it atop the book on
Buddhism.

"You said you had friends here, too?"
Bray asked, now fully focused on the

conversation.

"We had a team. One of them is my partner. . .Andy."

Bray looked Tori in the eyes. She'd expected to see some proof of sadness. Two months wasn't that long ago. But instead she saw an absence. Like something should have been there, but was hiding, as if Tori's tough exterior was a prison in and of itself, keeping inside the things that Bray figured weren't safe to feel in a place like this.

Two months ago. . .that was about when she'd stopped the transport truck, helped Alice and the living sows off the trailer so they could die in peace instead of being slaughtered. Around that same time, she'd first encountered Kage and Lana.
Lana. . .who had said she had a team that was captured. . .by S-Corp.

Wait a minute.

"Your team," Bray began, slightly hesitant. She wasn't sure if she wanted to know what she feared she already knew. "You didn't happen to work in Wyoming, did you?"

"Why yes," Tori replied, lifting an eyebrow. "How'd you guess?"

A click from an overhead speaker rattled Bray's attention. A female voice spoke: "Library closing in five minutes. Please gather any items you'd like to check out and bring them to the desk."

Bray grabbed her books and followed Tori up to the checkout desk. Bray was suddenly flummoxed, perhaps shocked, to the point of not knowing what else to say to Tori right now. She would need some time to think about what she had learned.

A woman with striking, crystal eyes sat at the checkout desk. Bray couldn't stop looking at the woman's eyes as she and Tori checked out their books. Before Bray could say anything, Tori waved to her and hurried out into the hallway. Bray also hurried along, grabbing her books and carrying them out into the hall where prisoners were lined up to return to their cells. She could not find Tori. Even if she could, it wouldn't have mattered. The guards were in control and corralling them through the halls, each prisoner dropping off into their cells. Bray arrived at hers, walked inside, and dropped the books onto the bed. She stood there waiting, her eyes facing the wall, hardening at the possible reality that she knew way more about the prisoners in this place than was comforting for her.

Chapter Eighteen

Kage

In Meeteetse, time was not *time* at all. Not by civilized standards. Time was not determined by numbers on a clock, or by needing to get to "this place or that." There was no rat race. Nowhere to go. Nowhere to be. The day was portioned out by breakfast, lunch and dinner. By an internal clock that worked in tandem with the internal clocks of others: Trevor, Emily, Dennis, Virgil, Ethan.

In Red Lodge, without them nearby, time was confusing for Kage. His cornerstones had been removed. In Meeteetse, he woke when his brain said to. Nowadays he woke because he had a job to get to. He ate breakfast silently in the kitchen, chewing on oatmeal and blueberries while Elliott slept in the bedroom.

Every day for the last week, Kage woke, ate, and walked to his work site. Lunch was provided inside the attic of the apartment building they were roofing.

The days went by fast because they all felt the same. The feeling reminded Kage of the hours he had spent each day working in the garden in Meeteetse, that feeling of truly mundane activity. He found he enjoyed the roofing job, the pure physicality of it.

But in the back of his mind, there remained an uneasy, unresolved question: what to do about Bray? He couldn't leave her to the uncertainty he'd left his disappeared parents. He'd been a teenager then; he was an adult now. He couldn't allow S-Corp to get away with Ethan's murder, among countless other things.

Kage sat thinking about this in Trevor's living room one evening after a week of steady, hard work. He was sitting in a kitchen chair beside Emily, Virgil and Lana, who sat slumped on a couch, eating potato casserole from bowls. The thoughts in his mind kept him pensive, quiet, while across from him Elliott sat on a love seat, laughing at something Virgil had said but Kage did not hear. Every now and then the scent of sage entered Kage's nostrils and brought him back to the room. But he did not want to be in the room, necessarily. Though he appreciated eating dinner with these people he had come to know as his family, he could not help but notice who was missing.

His indecisiveness loomed with each day that passed, and the week had swept by him so fast, Kage feared the time that might go by if he didn't act now. He had to find Bray, and that was that. How. . .that was the question. He didn't know where to start.

This was something he'd typically have spoken to Ethan about. Now, Trevor entered the living room and took the one free space beside Elliott. Trevor wasn't going to listen. It didn't feel right to breach the subject with Emily. Her bowl was empty, and as she sat between Lana and Virgil, she was looking down at the bare, hardwood floor. He wondered if she might be thinking about Bray. Emily had spent hours teaching Bray to meditate, and the two had become close in Meeteetse.

Who did that leave?

Kage's eyes scanned the room. Lana? No. That would feel too awkward. Being around her made him nervous, and he needed to focus.

His eyes rolled over to Elliott, and he suddenly realized Elliott had been looking his way. Elliott was not smiling. His lips were pressed into a thin line despite their thickness. His eyes seemed to be telling a story meant only for Kage.

Elliott motioned his head toward the door, which was on the other side of Trevor. Kage gave him a sideways glance.

Me? he asked with his eyebrows.

Elliott pulled himself up from the love seat, holding his empty bowl.

"That was a heavy dinner," he said, patting his stomach. "I'm going for a walk."

Elliott walked into the kitchen, passing Kage's chair as he did. He nudged Kage's arm with his finger.

"Care to join me?" he asked lightly. He set the bowl on the kitchen counter and started for the front door.

Kage did not hesitate. He returned his half-eaten bowl of food to the kitchen, for he was hardly hungry, and followed Elliott outside.

#

The sun had a way of admitting that the day was coming to an end. Here in Red Lodge, it did so by hugging the Beartooth Mountains to the west. As Kage and Elliott walked down 9th Street East, in the direction of the mountains, the sun looked into their eyes, but having weakened from the length of day, it did not bother them. If anything, Kage noticed the way its light hung around the place, dropping evidence of its power along the streets and buildings.

"I've been meaning to talk to you. . .away from everyone else," Elliott started. "I kept trying to catch you at home. Seems like it's been a busy week."

"Yeah," Kage agreed, walking side by side with Elliott, who matched him in height. "That roofing job is something else."

"I bet," Elliott said, nodding. They stopped at the corner. Kage half expected cars to pass, but remembered where he was. There were no cars, only random community members walking by, perhaps on their way home for the night.

They crossed the street, continued on.

"You seem kind of distant lately," Elliott said. "I've been wondering if you're thinking about what I'm thinking about."

"Bray?"

Elliott nodded.

They passed the General Store and Kage froze for a second. He was taken back to the time he'd first brought Bray here to find Elliott. They'd stopped at this store to ask the locals where they could find Bray's friend, and at the time Kage was not sold on finding the man. To be standing here with Elliott today, therefore, felt a bit surreal.

"I want to find Bray. . .get her out," Kage said, turning away from the store.

"I'm on board with that. Question is how." They'd passed the store and turned left on Oakes Avenue, the sun now disappearing over Kage's shoulder.

"I have no idea. I guess that's what has me distracted."

"I might have one," Elliott offered.

Kage glanced over at him. He found it suddenly amusing, how he'd come to trust Elliott a bit more than those he'd lived with for the past twelve years. There was something unassuming about the guy. Or maybe it was not knowing Elliott as well as the others, Elliott not yet having seen Kage in his worst, his less mature moments, that made it easier for Kage to be vulnerable with Elliott. Not to mention Elliott was Bray's best friend and so had his own stake in the game.

"I think it's time we reach out to Bray's dad, let him know we're safe."

Kage exhaled, then nodded slowly. He supposed Elliott was right. If it weren't for Cole, they probably wouldn't have had the time to go into hiding before S-Corp arrived in Meeteetse. Cole had contacted them through their website contact form to warn Bray and her friends that S-Corp was on to them, that they'd better hide. If not for him, they'd all be locked up by now.

"I was waiting for the right time to say this, and maybe there is no right time." Elliott paused. "But have you considered checking the email account we set up on that website?"

"You mean. . .the website about S-Corp?" Kage asked, having nearly forgotten.

"Yep."

"That's right," Kage said, his eyes widening. "We did add a contact page, didn't we?"

"We did. And if people have contacted us, they've been waiting. What if there are people who want to help? Or want S-Corp dismantled?"

"I guess I hadn't thought of that," Kage admitted. He'd lived so long in hiding. He'd long ago figured the country had given up, or that most people assumed he and the others were terrorists.

"But don't you think they're all assuming the same thing?" Kage asked.

"The terrorist thing?"

They turned a corner at 11th Street, heading back toward Trevor's apartment.

"I'm sure a majority of them believe
that. But what if there are some who agree
with what we did, or tried to do? I've just
been thinking. . .if there are people like
you in the world, and then there's Bray,
and Lana, and her team that got locked
up. . .there could be more," Elliott said,
shrugging.

Kage went quiet for a while. Elliott
did have a point. They'd set up that
contact page for a reason. Who was he not
to check it? Maybe that was the key he was
missing, the most direct way to continue
Bray's mission to stop S-Corp. Maybe
someone out there knew something, maybe
Cole knew something, that could lead to
finding Bray. And then there was the matter
of Ruben, the animal rights guy working
undercover at S-Corp, and his friend,
Bertan. What had happened to them?

"I think I've also been worried about
those other two guys that helped us. . ."
Kage's voice trailed off.

"The two S-Corp workers?" Elliott
asked.

They arrived outside Trevor's apartment
building, stopping at the front steps.

"I haven't told you, but I asked them
to help me save Bray," Kage admitted.

"What do you mean?" Elliott turned to
face Kage.

"Back in Idaho, when she kept talking
about how she might die. I felt like we
needed her. . .because she's the leader
here. And I honestly didn't think that
showing citizens the slaughter of cows
would make any difference."

Kage began to feel something heated
inside his chest. This entire week he'd
been going through motions, working,
eating, sleeping and repeating it all the
next day. He hadn't realized until this

moment that he had been keeping himself from facing some uncomfortable truths: his friend was missing, and he felt responsible if something had happened to Ruben and Bertan. If he found out they'd been taken, or worse, he'd blame himself.

"I asked Bertan and Ruben if they could help. They agreed to pause the slaughter so I could pull her out."

"I see," Elliott replied. "Can't say I blame you. I mean, I'm not even an animal rights person, so I definitely didn't believe the plan would be all that effective. I figured people might be enraged by what S-Corp had done, but that's all."

"I'm afraid to know," Kage said regretfully.

Elliott reached over and placed his hand on Kage's shoulder. The sun had disappeared behind the mountains, and those mountain caps were hovering over Elliott's head like a group of strong friends, offering the promise that everything was going to be okay, even if it hadn't felt like it.

"That's why I wanted to come out here and talk with you," Elliott said. "You and I. . .we owe it to Bray to find her. And to Ruben and Bertan."

They smiled at one another. Turning to enter the building, Kage felt slightly less alone. It was good to have a friend in Elliott, perhaps the only person he could trust to carry the burden of Bray's disappearance. Suddenly it didn't feel quite so heavy.

Chapter Nineteen

Bray

Afternoons in Bray's cell often passed slowly. She'd have bouts of energy but not much she could do with it. She'd returned from the library transfixed by her conversation with Tori. The air that hummed through the vent above her door gave her chills. She shivered. Tori had said she and her team had been located in Wyoming. Could that mean. . .no, *could* it? Maybe she knew Lana? Bray hadn't had a chance to learn the names of Lana's team members, the activists who were caught by S-Corp and disappeared. She hadn't taken the opportunity to learn about Lana because she was wrapped up in her own worries, hearing in her mind the voices of cows that had gained human-like awareness as a result of secret S-Corp testing-the S-Corp testing Bray then brought to the awareness of the entire nation, and as a result had ended up here in prison.

Was everyone in here for the same reason, for taking action against S-Corp? she wondered.

Her head began to spin. Her empty stomach seemed to leap into her throat and she felt slightly ill. She lay down in bed, on her side, facing the desk. Her thoughts raced back and forth between Tori and Valerie. For the first time since she'd received the injection, her thoughts became more lucid. She could remember things. Like the fact that Kage's mother was named Valerie.

No way.

Bray shook her head. She closed her

eyes, took some breaths, and opened them again. Her eyes landed on the desk and the books she'd brought back from the library. She read their spines, thought about meditation. She'd gotten into meditation in Meeteetse because her thoughts and the voices of suffering animals she heard in her mind were so powerful and intrusive, she needed solace. And during the two months she was there with Kage and Emily and the others, meditation had given her peace.

Bray sat up. Her head spun. She waited it out, stood up, and reached for the meditation book.

"Transcendental Meditation?" she whispered. She'd never heard of such a thing. She didn't realize there were *types* of meditation. She only knew about the meditation Emily had taught her, sitting and paying attention to breath, to thoughts, to sensations in the body. But this book, as she turned it over and read the back, suggested something different.

It would be more than two hours before she saw Valerie and Tori again. This gave her plenty of time to read the book and decide if it was something she wanted to try, to clear her mind, before she blurted out to Tori and the others that she might know one of Tori's team members, Lana. And *should* she tell her? That was the question. She had no way of confirming whether Lana was safe and in hiding somewhere. And if Valerie really was Kage's mother. . .well, that was something Bray pushed away from the forefront of her mind. When she considered it, her head felt like it might explode. She shuddered, shook off the thought, and opened the book.

#

Bray used time before dinner to read

the Transcendental Meditation book, once through. Always Bray had been a fast reader. As a child she read through books the way a racing heart runs through beats. She *loved* to read, and this book was no exception. Despite it having been published in the early 2000s, its message remained relevant: a simple practice that allowed one's mind to settle and to transcend consciousness.

That sounded good to Bray.

When she went to the cafeteria for dinner, her thoughts lingered on the meditation book. She'd elected not to say anything to Tori or Valerie about what she knew, or thought she knew. Not yet. She wanted to meditate, and to make it her primary focus while in prison to learn this transcendental piece. Then, she decided, when her mind had cleared more from the medication fog—and if, perhaps, she could *transcend* despite the medication—maybe then she would speak to them.

She'd learned from experience that she had to get quiet first, when she felt indecisive. When she had trouble hearing her instinct. The meditation book had given her a sense of purpose, for once, and so she sat quietly at dinner, eating only two helpings of salad soaked in olive oil, listening to Valerie and Tori discuss their work days.

She was quick to return to her cell. If she had any intrusive thoughts, they were the obsessive thoughts about getting quiet. About meditating. There was a time she would have fought this. But in prison, there was nothing better to do with her time. Meditation could, for one thing, make hours turn into minutes. For another, it was a test. To see if it could give her strength to fight off the effects of the medication.

That was what she really wanted.

Bray entered her cell and listened as the door automatically shut behind her. She sat on her bed, leaning back against the wall, the mattress providing comfort for her sitting bones. And bones were all she could feel with the continued weight loss from refusing to eat the prison's food. She paused, remembering the hard earth outside her home in Meeteetse, where Emily first taught her to meditate. Where the grass sometimes tickled her feet. The way the sky in the evenings revealed a vivid glimpse of the Milky Way. Stars layered upon one another in space and time, reaching beyond such elemental concepts, defining and transcending all human understanding.

Having read the book once through, she knew that students of this form of meditation were required to work with a teacher in order to practice it, but she was in prison without access to teachers. She would have to go it alone, hope for the best.

Turning to the chapter in the book that instructed how to practice this Transcendental Meditation, she read aloud:

"Sit comfortably for meditation. No need to focus on your breathing. For this first week, sit and silently repeat the mantra *so, hum. I am that.*"

"I am that?" she asked herself. "I am what?"

She shrugged, reminding herself she didn't need all the answers. That a meditation practice required a certain amount of faith, just like anything else in life. Faith that if she sat down, tried her best, and followed the instruction, whatever was supposed to happen would.

Bray closed her eyes. After taking a

few deep breaths, she began silently
repeating the mantra in her mind.
"*So. . .hum. . .so. . .hum. . .so. . .h
um. . .*"
Gradually, she fell into a rhythm. So
on the inhale. Hum on the exhale. Tiredness
came. Drowsiness attempted to take control.
She focused more fully on the mantra.
It developed into a kind of battle, or
dance, depending on how she looked at it.
As she repeated the mantra, with her eyes
closed, a sense of sleep enticed her,
whispered to her as if to say: *just stop
this and you can be asleep in seconds. You
can sleep through this pointless existence.*
Throughout the passing minutes, the
dance became:
*so. . .hum. . .sleep. . .sleep. . .so. . .h
um. . .sleep. . .sleep. . .*and so on until
the sleepiness became something Bray
accepted. She found that, in her second
round of Transcendental Meditation the next
morning, the sleepiness was given
permission to simply be there. No longer
was there any need to fight it. The dance
slowed into a kind of symbiotic
relationship, the way certain parts of
nature worked together to benefit one
another.
The mantra simply coexisted with the
drowsiness. Both could, and did, occur
simultaneously.
Within the spaces of this coexisting
relationship between mantra and medication,
Bray found solace. Maybe even brief
sensations of peace. . .quiet. The
sensation of not fighting, of working with
the medication's side effects rather than
trying to resist them. In the solace she
began to recognize a slow, gradual rise in
awareness. Of her in and out breath. Of the
spaces between breath, spaces where there

was no thing and no one, not even herself, the mantra *I AM THAT* ringing with truth in the core of her body.

Chapter Twenty

Oscar

Oscar was curled up on the floor when the guards came to get him. When they entered the cell and stood above him, one of them nudged his back with a steel-toed boot. Oscar flinched. He turned up and glanced at them, his eyes weary and weak.

"Come on!" The guard's voice boomed into his ears. "You're going outside."

"Ou-outside?" he asked. His voice was gruff from dehydration.

"You get one hour of fresh air. Take it, or leave it," the guard replied.

Suddenly he was pulled up to standing. It had been so long since he'd used his legs he'd nearly forgotten how to walk.

The guards *dragged* him out into the hall by his upper arms. He came to stand and they walked with him around a corner and to a steel door. He smelled the stench of urine on his pants.

"How long. . ." Oscar asked, but his voice trailed off with his mind before he could finish the question. He wondered for a moment who he was. . .where he was. Was his name Oscar? He wasn't sure.

"It's been a week, if that's what you're asking," the guard replied simply.

They stopped at the door. One guard held Oscar while the other unlocked the door and pulled it open. As the light slid into the prison, Oscar saw it and tears came to his eyes. He couldn't tell if there was emotion in those tears, he only felt them roll down his cheeks and stop. His chest was a cavern. His heart, a frail, weak child dying on the side of the road.

He was carried outside, one guard to each arm. The chains that hung from his wrists and latched to his ankles felt far away, as though attached to some other body he had gotten inside somehow.

Outside, a hot sun burned the earth. Oscar had lost all concept of a sun, having been trapped in the hole for a week that he did not know was a week. The time folded in on itself and disappeared into nothing.

He winced. The sun was painful. He shivered despite the extraordinary heat. The landscape was empty and stark. Surrounded by twelve-foot fences, Oscar was quickly entrenched with a view of miles and miles of dead earth. An uninviting color of sand-an expired yellow-blinded him and he looked up at the sky to divert his eyes.

He turned his head down from the sky. The guards led him to a fenced-in cage standing in the center of the yard. Its eight-foot fences were rusted and begged for attention. As the guards unlocked the opening to the cage, a thought crossed Oscar's mind to bash their heads into the rusted fence, yet his arms remained by his sides. He stood there in perpetual motion, as if standing in an ocean of water, moved back and forth by some force not his own. This body he was in, so foreign and so uncomfortable. Like a person inside a machine. He wanted out.

Oscar felt himself pushed into the cage. The door, enmeshed with fencing, shut quickly. The sound of a click hit his mind in a certain kind of way. Before he could register what was happening, one of the guards snickered at him from outside the cage. Oscar eyed the man, his mind set on wanting to do awful things with a vagueness that felt off-putting.

The guard chuckled, said something under his breath.

A swift and sudden wind picked up, seemingly out of nowhere, and kicked the harsh and desperate sands through the fences and into the cage.

"Hurry up, let's go!" the guard furthest away yelled back to the one staring at Oscar. The wind ripped through the fences and pushed the sand into the guard's face. He shielded his eyes, turned. The wind swirled around and around. Oscar lost his sense of sight through the spinning colors of sand and sun. The sand slapped his face and stung like a thousand needles. He crouched down and ducked his head as a sand storm blew through the yard. He saw that his cuffs and chains had been removed.

He heard the sound of running and opened his eyes. Through the heavy clouds of dust, he watched the guards run back toward the prison building.

"Good luck out here, asshole!" one of them screamed back. Oscar watched as they disappeared from sight.

The dust storm pushed down on him. He had no choice but to drop all the way to his knees. He covered his mouth with his uniform. Everything closed in on him. Despite being outside, he felt he might suffocate.

Suddenly, his t-shirt was dragged up and over his head, as if being pulled by the wind. The wind and dust and sand grew so intense he felt it push into his skin. It pushed and lifted, pushed and lifted. His hands now free, he used them to protect his head and stop his long hair from slapping against his cheeks and eyes. His eyes watered. Dust forced itself into his nostrils and into his sinuses and lungs. He began to cough. Distracted by the heaviness in his chest and the effort to breathe, his body was slowly dragged along the ground. A gust of wind swept in like a hand, lifted Oscar up onto his knees, and pushed him square up against the fence.

"Ahhh!" he yelled, pressed so hard the fencing scratched at his cheeks and embedded itself into his skin.

The wind was so strong, so steady, his body hung against the fence, knees digging into the ground. He tried to get his footing and slipped on sand, his body falling harder into the fence. A piece of rusted iron sliced his face. He started to bleed.

Something had come to destroy him.

His time was due.

"*Oscar*," it whispered. A man's voice, slipping into his ears without permission.

"*Open your eyes*," it hissed.

But he would not. And he sure as hell was not going to respond.

The wind was too strong. And loud. It burned his ears. It swept into his face, stopping his breathing, halting his lungs. Eyes forced closed, tears dropping from them and collected by the wind, Oscar's heart squeezed as if it, too, had been pressed hard against his back rib cage.

Then he felt something grasp his throat, but gently, and press his head into the fence. It held him there. No matter how hard he tried to move, he could not. He was stuck.

"*Listen to me, Oscar*." The voice spoke plainly. Clearly, as if someone was standing right in front of him. Oscar felt tempted to open his eyes to see, but the winds and sand were too much.

And then the wind died down.

As his body pressed firmly against the fence, everything around him dropped to silence. He let out a breath and then nearly hyperventilated as his lungs begged for air. He coughed. A taste of iron touched his tongue. Was it blood? Oscar lifted the lid of a single eye and peeked. Dots of red traced the ground, where no movement could be seen. Letting out a laugh of relief, he attempted to pull away from the fence, only to have some invisible force push him up against it.

"Do you not recognize my voice, dear Oscar?" the male voice spoke again. "*Or shall I call you by your true name. . .Bertan*?"

"Wha-" Oscar tried to speak, then went breathless. His eyes shot open, desperately searching the limited area he could see, unable to turn his head.

If there were no guards, he could try to escape. If he could get himself free of this paralysis.

"*The only escape for you is by leaving this body, and leaving it for good*," the voice said.

"What the hell is this?" He tried to yell but could only whisper. "Some joke to freak me out?! Someone's messing with my fucking mind."

Oscar brought his hands around to his throat to feel for whatever was holding him in place.

Right before his eyes, the dust particles lifted into the air. This time, there was an absence of wind. He froze, hands in mid-air.

The particles collected and gathered. They took shape. Suddenly he was watching a memory in his mind-someone else's memory, nothing familiar to him-of a dark, cold room. No windows. Thick, concrete walls. So dark he'd used a flashlight to see. Hands shaking.

"Who the fuck is in there!" he yelled.

He pulled a gun, stepped carefully around metal tables and strange instruments used to gut animals. Slowly, a ghastly image of a girl appeared. Her face had been shot through and a hole remained where an eye was supposed to be.

Then, Oscar's mind split in two. It felt that way, as though he were a part of someone, as if a twin or a second mind had been inside him all along. His head felt a crack in the middle, bending his identity sideways, tears escaping his eyes to ease some of the pain.

The body of dust particles formed into the figure of a man. Shoulder-length, flowing hair. White mustache.

Oscar began to shiver uncontrollably. His stomach turned. He opened his mouth to scream. Nothing came out.

"*Do as I say*!" the man yelled, echoing out into the landscape as if speaking from the sky. "*Leave my son, and leave him now!*"

The voice boomed into Oscar's head, between his ears, causing his temples to throb. He felt himself losing consciousness.

"Who. . .who. . .are. . .you?" Oscar begged, struggling to get the words out.

"Let me help you remember," the man said.

The man's hand lifted, pressed into Oscar's forehead. A cool feeling covered his skin, providing relief in the sweltering, desert heat.

Some part of his mind, Bertan's mind, remembered being a child. His father would read to him in bed. Classics from another time that seemed never to have existed:

Robinson Crusoe, Twenty Thousand Leagues Under the Sea, Treasure Island. Bertan would lie in bed, a fan whirring in the corner to stave off summer heat, and he'd listen to his father's voice. Baritone, yet soft. Kind. The sort of voice Bertan could fall asleep to, and often times he did.

The sound of the prison door opening jarred his brain. The cool feeling left his forehead, the scorch of heat quickly returning. Opening his eyes, he saw the ghost raise his head, turn to see the guards approaching, and twist into a swirl of wind, disappearing into thin air.

Chapter Twenty-One

Kage

Kage and Elliott returned to Elliott's apartment. It was night, and tomorrow Kage would have a day off from roofing. This gave him some relief, knowing he didn't have to jump right into bed to be up at daybreak to go stand on a roof all day.

Elliott flipped on the overhead light in the living room. As Kage pulled off his boots and left them beside the door, Elliott made his way to the desk, where he stood and clicked on his laptop. The two side-by-side screens opened to a background of a city at night. Kage hadn't noticed it before. It wasn't any city he was familiar with. It was. . .old. A city from before the 2030 Migration. From before the world had changed. He could tell this by its standard skyline, absent of the grossly uncharacteristic apartment buildings that suffocated cities nowadays. There were a number of skyscrapers, a Ferris wheel lit up in neon colors, and a bridge crossing a river, decorated in orange lights.

Kage approached the desk.

"All yours," Elliott said, motioning to the desk chair.

Kage took a deep breath and sat down. He watched as Elliott, who pulled up a chair and sat beside him, opened the internet.

The Quest browser popped up on the screen. Kage stared at it. He waited for Elliott to do something else. . .to bring up Kage's email, or do whatever he did to get to where they needed to go.

Elliott glanced at Kage. Kage glanced

back. Elliott grinned.

"You know how to use the internet, don't you?" Elliott asked.

"Of course I do!" Kage said, huffing. He leaned forward and looked at the screen; it was all white with a search browser in the center, and a large, blue Q in the center of that. He typed the word EMAIL into the browser, and leaned back.

Elliott laughed.

The browser displayed a list of email servers, the Qmail link at the very top.

"What?" Kage asked.

"Dude. . .here, let me show you."

Elliott leaned over and grabbed the wireless mouse. The arrow moved to the upper right corner where a dropdown revealed a photo of an envelope.

"Click on this," Elliott said, clicking on the envelope.

Kage felt embarrassed. To be twenty-eight and know little to nothing about something as basic as the internet was further proof of all he'd missed out on while living off the grid for twelve years.

"Put in your password," Elliott said, leaning back.

Kage sat up, looked down at the keyboard. He remembered the password, yet he still hesitated. What if, when he opened the email, there was nothing there? No responses. What would that mean? And what if there were several, but all nasty, snide remarks?

Kage slowly typed in the password, one letter and number at a time, and then clicked the NEXT button.

His breath stopped. His back was tight as he sat on the edge of Elliott's gaming chair and waited. Elliott leaned forward.

And then Kage's mouth dropped open.

"Holy shit," Elliott said under his

breath.

"No kidding," Kage replied.

There were hundreds of them. Emails upon emails. Subject headings like, YOU SHOULD BE EXECUTED FOR WHAT YOU DID. . .WHEN I FIND YOU, I'M SUING YOUR ASS. . .VEGAN FASCISTS.

Dispersed amidst the hate mail were a few more hopeful ones, the subjects stating: THANK YOU. . .S-CORP SHOULD BE DESTROYED. . .HOW CAN I HELP?

"Jesus," Kage said, his face growing hot. So many citizens, and as he scrolled down the list of unopened mail, most of them were not happy. In fact, it appeared as though most of them wanted Kage's head on a platter.

"He can't help us now," Elliott replied.

They both sat back.

Kage dropped his head into his hands, gave it a good shake. What was he supposed to do. . .respond? He didn't want to open all those nasty emails.

"There's no way I'll get through all these," Kage said, looking up.

"Here, let's do this," Elliott responded. He reached for the mouse again. Kage watched him create a new folder titled, HATE MAIL. He watched, still in shock at the enormous number of responses, as Elliott clicked here, clicked there, typed some phrases into a tiny phrase box.

"What are you doing?"

"We're going to funnel all hate mail into this one folder. I'm creating a list of catchphrases and keywords so, when any emails come in with those words or phrases, the system will catch those emails and send them to the folder. You won't even have to see them."

"Wow, you can do that?" Kage was

amazed.

"Thanks to AI, we can do more than we should," Elliott said, finishing and sitting back in his seat.

Suddenly, nearly seventy percent of the emails disappeared into the hate mail folder. What was left were more subtle, questionable or supportive emails.

And, Kage noticed, the email from Cole warning them about S-Corp, the one that had led Kage and the others to safety moments before Dianna Hoffman and her S-Corp hoodlums showed up in Meeteetse to try to take them all away.

Kage hesitated for a moment before opening Cole's email. He glanced at the words, remembering those final moments in the house when Bray was still unconscious after she connected with an entire nation of people through a minuscule implant in her arm, those final moments before Ethan was shot and killed.

Kage began typing, slowly tapping on the keypad as he found each letter he needed:

> COLE-
> THANK YOU FOR THE WARNING.
> WE ARE IN HIDING.
> BRAY WAS TAKEN. BY S-CORP.
> DO YOU KNOW WHERE
> SHE IS? WE ARE WORRIED FOR HER.

Kage paused. Was it wise to let Cole in on his name? Maybe not yet. He left the email as it was and hit send. Turning, he looked at Elliott.

"I guess it's time to start reading these emails," Kage said.

"Yup. Have at it, buddy." Elliott patted him on the shoulder and stood up. "I'm heading to bed."

Left alone with the emails, Kage fiddled with his hands. His eyes stared at the screen, at the fifty-plus emails that remained unopened, unread. Emails sent only days after the Embedicare takeover happened. Emails from strangers. Kage didn't like strangers. Before Lana, he never felt he could trust anyone outside his circle. But. . .then he'd met Lana, met her team, realized there were others out there like him. Kage shrugged. Maybe there were more people out there who were on his side. People who wanted to do the right thing.

There was only one way to find out.

Kage opened the first email, exhaled, and began reading.

Chapter Twenty-Two

Cole

One week passed and the nation's terror warning was reduced to yellow. Cole sat at his dining room table, which he had set up as his makeshift desk. A half-eaten salad sat beside his laptop. It was mid-morning, and he forwent coffee for a glass of ice water. A headache throbbed along his forehead and vibrated whenever he stood up, a product of caffeine withdrawal. That and an overall lack of sleep because at night he could not shake nightmares of the slaughter he witnessed, thanks to Bray. They always started and ended the same: an image of a cylindrical, metal box flashing on, shifting into darkness. An experience of immense pain between his eyes, followed by a feeling of vertigo as he was flipped upside down. A man with a sharp blade. Heat running along his neck. A sharp pain like he was being cut in two. Each time, he'd shoot up in bed, panicked and out of breath.

Enough time had passed since the Embedicare takeover for him to realize he was not going insane. Reports of other people recounting a similar experience dominated news channels for days, though today he saw stations returning to regularly-scheduled programming. He left the TV on whenever he was awake, to keep the edge off.

Cole rubbed his thinning hair. He hadn't yet showered, and without the usual hair gel, his hair was soft and lay flat on the top of his head. A stubble approached his chin and ran along his jawline. He was reading an email he'd received from Elliott. Or at least he assumed it was from Elliott. Whoever had written it did had not provided a name.

COLE-
THANK YOU FOR THE WARNING.
WE ARE IN HIDING.
BRAY WAS TAKEN. BY S-CORP.
DO YOU KNOW WHERE
SHE IS? WE ARE WORRIED FOR HER.

Bray had been taken. What he feared had indeed come true.

"But where?" he whispered. Thom had yet to respond to his request to find her, and he knew it would take some time. Three days ago, the president had given a press conference. He'd said the terrorists involved in the takeover had been detained. He'd said the lies told about S-Corp were just that: lies.

Cole shook his head.

He glanced down at his forearm. The skin was bare. He touched it with his thumb and a screen lit up. Nothing there. No messages or responses from Dianna. At this point, he wasn't going to get one.

When Bray was a child and first began exhibiting symptoms. . .telling Cole and Dianna that animals were asking her for help-"my animal friends cry," she would say-he wanted to believe her. He wanted to believe her because, when she'd said these things, he could see in her child's brown eyes a glimmer of sorrow the level of which no six-year-old could comprehend. Looking back now, he remembered the days when he was at home and they'd attempted family meals together.

"Bray, eat your food," Dianna said, cutting into a piece of baked chicken cooked by their assistant, Connie.

Bray did not reply. She looked away from her food, out the window. It was summer, and the sun was glancing into the living room. Birds landed on the blue spruce in the front yard. Cole watched his daughter smile.

"Bray!" Dianna shouted. "Eat or go to your room."

"Hold on now," Cole spoke up. "Bray, are you all right?"

Bray looked up at him and, when she did, her smile faded. She looked at him for the longest time, as if she were trying to say something without words, and only to him. She appeared so. . .downhearted.

Cole shook off the memory when his arm suddenly vibrated. He shivered and turned his arm over to view the screen of his Embedicare implant, where he saw a message from his campaign manager:

MIGHT BE A GOOD TIME TO
RESURFACE, COLE. YOU CAN ADDRESS
THE NATION. MAKE IT CLEAR WHOSE
SIDE YOU'RE ON. MAKE IT CLEAR YOU'RE
NOT ON THE SIDE OF TERRORISTS.

Cole exhaled in disappointment. What could he expect, that his campaign manager would see it any other way than how the majority of the country saw it? A terrorist attack? How could he believe that. . .when his own daughter was involved? His law background and years of service as a senator had taught him plenty about seeing both sides of an argument.

Moreover, he'd not yet received the information he needed to make a clear case for either: was this a terrorist attack or a cry for help?

"That's it," he whispered, nodding. "I need to get more information."

Cole leaned forward. He grabbed his phone and used his thumb to unlock it. He found the message sent by his campaign manager, and replied.

> NOT RIGHT NOW. I'VE GOT
> SOME THINGS TO SORT OUT.
> THAT WAS MY DAUGHTER, YOU KNOW.
> I'LL BE IN TOUCH.

Truth was, he wasn't sure he wanted to run for president anymore. He realized now it had been more Dianna's wish than his. Cole sent the message, turned the phone over, and set it back down. He returned his attention to the laptop and the email Elliott had sent. He would reply, and then he would get to work. Until Thom had something on his daughter for him, he would use this time to find out whether Bray was trying to tell him something. Something about S-Corp. Something about the truth that maybe, all along, he had been too afraid to see.

> ELLIOTT-
> I AM GOING TO ASSUME THIS
> IS ENCRYPTED. PLEASE BE CAREFUL.
> I WILL FIND BRAY. KEEP IN TOUCH
> IF YOU CAN.
> COLE.

Stretching, Cole stood up, grabbed the laptop, and brought it with him over to the door. He opened the closet to his left and pulled out his briefcase. He hadn't touched that since before the takeover. The time before seemed like a whole other life. A life he'd never be able to go back to.

Slipping the laptop inside, he set the briefcase by the door and returned to the dining room. He lifted the phone, chose not to look at the screen, and rushed it over and slid it into the briefcase's side pocket. He needed to get himself moving, or he feared he'd sit in this place forever.

Cole hurried down the hall into the bedroom. He opened his bedroom closet. His mind came alive with a flurry of activity, the things he needed to research and uncover from the website Bray mentioned in her video last week.

Cole called his assistant, Cassie.

"Hi, sir, I was wondering when I'd hear from you," Cassie said, having answered on the first ring.

"I need you to do something for me," he began, pulling out a pair of navy-blue slacks.

Cole went over to the bed. He placed the call on speaker, set the phone down on the bed. The sheets lay open on his side of the bed. The other side remained completely untouched.

"What's that?" Cassie asked.

Cole pulled off the sweatpants he'd been wearing for days and replaced them with the slacks, which felt cold and unforgiving against his skin.

"You know that website, the one my daughter mentioned?"

"The one about S-Corp?"

"I want you to start researching everything on there."

Returning to the closet, he selected a white button-up, sniffed his underarms, realized he needed deodorant and a clean undershirt.

"You want to know if she was telling the truth?"

"Of course. This is my daughter we're

talking about," his voice suddenly shaky. He pulled open his dresser and slid on an undershirt, running into the bathroom and rubbing deodorant under his arms before returning to the phone.

Cassie had gone silent.

"You there?" he called out, walking over to the closet and finding a black button-up shirt, turning to a mirror on the inside of the closet door.

"Yes, sir," she said, clearing her throat. "I'll get right on it."

Cole grabbed a purple paisley tie from the tie rack hanging beside the mirror. He twisted it into a double Windsor, searched out a navy-blue jacket to match his pants.

"Great," he replied. "I'm on my way into the office."

"Oh." Cassie paused. "I'm still at home."

"That's fine. I'm sure you have everything you need there to do the research. Whatever you have trouble finding, let me know and I can help."

With that, Cole ended the call. He walked into the bathroom, looked at himself in the mirror. He hadn't showered, but he doubted many people would be in the office. As a matter of fact, the more he'd looked at himself, the more he realized he liked his hair the way it was. The gel had made it appear too stiff, like he was trying too hard. He found himself not really giving much of a shit. His daughter was in custody, and what mattered was finding her and finding out why she'd done what she'd done.

He opened the medicine cabinet and took out a dark green prescription bottle. He'd had one heart attack already, and decided it was time to get healthy. His daughter needed him. He opened it and peered inside.

Dropping two pills into his palm, he popped them into his mouth. Using the sink water to wash them down, Cole took a deep breath, relieved himself, and exited the room.

It was time to return to the office. Time to get back to work.

Part Two:

The Missing Link

Chapter One

Bray

Meditating did not come easily, at first. Or at second, or third. Five days into attempting to sit and remain alert, Bray was about ready to give up. She was sitting on her bed, her bottom sore and a dent sinking into the mattress where every day, twice a day, she sat, diligently, and practiced Transcendental Meditation.

This morning was no different. It was cold in the room and she felt the air against her skin. It crawled with gooseflesh. She didn't bother with her blanket because it felt like sandpaper. Everything felt so. . .uncomfortable. The side effects of the medication continued to hamper her mind. Each day, the moment she felt the meditation deepening, she fell asleep.

She'd wake when the meal bell rang.

The frustrations continued every single day.

Now, she thought about Emily. How Emily had taught her that the starting point of anything in life was in this moment, to start right where she was, whether she was happy or sad or angry.

"Okay," she whispered, dismissing the teachings of Transcendental Meditation for a moment. "Let's see where this goes."

Her eyes closed, Bray focused in on her frustration. It felt hard in her chest, in the space between her abdomen and her heart. It took up this space as if it had moved in and was never leaving. Bray's attention dropped to this area of her body.

She breathed into it. Its hardness reminded her of a stone sunk deep into the earth, beneath the soil. She thought of the way Kage would till the ground with a sharply-bladed mechanism, turning the soil, pulling up rocks and roots and weeds in its wake. Tilling the soil was what one did to prep it for planting. For newness. For life.

Yes, Bray thought, *the soil needs tilling*.

As she focused in on the frustration, it hovered in her chest and began to burn. The burning warmed her skin. She welcomed that. The burning turned into a deep anger. A. . .*rage*. Suddenly she saw in her mind an image of the day her mother left her here, in prison, and walked away without saying goodbye. Her mother had abandoned her.

She began to whimper.

Tears edged out of her eyes. She felt the salt of them as they rolled calmly down her cheeks. She felt a deep, cleansing breath, the frustration transmuted into sadness.

Finally, for the first time since she had been injected with that hideous medication, she could feel again.

The breakfast bell rang. Bray leapt in response. Her heart raced. She opened her eyes, and in a heat of rage she reached for her pillow and threw it toward the door, letting out a scream. The pillow landed in the middle of the floor. She stared at it. *Pathetic*.

She wanted to break something.

Meditation would have to wait. . .again.

#

That evening, Bray returned to meditation. This time she waited until after dinner so she would be less likely to be interrupted. Already she had found that

the Transcendental Meditation had elevated
her senses in many ways. When she walked
the halls and looked upon the other
prisoners, everything was brighter, as if
she were seeing things for the first time.
Vivid, close. When she sat with Valerie and
Tori in the cafeteria, she felt more
present. The scent of food was more potent,
making her feel both more hungry and more
nauseous. The burning smell of animal flesh
coming from the kitchen sometimes made her
so sick she had to sit with her head
between her legs, taking deep breaths.

"You need to go to Health Services?"
Valerie had asked her at dinner.

"No," Bray whispered, her head dropping
toward the floor. "The smell of those
burgers cooking is making me sick, that's
all."

"Right," Valerie replied, rubbing
Bray's back but saying nothing more.

Bray had finally told Valerie and Tori
about her abilities as an animal empath.
Over the last week they'd had a number of
conversations about it. Only now did Bray
wonder, while she was practicing deep
breathing and smelling every smell and
hearing every conversation and noise, why
it was she couldn't hear any voices in her
mind. No animals calling out for help.
Inside her mind there was a silence,
nothing but her own thoughts, the other
voices behind a soundproof door that would
not open.

That, she knew, was a result of the
medication.

Seated on her bed once again, Bray
closed her eyes and pressed her back
against the wall. After a series of deep
breaths, followed by several minutes of
chanting, "so. . .hum. . .so. . .hum. . .I
am that. . .I am that. . ." everything

quieted.

Bray fell into a trance. Her mind ceased. Suspended. Feeling as though she was in air and about to fall, yet trusting there was no fall because there was nowhere to go, no one to be. An interesting experience began to develop.

Very slowly, building up toward her—whatever or whomever *she* was, the awareness inside that called itself Bray, identified as human yet aware that it was all things—*something* rose from beyond that place. A something else, a presence.

This presence marched up, up, like climbing stairs or a ladder. Building, increasing in depth and substance as it came nearer. It rose up into Bray's consciousness. Another consciousness. . .*connecting* with her own. It brought sound. First, like an echo. Muffled. Under water. Taking form. Pushing through. Expanding up. Into her ears. Taking on identity. A lower pitch. Masculine.

A voice.

"*Please help me. . .Please God, help me. . .please.*"

It whimpered and shook.

Bray's eyes shot open.

The room around her was quiet, unmoving. For a second she'd forgotten she was in prison. Frantic, her heart racing, hopeful and afraid all at the same time, Bray closed her eyes again. She waited for the voice to return, but where the voice had been there was nothing. The feeling of another consciousness was gone, too.

Chapter Two

Bertan

A dull, evening sun crept inside Bertan's new cell. He had been removed from solitary confinement a week ago. This time, he had no cellmate. This cell had a single bed, twin-sized, up against a wall perpendicular to a narrow window. Bertan was lying in bed, facing the wall.

He tried recalling the day before and the day before that. But again, he didn't understand time anymore. The only things he could recall were memories of his past, of the time before his mind split. Before the fugue. He remembered a time in Honduras when he was young and in love with Carmen. They'd gone to the cinema on a date. He had to have been only a teenager. They were in the theater, waiting for the film to start. The screen was black and there were groups of kids and families filling the spaces around them. Bertan thought about that movie screen, that date, how as he sat there he had been filled with angst for Carmen, a yearning and a waiting and an anticipation in his groin.

Gradually the sun disappeared. Night approached. Bertan rolled onto his stomach, looking out into the night. He couldn't see the moon from the narrow window, but remnants of its chalky light edged along the fences, and in the distance he could see the prison's guard tower. He frowned. The worst punishment was to have a good life just within reach, but not be able to touch it. To have had it once, and then to have lost it. To still live to know it was lost.

Bertan shuddered. He grimaced at the outside world and turned away. Curling into a fetal position, he stared into the darkness. This was the only reality, wasn't it? Darkness. It was what he deserved all along, he surmised. He'd made his choices. The choice to work for Medina. The choice to leave his family and come to this country. To become so afraid of Medina that he abandoned his family.

"Coward," he whispered.

To have met Ruben, a good man, and then turned and lied to him. And now where was his friend? Dead seemed the only logical answer. Dead or in some other prison.

What a shit it would be, he thought, *if Ruben was in this very prison.*

Bertan laughed and then stopped laughing. He began to rock back and forth in bed. A pain filled his chest, but it was not physical. It was familiar, like the way his daughter's voice was familiar. It was heavy as an anvil, and it sat on his heart. This pain was the pain he'd tried running from over all the years. The stuff he knew he'd done to people and could no longer escape. They'd put him in here with nowhere to go, no one to talk to, and all he had was his own self to face.

And he realized he hated himself.

He began to cry. The pain was immense. It was not like any physical pain he'd ever experienced. He had scars to prove the sharp knife blades and the near misses. But that pain was temporary. It came and it went. This pain was always there and he believed it would never leave him.

He did not deserve for it to leave him.

What he deserved was to be gone. To be rid of the pain by death alone.

"Please help me. . .Please God, help

me," he whimpered. The tears washed over his face and he felt like a child. "Please. I don't want to be here anymore. . .Not like this, please. Take me. Please make it stop. . .please. . .just kill me, please."

Bertan continued on like this until there were no more tears to cry and no more words to speak. Until he found there was no one to respond.

Not even God.

Chapter Three

Kage

Kage's eyes struggled to remain open as he sat at Elliott's desk, staring at the laptop screen. His arms felt heavy. He'd slept deeply, yet every morning for the past couple of days, he'd awoken exhausted. He'd planned to stay away from the hate mail that disappeared into the folder Elliott had created for it, but he couldn't help himself. He wanted to know what citizens were saying.

This email in particular had no name attached. Only a message that read:

YOU'RE A BUNCH OF HIPPIE COWARDS. SPINELESS DICKS. I HOPE YOU END UP IN PRISON BECAUSE IF I FIND YOU, YOU'RE GOING TO WISH YOU DID.

Ouch, Kage thought. He closed the email, a cringe hitting him in the heart. The hate folder was reaching one hundred and fifty messages and counting. He clicked over to his inbox to find fifty more unread messages. And he'd spent all last evening catching up on emails from the day before. What day was it? How many days had gone by? He couldn't think. He rubbed his eyes. The screen was blurry for a moment. He'd been looking at it so long this evening it was making his eyes burn.

But he still could not stop reading the emails. It was. . .fascinating. Countless citizens reaching out. He never thought they actually would. Maybe one or two, but not more than fifty, one hundred, *many* hundreds. People were angry, scared, uncertain. Most of the contacts were people who'd lost family members or friends in what had been dubbed the "S-Corp Fertilizer Disaster," where thousands of people died after S-Corp accidentally released a new form of oxygen, called Oxygen-11, into a new fertilizer they'd developed for drought-resistant crops. It happened in 2027.

Kage wanted to do something to help these people, of course, but he felt so out of sorts and disorganized, he didn't know where to start. And so he just sat, each night, reading the emails, not knowing what to say because he wanted to say everything.

Behind him, Elliott and Trevor were sitting on the couch. Trevor had stopped by to check in on Kage, and while Kage managed to step away from the laptop long enough to eat dinner with his uncle, he was obsessed with the emails. He didn't want to do anything other than read them and try to come up with a plan to find Bray and finish what they had started: exposing S-Corp. After dinner he'd returned to the laptop while Trevor lingered, Kage hardly noticing he was still there.

He was thinking about one of the emails he'd read earlier, this one sent by a citizen from New York state who'd said his grandfather was a vegan and an animal activist, too:

. . .HE DISAPPEARED WHEN I WAS TEN AND I NEVER DID FIND OUT WHAT HAPPENED TO HIM. NOW I SEE THIS STUFF YOU ALL DID, AND IT'S MAKING ME WONDER. . .I LOVED MY GRANDFATHER, WE WERE VERY CLOSE. BUT MY MOM WAS ESTRANGED FROM HIM BECAUSE SHE SAID HE WAS OFF HIS ROCKER. I NEVER SAW THAT IN HIM BUT I WAS TOO YOUNG TO UNDERSTAND. SORRY,

THIS MESSAGE IS GETTING LONG.

That was it. End of message. It had lingered with Kage all through dinner, bringing more memories of Ethan, and of his own parents. For so long he thought he was the only person with loved ones who disappeared as a result of being animal activists. He thought he was alone.

To see that he wasn't, that there were other people, many people, in this country who'd faced the disappearance of loved ones evidently at the hands of S-Corp, left him with feelings of catharsis and sorrow simultaneously.

Kage hit *Reply* to the email and watched the cursor blink at him. Rarely was there a time he didn't know what to say. Usually Kage was the one putting his foot in his mouth, not thinking before he spoke. But emails were different creatures. Here he could watch a blank screen and, because it took him so long to type a word, the act of typing forced him to think.

The longer he thought, the harder it was to know the right thing to say.

"Kage?" Trevor called to him from the couch.

Kage startled when he heard his name. He'd been so immersed in this email that he wasn't picking up any sounds around him.

He turned swiftly in Trevor's direction. Trevor looked him over with forlorn eyes. He stood up and approached Kage, placed his hand on Kage's shoulder.

"Can you take a break? I want to talk to you about something," Trevor asked.

"If it's to try and stop me, then no," Kage replied. There was that foot in mouth thing again.

"It's not. I promise," Trevor said.

Kage took a deep breath. He supposed it

wasn't such a bad idea to take a break. He'd been sitting here for. . .he turned and checked the time on the laptop. . .three hours! He'd worked all day at the roofing job and came directly home to get on the laptop.

Geesh, he thought.

Kage stood up. His bottom was raw, his lower back tight. Glancing around the room, he realized Elliott was not there.

"Where did Elliott go?" he asked.

"Bedroom." Trevor nodded toward the hallway.

Kage hadn't noticed.

"I guess I do need a break," he said, stepping away from the chair.

"Outside?" Trevor asked, motioning toward the door.

As soon as they stepped outdoors, Kage got a whiff of the evening air and felt instant relief. His shoulders released and his body relaxed. Still he had a million thoughts running through his mind about how he needed to respond to this email or that, a to-do list miles long making him feel he should return to his work at the computer.

"Kage?" Trevor said.

Kage looked over at him.

"Come sit."

Kage followed Trevor over to a bench between apartment buildings. On either side of the bench, tall spruces added darkness to the area to deepen the coming of night.

"I wanted to check in on you, ask how you're doing," Trevor started.

"Definitely busy," Kage replied. "So many emails, so many people who need help or want to help. It's amazing."

"I'm sure it is." Trevor paused. "What I meant was. . .how are you feeling? After. . .everything. Losing Ethan. And Bray? You and I haven't had a chance to talk since we left Meeteetse."

"Because I've been busy," Kage snapped. "We have a lot to do. The more time that goes by, the less time we have to save Bray. To stop S-Corp."

"I hear that." Trevor leaned back on the bench, looked up at the sky. "Have you ever heard of burnout?"

"No."

"Back in the twenty-teens when we were working to end factory farming, there were a lot more animal activists to help with the work than there are now. These activists worked night and day, tirelessly. . .witnessing horrible, unspeakable acts against animals. They really had no one to process it with because few people understood. And so, eventually, they would burn out. They'd get so stressed. . .traumatized. . .that they'd have mental breakdowns. Many of them just quit the work altogether and shut themselves in their homes, not able to do anything after that. Over time, there became fewer and fewer of us, even before the disappearances began."

Trevor stopped. Kage glanced over at him, noticed his eyes now seemed vacant.

"I didn't know that," Kage replied, aware of his own urge to get back to the computer, feeling as though the work could not wait.

"I don't want this to happen to you, Kage. I've been watching you since we arrived here. If you keep going at this rate, you'll burn out and I fear you'll shut down."

"What am I supposed to do?" Kage asked, throwing his hands in the air. "It's like you said: no one else is helping us."

"That's not true," Trevor refuted. "You have plenty of help. All those people who've emailed you. They sound like they want to help. I say, let them."

"But they're not animal activists."

"If you let them, maybe they'll *become* activists. We all started somewhere. Besides, we don't have the luxury to pick and choose our help anymore. You can't do this alone."

A pair of bats flitted about beneath the trees, feeding on hidden things Kage could not see from here.

"So what do you suggest I do. . .to let them help?" Kage wasn't sure he trusted complete strangers to help with something so important. These people had remained complacent for so long, and, in his opinion, they had *chosen* that complacency. They were weak. He couldn't see how handing over any of the work to stop S-Corp to the general public would accomplish anything when they were the ones who allowed S-Corp to gain control of the government, and society, in the first place.

"I have an idea, if you'll let me help," Trevor said, leaning forward. Kage turned and met eyes with him, waiting.

"We select one person in each major city. . .to step forward as a representative. We pass information on to the representatives, who then pass the info down to their contacts. Like a phone tree. Think of it as a grassroots campaign, if you will."

Kage paused to think. A memory of Ethan telling him about the Animal Rights Movement suddenly came to him. Ethan had said this was how he created the movement: he elected others-people like Trevor, Emily, Dennis-to be on his team and help spread information.

"Why hadn't I thought about that?" Kage replied, shaking his head.

"You can't think of everything, Kage. We aren't meant to do things alone."

"It all feels so overwhelming," Kage said. "I don't know where to start. So many emails and I haven't replied to a single one."

"Let me do it," Trevor replied. "Let me be the manager, so to speak, to keep track of the representatives and disseminate information."

"You mean. . .you actually want to help?" Kage asked, shocked. For years his uncle had pushed back against Kage anytime he made mention of something as important as finding his parents. And when Bray had come up with the plan to expose the nation to S-Corp's secrets and horrific practices against animals, Trevor had been against it.

Trevor looked up at the sky before speaking.

"I never told you this but. . .when you were a teenager, do you remember Amanda?"

"The girl you brought over to our house every now and then?"

Trevor looked at him and nodded. The blue of his eyes deepened, became a shade darker.

"I was about to propose to her. We were supposed to go camping, but it was 2028, and President Walker was assassinated right before that weekend. She wasn't a vegan, but that didn't matter. I loved her." Trevor paused. His head dropped and his eyes met the ground. "When I realized we had to leave, to get you to safety, things were so chaotic I couldn't get ahold of her in time. We left before I could even say goodbye to her."

Silence overtook them both. Kage watched Trevor rub tears from his eyes. He recalled that time in his life. He was a teenager. His parents were at risk of being arrested by authorities, and they begged Trevor to take Kage to Ethan's, to get Kage as far away from home as fast as he could. His parents said they'd be right behind, but Kage never saw them again. He often forgot that he wasn't the only one who suffered their disappearance.

"Ah. . .uncle. I had no idea."

They met eyes.

"I never told you because I didn't want you to feel responsible, because you're not," Trevor said. He sat up, placed his hand on Kage's.

Kage took it, held it tightly, feeling for his uncle.

"I only tell you now because Amanda was the reason I hid away for so long. I never quite got over losing her, not to mention losing your dad. I know I don't process emotions well. It closed me up inside, made me hard. So I was too afraid to let you go out and find your parents. That was selfish of me. I just want you to know. . .I'm really sorry. I'm sorry I wasn't more supportive. I'm here now, and I want to help."

Kage reached over and hugged Trevor. He felt Trevor's body shake. Trevor began to cry. Trevor's crying led to Kage doing the same, realizing how much he, too, had been avoiding the pain of losing Ethan, of missing his parents, missing Bray.

The two of them sat there together until the crying eased off.

Chapter Four

Bray

Bray did not sleep. She sat up, back tight against the wall, and she listened. Off and on, the voice returned.

"*Please help me. . .Please God, help me. . .Please. I don't want to be here anymore. . .Not like this, please. Take me. Please make it stop. . .please. . .just kill me, please.*"

The voice was male, accented with Hispanic tones. Bray's heart pumped loudly in her chest and ears. Never had she heard an animal with an accent. It made no sense. An animal would not plead to a god that humans had made up for themselves.

This meant only one thing: she wasn't hearing the voice of an animal.

This was. . .*human.*

Again? she thought as she opened her eyes.

She stared into the darkness of her cell. The sound of muffled music came up against the cell door. Country music, which she hated. Must be the guards. She could hear some of them conversing in the spaces between musical notes.

Bray closed her eyes, but not to connect with the voice. No, first she needed to consider the implications. If the voice was indeed human, who was it? This did not sound like any of the citizens she had connected with during the Embidicare takeover, none of those voices she had heard when she first arrived at the prison. And what human would ever believe her if she responded? Most humans she'd met had a hard time believing she had this gift at all.

"*I just want it to end. . .please.*"

What did they want to end? Their life? she wondered.

Silence. Bray's mind went quiet. The silence was so palpable she stilled herself completely, to the point her heart began to slow.

"*What was that?*" the voice asked.

Bray heard that, too. Her eyes flew open again. Was this happening? Had she found a way to communicate again? Had she somehow managed to overcome the medication?

Should she say something?

"*Say something? Who. . .who is there?*"

"They heard me," she whispered. Her eyes watered as a kind of fear filled her body. A fear and a wonder and a curiosity. Bray gulped, closed her eyes, and decided to speak.

"Hi. My name is Bray. What's your name?"

Another silence. Bray listened intently, waiting for a response.

"*I-I don't know what's going on,*" the voice hissed into her mind, as though they had been whispering.

"You probably won't believe this, but I'm another human. Like you. . .are you a human?" Bray asked innocently. She'd never been so afraid to talk to a voice before. This was downright intimidating.

"*I'm going mad,*" the voice said, but not to her. To itself. "*This place. . .it's destroying me and I am losing my mind.*"

What could Bray say to get the voice to believe her? She didn't want them thinking they were hearing things. Well, they *were* hearing things, but this was real. Not imagined. If only she knew their name. Who they were. Something about them.

Bray's mind returned to the sound of the voice. The accent. She'd heard an accent like that before. Maybe from Mexico or. . .where had she heard it? Bray thought back. Her mind traveled through memories, all recent. Memories of her time here in prison. There was no one she'd spoken to here with an accent. She thought about the voices she heard before the psychiatrist ordered her medicated: Dawn, Mateo, Elisha, Tim-citizens whose voices she had heard while implementing her plan to connect ordinary people to suffering cows via the Embedicare implants. The citizens she'd listened to sounded mid-western. One, she recalled, sounded as though she was from New York.

But Hispanic?

Bray's memory landed on the trailer in Idaho. The space that she, Elliott and Kage had used so they could remain in hiding while they finished putting their plan into place.

"Can't be," she whispered. She opened her eyes and stared down at the bed. In the darkness, the blanket appeared so dark she was glancing into a deep cavern with no bottom. It helped her focus.

There were two men at the trailer in Idaho. They both had accents, Hispanic. What were their names?

"Ruben," she said. He was the one who had given them the trailer to use. He was one of Lana's activist partners, undercover at S-Corp. He had a friend. . .a man who worked at the slaughterhouse, the same slaughterhouse where the cows she was linked to were headed for slaughter.

What was his name?

Bray suddenly recalled a moment outside the trailer when she'd taken a break to get fresh air. That man, Ruben's friend, had come out and asked to sit with her. He'd had these green eyes that were as beautiful as they were off-putting, and he talked to her about his wife and daughter.

He was from. . .Honduras. Yes, that was it. He'd had family down there.

"You remind me of my daughter," he had said.

But when he showed her a picture from his phone, Bray didn't think she looked one bit like his daughter. The girl appeared to be about five years younger than she was.

What was his name? she asked herself again, a brief frustration that she could not remember. Bear. . .something?

A moment of hope struck her heart and she smiled as she remembered. Closing her eyes, she called out to him:

"Bertan? Is that you?"

Silence. Silence on top of silence. Silence paired with silence somewhere else, away from here. Wherever *he* was. Two humans, separated by place, possibly by time, in this moment aligned. Both had gone silent. The one, the voice she had been trying to connect with, she was slowly beginning to sense. He too, had gone quiet. It was the silence on his end that she had noticed, not her own. She could feel him *beside* her, as if he were in the cell with her.

Bray's arm hairs stood on end. Her consciousness rose to the ceiling of the cell and looked down upon her body. There she watched herself in meditation pose, back against the wall. She felt her consciousness meld with that of another.

For the first time in Bray's life, she felt herself linking with something being she never thought she could. She had linked with another human, which was not the same as hearing their thoughts. With Bertan, she sensed that she would also be able to feel his feelings, experience his physical sensations, just like she had with Rhea before him, and Alice before Rhea.

#

No time to hesitate. Morning was coming and she could not miss this chance to connect with Bertan, if indeed it was him with whom she had linked. She had to know if her instincts were correct.

"Bertan, can you hear me? Is that you?" she asked.

"*Wh—who is that? Another voice in my head?*" he replied. "*I'm definitely losing it.*"

Bray heard him crying.

"Bertan," she said softly. "If that really is you, please trust me when I say you're not losing it. I am here. Do you remember me?"

The voice stopped its crying. It seemed to be asking its own consciousness what it remembered. Did it remember anything? Could it trust itself?

"Let me help you to remember," she continued. "There was this trailer out in Idaho. A man named Ruben helped us find it. My friends and I, we used it as a hidden place to stage a plan—"

"*What?! Who is this? How do you know about Ruben?*" the voice asked, accusatory and harsh. Bray felt the anger. She proceeded, but with caution.

"Ruben's your friend, right?"

"*Where the fuck is he? Who are you and what do you know about Ruben?*"

This confirmed it. The man was not Ruben, so it had to be Bertan. Ruben was the only other human she had ever met with that kind of strong accent. But now she was losing Bertan. He was getting angry, she could sense it with precision. The anger was exact and strong, like a knife blade cutting through skin. If she wasn't careful, she'd lose him for good.

Maybe something factual would help bring him back.

"Bertan, please. This is Bray Hoffman. I am in prison. In Arizona. S-Corp. . .they tracked me down and found me."

Bertan paused.

"*How could you be in a prison in Arizona and I can hear you?*" he asked.

"Fair question." She told herself to tread carefully. "Do you remember the time we sat outside that trailer in Idaho? You came and sat with me and told me about your daughter."

"*How do you know my daughter?*" the voice spat. The anger had not ceased. No, it wasn't anger. What Bray sensed was something deeper, under the anger.

What Bray sensed was fear.

She opened her eyes. Outside the window, a slither of yellow, the color of a canary, began to appear along the dead earth. She was running out of time.

Ages ago when Bray linked up with her friend Alice, a pig that had been confined in an undisclosed factory farm, Bray would often imagine a beautiful space with a barn and rolling hills of green grass. When she connected with Alice, she would imagine the two of them sitting together in this open prairie of grass. Somehow she could communicate this vision to Alice, and the pig could see it, too. Even though they were not physically in the same place, Alice would lie beside her with her head resting on Bray's leg. This was where they'd meet and talk.

Bray wondered. . .if she was linked with Bertan, could she do the same thing? Could she help him see what she could, in order to get him to remember?

Suddenly a bell rang, startling her from meditation.

"Dang it," she whispered.

Bray had about five minutes before they came to her cell. She hadn't slept all night, so her bed was already made. All she needed were these few last minutes with Bertan before the guards unlocked her cell door.

She closed her eyes. Focusing inward, she imagined the trailer in Idaho, the three boulders behind the trailer where she had gone to take a break. This had been her first time in Idaho, and the starkness of this new environment had made it deafeningly real: that she was following through on the plan to connect to hundreds of citizens through their implants.

Bertan came out behind the trailer and asked if he could join her. She said yes, though she didn't want to. They started talking. The sound of clacking invaded Bray's ears. A click and then a turn. With her eyes closed, Bray turned and dropped her feet down onto the cold floor. The memory dissipated. She stood up as the guard entered her cell. She shook off the memory, feeling it fade, holding out hope that she could connect with Bertan again. That he would believe her.

Chapter Five

Bertan

It was afternoon. A blinding sun pierced Bertan's eyes as he exited a trailer and saw the young girl, Bray, sitting beside a set of boulders. He walked toward her. He could see that she was tired by the way she used the boulder to support her head as she leaned backward against the rock. Her lengthy, brown hair reminded him of the way his daughter's hair had grown thick and beautiful in the photos Carmen used to send him. How Gabriella had arrived at the same height as her mother, and seemed to be aging faster than he could track. He stepped up to Bray and thought how, if this plan of hers did not work, he did not see his way back home. He did not see a future for himself.

This was his last chance, and so he wanted to know this person, only a teenager yet claiming she had some kind of. . .gift?

"Mind if I join you?" he asked her, and he was surprised that she obliged.

He asked her how long she'd known she could talk to animals, and how did she know she wasn't losing her mind? These were answers he needed for himself, perhaps to validate that maybe he wasn't losing his. Someone else, someone young and innocent with no tainted years behind them, maybe she could tell him he was okay.

As he spoke to the girl, her eyes, the irises, changed as the sun peered into them, from hazel to a tint of copper. The shade of copper was electrifying, and in it Bertan recognized something from his past.

A time when Gabriella was lying with him in bed and holding a stuffed elephant he'd gotten her. Carmen was out at the store. It was mid-morning, and through the window above his head, hot air rose and entered the room, a fan on the bedside table moving it from one side of the room to the other. Gabriella was talking about something he could not recall, but what he did remember was how she'd sat up and look down at him, and when he saw her face, he saw a piece of himself, mostly in the honey-brown of her eyes, and it humbled him.

An ease fell over him now. He turned his attention back to Bray again, and, as he showed her photos of his daughter, having told her she reminded him of Gabriella, he felt his shoulders release some tension, and a sense of pride come over him. Something he hadn't felt in ages and wanted to hold on to. But he knew this was not real. He knew because he'd grown calm enough to remember. . .to remember that this flashback was from the past, from weeks ago when he'd first agreed to help Bray with her plan. When Ruben was still alive and well.

"What's happening?" he whispered. His eyes were closed but he sensed the room becoming lighter.

Morning had come.

And this memory was not something he'd constructed in his mind. He knew this. It came from somewhere else. That voice in his head, the girl who claimed she was Bray. It made no sense, yet it was the only thing that did-that she'd been communicating with him the way she claimed to communicate with animals, and she'd sent him this memory. She was trying to get him to believe.

The tray slot slid open and sent a shriek, metal against metal, into the cell.

Bertan's eyes shot open. His heart raced in fear. He sat up and turned. He realized he was still in his cell, and he saw the tray of food left for him, the slot shutting immediately. From here he could see and smell the scrambled eggs and a piece of toast. He considered whether he might be falling deeper into insanity, yet he felt calmer now than he'd felt in. . .he didn't know how long.

"Hello?" he said out loud, looking around the cell and up at the ceiling as if that would bring the voice back.

But there was nothing.

Bertan remained still, confused. How could someone be in another state, locked away, yet sound as though they were right beside him? The voice even *sounded* like the young girl, at least what he remembered of her.

He was certain he'd had some kind of mental breakdown over the past few months, where he'd dissociate and lose track of time, and become like a whole other person, but as he thought back, the voices he heard in the past were not like this one.

This was something different.

Was this real? Was he speaking to another human? And if so, where had she gone? Why had his mind suddenly gone so quiet?

Bertan stood up and went over to the tray. He slowly drank the milk. He considered the food, but still had little appetite. He grabbed the toast and bit into it. It was crunchy but tasteless. He found he liked the crunching and so he ate it, then returned to bed. He sat down on the edge and looked outside, taking a deep breath.

"If that's really you," he said aloud. "You'll have to prove it. Please tell me

I'm not going insane."
    For the longest time, there was no
response.

Chapter Six

Cole

"Mr. Hoffman. . .you better come take a look at this."

It was Cassie, his assistant. Cole had been in his office, reading the manuscript that had been posted on the truthaboutscorp.com website. It had been written by an animal rights activist more than ten years ago and provided details upon details of instances in which activists were detained, without court dates, held in high-security prisons, marked as terrorists. One of those prisons was located in Arizona. Arizona was one of those states, similar to New Mexico, that had been deemed uninhabitable prior to the 2030 Migration. "Uninhabitable," in this case, meant no one was permitted to move into the state due to the increasing burden of drought. Phoenix was the last remaining city in Arizona, grasping for every last bit of water and energy for its current population of one million. During the migration, three million people fled the city. It had since fallen into decay, riddled with crime, rioting and impoverished families. And in that case, Cole thought, perhaps it made sense to lock eco-terrorists away in a state where no one would ever think to go.

He'd been staring out the window, thinking about his own city, Denver, and how, if things did not improve, it would be on its way to becoming another Phoenix. Cassie called for him again.

Cole shook off the thought. Relieved to

be pulled away from the heaviness of this world, he looked out into the lobby.

"What is it?" he called back to Cassie.

"Dianna Hoffman just did a press conference."

"What?" Cole jumped up from his desk and hurried into the lobby. There, Cassie's round face peeked out over a standing desk, a laptop open before her. Cole approached the desk and came to stand behind her. She rewound the video on the laptop screen and pressed play.

There stood Dianna, standing at a podium with the S-Corp red insignia on it: a circular symbol with a tree in the center. An American flag hung from a standing pole to her left, and behind her, a plain, gray wall. She was inside S-Corp's press room. Cole knew it because he'd been there many times. This was the space where she issued her press conferences. It was convenient to have reporters on her turf.

"Good morning," Dianna began. "I am here today to speak on behalf of S-Corp, and myself. First and foremost, our hearts go out to the people of this nation who were impacted by this heinous act of terror-"

"Hmph," Cole voiced, crossing his arms.

"It is true that Bray Hoffman, my daughter, was somehow a part of this eco-terrorist group that we have successfully captured. . ."

"What a lie," he said, and then stopped himself. How many times in his own career as a politician had he bent the truth, or lied outright to his constituents? He was a part of the same system she was. This reality was becoming harder and harder to swallow.

"This includes my own daughter. As painful as it was to watch her be taken into custody, I knew it was the best thing for our country. S-Corp is working tirelessly to get to the bottom of what happened, in order to keep our country safe and clear of future attacks. For over ten years S-Corp has been the leader in providing safe, accessible drinking water and food products, and we will continue doing so. Please do not be swayed by the lies of eco-terrorists who aim to make you feel less safe, whose goal is to create imaginary terror, and what better way than to suggest that our soil is somehow safe for use. Please, do not believe these life-threatening lies. . ."

"You have to admit she's good at it," Cassie commented.

Cole nodded, watching his ex-wife, a woman he once loved, deny all the things he was beginning to believe were true. That Bray was telling the truth.

"I'll open the floor for a few questions," Dianna finished.

She pointed to a reporter in the audience as cameras flashed bright lights into her face. Cole noticed how tired the woman looked. He knew that look. That was the look of a woman who was under a lot of stress. He wondered what kind of heat she was taking from S-Corp CEOs and the like.

A reporter shouted from the back of the room. Cole leaned forward, listening haphazardly, figuring Dianna had screened all questions prior to the press conference as was customary.

"How were you not aware of what your daughter was doing?" the reporter asked.

Dianna glanced down at her notes, then looked up in the direction of the reporter.

"I'll be honest; Bray has a mental illness. As I've stated in the past, she escaped Denver Health and I did all I could to find her, exhausting all of my resources. I suppose being an S-Corp president has the disadvantage that I was unable to put as much attention into her life as I would have liked, and I didn't know what kind of activities she was getting into. . ."

Gooseflesh ran down Cole's back.

"The person you'll want to direct these questions to is Bray's father, Senator Cole Hoffman."

"What?!" Cole blurted. His hands dropped to his side at the mention of his name.

"It was Senator Hoffman who intervened on Bray's behalf and made sure I was not notified when she was discovered miles north in Wyoming. He assisted her in going into hiding with the eco-terrorists."

Cameras flashed vigorously. Reporters raised their hands and shouted for Dianna's attention. Cassie turned and glanced up at Cole, one of her eyebrows lifting in curiosity. Cole met eyes with her and shook his head.

"She's trying to ruin my reputation," he grumbled. "I can't believe her." His face turned red.

"It was Cole Hoffman who did not believe Bray was mentally ill. If there is anyone in this country the authorities ought to consider questioning, it is Senator Hoffman, not S-Corp," Dianna said, glaring into the camera.

The look in her eyes of pure disdain filtered through the laptop screen and pierced Cole's chest. Anger rose there and lifted into his throat. He felt he might burst.

"That is all," Dianna finished. She picked up her notes and walked away.

Cole's forearm vibrated immediately. He

turned it over and glanced as a series of messages popped into view.

The phone on Cassie's desk rang.

"Take messages," Cole said, stepping away from the desk. "If it's a reporter, no comment, for now."

"Got it," Cassie replied. "What are you going to do?"

Cole hurried into his office, grabbed the door by its knob.

"I've got a mess to clean up," he said, slamming the door.

Chapter Seven

Bray

After breakfast, Bray's day began with her new job. They'd placed her on laundry duty. She was currently pushing a laundry cart down the hall, opposite the cafeteria. Outside each cell, prisoners had left mesh bags containing their dirty clothes and sheets. Bray used her gloved hands to pull the bags up by their strings and carefully drop them into the cart, rolling it down to the next cell. It was a simple enough job that she could think about other things while doing it. . .things like what happened with Bertan, or the voice she assumed was Bertan's.

Since leaving her prison cell this morning, she hadn't heard any more voices. Breakfast made that challenging, given she was listening to Valerie and some other prisoners explaining to Tori how after all these years none of them had received opportunities for parole. Tori, of course, could not believe it, and for Bray it was so hard to imagine never getting out of this place that she simply tuned them out until the meal had ended.

Bray rolled the cart around a corner, the laundry bags filling it halfway. She rolled it past a set of offices. One belonged to the unit supervisor, the other, to Jacob, whom she'd have to see the next day.

Before reaching the laundry room, Bray stopped in the middle of the hall. She closed her eyes and called for Bertan in her mind, as if passing a thought.

"Are you there Bertan?"

"*Yes, but how do I believe it's really you, and not my mind playing games?*" he replied instantly.

"Did you get the memory I sent?"

"*Yes.*" Bray noticed a pause. It felt like a hard stop in her chest. She took the opportunity to continue down the hall, the laundry room coming into view.

"Don't you remember me?" she asked.

"*I remember Bray. And you sound like her. But my mind. . .I can't trust it.*"

"How come?" It suddenly occurred to her that she knew almost nothing about Bertan, only that he had a wife and daughter in Honduras and he had worked for S-Corp when she met him at the trailer in Idaho.

Bray shifted the cart through an open door into the narrow laundry room with low ceilings. Front-loading washing machines sat heavily atop identical-looking dryers. The sound of machines running gave off a consistent hum that Bray found soothing. In the center of the floor was a long, stainless-steel table where a group of women stood sorting clean uniforms.

One of the women was Tori.

Bray pushed the cart over to a nearby corner and set it against the wall. She began pulling out the dirty laundry bags. A stench of body odor struck her nose and she cringed. All the while, she was awaiting a response from Bertan. She sensed he was hesitating, that he didn't want to tell her certain things, either for fear of what she might think or fear that she would tell the entire world.

"If you don't want to tell me, I understand," Bray said in her mind.

She emptied the laundry onto a table nearest the door, waiting for the first washing machine to become available. Tori glanced over at her and waved. Bray glanced back. She wondered what she could do to get Bertan to believe her. She watched the washing machines turn and flip clothes around, water and soap mixing as the uniforms flopped around like dead bodies being tossed to and fro.

"Bertan," she said finally. "Can I tell you what happened after our plan went awry? Maybe that will help you believe this is real."

"*Okay.*"

This was going to take all of her concentration, communicating with Bertan while doing laundry and trying to act as if her mind were in the same room as her body.

"After the cows went through slaughter, I went unconscious. Kage and Elliott took me to our hideout in Wyoming. I'd been living there with Kage and a group of other activists before you and I met."

The sound of a machine buzzing forced Bray to pause.

"Hold on," she said to Bertan. "I'm on laundry duty so I have to work while talking to you."

"*How is this even possible?*" she heard him whisper. She imagined him shaking his head in disbelief.

Bray bent down below the steel table and pulled out a footstool. She placed it in front of one of the dryers and stepped up, opening the washing machine door.

"Could you maybe just give me the benefit of the doubt?" she asked him.

"*I'll try.*"

Bray focused on removing heavy, damp uniforms from the machine and landing them in an empty dryer. Meanwhile, the group of women in the room with her continued their folding, talking amongst themselves.

After she got a new load of clothes

into the washer, feeling exhausted from that one load alone, Bray took a deep breath and came down to the floor, pushing the stool back under the table with her foot.

Turning to stand beside Tori, she went to pick up a clean, wrinkled uniform shirt and took a deep breath, focusing inward on Bertan.

"When I woke from being unconscious, my friends had taken me down into a cellar beneath the ground. We were hiding there because S-Corp discovered our hideout." Bray paused.

She felt a nudge against her shoulder. She turned to see Tori looking over at her.

"You seem really distracted lately," Tori said. She was picking out clean clothes from a pile and folding them, one by one. "Are you holding up okay?"

Bray didn't know what to say. Of course she was distracted. Communicating with a human telepathically wasn't something she wanted to reveal to people in this prison.

"I have to see Jacob tomorrow and I'm just nervous about it," Bray lied.

"Ah, I see." Tori nodded. "He can certainly have that effect on people."

Something in Bray's mind switched, as if there were a paused video and someone had just pressed play.

"*I'm sorry.*" It was Bertan. "*How is it that you can communicate with me? If this is really Bray, how is this possible? Is it like, ESP, or something?*"

"Yes!" Bray said, so excited she'd accidentally spoken it aloud. Her eyes lifted in shock.

Everyone looked over at her.

"Sorry, that was loud," Bray said, smiling. "I meant yes, like that's why I'm distracted. They think there's something wrong with me and there isn't."

Bray stopped talking. The two women opposite her smirked. One turned and placed a stack of clean, folded clothes into a mesh laundry bag, a prisoner's number sewn onto the bag, and tossed the bag into a cart beside the door, clean clothes ready to be returned to prisoners.

Bray took a deep breath and thought carefully before directing her thoughts to Bertan.

"Yes, it's basically ESP. Does that help?"

"*I guess,*" he replied. "*But I never much believed in the stuff.*"

"But you believed I could communicate with animals. . .at least enough to help us carry out the plan back in Idaho."

"*I don't know what I believed back then. I wasn't exactly. . .in my right mind.*"

Bray noticed something about Bertan. He seemed to retreat into himself, like he was thinking about what he'd said. He was worried.

She began folding clothing. It was repetitive: spread the shirt out, fold the right side into the middle, then the left. Fold the shirt in half, and *tah-dah*. A brainless activity that allowed her to continue communicating effortlessly. As long as Tori did not interrupt.

"Bertan," she said. "I just want you to know I am a friend. You can talk to me about stuff, if you want."

"*You're just a kid.*"

That stung.

A buzzer went off. One of the dryers had completed its cycle. Frustrated by the interruption, Bray turned and glanced back at the dryer. Tori opened it and began pulling out the clothes and setting them on the table. Heat emanated from the dryer and Bray felt it on her back. She closed her eyes for a moment.

"I may be young, but I've been through a lot. I can handle more than you think," she replied to Bertan.

He did not respond. She felt him pulled away by something, either within himself or something happening wherever he was. And where was he? She hadn't asked. One of the challenges with this gift was that, although she could communicate with others, rarely was she linked enough to see where they were. She had only been able to do this with Alice and Rhea. No other animals, and certainly not humans. The fact that she was communicating with one right now still boggled her mind.

Chapter Eight

Kage

Kage woke to the sound of typing. He sat up from his air mattress, which was on the floor beside the couch.

"You're up?" he asked, wiping his eyes and stretching.

"I had an idea," Elliott replied, his eyes fixed on the computer screen.

Kage stood up. He pulled two blankets off the mattress and tossed them onto the couch. Picking the mattress up from one end, he dragged it over and pushed it up against the wall. Turning, he watched Elliott.

"What idea is that?" Kage ambled over to stand beside Elliott.

He saw a spreadsheet with a list of names and email addresses.

"We need to tell them something," Elliott said. "We've got momentum and we need to keep it. The way to do that is to keep communication going."

He then used Kage's encrypted email address to create one new email. He switched over to the spreadsheet, highlighted all the email addresses, then pasted them into the blind copy field of the new email message.

"How about this for a subject heading: 'Thanks for reaching out-more to come'?"

Kage understood little when it came to email etiquette. He had only been sixteen when he went into hiding with Trevor. His parents hadn't approved of social media, so he'd never had an account. He had only sent a handful of emails during his teenage years. And once he arrived at Meeteetse, any form of online communication was out of the question.

This made him appreciate whatever life force had brought Elliott into his trajectory. He'd have been completely lost without the guy.

Elliott set up the email, which read:

HELLO,
THANK YOU FOR YOUR EMAIL. WE ARE IN THE PROCESS OF SORTING THROUGH THE ENORMOUS NUMBER OF RESPONSES TO OUR TRUTH ABOUT S-CORP WEBSITE, WHICH WE WERE NOT EXPECTING. PLEASE BE PATIENT WHILE WE DETERMINE NEXT STEPS.
WE WILL BE IN TOUCH IN THE NEXT FEW DAYS.
REGARDS,

"All righty," Elliott said, swiveling in his chair to face Kage. "This is where I suggest you come up with a code name."

"Code name?" Kage asked, smirking.

"You don't want anyone knowing your real name."

Kage read over the email.

"Regards?" he asked, huffing. "People actually say that?"

"If you want to be professional, yes."

Kage snickered. He stepped into the kitchen, deep in thought as he grabbed some grapes from the refrigerator. Holding the bowl of grapes, he stood beside the dining room table and stared at the screen, thinking. The only thing coming to mind for a code name was his love for motorcycles, for the one he'd lost in Wyoming, the last remaining thing from his father, the man who'd taught him about bikes when he was just a kid.

"I like Triumph," Kage said, tossing a green grape into his mouth. When he bit down on it, the sourness punched his teeth and he shivered.

"Really? *That's* what you're going with?" Elliott asked, grinning.

"Yes." Kage smirked. "It's a type of motorcycle. At least it's not Surge. . .whatever."

"Surge McPhee," Elliott replied. He turned back to the computer screen. "It has a nice ring to it."

"If you say so."

They both went quiet as Elliott reached for the computer mouse. He typed in the name, clicked Send, and closed out of the email.

"There we go," he said, leaning back in his chair.

"I guess now the real work begins," Kage said, quickly downing a bunch more grapes and starting for the bathroom. He had to be at work in an hour.

Elliott nodded.

"That reminds me," Elliott said.

Kage stopped in the hallway, turned, and glanced back into the living room.

"Trevor asked me to help him create a list of contacts. . .one person from each city. . .to be some kind of *representative*. He said he was going to be the one to start emailing them when we had new information."

"Yep," Kage said, smiling. Finally, Trevor was stepping up to the plate.

"I thought you said he was always rigid about getting involved with our plans."

"He used to be, but I guess he changed his mind."

Kage turned and headed for the bathroom again, noticing one missing piece to this whole situation. He stopped at the bathroom

door and turned back to Elliott, who had
gotten up and moved into the kitchen.

"I wish Bray was here," Kage said,
projecting his voice.

Elliott popped his head out from the
kitchen and half-smiled.

"Me, too."

Kage remembered how determined Bray
was. How she'd come up with a genius plan,
and each time an obstacle got in the way,
she'd found a way around it. Kage suddenly
had the outlandish hope that she'd find a
way out of wherever she was, wherever they
were keeping her. He turned into the
bathroom, closed the door, and started the
shower.

Chapter Nine

Bray

The next day, Bray sat in Jacob's office.

"It's been two weeks since your injection, and I wanted to see how you're doing," Jacob started. He sat across from her, notepad in lap. He wore a long-sleeved, purple button-up shirt, an indigo shade that Bray found pleasing.

"Fine." Bray shrugged. She sat in the chair across from him, her hands dug down under her thighs. It was cold in this office, and a faint sound of classical piano drifted through the room. It was coming from Jacob's laptop. She wished for silence, so it could be easier to listen for Bertan.

"Any grogginess, light-headedness?"

"In the beginning, yes. It's not as bad now."

"Have you gotten your appetite back?" Jacob was jotting on his notepad.

Bray paused. In the space where she considered how to reply, she heard what sounded like a subtle whisper, but she couldn't make it out.

"Hello?" she called out in her mind. "Bertan?"

While awaiting Bertan's reply, she responded to Jacob.

"Like I said, I am not eating the food until they give me something animal-free. I stand by that."

The words spat right out. It probably wasn't going to help her case, but as time went on it was getting harder to filter her mind.

"Hmm." Jacob nodded. He made another note.

In perfect timing, Bertan said something.

"*You're still there.*"

"Where else would I be?" Bray asked him, a smile approaching her face. She was relieved to finally hear from him again.

"Something amusing you?" Jacob asked, looking up at her.

Bray quickly dulled her smile.

"I was just enjoying the music," she said, cringing inside. She never was much a fan of piano music. It most often put her to sleep.

"Oh, you like Bach?"

"The piano is. . .relaxing," she replied, placating the man.

"How's your mood been?" he continued. "Being in prison as a teenager must be hard."

Bray shrugged. She met eyes with Jacob. He looked considerably tired, wrinkles drooping beneath his eyes.

"I've been in and out of psych wards all my life. Being locked up is kind of normal for me."

Jacob's hand went wild on the notepad.

"Bertan," she called out quickly, while she had the chance. "I've been wanting to ask. . .where are you?"

"Can you say more about that?" Jacob asked. "What it must've been like to be locked up all the time?"

"I don't know." Bray shrugged. "I don't have anything to compare it to."

She thought about Meeteetse. Her two months living there were the closest to freedom she'd known. Only, she'd been in another kind of hell: hearing confined animals reaching out to her for help and, for the longest time, feeling afraid to do anything to help them. The more she thought about it, the more she realized there were elements of her life that had always felt like a prison wherever she was.

Until everyone was free, animals included, she wasn't sure she ever could be.

"There were times when you weren't locked up, right? Like before you ended up here. Where were you?"

"I'm not telling you that," Bray replied, laughing.

"Fair. Wherever you were, was it a place you called home?"

"For a while I did. Until I got caught by my own mom and brought here."

"How is your relationship with your mom?"

Here we go, she thought. But before she could respond to Jacob, she heard Bertan's voice.

"*I'm in prison, too.*"

Holy what? Bertan was also in prison? What did that mean for Ruben, for the rest of her friends? Kage? Elliott? What if they had all been locked away. She needed to know more, but first she had to get away from this session with Jacob.

"Bertan," she said. "I'm in the middle of something. Can I get back to you later?"

"*Okay*," he replied.

"I don't have a relationship with my mom," Bray answered Jacob matter-of-factly. She shot a glance around the room for a clock, something to tell the time, and then remembered there was a digital clock on the bookshelf behind her. She wouldn't be able to check without making it obvious.

The conversation went back and forth for a while. Jacob asked her to tell him more, and so she added that her mother was the one who always put her back in the psych ward when she stopped taking her meds, and it was her mother who never listened to her. Jacob jotted notes, asking her how she felt about that. She didn't really feel much about it. She was used to her mother being an unemotional tyrant, she told him. That made him write more notes. It became a game for her, to see what she could say to get him to vigorously take more notes. Not that she was lying, because she wasn't. But anything to pass the time more quickly. All she wanted was to talk with Bertan.

Eventually, Jacob's questions subsided.

"That's our time," he said, turning in his seat and setting the notepad on his desk. "I'll see you back here in a couple more weeks."

Bray hurried out of his office. She had five minutes to get back to her job, where she would stay for the remainder of the afternoon. Past experience taught her that communicating telepathically caused her to lose track of time. And that wasn't something she could do in a place where guards were keeping an eye on her. She had to keep moving.

She started down the hall for the laundry room. On her way, she checked back in with Bertan.

"Bertan," she said quickly. "Can you please tell me more? What happened to you? I'm on the way now to my prison job, but I am listening."

There was a pause, as though he'd heard her and was coming to the surface to reply.

"*I can't remember everything that happened,*" he admitted. "*I was taken to a detention center in the desert. Then. . .I was sent here, to a prison. I think I'm somewhere in Texas.*"

Bray arrived at the laundry room. Inside, Tori and the other three prisoners assigned to this shift were sorting and tossing dirty uniforms into the washing machines. Bray's shoulders slumped. The more information she received from Bertan, the more she wanted to be alone to parse through it the way she was beginning to parse through a pile of clean uniforms, taking one out at a time and folding it, noting the prisoner number sewn into the back, and placing it into a corresponding mesh laundry bag.

Her mind was getting jumbled. She closed her eyes a moment, took a deep breath.

"Was it that bad?" Tori called from the other side of the table.

Bray opened her eyes and grinned.

"Yeah. At least folding laundry is peaceful enough that I can recoup," she replied, hoping Tori would get the message she didn't feel much like talking.

Tori nodded, stopped what she was doing, and walked around the table toward her. Beside the door, a laundry cart was nearly full with clean laundry. Tori reached for it, stopping beside Bray.

"Did you get to see the news?" Tori whispered.

"No, not yet."

"Your mom. . .she did a press conference."

"Oh geez." Bray felt her face going flush.

"She basically pinned everything on your dad."

"What?" Bray stopped folding and looked at Tori. "What do you mean?"

"She said it was your dad's fault, that

he was the one who didn't believe you were mentally ill, that he assisted your going into hiding. I thought you'd want to know."

Bray went hot with anger. Of course her mother would do that. Why was she surprised? She squeezed the pair of pants she was holding, her knuckles whitening. She inhaled, held her breath a moment. It must've been Dianna's way of trying to get the heat off S-Corp after everything Bray and Kage had done to expose them.

Tori disappeared with the laundry cart. The remaining prisoners stood around the table, quietly folding and talking.

"*Bray?*" Bertan called.

Shoot, she thought.

"Sorry," she replied in her mind. "I just got some news that made me really angry. I've been distracted today. I'm sorry to hear you also ended up in prison. What about Ruben?"

Bray's thoughts raced back and forth. Her mother. Her father and what his reaction to the press conference might've been. Bertan. . .in prison. It was becoming increasingly more challenging to keep up, and especially frustrating not to be able to do anything about anything while locked up in this place.

"*I don't know what happened to Ruben,*" Bertan replied. There was a long pause. Bray sensed a faint feeling of sorrow. "*Last I saw, he was beat up pretty bad. And unconscious. Someone was onto us. . .knew what we were doing.*"

Bray knew exactly who that was. S-Corp, of course. No guessing. Things were coming to light. Bertan, in prison. Her, as well. Ethan, murdered. Ruben, gone. There was no way to find out about her friends. The longer she spent here, the more power S-Corp could gain back. What she'd worked so

hard to create might fall apart.
     Bray was beginning to realize she needed to find some way out of here.

Chapter Ten

Bertan

It was night. All the same to Bertan. Only difference was the disappearance of daylight from his window, exchanged with a deep, dark sky and no moon. Sounds of whistling in the hallways, which he had grown accustomed to. Some music from far down a hallway. He lay on his back in bed, experiencing hunger pangs.

A tray of food had been placed inside the door, but he still would not eat. He felt too low a mood to have any desire to eat, despite the hunger. And this thing that was happening-this conversation with Bray-had confounded him. He was transfixed by it. Unlike his familiar fugue, he didn't think he was losing track of time now. He'd been awake and alert in his prison cell all day, lying here talking with the girl intermittently.

If it was true that she was real and she was in Arizona, he could believe it, for she had told him that she, too, was in her cell, that it was night, and lights would be going out in one hour.

They would have time to talk, without interruption.

He was surprised that a part of him wanted to believe her. Wanted to believe this was all real. A fraction of his old self lay inside him somewhere, and when he spoke with Bray, it came up closer to the surface, as if being heard for the very first time.

Bray began their nighttime conversation by stating how sorry she was about Ruben, how she knew he was Bertan's friend. He searched her voice for some kind of insincerity, but could not find it. It was much harder to tease out a liar without seeing their face. Therefore, he found himself opening up, without cautioning himself that he shouldn't. Besides, he was in prison, and what, if anything, could someone do who was communicating with him telepathically? His mind was already fucked up enough as it was. If anything, he thought maybe he should warn the girl to stay away from him.

"Aren't there other things you'd rather be doing than talking to me?" he asked.

"*Ha!*" Bray laughed. It sounded odd to hear it in his mind. "*They give us books to read. But if I wanted to read, I'd read. Right now I want to talk to you.*"

"What books? We don't get any here."

"*Really? There's no library at your prison?*" Her voice was so. . .unassuming. She did sound like a young girl.

"Hell if I know. They don't let me leave my cell."

"*What? But what about meals? Showers?*"

"They leave my meals on a tray inside my cell door, then take it when I'm done." He left off the part about not eating. "And they take me to showers in the mornings, but then bring me right back after."

"*They don't put you to work or anything?*"

"No."

There was a pause. Bertan's eyes searched the ceiling the way his mind was searching for her response, for some proof that she was or was not real. Yet everything she was saying made sense.

"*So you're just stuck in your cell all day, every day?*" she asked.

"Yes."

"*I hope you at least have a window.*"

"I do, but I don't pay it much attention. It's almost worse. . .to see a piece of the world but not get to touch it or feel it. It's its own kind of torture." Bertan stopped himself. "Sorry, that was a lot."

"*It's okay. Like I said, you can talk to me about whatever. I've seen and heard a lot of things.*"

"But you're so young. If you are who you say you are, that is. Seventeen-year-olds are just learning the world. Or should be. . ." Bertan's voice trailed off. He thought about his daughter, down in Honduras without her dad, not knowing where he was. Was she thinking about him?

"*All my life,*" Bray said, "*my parents put me in psychiatric wards. They believed I had schizophrenia.*"

"I'm sorry, I'm not too familiar with what that is," Bertan admitted.

"*They thought I was hallucinating and hearing things. . .because I told them I was talking to animals and could hear animals calling out to me in pain.*"

"That young?" he asked, and stopped himself. He was beginning to remember this conversation. The one where she said she had been able to communicate with animals for as long as she could remember. He shifted onto his side, and when he did, he noticed his stomach pangs had lessened.

"*Since I was a kid, yes. And so they put me on medication, and the medication would dull my senses, so I'd stop taking it. Then I'd end up back in the hospital again, forced to take more medication. It went back and forth like that for years.*"

"How did you end up in Idaho?" he asked, more curious now than suspicious.

"*Well.*" Bray's voice paused. "*I managed to escape Denver hospital. I think I may have told you about my friend, Alice? The pig?*"

Bertan did recall her mentioning a sow. "You said it got shocked in the back and then you ended up hurt in the same place?"

"*Yes. That was actually how I managed to escape the hospital. They took me down to the emergency room and on the way, I made a mad dash for the exit.*"

"Huh. . .and no one caught you?"

"*Almost. I hid in a church and I found a knife to cut the implant out of my arm, so they couldn't track my location.*"

"And then?" Bertan was staring down at the floor, completely immersed in this story. He liked that it was helping him pass the time. Helping him forget where he was.

"*I made my way to my friend, Elliott. You remember him? The Black guy that was with us at the trailer.*"

Bertan recalled meeting Bray's friends at the trailer. Two young people, one Black, the other he thought was a woman but later realized was transgender. That time in his life seemed so foreign to him, so removed, as though he was not really there. When he pictured it, he certainly saw his body standing inside the trailer, beside Ruben, as Bray explained her plan to them. She needed to be close to the S-Corp slaughterhouse in order to connect citizens who were using Embedicare implants to cows going through slaughter. The plan sounded completely ridiculous to him, but he was so obsessed with ending S-Corp, he was willing to help her. He felt a new sense of purpose when he heard about the secrets and incriminating evidence they were going to share with the entire nation, hoping it would be enough to destroy S-Corp so he could go home and be with his family.

When he thought of that meeting, he thought how his body was there, but his self was somewhere else entirely. Somewhere lost. The fugue had been more in control of him than he was.

"Yes, I remember," he said finally.

Everything came stumbling into his memory the way beefs would stumble into the knock box on their way to be slaughtered. Unwilling and resistant at first, because the memories challenged the notion that this couldn't possibly be real, but that conversation he'd had with her in Idaho was as real as anything. She'd said she helped get that pig off a transport truck, and some other pigs, too, but he didn't remember her telling him how.

Bertan stood up in his cell. Dizzy, he held onto the bed until the spell dissipated. He began pacing the floor.

"How did you stop that transport truck?" he asked.

"*You do remember*," she said. He imagined she was smiling. "*I got help from a group of wild horses. I rode one of them, got close enough to the truck, and climbed up onto it. The horses forced the truck off the road. That's what happened.*"

"Okay," Bertan said, gleaming from the ridiculousness of it. "I don't believe you, but the story is entertaining. And I do enjoy stories."

"*It's no story*," Bray said. Her voice did not waver. "*And you don't have to believe me for it to be true.*"

Fair, he thought to himself.

Bertan returned to his bed and sat back down. He felt a bit. . .deflated. He wanted to believe that Bray was real. But it was beginning to sound like crazy talk, and crazy talk usually led to other things, such as him losing track of time and becoming violent. He did not want that to happen now because it would get him nowhere but more hurt. He debated ignoring the girl's voice, seeing if it might go away on its own.

"*You said you don't get books in your prison*," spoke the voice that called itself Bray. "*Do you like to read?*"

"Yes. Why?"

"*I can get a book from our library. Maybe I could read one to you.*"

Bertan's eyebrows lifted at the thought. He did love the escape of a good book. He would welcome any escape from this stinking hole. And if he could get her to read something to him that he'd read before, something he knew, maybe then he could test whether she was real or not.

"Okay," he replied. "See if they have *The Revolution of Astra Hayda*."

"*I'll check tomorrow. I've got to go to sleep now, get some rest.*"

The voice faded away. Along with it seemed to disappear a kind of *essence*, a feeling or a sense of someone else, but not like the fugue. Almost like. . .the opposite of it. He could only notice it by noticing its absence whenever Bray's voice left.

Maybe she was real, after all.

Chapter Eleven

Bray

The next day moved into night with ease. It began as usual, with twenty minutes of meditation before the 6 a.m. bed check. After breakfast, where she ate a meager piece of dry toast and some fruit, Bray willingly completed her laundry duties. She hurried to the library during her hour-long lunch break, knowing she still wasn't going to eat. She had become quite used to her empty and ever-shrinking stomach. She wanted to find that book Bertan had requested. In her conversation with him the night before, she got the sense he did not-or would not-believe her. Was it such a stretch of the imagination to believe in telepathy? She knew for many people it was, especially her mother. But there had been enough documented accounts of ESP, ones she had read about during her times spent in psychiatric wards trying to understand her strange abilities, wishing she could prove it was possible.

Still, Bertan seemed to doubt her.

The library did not have the book he'd requested. She'd heard of it before, knew it was about a young woman who'd journeyed to Central America to learn about her family history, only to become seduced by a revolution of the people, and how the experience unraveled the beliefs she had about herself, her family and the world as she knew it. Bray had always wanted to read the book, but she would have to select something else.

She'd reached out to Bertan to see if any of the books in the library might suffice, listing each one off silently to him in her mind as she perused the fiction section. He'd settled on a book he said he had started reading prior to meeting her, a book titled *Civilization*, and asked her to start it from the beginning.

Bray eagerly awaited nightfall. She returned to her cell after dinner and sat down at the small desk, pulled out the book, and called for Bertan.

"Bertan? Are you there?" she asked, staring at the wall.

"*Sí. Where else would I be?*"

"I guess it would be nice to reach out and find out you've been released."

"*Hmph.*" He grumbled. "*I doubt that will ever happen.*"

"Have they not said anything about a court date?"

"*No. They tell me nothing. I don't even get to speak to anyone. Not my family, not a lawyer. They just leave me in here, day in and day out.*"

Bray felt a pain in her chest. It was the pain of powerlessness. She understood it well.

"They haven't given any of us court dates, either. No contact with the outside world, no emails. We get to read books, watch the news, and things like that, but otherwise it's like they've just abandoned us in here."

"*At least you get that much. If it goes on this way much longer,*" he said, "*I may really lose my mind.*"

Bray frowned. *How could he not*, she thought.

"*Who are you talking to?*" Bertan

suddenly asked.

"Oh, did you hear that? I was talking to myself."

"*You said, 'how could he not?'*"

"I did. I was thinking I'd be surprised if being in a cell by yourself all the time didn't lead you to losing your mind. It's sad to hear they can just treat people like that."

"*Huh,*" he huffed. "*I've seen, done and been through worse.*"

"I imagine you have," she replied, nodding. Her shoulder released in a kind of ease.

Bertan was quiet. Bray suspected he wanted her to carry the conversation.

"I've got that book, *Civilization*. You want me to start reading?"

"*Yes, please.*"

Bray opened the book to the first chapter, sat back in the chair, and began to read.

"Chapter One. . .In all directions, no sign of humanity. Plenty of life, of course. Broad fields of farmland surrounded by pine trees that dotted the landscape in a green so deep it could render its viewer windless. It was out here, in the mountains of Maine, that one could become free of the suffocation of humanity. One could truly live. . ."

Bray read the sentences, one page into the next, silently, but as if she were reading it in thought, so that she was certain Bertan could follow along. At first it was disorienting, to consciously remember to say the words in her thoughts. At the first break in the chapter, she paused.

"Are you getting everything?" she asked him.

"*Sí,*" he replied.

Bray smiled. She continued on, reading slowly through the chapter as the sun faded away outside. She did not notice the coming of dark until the cell's fluorescent lighting became more evident. Bray brought the book up to block the glare.

As the reading continued, Bray found herself becoming immersed in the story. Not only that, she found herself immersed in the connection between herself and Bertan. Immersed in wonder that there was any connection at all. That he was right there, so close. She'd never felt this kind of proximity with Alice or Rhea or any animal. Perhaps it was because they were both human, of the same species, she could only guess. This was foreign to her. Gooseflesh ran up her arms. She felt cold. She ended the chapter and went over to lie down in bed, bringing the blanket up over her body and lying on her back. She stood the book up on her chest and turned to Chapter Two.

"How far into the book did you get?" she asked.

"*About five chapters. It's very addictive.*"

"I can see that."

Bray took a moment to get warm. The air that flowed through the vent in her cell never seemed to ease up. At the same time, she knew the coldness she felt wasn't due entirely to the temperature. She felt both a sense of unease and calm. The unease came from her sense of someone else being in the room, even though she knew that someone else was Bertan. But the calm. . .that was him. She could sense what he was feeling. The book was calming him down.

So she kept on reading into the night. Her eyes grew heavy. Eventually the lights would shut off and she would have to stop. But for now, she fell back into the story, three chapters in, and something began to happen.

Something very close
to. . .frightening.

Somewhere in between the reading of the book here in her cell and the connection with Bertan, a chasm developed. A space in which there was complete unknown. She felt it first in her chest, and as the reading became like a meditative chant, this chasm rose up into her mind. For a while she had been imagining the story taking place: two characters alone in the wilderness, backpacking for days, with no awareness that the world around them was about to fall into disarray. Then, these images began to change. But she was not the one changing them.

Bray stopped for a moment. She considered calling out to Bertan, but figured he'd say something once he noticed she had stopped reading. But he said nothing. He'd fallen to sleep. She could feel it. She could feel a chemical shift. The melatonin had calmed him into a quiet yet restless space, that transition between wake and sleep.

Bray closed the book. She turned and set it down on the floor, and then lay there on her side. She hadn't realizes how tired she was until she'd stopped reading. Her eyes closed. The chasm broadened. The tiredness overcame her, and she fell right into it.

#

It was dark. Humid. A feeling of dripping heat, as in a jungle. Yet Bray had never been to a jungle. She felt the trees all around her. A forest of mangroves and oil palm trees grew like giants and hid the moon away.

Bray found herself kneeling in the

grass. The earth pulsated beneath her, alive and angry. It quaked. Finding the sensation uncomfortable, she stood. When she did so, she felt taller. Bulkier. Strong. She glanced down to look at her body but could see nothing but darkness.

Suddenly she began to move. Ahead of her was a chain-link fence, twenty feet high with barbed wire at the top.

Apparently she was dreaming.

Arriving at the fence, her breathing deep and long, she saw that a hole had been cut wide enough for her to get through. She had the sense she should not do so; nevertheless, she stepped through with stealth and quiet determination.

There was something in here she needed.

Her vision turned toward a single-level house made of concrete blocks and a tin roof. The house, a perfect square, stood tucked away beneath more oil palm trees. Beyond it, a crop of plantains. The scent of pungent vegetation hung in the unmoving air.

Seconds later, she was outside the house, standing against a wall. Above her head, an open window revealed the noise of someone snoring inside. As she felt herself pull something cold and hard out from a holster strapped to her pants, she began to feel sick. More accurately, she began to feel not herself.

The world grew smaller in her mind. Narrow, like tunnel vision. Falling in place. Falling away. Leaving consciousness. Remaining standing, still, a transition pulled her from all she had ever known of herself, into someone else.

A switch, as subtle as a light gone off.

Bray witnessed as the someone she inhabited moved around to the door, gun aimed. The door was open. Inside, the house was full of shadows and the air dense as an untamed mind. A thin light crept down a hallway. Following the light, heart pounding, gun raised. The door pushed open to reveal someone standing in the bathtub.

   Trigger pulled, looking up, she was faced with close and present horror. A young girl, younger than herself, whose eye had been shot out. Blood on the walls. Blood rising up from the bathtub drain. The body dropped. Blood consumed the body and swallowed it whole. The feeling of constriction. Pain in the back of the head. Extreme pressure, pounding, and a loud scream. The blood curled over the edge of the bathtub. It came closer. There was nowhere to run. Nowhere to go. Suddenly there were no doors. One room, with walls covered in blood that darkened into black. The blackness sucked everything into it, including all sense Bray had of herself.

Chapter Twelve

Bertan

Bertan had been here before. It was an atmosphere strikingly familiar. Tall, concrete walls of drab gray. No windows. Mechanical sounds. Clinking, sharpening of knives, swooshing sounds. Industrial fans along the ceilings, turning in slow and methodical movement. The floor opened out beneath insufficient lighting. Stainless-steel tables, conveyers running below the ceiling fans, leading to a set of metal stairs whose steps climbed one level to an office. Workers in smocks and rubber boots howled and shouted, whistled.

Yes, he had seen all of this before.

Beside him, a six-foot-high, metal chute angled slightly upward toward a cylindrical metal box.

"The knock box." He knew.

The sounds of animal cries came from the chute. Suddenly his vision rose up toward the ceiling. It felt disorienting. When his view shifted downward, pointing at the floor, dizziness led to a sweaty feeling of nausea.

Inside the chute, *beefs* stood in a single line. Someone or something in his mind kept referring to them as cows. As if there were a second voice in his mind, something else referred back to them as beefs. Like an argument.

The beefs had stalled and were not moving. One of them climbed up onto the

back of a beef in front of it, used the
beef's back-end for support, and managed to
get itself up to the top of the chute. It
struggled and Bertan began to feel the
weight of it. He felt as heavy as a beef's
corpse.

When the beef hurtled over the chute
and landed on the other side, Bertan felt a
pain in his side. It ran from his shoulder
down his torso and through one leg. He'd
never had a dream where he could feel
physical sensation, and this disturbed him.

Suddenly a worker pushed a gun right
between his eyes and he panicked, pleaded
for this not to happen.

"Please! No, no, no!" he cried.

The gun went off and his ears popped
and his eyes rolled up into his head. His
heart stopped a moment. When it started
again, his breath shot up into his mouth
and he convulsed.

He whimpered and begged for a way out.
He wanted to open his eyes and end this
nightmare, yet no matter how much he willed
it, the vision remained the same.

Workers prodded and shocked the beefs
in the chute. The beefs shrieked and his
own throat went sore. A second beef climbed
itself up to the top of the chute and got
smacked in the face with a prod, making
Bertan's teeth shake and sting, right down
to the gums.

He wanted to scream.

Everything went dark. He was not
expecting this. That was the last thought
in his mind before it, too, went dark. What
remained was a rapidly-beating heart and
extremely loud silence. Dry mouth,
terrorizing heat and a sense of being
unmoored in space.

A vision of a square opening replaced
the darkness. He was forced through it,

where before him there hung the bodies of beefs, upside down, being bled out one by one. There were no thoughts. Only animalistic fear. Eyes wide, wet. A worker standing above him, eyes hidden behind goggles. The sudden feeling of pressure between his eyes.

When the stunning happened, it happened both in seconds and in ages and seemed to never stop happening. It began with the crack of bone, like a nail being hammered into his head. His head split into a million pieces. Pain pushed with unbelievable speed through veins, into his frontal lobe.

It went beyond pain and into abject nothingness. Spaciousness mixed with overwhelming sensation. A lifting up. Heat rolling slowly down somewhere. The scent of iron and decay. A screaming and blinding sharpness in the heel. Flipped upside down. Pressure, hovering and more stinging. Something falling. Blindness.

It was then Bertan lost any remaining sense of humanity and fell away from himself.

Chapter Thirteen

Kage

The midday sun hit Kage's back, heating his skin beneath the vented, button-up blue shirt that Chad lent him. He'd been assisting another worker in attaching ribbed, metal roofing panels to the roof. Chad had been handing the metal pieces to them, one at a time, through the window of the attic. Now he climbed out onto the roof along the plywood surface, careful not to slip, and came to work beside Kage.

Two of the roofers paused and stood up. They used their hands to block the sun from their eyes as they looked out along the valley. Chad stopped working and did the same.

"Well, would you look at that," Chad said.

Kage turned in their direction to see what they were looking at.

Below the Beartooth Mountains, a band of horses galloped along the exposed earth. Their bodies were the color of sand. Their muscles vibrated beneath tight skin as they moved with dexterity and purpose. Kage could hardly believe his eyes.

"Are those horses?" he asked.

"Yep," one of the workers replied.

Kage smiled. He'd never seen such a thing. So beautiful and rugged and free. It was as though he could feel the rhythm of their hooves pounding against his heart.

His eyes watered in excitement.

"Those must be Pryor Mountain horses,"
Chad said.

"Way out here?" asked the worker.

Chad watched them run. His smile began
to droop.

"I bet they're headed for Washington."

"Water?"

"Yeah." Chad nodded slowly. "There's
not much here in Montana for them anymore."

Suddenly Kage's heart sank. The horses
passed through quickly, their bodies a wave
of gold against the green and yellow
ground, their manes and tails snapping and
twisting in the wind. A sadness approached
Kage, hearing that these beautiful animals
had to migrate elsewhere for their
survival. Of course, wasn't that what he
had done? If things did not improve, wasn't
that going to be the continuation of
humanity until all of humanity burned
itself out?

The horses disappeared into the
horizon. The sun became too blinding for
him to follow their journey westward. A
feeling of loss and regret resonated with
him and Kage wondered if that was how the
horses had felt.

"Looks like that wasn't the only reason
they're migrating," one of the workers
noted.

Everyone turned in the direction from
which the horses had come. Beyond the last
of the foothills, Kage could make out a
faint cloud of smoke.

"Another fire," Chad stated. His hands
landed on his hips. His eyes narrowed.

Kage knew what he meant by that. When
he'd first begun this roofing job, the
workers had given him a crash course in the
current state of the climate in these
northern states. Dust storms, wildfires,

extreme storms, and flooding.

Kage knelt against the roof, watching silently as the smoke billowed against the sky, barely differentiated from the cumulous clouds that hung beside the foothills. He watched it for the longest time, while Chad and the others got back to work stapling the fire-proof panels onto the roof. The smoke concerned Kage gravely, giving him a sinking feeling, like what he had already lost was being lost again. And then he thought about Meeteetse. The empty house. The garden, which by now had probably died without care. The cellar where they'd buried Ethan.

Kage shook it off so he could return to his tasks. The physical labor kept his mind off things, helped him hurry the hours along until night.

He had something he needed to discuss with Trevor and the others.

#

Everyone sat in a haphazard circle in Trevor's living room. Kage sat beside Elliott on the love seat. Lana, Emily and Virgil sat on the couch across from them. Kage hadn't seen Lana in what felt like months, and he was regretting not getting to spend more time with her.

In the two kitchen chairs, blocking the kitchen doorway, were Trevor and Dennis.

They had completed dinner, and those closest to one another, such as Lana and Emily and Trevor and Dennis, were talking amongst themselves. Kage's foot began to bounce against the floor.

"I checked your email this morning," Elliott said to him. Kage had left his password with Elliott for extra help, in case Elliott wanted to check the emails from citizens himself. At this point, as busy as Kage had become with his job, he

was happy to have help from Trevor and
Elliott both.

"Anything exciting?" Kage asked.

"A response from Cole," Elliott
whispered. "He's got people looking for
Bray, but hasn't found her yet."

Kage glanced over at Lana, then Emily.
He wasn't sure how to feel about the news.
No news. Discouraging, of course. He didn't
want to give up on his friend. He'd watched
Bray's dedication to the animal friends
she'd made, how she'd stopped at nothing to
save them. How she had been willing to lose
her life. She deserved the same dedication.

Kage gave Elliott a side eye, but said
nothing.

"Also," Elliott continued. Kage shifted
closer so he could hear the man speak.
Everyone else continued their individual
conversations, and he gathered that Elliott
didn't want the others to hear what he was
about to say. "I added something new to the
website."

Elliott turned toward Kage. They eyed
one another.

"A separate comment page for families
who've lost loved ones to the S-Corp
fertilizer disaster."

"Really?" Kage said, then remembered to
keep his voice down. He looked around, but
no one seemed to notice.

"It's my own thing. . .something I need
to do. Partly for my parents, and it's
something I can maybe help with, to stop S-
Corp."

"Have you gotten any response?"

Elliott nodded emphatically.

"Lots," he replied. "So many I had to
start a spreadsheet with their names and
contact info."

"What does this mean?"

"It means. . .maybe. . ." Elliott

hesitated. He glanced in Lana's direction, then back to Kage. "Maybe we could sue them."

"S-Corp?"

Elliott nodded, a broad smile approaching his face.

"But I thought you'd said families had tried to sue S-Corp already."

"They did, ages ago. And nothing came of it. But this time, we have more families. More people coming forward. This time, we have power in numbers."

A burning struck Kage's heart, like the way he'd felt the first time he left Meeteetse to hit the road, searching for his parents. A sense of something starting, like the lighting of a match.

"Have you talked to Lana?"

"Yeah, she's going to help me."

Kage turned and looked over at Lana. She was sitting at the end of the couch closest to Kage, leaning back against the cushion, her bare feet hidden beneath her legs, which were crossed. Kage felt that affection he'd always had for her.

Lana exchanged a glance with him, and then a smile. He smiled back. He remembered the first time he'd gotten a chance to talk to her, when they drove out to Boysen Reservoir in Wyoming and took video and photos of S-Corp's dirty little secret.

He decided it was time to get everyone's attention.

"Eh-hem," Kage said loudly.

Lana and Emily turned to him in unison. Trevor and Dennis were still talking.

"Hey, ho," he raised his voice. "I need to talk to everyone."

The room went quiet. Trevor turned to him and looked on, his hands resting in his lap. He gave Kage a wink.

"I have something I need to do, and

right away," he said.

"What's that, Kage?" Emily asked.

"I think it's time I return to Meeteetse, see what shape it's in."

"You sure it'll be safe?" Dennis asked.

"I mean. . .there are no guarantees, but I think it's time we get some video of the place, show our supporters--maybe even the neigh-sayers--that food can be grown in the soil, and consumed."

"Not a bad idea," Trevor said.

Kage was relieved to finally have his uncle on his side.

"If you're going to do that," Lana said, "why not stop by the Boysen Reservoir dam in Wyoming, get some video of that, too. People ought to know about the Wyoming water situation."

Kage opened his mouth to reply, but Trevor jumped in before he could.

"What Wyoming water situation?" Trevor asked, looking over at her.

Lana shot a glance over to Kage. Kage's eyes widened. He let her have the floor.

"For the past few years, S-Corp has been illegally extracting water from Wyoming's reserves. They'd been given permission to extract monthly, but we had proof they were doing it every day. . .until S-Corp caught our team and took all of our evidence."

"Unbelievable," Virgil said, shaking his head. His eyes sank to his lap.

"If we let them continue, they may very well destroy our climate. Or at least, what's left of it," Lana finished.

"So when were you thinking of going?" Trevor asked him.

"I could go tomorrow." Kage shrugged. Tomorrow was his day off. "The sooner, the better."

Dennis got up and left the room,

entering the kitchen and beginning to clean up the dinner dishes.

"Only if I can come with you," Lana said, gazing pointedly at him.

Kage's eyes trailed back to Lana. Her eyes remained on him. They were as green as ever, and disarming as always. She had this way of looking at him that made him feel she was seeing into the parts of himself that no one else could see. He liked it, and he also feared it. Nonetheless, there was no one else he'd rather have had with him, other than perhaps Elliott.

"Deal," he replied, smiling.

Chapter Fourteen

Bray

The obnoxious buzzer of Bray's alarm forced her up from a restless sleep. When she got out of bed to prepare for the morning check, her head felt like it had been squished by a powerful pressure. She felt hunger pangs in her abdomen. This surprised her, given she'd grown accustomed weeks ago to not eating, Until this morning she had hardly felt any pain at all.

After the bed check, she headed to the cafeteria with the other prisoners. She stood in line behind them, in a complete daze. Like she was only half-alive, yet there was a strong presence within her. She couldn't quite place her finger on the feeling it was giving her. It was. . .unpredictable.

Typically, when Bray had done stints in the psych ward as a teenager, they'd give her internet privileges as a part of her "learning," as they called it. At the age of sixteen, she'd come upon a news article about conjoined twins. It was the closest she'd ever come to a description of how she felt while linked telepathically with her friend, Alice, the sow. It was like having a twin right beside her, who was different and very much their own being, yet conjoined with Bray in a way that only death could separate.

That was how she'd felt from the time she'd woken up this morning.

What had changed?

She sat and ate breakfast, but hardly

said a word. She was too consumed with what
had happened last night. She remembered
reading aloud to Bertan, and then she
sensed he'd fallen asleep. Somewhere in
there, she fell asleep, too.

And then she had that nightmare.

Or maybe it wasn't a nightmare. It felt
like the times she'd linked with Alice to
find out where Alice was located, so she
could try to rescue her. In those
experiences, everything became so real, so
palpable.

She had to get herself through
breakfast before she could reach out to
Bertan. . .to confirm what she believed may
have happened last night.

#

"Bertan?" she called out in her mind.
She was rolling the laundry cart down the
hall, collecting dirty laundry bags and
taking her time doing it.

The response was muffled. It reminded
her of something she'd seen, in television
shows, someone being taken or kidnapped and
their mouth taped shut. How they'd try to
talk or scream and all that came out was a
moaning voice.

She stopped in the hallway.

"Bertan? Are you okay?"

Again, the muffled sound.

He was there. She could feel him. This
was exactly how she felt when she was
linked to Alice. Admittedly, it stunned
her. This meant she had found a way to tame
the medication. The consistent,
Transcendental Meditation must have worked.
There was nothing else to explain her
sudden capacity to *link*. . .and with a
human, no less.

It also frightened her. She was in new
territory, and, not knowing much of
anything about Bertan, she began to grow

nervous. How linked were they?

"Keep a move on," a guard called from the opposite end of the hall.

Bray sauntered over to the nearest cell, picked up another bag, and dropped it into the cart. She kept moving, turning a corner out of sight of the guard. She stood against the wall, closed her eyes, and breathed.

Despite having eaten a few pieces of toast with strawberry jelly for breakfast, the hunger pangs hit at her stomach. She scanned her body and noticed congestion in her head. She noticed a subtle, pulsing pain in both her wrists, yet they were not injured. They were free of markings.

She had to assume she was feeling Bertan's pain. She didn't want to think that's what was happening, but it was the only thing that made sense. Trembling, she gave herself a little shake and opened her eyes. She turned and reached for the cart, placing her hands on it and beginning to steer.

"*Ah,*" came a voice from very far away, as if from the bottom of a well. "*What's happening to me?*"

"Bertan?" she called for him. She pressed on down the hall, but it was more difficult than usual to focus on him while also doing her job. She would have to delay as long as possible before returning to the laundry room. Once Tori or one of the others began talking with her, she'd have to do her best to act as if nothing was wrong.

"*I—I'm losing it. . .again,*" he whispered.

"Bertan? Can you hear me?"

"*Barely,*" he replied. She got the sense that he was pushing the words out, with great effort. He sounded in significant pain, but not the physical kind.

"I had a vision last night," she said, hoping he would hear. "I was in this jungle. . .with a gun. Then there was this house, and inside there was a hallway with. . ." Bray stopped, tried to recall. "Where a bathroom light was on. I entered the bathroom and there was this little girl, in the bathtub-"

"*Stop!*" Bertan pleaded.

"I'm sorry?" she replied. She thought she'd heard him say stop.

"*I know what it was. That was Chino's daughter. I murdered her.*"

Bray's eyes widened. She froze in the hall, her heart beating through her chest.

"What? You mean. . .that was your memory?"

"*What else?*" Bertan let out an exhale, as struggling to speak. "*Did you see?*"

"She had a gunshot wound in her eye. There was blood everywhere," Bray said, shivers running down her back and legs.

Bertan let out a wail.

Bray felt a sudden sickness in her stomach, followed by light-headedness. She grabbed the last bag in the hall, dumped it into the cart, and pressed herself against the wall. Glancing around for guards, she closed her eyes and took a few deep breaths.

"Bertan," she said. "Are you okay?"

"*I don't know.*" His voice was moving further away.

Bray grabbed the cart and moved down the hall, wishing he would say something before she got to the laundry room. Her face was flushed, and although the dizzy spell passed, the nausea continued. She sensed she wasn't going to throw up. She sensed it because she understood it wasn't her nausea.

". . .*had a vision, too*. . ." Bertan's voice went in and out. "*Beefs. In a. . .for slaughter. . .tried to escape. . .shot between. . .eyes. . .*"

"Beefs?"

There was no response. She was lingering, focusing on Bertan. Hanging on to every word he'd said. Something about a slaughter. Was he referring to cows?

Suddenly it hit her. She stopped outside the laundry room door. Inside, two women were laughing. The laughter seemed miles away.

Bray closed her eyes for a brief moment before entering. She remembered Rhea, the cow she'd linked with back in Meeteetse. The one who'd reached out to her and begged her to help. The one Bray had tried to save, who had tried to save herself by attempting to escape slaughter. Suddenly she remembered how Rhea had rallied all of the cows in one desperate plan to escape. One of them had gotten close enough by jumping the chute and falling over onto the other side.

And then. . .Bray remembered. . .it was shot between. . .the eyes.

Oh, no, Bray thought. Any blood still left in her head rushed in a downward motion. She felt simultaneously cold and hot.

This had never happened before.

"*Wh-what?*" Bertan asked, his voice quavering.

"Bertan," she whispered in her mind. "I think we're linked."

Chapter Fifteen

Bertan

Bertan lay on the floor in fetal position. Until he opened his eyes, he had not known his body was on the floor. It must have happened when he was entrapped in the nightmare, when the beef had attempted to escape the chute and landed hard on the concrete floor. He'd landed hard on the floor, too, gaining a resurgence of pain in his injured wrists.

His body was covered in sweat. His stomach pained with hunger. His head felt like a balloon. Inside, he felt like he was still falling.

When Bray reached out to him, he could barely understand her. He covered his ears as if some burdensome noise was attacking it from the outside when, in reality, the cell was as silent as the inside of a freezer.

Bray had said something about a vision. . .he was barely aware of her words, but he knew she'd mentioned the little girl and her blown-out eye. He'd done that. He'd shot the girl in the eye because he thought she was someone else.

And he had never been able to forget the horror of it.

Now, the pain went deep. Deeper than it had ever gone before. He didn't think it could go any deeper. He was alone, locked away, forgotten, left with the confirmation that he was no good. It pained him deeper this time because, for a short while, he had begun to *believe* he wanted a way out. That he wanted to be better, for his family. In those few interactions with Bray, he'd felt. . .*normal* again.

But then he'd had this nightmare. The terrible vision of beefs going to slaughter, haunting him from a lifetime ago when he hadn't known who he was, had felt himself a whole other person. A person he wanted to forget. And the images of that kill floor, that chute. . .that, that *knock box*. It was all coming back to him again, as if to terrorize him, and he grew hot.

Remembrances played through his mind. How the girl told him in Idaho that she'd linked with some pig and was able to feel what the pig felt. She was able to experience its pain. Had she left something out? Had she not mentioned that maybe the pig also experienced something on its end? No, that was ludicrous. Something had happened last night, when he fell into slumber. It made little sense, but it was the only logical thing. The nightmare was not his. It felt like a movie he'd watched. The setting of the kill floor did not reflect the reality of the place he remembered from his time working there. And never had he seen beefs attempt an escape like that.

This was her stuff. It was coming from her. Was she maybe not real? Was she another fugue, some other identity tricking him?

"She's definitely playing you, man," came a scathing, masculine voice. It moved closer as if to sit down beside Bertan in the cell. *"Don't let her get to you."*

"How do I stop it?" he screamed.

"Bertan?" The girl's voice popped back into his mind. *"Are you scared? I'm here.*

You're not alone."

Her words calmed him for a moment. He fell still. His chest eased and his heart softened.

"It's a trap," the male voice spoke again, this time with increased firmness.

Bertan felt himself lifted, but by the will of another. As if something had come through the window, had thrown him a rope, a promise of escape.

"Come with me. We can leave all of this," the male voice whispered.

Bertan felt himself between two worlds. He was in space, losing oxygen. His identity faded in and out like a slow, dying pulse.

"Take my hand and come with me."

"Bertan," Bray returned. *"I can tell you are hurting. Maybe. . .maybe I can help somehow."*

*Hurting. . .*the word reverberated through his soul, through spaces and places of translucent smoke and mirrors. A place that *sounded good.* The way it had sounded good to leave his family in Honduras and come to work in the U.S. Her voice could not be trusted any more than he could trust his own.

"I can take all the feelings away," the male voice persisted. Bertan heard a luring, seductiveness in the man's voice. *"She will only make them worse. There is no time to talk. I can get you out of here."*

It was becoming hard to focus. Bertan wanted to give up. To give in. This back and forth in his mind sapped all of his energy. He lay there, eyes closed, and whimpered.

"Just give me a sign," Bray encouraged. *"Just an okay, or something, and I'll do what I can to help you."*

"She will leave you. Just like all the

others. Your father. Your wife. Ruben. I'm here with you. If you let me, I can take it from here." The male voice grew strong and reverberated through his mind, an echo bouncing off walls. So much that it hurt.

Bertan exhaled. The female presence faded slightly, but he could tell she was still there, in the back of his mind, waiting.

"Okay," he murmured, and fell away.

Chapter Sixteen

Kage

Kage and Lana left the next morning. Elliott had equipped them with an RF repeater, a square instrument that jammed drone signals for a five-mile radius. He had also given them a palm-sized camera, which they were to use to record video. They placed these in the back of the black truck they'd driven to Red Lodge from Meeteetse. The truck had belonged to one of Cole's friends, one of a group of men who'd helped Bray after she rescued the sows back in Wyoming. When Bray passed out after her sow friend, Alice, died, Kage and Lana had used the truck to get Bray to safety in Meeteetse, and they'd held onto it ever since.

Kage got into the driver's seat, and the sun met his eyes. It grazed along the top of the windshield, blinding him with a golden-white, fierce presence. Today was sure to be hot, just as all the others had been. He pulled the visor down and waited as Lana opened the passenger door. She was wearing a long, flowing floral skirt and a white t-shirt.

"You look nice," Kage said, smiling at her.

"Thanks," she replied, closing herself in and clicking her seatbelt into place. She sat back, her feet barely touching the black floor mat. Sometimes he forgot how small she was.

They headed south on Route 310, bypassing Marshal checkpoints. Once they entered Wyoming, the land didn't change. They traveled through miles and miles of old ranch land. Abandoned barns and farm equipment dotted the golden, parched ground.

"We haven't had much of a chance to talk since we left Meeteetse," Lana spoke, her eyes set on the view beyond the windshield.

Kage glanced over at her, then returned his eyes to the road.

"That's true. We haven't." He cleared his throat.

"I feel really awful about what happened," Lana continued.

Her hands were resting in her lap, and for a moment, as Kage watched her out of the corner of his eye, she seemed a different person from the lawyer he had first met back in Cheyenne. She seemed less guarded now, even unguarded.

"Me, too."

"I mean. . .how S-Corp found us," she said, turning toward him.

Kage wanted to look at her, but he felt the nervousness climb deeper down into his ribcage, so he kept his eyes on the road. Not much to see. No other cars. Miles and miles of blue sky with lines of jet stream, clouds as thin as paper, and a sliver of foothills in the distance.

"I feel like it was partly my fault," she continued.

"How?" he asked, confused.

"I didn't even take into consideration that contacting Ruben might lead them to us." She paused and looked at Kage, then continued. "Because my phone could still be traced. I didn't know."

Kage's eyes widened. He remembered. After Bray had passed out during the Embedicare takeover, Kage and Elliott rushed her back from Idaho to Meeteetse. Kage received a warning from Bray's father, Cole, that S-Corp was searching for them, so Elliott had checked all their devices. That's when he had discovered that Lana's phone was not as encrypted as she thought it was. But in no way did Kage feel Lana was responsible for S-Corp flushing them out of their hiding place.

"Oh," he breathed. "It wasn't your fault. Please don't take that on."

"I'm trying not to, but it's all I can think about." Lana turned away and looked out the window, to the sky.

"There's more to it, isn't there?"

"I feel like we've probably lost Ruben, and that's on me, too," she said. She wiped her face.

Kage glanced over at her and saw the wetness of tears lining her cheeks.

"Come on," he said gently, taking her hand in his. "Remember when I was staying with you and your team back in Medicine Bow?" After he'd left Meeteetse to search for answers around the disappearance of his parents, Kage got into trouble with the law and ended up in jail. It was Lana's team, and her colleague Tori, in particular, who took Kage into their hideout in the mountains. This was how he'd learned there were more animal activists out there, that he and his uncle Trevor and the housemates in Meeteetse weren't the only ones.

"How could I forget?" she giggled.

"And remember how I stole one of your cars and tried breaking into S-Corp on my own?"

She nodded.

"And then your entire team was captured." He paused, wondering for a second how devastated he would have been if he'd lost Lana. "And you and I almost were."

"Except you got us out," Lana replied. She freed her hand from his and used it to wipe away the remainder of her tears. She dropped her hands into her lap, releasing a sigh.

"Yeah, well I carried guilt about your team for a long time after that."

"You never told me."

"Didn't know how, I guess," he replied. "My point is, I carried that guilt-and then more guilt after Bray was captured. I decided that I could carry guilt forever, or I can do something about it. Which is why I'm glad we're out here, so we can maybe transfer that guilt into something more. . .productive."

"Wow." Lana nodded, nearly smiling. "You sound very. . .mature."

Kage rolled his eyes and suddenly felt insecure. Lana was six years older than him. Another reason he figured she'd never see him as anything more than a friend.

They continued on for another two hours, passing through Meeteetse but not stopping. Kage had thought it best to drive to the Boysen Reservoir dam first and then return to Meeteetse on their way back to Red Lodge. Save it for the end, when he felt he could have more time there. More time to say goodbye to his former home, if that's what it would come to.

Finally, the Boysen Reservoir appeared to the truck's right, a broad expanse of water, lively blue water juxtaposed against dead brown and yellow earth. Islands of brown land popped up amidst the water. Abandoned trailers sat along the reservoir's edge.

Kage turned off the road and into the dirt. The truck bounced along rock and dead grass, toward a couple of foothills. He felt the steering wheel shake beneath his hands, so he eased up on it while gently directing the truck up along the edge of one of the hills, then down the other side. He stopped and placed the truck in park. Never had he thought he'd enjoy driving a truck, but it made him feel lively and in control, and it brought a warmth to his groin that made him grin.

As much as he didn't approve of gender norms, the thing sure made him feel manly.

"Let's get out here," he said, shutting off the engine. "Good place to keep hidden."

Lana walked around to the truck bed and pulled out a tripod and the bag with the camera. They walked across the road. When they reached the edge of the reservoir, away from the road and beneath scattered trees, they headed north toward the dam. Kage noticed a scent of dead fish, gasoline and dirt that spun around in the increasing winds.

They walked about a mile and came upon the turn-in to the S-Corp substation and dam. The sound of rushing water and humming turbines set Kage on edge. They were close, very close. He hadn't expected that coming here would make him nervous. With all that had happened with Bray, losing Ethan, his whole group having to uproot and leave Meeteetse, he had seen what S-Corp was capable of, as indicated by the brilliant structure and power of the dam itself, a concrete divide rising more than 200 feet. Kage and Lana now stood on the dam, overlooking the water. Kage's heart began to race as he glanced past the fences and down at the substation, a gray, square building.

"This is making me super nervous," he admitted.

"I know. Me, too. Let's hurry and get this video."

Lana set up the tripod and camera, pointing the tripod slightly downward in the direction of the S-Corp building. The wind picked up again and threatened to push it over. Lana stood holding the camera, calling over to Kage.

"Do you know what you're going to say?"

"I'll wing it," he replied. Kage walked over to the fence, Lana waiting behind him with the camera. He stared at the building. Along its outer wall, the S-Corp insignia was painted in thick, red: a circle with a tree in the center. It made him sick to look at it. Although he knew the dam helped prevent flooding and provided electricity for Cheyenne, he also knew that S-Corp had been illegally extracting water, which was what they'd done in other western states before those states fell into severe drought.

"I thought you might say that," Lana said. "I wrote up a few talking points last night."

"You did?" He turned and looked back at her.

"Yep," she replied, winking. She had a playful smile on her face. "There are things we don't want to miss. Important details about the history of this extraction project, things you don't consider in that thick skull of yours."

"Hey-" he started, feeling teased. But he had no rebuttal. She wasn't wrong. He appreciated how well Lana seemed to know him, despite how little time they'd spent together.

They wasted no more time recording the video. Kage used Lana's speech, describing the brief history of the water extraction program. How S-Corp had gone behind the state's back to take an additional ten megaliters of water above the legal twelve megaliter amount as contracted to them by the state of Wyoming.

"The proof of these water extraction programs, which my team spent years gathering, is now gone. Two months ago, S-Corp followed my team to its hideout in the Medicine Bow Mountains—" Kage paused. He glanced up from the paper Lana had given him.

"You want me to read this?" he whispered.

The wind began to gather again, pushing at his hair and face. Lana grasped the camera and tripod while she silently nodded to him.

Kage continued. He talked about how S-Corp found and took Lana's team, and he named the missing teammates: Tori Banks, Andy Capulin, Ben Sallow.

Suddenly, an obnoxious alarm sounded from the building below. It rang out in threes. *Wert. . .wert. . .wert.* Then a pause. And continued the sequence off and on. Kage shot a look at the building. Two security officers popped out from tiny doors along the side.

"Grab the equipment!" Kage yelled over the wind. He ran over to Lana, picked up the camera bag. Lana folded the tripod. She was visibly shaking. The camera fell to the ground. Kage grabbed it, shoved it into the bag. They ran off down the road, away from the dam. Lana slipped on the gravel. Kage reached for her wrist, catching her before she hit the ground. His body was hot with sweat and fear.

He couldn't let anything bad happen to Lana.

Kage slid his hand down to meet Lana's fingers, and clasped onto her tightly. He led her down along the embankment, through trees, to a nearby trailer. The sound of the alarm faded slightly.

"We need to hurry," Lana said, out of breath.

Kage shot a look at the road from behind the trailer. She was right. They couldn't stay here. If they could reach the truck, the RF repeater would block any drone signals, and he could get them out of here.

His heart racing, his eyes alert, Kage started for the foothills. Lana followed behind.

"Drop the tripod!" he yelled back to her.

As they crossed the road, Lana let the tripod go. It crashed against a set of rocks. She picked up her pace and they both ran hard and fast, scrambling up rocks and gravel, slipping, then picking up speed again.

At the top, Kage stopped. He turned and glanced down at the road. The dam was perhaps a mile away, and he saw an S-Corp-issued truck exiting the dam.

"Come on!" he yelled. They ran down the hill, where their truck was waiting. Lana jumped into the passenger seat, slammed her door. Kage ran for the driver's-side door. In his urgency, he slid and fell just beside the front tire. He landed hard on his bad wrist, remembering immediately the fight that had caused it to break. In this moment and always, it seemed like the fight with S-Corp would never die down.

Kage got up, winced, and climbed into the truck. He pulled the keys from his

jeans pocket and started the truck
instantly. The camera bag rested between
Lana's legs. He looked down at it, up at
her, smiled, and drove down the hill, away
from the dam.

At least the trip was not for nothing.
At least this time, they got away.

Chapter Seventeen

Bray

Bray knew what she had to do and what it would mean. She had just finished lunch and was sitting at a table in the cafeteria, staring into space. Tori had taken Bray's tray, the cheese pizza dripping in grease untouched, and went off to her afternoon duties.

Valerie sat with Bray as everyone else got up to start for the hall.

"Bray, what's going on with you?" Valerie asked.

Bray did not look at Valerie. She heard her question, but her eyes remained set on nothing in particular. She was deep in thought, concerned about Bertan. He'd sounded wounded. Like something was eating away at him, and slowly. She wasn't thinking when she'd impulsively offered to help somehow. In the past, when animals reached out to her for help, she found a way to physically get to them. She'd even found a way to escape the psych ward to get to Alice. It was a miracle that she had accomplished that. But she was in *prison* now. How was she going to get out? How was she going to help Bertan from here?

What was bothering her was that, on some level, she believed she could help him. She was beginning to believe nothing was impossible. She had, after all, linked to an entire country of citizens through a satellite, of all things.

She *feared* that she could help Bertan, that she *would* help him, and that it would mean certain solitary for her—or worse.

"I think I'm going to be gone for a while," Bray responded finally.

"What do you mean?"

"No time to explain," Bray said. The afternoon buzzer had gone off, and Valerie had somewhere to be, as did she. She pulled her eyes away from the wall, brought herself back to the present. She gazed at Valerie.

"There's something I need to do," Bray whispered. "And they're not going to like it. I'm sure I'll end up in solitary."

Valerie's head downturned slightly. Bray could see she was concerned. Yet Valerie did not reply, almost as though she'd expected it.

Valerie placed her hand on Bray's shoulder and gave her a squeeze. When she got to the double doors, she turned to Bray, nodded, and disappeared down the hall.

Bray waited until the guards called her out. She obliged them by getting up and starting down the hall, which was now empty of other prisoners. She was scheduled to return to laundry duty. She passed the turn to her cell, and stopped. Looking back, she watched the two guards standing at the cafeteria doors. They struck up a conversation and started laughing. Bray swiftly edged herself around the corner and disappeared down the hall. She quickly jogged back to her cell and hid in the corner, away from the door.

Sitting on the floor, she closed her eyes. She knew that once she went into her meditative trance, there was no telling what might happen. This was her first time attempting to connect with another being

with the intention of helping them
internally, rather than on the outside. She
had no idea what would come of it. If this
idea worked, she would lose track of time.
Hours could pass, and the guards would come
for her. If they deemed she was not obeying
rules, they'd send her to solitary
confinement. Or, she supposed, she might
end up in Health Services, under an
assumption she was in some kind of coma.

Sometimes there were more important
things to do than obey rules.

Bray practiced some deep breathing.
After a while, she fell into her rhythmic
mantra.

"So. . .hum. . .so. . .hum. . . ."

It did not take long for the rhythmic
chanting to drop her deeper into herself.
Noises outside her cell faded. Her body
temperature dropped, though she did not
feel cold. Everything was dark. The beat of
her heart drummed in her ears. It slowed.
Everything became still.

She called out to Bertan.

Chapter Eighteen

Kage

The dirt path that led to the Meeteetse house was still intact since they'd left over two weeks ago. It was noon when they arrived, marked by the clock inside the truck as it bounced through thickets of grass and weeds. When the familiar path jumped out at Kage, his heart did the same. He turned the steering wheel sharply to the left, guiding the truck toward his old home.

As they approached, the corn stalks came into view. Rising above them was the house, or what was left of it. Kage's eyes widened with shock. He slowed the truck.

The closer they came, the more the corn stalks appeared. . .blackened. Nothing more than frail bodies. . .burnt to a crisp.

Kage's mouth dropped open. Heat rose up from his chest into his throat. He could feel the anger coming on. He slowed to a stop alongside the corn.

"Wha-" Lana started.

Kage rolled down his window. Reaching out and grabbing one of the stalks, he felt it crumble in his hand. He clenched his fist, held the ashes in his squeezed palm, and let go.

"No, no, no," he whimpered.

Kage turned off the engine. He jumped out of the truck and stood amidst the burnt crops. A scent of smoldering leaves wavered into his nostrils and made him nauseous. It

wasn't the scent that sickened him, it was
the reason for it.

The house! Kage thought. Were his eyes
fooling him, or was he seeing what he
thought he was seeing?

Kage ran through the stalks, ash
falling onto him as he did, and then he
stopped cold. All around him, everything
had been completely incinerated. The wood
fences Ethan and Dennis had erected were
broken and black. The grapevines in the
back of the property hung frail against the
chicken wire.

He could barely look at the frame of
the house. It was as though something had
taken a huge bite out of the front corner.
The roof was half gone and all that was
left was wood frame, burnt to nothing. The
guts of the house, piles of singed wood,
siding, panels, shelves, and other things
so destroyed Kage could not recognize them,
stumbled out into the grass as if the house
had bled out. Kage approached, reached his
shaking hand down to touch the remains.

Footsteps came up behind him. He leapt
in fear, turning to see it was only Lana.
He'd already forgotten she was with him.

"Oh. . .my. . .oh, my. . ." she
whimpered, then went silent. She fell to
her knees, looked up at Kage. He saw tears
develop in her eyes.

Everywhere he turned, the land had been
reduced to ash. Black, dense, hard burnt
crisps of a life he once had and would
never have again. The front porch, and his
room, which had been directly above it, all
gone.

Kage took another step, and the burnt
grass crunched beneath his boots. He
cringed. The sound of it ran up his spine,
as if he'd been stepping on bones. His
heart dropped down into his stomach while

pain shot up into his throat. It rolled out
of his mouth into a scream.

"Ah!"

Kage ran over to where the gardens used
to be. He froze again. He dropped to his
knees, grabbed at the crisped zucchini
plants. All of the tomatoes were ruined. He
grabbed one of the tomatoes and it fell
apart in his hand. He trembled. Everywhere,
death.

As if feeling the fire burning him
inside, Kage grew hot. This was S-Corp's
doing. They'd burned the place down. To
hide evidence, he supposed. Or to show Kage
and the others who they were dealing with.
He believed S-Corp to be that callous.

He stood up quickly. He kicked the
ground, and a spray of ash hit him in the
face.

"Fucking shit!" he cried. How they'd
worked so hard to build this garden, tend
the house, create a sustainable, self-
sufficient life here. How Ethan had
discovered this place, made it his home,
turned it into a safe haven for animals,
and eventually, for Kage. He kicked and
kicked and kicked at the ground.

Suddenly Kage halted.

"Ethan!" he shouted.

Kage ran over to the spot where he knew
the door to the cellar hid. His heart
racing and splitting in pain, he pushed
away at the burnt rubble. Crying, his tears
fell down and wet the dead earth.

Lana came up behind him, placed her
hand on his back.

"What can I do?" she asked. Her voice
cracked. It had been her home, too.

"Help me get this open," he replied,
shaking as he searched the ground,
desperate for the door latch.

Lana knelt beside him. She began

pushing at the ash and dirt. Finally, the rusted cellar door revealed itself. Kage exhaled with relief. He wiped his eyes so he could see better.

Together, Kage and Lana pulled the door until it popped open, causing Lana to slip backward. Kage managed to catch her with his free hand.

"You okay?" he asked, sniffling.

"Yeah."

Kage let the door fall open onto the ground. An unfathomable scent of rotten meat and fruit hit him in the face. He held his breath and stared down into the dark, a set of ladder steps looking up at him.

"Can you give me a minute?" he asked, looking over at Lana.

"Of course," Lana replied, stepping away.

Kage turned and carefully started down the ladder into the cellar. He nearly doubled over from the odor as he reached the ground. Taking off his jacket, he wrapped it around his face, leaving his eyes exposed so he could see.

The shelves of pickled vegetables and beans remained intact. In the corner sat a barrel topped full with water. Along the dirt floor across from the shelves, bags of rice waited. . .and right there before him, lying placid like a dead tree, was the body of Ethan Calter.

Kage bent down beside it. Taking a deep breath, he reached out, placed his hand on Ethan's chest where a perfect hole the size of a quarter dug deep down. The stillness was unsettling. He dared not move for fear that something might jump out at him from the dark. But as his hand warmed the cold, hard body beside him, he was able to close his eyes. He allowed the stillness to relax him.

"Ethan," he whispered. "The world doesn't seem right without you in it. They took Bray. They destroyed the house, the garden. But. . ." Kage paused. Opening his eyes, he stared off into the dark. "Maybe you'll be pleased to know. . .our plan worked. I don't know how she did it, but Bray managed to connect those cows to hundreds of civilians. They're reaching out to us now, at least, some of them. Some of them don't believe us. And even more of them want my head on a plate," he said, laughing. The laugh ended as quickly as it began, and he slowly looked down at Ethan's face. The skin had turned green. The body, bloated. Kage shivered, looked away.

He was not a believer in an afterlife. To him an afterlife was only what could be seen right here, before him. An empty body and darkness. Death was a wall over which no soul could climb. No one got past it. There was no great beyond. No heaven. No hell. This was it. Thinking there was some place where Ethan was now enjoying life seemed disrespectful of the life he had lived while he was here. This man had dedicated his life to saving animals and helping others do the same.

Kage closed his eyes again. If a heart was capable of breaking in two, that was how his felt. The loss of his parents, and Ethan, had made a cut right down the middle of his beating life force and tried to destroy it.

He could not allow that to happen. He had people to live for now. Or, in Bray's case. . .to die for, if that was what it came to. The pain in his chest released like a valve opening, and he felt the pressure rise up and exhale from his body. He let out a good cry.

Looking back down at Ethan's body, Kage

whispered through tears.

"I wish you weren't gone. Sometimes I don't know what to do. . .without you in the world. But I'm going to try. I'm going to try to be there for Bray, to do what you and my parents no longer can. Thank you for showing me how to live."

With that, Kage pulled his hand away. He stood up, turned for the ladder. He climbed a few steps up, then glanced down one last time. He hoped maybe, just maybe, Ethan could somehow rise from the dead, come back to him.

Let's not be delusional, he said to himself as he turned and climbed back up to the surface.

He closed the cellar door, used his boots to push the dirt back on top of it so it could not be found. He removed his jacket from his head and slid it back on, noticing how much cooler it had gotten outside, and darker.

He searched around for Lana.

"Lana?" he yelled, concerned.

"Over here," she yelled back.

Kage turned to the sound of her voice, which came from the front of the house. He walked over to front where half of the house remained standing, yet probably extremely precarious.

"You okay?" she asked.

Kage noticed himself feeling more. . .resolved. Like his plan to end S-Corp became more crisp, more clear and immediate.

"Yeah, I am. Let's get this video done. If I stay too long, I may never leave."

#

Lana held the camera in her hand as she faced the ruins of the house. The truck sat behind her, its black exterior blending in with the death around it. The wind had died down, and the evening sun disappeared behind the house, extending the last of its rays over a land of rich and fertile soil, the likes of which most citizens believed no longer existed. It was S-Corp and the government who'd led people to believe the entire nation's soil was tainted. Kage hoped this recording would convince the public of the danger of S-Corp, but also the promise of a soil ready for planting. Ready to sustain life.

His arms crossed, Kage waited as Lana pressed a button and pointed the camera at Kage.

"Recording," she said. "Say whatever you need."

Kage stared into the camera. The house stood behind him like an old friend saying goodbye, and for good, this time.

"I wanted to show you my home. . .here in Wyoming," Kage started, raising his hand at the house. "This is the hideout that my friends and I used, until S-Corp found us here. We lived here for many years, in peace." He paused.

Lana quietly tiptoed in his direction, filming him as he spoke.

"This was our garden." Kage paused again. He knelt beside the crisp tomato plants, their leaves cracking, smoldered and gray. Lana came close, bent down beside him. The camera turned and looked up at him, then down at the tomato plants.

"These were tomatoes. We grew all of our food, yes, in this soil. Take a look," he said, picking up one of the burnt tomatoes. Its once-red exterior was completely molten. He squeezed it between his thumb and forefinger. Its juices poured out, ran down his finger. How he missed the days of tending to this garden.

"Psst," Lana sounded. She made a

rolling motion with her free hand to encourage him to move along.

"I wanted to show you proof that S-Corp-and our government-have been lying to us. This food was once perfect for eating, as recently as a few weeks ago. As pure as the soil itself." Kage paused, brought the burnt tomato close to the camera, and continued. "Before S-Corp set fire to this garden, we grew good food and it was all safe for eating. The soil is not tainted. The fertilizer disaster. . .that was S-Corp's story. They made a mistake and they lied to cover it up. And when they came here and saw what we had grown, they burned all of this to a crisp. Now it's all gone. Nothing left. S-Corp killed one of our activists and would have taken us all, but we managed to escape. We're on the run and we're in hiding because S-Corp knows we're telling the truth. And we will continue to give you the truth, whether you believe us or not."

Kage ran his finger along his throat to request Lana stop the camera. She clicked a button and slid the camera into her back pocket.

"Nice work," she said. "Very impassioned."

Kage forced a smile. He wished he didn't have to do this, to tell an entire nation they'd been lied to. He figured most would not believe him, but it was his responsibility to give them the information. He could only hope they would do right by it.

Back in the truck, Kage started the engine. He glanced up at the house.

"Sorry old friend," he whispered to it. "It wasn't supposed to end this way."

Kage continued staring at the house, how sad it looked with its insides on display in the front yard. The way the fire had gutted it like that. What deep regret he felt in that moment. This place had kept him and so many others safe for so long. And before him, it provided safety for countless animals. Seeing it all burnt to a crisp left Kage feeling at a loss for his future, wondering where he might end up. Would he ever find a place as safe as this, where he could settle down? Where maybe he could do for animals what Ethan had done? He didn't know. The only thing he could do now was take the memory of this special place with him, and use that memory to fuel his plan to find Bray.

Some things just can't go with you, he realized.

Kage had learned from years of gardening that things had to die in order for new things to take their place.

A single tear rolling down his cheek, Kage pulled the truck away from the cornfields, watching the rearview mirror as the house slowly disappeared from view. He shook his head and pulled his attention away from it. He turned to Lana.

"What?" she asked, her eyebrows raised.

He thought about what he'd said in the video, about the soil and S-Corp's lies.

"Elliott said something about possibly suing S-Corp, because of the fertilizer disaster. Is that true? Can we?" he asked.

Lana huffed, then went silent a moment. She looked at Kage. He looked back, pointedly. The expression on her face became serious.

"Well, I mean. . .they should be sued for many things. But hypothetically, if we got enough people to agree to testify about their financial losses, due to medical bills and such, their inability to work, then yes, we could sue."

"That's great, isn't it?" he asked, starting down the path as the house disappeared behind them.

"Only one problem."

Kage kept his eyes set on driving, waiting for her to say more.

"We need a lawyer. Someone to take on the case. Not sure who would be willing to do that."

Kage fell into thought. He shifted the truck off the dirt path and onto the single-lane road that meandered slowly into downtown Meeteetse. There was something about driving that cleared Kage's mind.

"What about Cole?" he asked finally. "Isn't he a lawyer?"

"He's a politician, but I don't know his background."

"Maybe you should ask."

"Maybe I will," Lana said, smiling over at him.

They continued in silence, returning north to Red Lodge with a world of open sky and untamed land around them.

#

They arrived in Red Lodge in time for dinner, leaving the truck parked outside Trevor's apartment. Everyone had filled Trevor's living room, as usual. It was becoming a new tradition; eating end-of-day meals at Trevor's each day, where everyone could be in the same space at the same time.

Kage and Lana sat together on the love seat. Kage was starving, and he had shown it by scarfing down a plate full of two lentil loafs, fried zucchini and baked sweet potato fries. It was all delicious, and when he was done, he carried his plate into the kitchen, where Trevor was standing with his own plate of food. Elliott stood beside him.

"Why don't you two catch me up on what's been going on while we were away," Kage said to them. "I need a little time before I can talk about what happened."

"There's not much to report," Trevor said. "I've had emails from a few people who've agreed to be representatives. One guy named Tim out in DC, and a woman named Mandi down in Texas. Plus one other in Cincinnati, name's Elisha."

"Cincinnati?" Kage asked. He'd never heard of the place.

"Ohio," Trevor remarked. He watched Elliott push a forkful of fried zucchini into his mouth. "Anyway, she says she has a couple of friends who used to be animal activists. That they used to rescue animals from factory farms a number of years back."

"Did she say the names of the other activists?" Lana called from the couch, getting up and walking into the kitchen.

"Your ears are razor sharp," Kage said to her, grinning.

She rolled her eyes. Leaning against the counter, she turned her attention to Trevor.

"Emerson something-or-other," Trevor replied. "She said he had a website. . .The Animalist Code, I think." Trevor looked over at Lana.

Lana's eyes dropped to the floor.

"So he's alive," she said in a near whisper. She shifted and faced the others, grinning.

"Who's *he*?" Kage asked, not sure if he should be jealous. But then again, jealous of what? It wasn't like he and Lana were dating.

"He's the activist I told you about. That S-Corp president. . .Carl. . .he murdered Emerson's father," Lana replied.

"Oh, yeah," Kage said, feeling a twinge

of anger. He did remember. Emerson had been a rogue animal activist back in 2035. He tried alerting people about the dangers of S-Corp, tried saving animals, but he had to go into hiding, and as far as anyone knew, he'd never come back out.

"Elisha said she might be able to get him to help, but he's been in hiding for years." Trevor paused. "We know that all too well."

Kage nodded in agreement.

"You got video for us?" Elliott asked Kage.

Kage exhaled, set down his empty plate on the counter, and stepped past Lana. He turned toward the living room where Virgil, Dennis and Emily had been sitting.

"There's something we need to talk about first," he said. "If I can have everyone's attention."

The three on the couch looked up at Kage in unison. Lana came to stand beside him. Elliott and Trevor stepped into the room and remained standing beside the wall.

"What's going on?" Emily asked. "You look. . .tense."

Kage shot a look over at Lana. She gave him a nod. In her eyes was a look of sorrow.

"We got video of the Boysen Dam. That was no problem. But when we got to Meeteetse. . ." Kage's voice trailed off. His eyes dropped to the floor.

"What is it?" Trevor asked.

"They burned it all down," Kage said. He wasn't much for subtly.

"What?" Virgil asked, his voice quivering. He dropped his arms to his sides.

"The garden. The house. It's all gone," Kage replied. His voice was quivering too.

"Jesus," Trevor replied.

"I'm assuming it was S-Corp?" Dennis asked.

Kage felt the anger and sorrow rising into his chest. He struggled to reply.

Lana spoke. "We believe it was, yes."

"Let's get that video uploaded to the website," Elliott said, shooting a glance at Kage.

Kage looked up at him, holding back the tears.

"It's in the truck," Kage replied. "I'm ready when you are."

With that, the two of them left, stopping for the camera and walking over to Elliott's apartment. Out beyond the buildings, the sun was making its way toward the horizon. Its round shape glowed the color of the corn that would've been growing and ready for eating by now, had S-Corp not destroyed it.

Chapter Nineteen

Bray

Bray was immersed in darkness. This darkness felt more real than the darkness behind her eyes, the darkness she experienced when she simply closed her eyes to meditate.

This darkness was a place. A place undefinable, a place she did not try to understand. She was here for one thing and one thing only, and that was Bertan.

Bray recalled a moment when she was ten years old, sitting in her mother's car outside a restaurant in Denver, waiting while her mother ran inside to grab a to-go order. Dinner. She never cooked. Always the food was ordered or prepared by one of their assistants.

While Bray sat in the car, she caught a glance outside of a dog chained to a bike rack. It was standing on the sidewalk next door to the restaurant. The dog was black, sleek, with a long snout and ears raised. Its ribs showed beneath its skin. Its tail had been cut and scabbed. When people walked by, the dog snarled and barked at them. They pulled back, hurried past the dog, and went on. Bray closed her eyes and placed her attention on it. In her younger years that was how she connected to animals. She pictured the dog in her mind and, while doing so, began communicating. She learned that the dog was full of rage. It was also scared. It had been left there for a very long time, probably hours. Its energy was pained, gritty and, at the same time, desperate for something better.

She recognized this same energy now in Bertan. She knew some wouldn't like that she was comparing a complex human to a dog, but at the same time, in her mind animals were equal to humans. To her, the comparison was not an insult.

Since she was alone in the dark, it didn't matter what her thoughts were. No one here was going to judge her.

Bray heard Bertan whimper. She felt some part of him crying, but he couldn't get in touch with it. It almost felt as though there were two entities inside of him: Bertan and someone else. That someone else was *not* Bray. She sensed it as some other life force, one that seemed to have its own agency. Agency more powerful than Bertan's.

"Bertan?" she called out to him.

No response. Bertan was close to touching who she was and, at the same time, he was falling. She thought this might be comparable to watching someone sink in quicksand. In her mind she watched powerlessly as Bertan was gradually overtaken, a storm cloud moving in on a sunny day, covering the land in a shade of darkness before it pommeled everything with lightning and rain.

How was she going to save him? There was no way to get to him. This was not something that could wait until she got out of prison, *if* she ever did. She would have to try to pull him out with her mind.

The key here, she quickly surmised, was less about bringing Bertan out and more about clearing the dark energy that had overtaken him. Bertan was too submerged at this point to hear her. She could tell how

minuscule his energy was compared to the
dark energy.

Bray would have to go directly to the
source and clear it out. She thought back
to times spent with Emily in Meeteetse. How
Emily had cleared her energy through a
cleansing chakra meditation.

Bray wasn't sure this would work, but
it was the only thing she knew to try.

Seeing only darkness, she focused on
that darkness while cleansing each of her
seven energy centers, from her lower back
all the way up to the crown of her head.
She imagined the color associated with each
energy center, colors that, when connected
in sequence, made a perfect rainbow. She
chanted a word that corresponded with each
chakra, feeling it vibrate through her
body, while imaging a golden light clearing
out the chakras one by one. When her
attention finally rose to the top of her
head, she felt more cleansed, but nothing
else had changed.

The dark energy consuming Bertan began
laughing.

This made Bray angry. She felt the
anger, let it filter through her, and flow
out, as though she were nothing more than a
sieve.

"That's it," she whispered.

Bray needed to get in there. She needed
to get *inside* Bertan's mind. She recalled
all she knew about him. How he was from
Honduras. . .undocumented in the U.S. A
family. Wife, Carmen.
Daughter. . .Gabriella? How Bertan had
worked for S-Corp for such a long time. How
he wanted to stop them as much as she did,
enough to risk his life. How that must've
felt. How isolated he must've been living
the life he was living. And now here he
was, imprisoned, twice over. She knew, to

some extent, what that was like.

Gradually, her identity transitioned. It shrank as she continued to pull Bertan forward in her mind, visualizing herself entering the dark mind in which Bertan was now trapped.

Standing up, eyes closed, Bray felt herself step inside that dark mind, and a rush of cold hit her skin. She shivered. It was both endless and full of walls. In its darkness she could still see things, things she shouldn't have seen, and that was why they were hidden away in the darkest recesses of his mind. Horrible memories, brokenness, fractured thoughts. She didn't much like what she was seeing.

But she had to get Bertan out.

The ground beneath her felt wet, something seeping over her bare feet. Looking down, she saw she was standing in a black puddle of liquid. Too black to be water, the consistency of blood. When she looked down into the liquid, she saw only a reflection of herself.

The puddle morphed into a more dense liquid. . .like melted metal. It transitioned from black to kinetic chrome, in which all the colors of the chakras she'd envisioned a moment ago mixed and twirled. A melding of red, orange, yellow, green, blue and violet, all separate while appearing together simultaneously. This left an effect of pain on her eyes. She wasn't in meditation anymore. She was inside something. Or someone. An energy, an *entity*. The feeling was of floating and spinning while also remaining still. The disorientation of it made her sick to her stomach.

The colors died away to reveal pure, metallic liquid. In it was the reflection of darkness, which Bray did not know was possible.

"*You shouldn't be here*," a voice called out. It sounded androgynous and grainy, as though broadcasted through a radio with a poor signal. "*You are far too young for such places*."

The liquid beneath her feet swept along the floor and rose up into the air. It towered above her and slowly took form. A perfect, circular head, broad shoulders. A body stood before her, its metallic color bouncing back a reflection of herself, like a mirror. It came closer, and when it did, the head seemed to glare down at her. A feeling of entrapment grew around her heart, like ivy. A squeezing sensation constricted her arms and legs. She could not move.

This was something far beyond anything Bray felt she could handle. She was beginning to feel she had made a huge mistake, fearing she might not be able to get out of whatever limbo she'd led herself into.

Chapter Twenty

Bray

Bray felt a startling sensation of being carried. It was as though the entire room, or whatever space she was inside, had been picked up, as if inside a vehicle. The sensation led Bray to stumble, and she realized she'd regained the ability to move. She caught herself and came down to her knees to give herself some stability. She wondered if the guards had found her by now, and if they had taken her body to Health Services. That body felt very separate from where she was right now.

Bray was afraid. Could she hide her fear from this. . .this thing before her? She thought to call it an entity, for lack of a more accurate description. It stood above her, its mirror-like exterior hovering.

Closing her eyes, she found that, just as in her waking life, she could breathe, and breathe deeply. She did this for a while, until the entity began to laugh. The laugh brought a shiver and a sting to her skin. The entity was deep and hollow, and a putrid scent hit her nose.

"I want you to release Bertan," she said in a calm, composed voice. She opened her eyes and looked up at the entity, metallic and reflective.

"Release? He made a choice, little girl. I'm not the one who locked him away.

You did that yourself."

"How so?" Bray asked. She glared at it.

"*You set him up. . .devising this plan to tell the entire country about S-Corp.*"

"As you said, it's not like I forced him. He helped us of his own accord."

"*Not you. . .your little friend. Kage, was it?*" the entity replied. It remained in place, hovering but unmoving, unwavering.

"What are you talking about?" Bray was confused. Her heart rate picked up. She exhaled fully and, for a moment, remained still, in perpetual exhale, waiting.

"*Kage asked Bertan to help you. You didn't know, did you? To stop the slaughter. . .so you wouldn't die,*" the entity hissed. "*Bertan was a sacrifice.*"

"That's a lie," Bray said, inhaling as her anger built along with the intake of breath. She reminded herself to exhale, to keep breathing.

"*Is it? How else could I know what I know?*"

"You aren't real. You make things up," she responded, desperate. "And if you know these things, you got them from Bertan, which means Bertan is here, somewhere." Bray paused, glanced at its metallic form. "Bertan? I know you're there. Can you hear me?"

The entity recoiled, and she knew her words had affected it. It made some kind of sudden, unnatural movement at the mention of Bertan's name. She called for Bertan again, this time keeping her eyes set on the entity, to see what it would do.

"Bertan?! I'm here to help you. Don't let this thing take over!" she yelled. Her voice boomed *through* the entity. This time its movement was a blip, as if on a computer screen.

Bertan still did not reply. Bray

couldn't sense his presence, his feelings.
But he was here. He was here because this
was his mind. Not hers. It felt too foreign
and off-putting to be her own. This entity,
whatever it was, perhaps some part of him
or piece of his psyche, *was* Bertan.

"I know you can hear me, Bertan. There
is a way out of this. You are stronger than
this," she persisted.

"*What makes you think he needs your
help?*" the entity asked.

Bray looked at the entity. She looked
really closely. This thing was just a kind
of fear, something she couldn't quite
identify, but she was getting closer to it.
She had to be careful with her replies.
Destroying this thing would require the
right words and intentions, not actions.
This wasn't some superhero movie. This was
real. She was inside another human's mind,
and she would have to tread carefully.

"What makes you think he doesn't?" she
asked.

"*I got Bertan through his worst times,*"
the entity replied, slowly circling Bray's
body. She turned to watch it, felt slightly
dizzied.

"*All the years he did horrible things
for Medina. . .that was me. His wife and
child are gone. Your team led him astray.
Ruben is gone. Who do you think can really
help him? Some seventeen-year-old white
girl who knows nothing of the cruelty of
this world?*"

Bray went hot with rage. She closed her
eyes, breathed the rage through her
bloodstream. She knew cruelty, had
experienced the suffering of animals at the
hands of humans, the suffering of her own
friends. That didn't feel much different
from this suffering Bertan must have been
experiencing. Something she could not

understand first-hand, but she felt it within the lives of friends now dead and gone, friends like Alice.

She knew what suffering was.

"Call me what you will," she replied, unfazed. She'd been called worse. "But Bertan doesn't need you anymore."

"*That's the problem with people like you*," the entity said, no longer circling, but sliding closer to her. "*You don't want people like Bertan to have choices.*"

"That's not true," she replied, shaking her head as though she were reassuring herself.

"*You pompous little girl. You don't know anything about him, what he's been through. But I know everything about him, and I know he chose me. I am Bertan's creation. This was a necessity for him, for his survival.*"

Bray did not reply. She had to admit. . .the entity was not entirely wrong. She didn't know much about Bertan. But she wanted the chance.

"*What you really don't like*," the entity continued. "*Is that people like Bertan have choices. And the one choice that really gets under your skin. . .*"

Suddenly Bray felt a jolt of heat penetrate the skin of her forearm, in the area of her implant. A feeling of hard pain, like a heavy liquid, pulsed through her bloodstream. It reminded her of the injection she'd received.

She let out a whimper and keeled over, her head on her knees. The liquid feeling coursed through her arms, down her legs, and up into her chest.

". . .*is that he chose me over you.*"

The painful liquid rose up into her heart. She felt suspended. The pain jolted into her throat. Her mouth opened in response yet made no sound. She couldn't breathe. The liquid rolled up into her eyes, which began to water profusely. Once the pain edged toward her forehead, her ability to think fell away, and she fell with it.

"*You sad, sad, little child*," the entity mocked, its voice now distant.

The darkness spun and twisted into a tunnel. The entity disappeared, and Bray was jolted through the tunnel, hurled at a frightening speed. The sound of voices approached. Her eyes shot open. She found herself lying in bed. She was in the Health Services Department.

Chapter Twenty-One

Dianna

In ten minutes, Dianna would be meeting with her boss. Dr. Michael Brisbon, a sixty-year-old average white man, had been with S-Corp for forty years, and he was unforgiving when he felt crossed. He was rarely compassionate, his decisions consistently driven by what was best for the corporation. Dianna admired this about him, until the decision in question had to do with her own future. He hadn't mentioned it in his earlier email, but he didn't need to. He'd called the meeting, and that was enough.

Her job was on the line. He would want answers about how the Embedicare takeover could have happened. She didn't have those answers.

Her cell phone vibrated.

Dianna turned and picked up the phone, which had been sitting on her desk beside a stack of files. Morning sunlight grazed the desk, hit the back of her chair and ran along her shoulders. It was warm, balancing the cool air coming in from the ceiling vents. For a moment Dianna felt briefly comforted, until she saw it was the prison calling.

She answered immediately.

"Mrs. Hoffman?" She heard a man's voice, older, gruff.

"This is she," Dianna replied.

"This is Jacob Stalzky, psychiatrist at Arizona Correctional."

"Is everything all right with my daughter?" Dianna asked, suddenly concerned, her heart pausing for an answer while her eyes glared at the time on the laptop screen.

Seven minutes.

"Ma'am." Jacob hesitated. "The guards found her unconscious in her bed this morning. She's currently in Health Services, but she's still unconscious."

"How in the world did my daughter end up unconscious?" Dianna stiffened. She put the phone on speaker and set it down, dropping her head into her hands.

"She hasn't been eating much since her arrival. We did place her on the injection medication to treat the schizophrenia. I am running some blood work, but that's all I know right now."

Dianna glared at the phone. Five minutes. She pulled up the camera on her phone, checked her makeup and hair. She rubbed her forehead. Her hair had been down, and she had yet to shower. She reached into her desk drawer and searched for a hair tie. Her heart began to race. She quickly pulled out a hair tie and began squeezing her hair back into a ponytail, feeling her scalp pull.

"My concern, ma'am, is that she may need more intensive care than what we offer in this prison. She should really be in a psychiatric facility. And if she doesn't wake by end of day, we'll need to take her to the hospital."

"I don't disagree with you," Dianna said, reminding herself to breathe. "But she's also a flight risk. I'm open to suggestion but only if there are places that can offer the highest level of security possible."

Four minutes. Dianna began to feel panic. She wanted to have the time to figure out what to do for Bray, but she couldn't miss this meeting. It would mean her job if she did.

"I can do some research and let you know. But if we need to send her to the hospital, we'll need you to sign off on it," Jacob explained.

"Send over whatever you need," Dianna said quickly. She opened her email with the meeting link. She gulped. Her mouth went dry. She reached for the link with her finger, touching it. "Do you have my email address?"

Dianna watched a video box pop open, revealing her face on the screen. There was no more time; she had to click on the LAUNCH button. Her breathing suspended as her face went flush. She prayed Michael wouldn't see that she was on the phone.

"Yes."

"Great. Now I've got to get to a meeting. Please." She paused, lowering her voice. "I'm counting on you to watch over my daughter."

"Yes, ma'am."

Dianna abruptly hung up.

As Michael's face popped up on her screen, she saw it was contorted into a tough frown. His shoulders were slumped over his desk, and in his hand he squeezed a ballpoint pen.

"Good morning, Michael, how are you?" Dianna asked, forcing a smile.

"I have no complaints," he replied, his voice monotone. "This won't take long. I just wanted to check in, hear from you what's been happening with all this Wyoming water business, and what you're doing to help resolve this eco-terrorist nonsense."

Wyoming water business? How did he know about that?

"I'm sorry," she began. "What's going on in Wyoming?"

"Did you not see the latest video?"

"No, sir," she replied. She hadn't seen any videos. Not since the Embedicare takeover. She assumed that was what he'd been calling about, the eco-terrorists.

"They posted another video. This time, it's the dam at the Boysen Reservoir in Wyoming. Proof that S-Corp has been extracting too much water. You can't tell me you didn't know."

Dianna's face went sheet-white. *Goddamned terrorists*. If she could, she'd search her computer for the video right now, but she was trapped. She couldn't take her attention off Michael. The best she could do for herself was to tell the truth.

"I didn't know about this video, but yes, I did send a team out to extract water."

"But did you extract more than the legal amount?" Michael set down his pen and clasped his hands.

"Yes, I did," she admitted. Her underarms began to sweat.

"What was it that made you feel it was okay to proceed with this project without informing me first?"

And there it was.

Dianna exhaled. What could she say? Excuses were not the way to go with this man. What did he want from her? An apology? She didn't think so. Apologies didn't fix things. What S-Corp looked for were *solutions*. She was running out of those.

"I don't know," she admitted. The truth was all she had left.

Michael closed his mouth and looked at

her. The meeting went silent for a moment.

"Dianna. . .I'm being pressured from all directions to fire you. The only reason I haven't yet is because you have a history of being an outstanding regional president."

Dianna nodded but chose to keep her mouth shut. Her heart raced and she feared that opening her mouth might expose the emotion she was experiencing.

"S-Corp is in the process of restructuring. . .after that Embedicare takeover. Things look really bad. I probably don't have to tell you how our stock has plummeted. How frightened the general public is."

"No, sir." Her world was quickly closing in on her.

"And I imagine it's been hard. . .seeing you daughter as the culprit."

"I really believe she was-"

He cut her off. "Let me finish, please."

Dianna took a deep breath. She let the tension in her shoulders ease a bit. There was no room here to defend herself.

"I appreciate that you sent her to prison. That must've been very hard. Obviously, you're not the one to blame for all this, but there are other recent behaviors that have been brought to my attention, and I need you to tell me the truth."

"Okay," she agreed, feeling she might implode.

"First: did you provide S-Corp funding for project SC-118 without approval?" She saw him glance down at a paper on his desk.

The only person who knew about that project, other than the scientist, was Carl. It was *Carl's* project. And the scientist had signed an NDA, stating he would not share information about it with S-Corp. Dianna suspected it was Carl who had informed on her. Maybe that was why he'd stopped taking her calls recently.

"Yes," she admitted. The room began to spin. She reached for the bottle of water sitting on the desk, took a gulp. Michael jotted some notes down where she could not see.

The questions continued: "Did you use S-Corp property, such as helicopters, for personal use. . . Did you use S-Corp security, including staff hours, without first getting approval. . ."

"Yes, yes, yes."

Dianna had done all those things. There was no sense in denying it.

"Do you see the pattern emerging here?" Michael asked.

Dianna nodded silently. Her decisions, no matter the motive, had caught up with her.

"Countless times you have gone behind me to make unilateral decisions for your own personal issues. I am not sure I can trust you."

"I understand."

Dianna was stuck. She couldn't mention that there were other S-Corp presidents, CEOs even, who'd done the same or similar things. She supposed the difference was that they hadn't gotten caught. Their decisions weren't connected to a dirty scandal gone public. Their daughters hadn't become eco-terrorists and attacked S-Corp in the media.

For once in Dianna Hoffman's life, she did not try to defend herself. What was done, was done.

"I'm going to need you to take some time off," Michael said. "Think things over while we come to a decision."

"A decision?"

"You're an intelligent woman. You can figure it out." Michael glanced at his forearm. "I've got to go. The time off is unpaid, just to be clear."

Dianna fumed. Anger twisted her stomach in knots. She tried not to let it show, reminding herself to breathe.

Without speaking, Michael ended the video call. Dianna sat and stared at the black screen, demoralized. She slowly moved her hand over to the mouse, clicked off the screen, and shut down her laptop. Her eyes moving around the office, she thought of her career, her lifeblood.

What would she do. . .who would she be. . .without it?

Chapter Twenty-Two

Bray

Bray's vision was blurry. She rubbed her eyes, blinked them several times, until they revealed a confusing and unsettling sight.

She was not in her cell.

This was far worse.

Four walls. Glaring white. A fluorescent light shot a forceful glance down upon her, with no plans to ease up. No bed. No toilet. Not even a door. *Where was she*? This was not Health Services, with no bed, no table or chair.

Bray leapt up from the pool of sweat beneath her. Heart racing, she turned and turned, desperate for a way out.

"*There is no way out,*" came the voice of the entity, from somewhere above her.

She paused, listening to the voice. She looked down to see she was naked. Embarrassed, she wrapped her arms around her chest, wishing for something to cover herself. Gooseflesh ran up her arms and then crawled down her back. She had to remind herself to breathe.

"Where am I?" she whispered, not wanting the entity to hear her.

"*Now you can experience what it is to really be trapped, the way Bertan has felt all his life,*" the entity said.

How had this happened? Last she remembered, the entity seemed to have seeped into her bloodstream—or so it felt—and she woke up here, no longer in her cell. Where was here? She told herself right off that it wasn't real, so as not to lose her sanity. The entity was controlling this. She'd somehow gotten stuck between her mind and Bertan's.

Then, a nudge. It pushed at her back.

Yes, that was it. Entering Bertan's mind to try to stop the entity had pushed her into some kind of. . .limbo.

And now she had to find a way out, and she needed to take the entity with her.

#

"*Ha!*" the entity laughed. Laughter bounced off the walls, hitting Bray with ridicule.

If she was going make this to work, she'd have to go back to square one. The basics.

She sat down, right where she was. The fluorescent lighting was causing her head to ache. She closed her eyes. There was significant discomfort in knowing she was naked, but as she began breathing deeply, it made sense. Being stuck in this limbo—between realities-it was logical that her clothes were missing.

Bray spent some time focusing on her breathing.

"*I will never let you leave, little girl,*" the entity said. Its words hit her in the chest, leaving a feeling of fear.

But Bray knew how to manage her feelings. Emily had taught her well, and now it was time to put all she'd learned to the test. She focused in on her chest, on her breath, on the sensations within her.

"*Nothing will help you now,*" the entity spoke again.

"I wish you would be quiet," she

retorted, surprising herself for doing so.

"*Pompous little bitch. I'll destroy you*," the entity hissed.

Go right ahead, were the words that ran clearly through her mind, like the clearest of water, the fresh water she'd sometimes watched pouring out of the garden pipes back in Meeteetse.

And then another nudge brought her back to this place.

What was that nudge? Or more accurately, *who* was nudging her?

"I'm here," she said with her mind, finding she didn't much care if the entity heard her. As long as she acknowledged the sensations and fears inside, and sat with them, she discovered how quickly they passed, simple moments in time, and how quickly she returned to a calm stasis. "Please make yourself known."

The blankness within her mind transformed into intense light. It was warm, expansive and safe. It pulled her along. . .up, up, through the earth's atmosphere, into absolute stillness. It was a level of quiet Bray had never experienced. Dropping slowly, she felt wind pressing against her body, pushing her back down to earth.

She opened her eyes. She was lying in a meadow. Wildflowers, yellow and lavender, covered the ground. She sat up. Lightheaded, she waited for the dizziness to pass. A blue sky hung close to the ground. There was no sun in sight, yet the day was bright and remarkable. She heard a rustling beside her.

Turning her head, she smiled instantly when she saw the image of Rhea, the cow, sitting beside her.

"Rhea!" Bray greeted, relieved to see a familiar face.

"*You can call me that, yes*," a soft, feminine voice replied, yet the cow's mouth did not move.

"You mean you're not Rhea?" Bray asked, confused.

"*I am no one and everyone and everything. I come to you as an image of Rhea.*"

"Okay," Bray replied, her skepticism edging in. "This again."

"*You're learning*," Rhea replied. The cow seemed to be smiling.

Bray remembered the conversation she'd had with Alice and Rhea when they'd visited her together. It was right after she'd passed out from the ordeal of Rhea's slaughter. They'd given her a chance to leave this world and go with them, but she'd chosen to return to earth. Even if the chance were given to her again now, she'd still choose to come back, knowing her work was not done.

"*It is true. Your work is not done*," Rhea said, as if knowing Bray's thoughts.

"I suppose I am talking to God, then?" Bray asked, slightly unconvinced.

"*Let's not get into semantics. I am here to help you.*"

"Were you the one nudging me this whole time?"

"*That nudge came from you. . .and us, yes.*"

"Us?" Bray asked, already thrown off by what Rhea might have meant when she said the nudge had also come from Bray herself.

"*The everything and everyone. Alice. . .the other sows you saved. . .Rhea. . .the other cows. . .Ethan. . .all of the animals that went before us and will go after. All who have come, gone and are yet to be.*"

Bray was dumbfounded.

"Can I see Alice?" she asked.

"*Alice has moved on, dear child.*"

"What do you mean?"

"*She fully transitioned. Her task was completed once she helped you,*" Rhea replied. She was lying on her belly, her hooves hidden beneath her body.

"I'm so confused," Bray said, befuddled by all this spiritual after-life mumbo-jumbo.

"*Don't use your human mind to understand. It is limited. Use your heart, your instinct.*"

"What do I do? I need to get out of this place and help Bertan," Bray said, a sense of urgency returning.

"*I can't tell you what to do. Only you know what to do. I can help you find it within yourself.*"

Bray took a deep breath. She was frustrated. This thing. . .this entity. It was beyond her. She wasn't confident that anything she could conjure would be enough to destroy it.

"*My dear child,*" Rhea said. "*Move past your thoughts, beyond doubt. Go to the quiet places, and there you will find your next steps.*"

"I just have one question," Bray responded, perplexed by this image before her, whether it was really God, whether one truly existed.

"*What is that?*" Rhea asked, her eyes wide and full.

"If you are God, or there is a God, then why not do more? Why have us do all the work when we're so messed up as humans, we don't even know what we're doing?"

Rhea laughed. The laughter bellowed out of the cow's body, making a deep, rolling sound.

"*That is the perfection in it, my*

child. It is your fallibility that helps others, your imperfections. It is a paradox. One day very soon. . .you will come to understand that you are not separate from God. This you will use to help others, to help Bertan."

With that, the image of Rhea grew increasingly transparent. She was fading away. Bray did not try to stop her. She sat there simply watching the wildflowers in the meadow. They, too, began to take on a translucence, fading until all she had seen drifted away.

Chapter Twenty-Three

Kage

Kage was sitting beside Elliott at the desk. He was picking away at a bowl of blueberries. It was evening, and they were checking in on Trevor's progress with the representatives he'd been organizing. Three days had passed since Kage had gone out to Wyoming with Lana. They had uploaded their video to Kage's website exposing S-Corp's water extraction project and the destruction of the Meeteetse property. Since then, they'd received a surge in new emails, citizens requesting more information. One of the emails included a video of a press conference by Dianna Hoffman, in which she'd exclaimed that all remaining eco-terrorists involved in the Embedicare takeover had been captured.

"No shit," Kage said, smirking as they watched Dianna's press conference.

When it ended, Elliott reached over and grabbed the plate of scrambled eggs he'd been eating. Kage watched him eat the eggs without concern, checking emails and adding more citizens to his growing list of those who'd lost loved ones in the fertilizer disaster. Kage wasn't very good about keeping his mouth shut on certain subjects. He turned to Elliott and eyed the plate of eggs.

"How can you eat that. . .with everything that's going on?" Kage asked. He'd finished his blueberries and set the bowl down on the desk.

Elliott stopped eating. He looked at Kage squarely. His lips formed into a sideways grin.

"Really? We going there now?"

"It's an honest question," Kage replied, shrugging.

Elliott set down his plate. He folded his hands together, leaned back in his chair. His eyes remained set on Kage.

"Killing animals for food isn't a big deal to me. I don't want them to suffer, of course. You know I'm not a sadistic person. But animals kill animals all the time for food."

"But we're human. We understand when we're causing suffering."

"Yeah, I know. I guess what bothers me is when someone tries to tell me what they think I should or shouldn't do based on their own moral code, without respect for my own values, which may differ. I want us to be able to have a difference of opinion and have that be okay."

Kage had no rebuttal. The man was not wrong, he decided. Why argue with someone with whom he was becoming friends. *Good* friends. Maybe someday Elliott would change his mind. Maybe after—

"Hey, take a look," Elliott interrupted Kage's thoughts. He had leaned forward and was glancing at the screen.

"What?" Kage sat up and squinted at the email Elliott had open on the screen. It was a message from Trevor.

"He's emailing us now?" Kage asked, smiling. The man lived only a block away, and he was emailing Kage?

"That's what people do. Text from the next room, even," Elliott replied.

They both read the email.

KAGE-
WE NOW HAVE 15 REPRESENTATIVES,
FROM CITIES ALL ACROSS THE NATION.
THEY'RE CALLING FOR ACTION. AGAINST
S-CORP. WANTING TO KNOW WHEN WE'RE
GOING TO ORGANIZE. WHAT WE'RE GOING
TO DO. I SAY WE MARCH.
A MARCH FOR FREEDOM. FREEDOM FOR BRAY.
FOR THE ANIMALS.
WHAT DO YOU SAY?

TREVOR.

"You're kidding me," Kage said under his breath. He never thought his uncle would be the one to propose something so grand, something so *visible*. There'd be no more hiding after a march.

"All yours," Elliott said, grabbing his plate and standing up. He stretched his arms and sauntered into the kitchen.

Kage took his seat and began typing. His heart raced and he felt so excited he blinked and reread the email, to make sure he wasn't seeing things.

"Who are you," he said aloud while typing. "And what have you done with my uncle?"

A laugh came from the refrigerator. Elliott had opened it and was moving things around inside, probably looking for more food.

"Okay," Kage said, finishing his typing. He'd said yes to Trevor's idea, of course. He didn't know he'd been waiting for a march until Trevor suggested it. The idea was perfect. *March for Bray. March for freedom. Freedom for everyone*. That would be the message.

"No one is free until everyone is free, right?" Kage said aloud, trying to remember where he'd heard that quote before.

"Quoting Fannie Lou, are we?" Elliott asked, returning to the desk. He stood over Kage, looking down at him. "That's a civil rights quote. Not sure how I feel with you using it."

"Fair." Kage thought for a moment. He remembered sitting in the dining room back in Meeteetse. Trevor homeschooled him as they sat together at the table Ethan had made. He'd learned about the civil rights movement, and it probably was Trevor who'd taught him about it. What he was also taught, and had now come to believe, was that Fannie Lou Hamer could not be more right. . .about everyone. Absolutely no one could be free until everyone was free. And that had to include animals. Something Elliott might never understand.

Chapter Twenty-Four

Bray

Bray came to. Everything surrounding her quickly transitioned to white. She was in limbo. Again. She hadn't expected to end up back in her cell, but she did feel somewhat dismayed, maybe even a little resigned, to find herself here.

What was she going to do now?

"*I told you there was no way out,*" the entity said, laughing.

The room was ghost-white. It was hard to tell what was floor, wall or ceiling. It all came together as one. It hurt her eyes. Her stomach felt queasy. Naked again, she began to shiver.

Maybe there *was* no way out.

It felt odd, to be thinking that. Odd because it also brought her a sense of calm. Of surrender. Just as she had no control over the lives of animals she'd tried to save in the past, she had no idea how to get back to her reality. And she had learned that forcing things just made them worse.

So, she sat down, positioned herself into meditation pose, and did the only thing she could. She meditated.

Her eyes closed, breath steady, she recalled what Rhea had said to her.

"*You are not separate from God. This you will use to help others, to help Bertan.*"

There was something in that statement. Something Bray needed. Some. . .answer.

Bray continued to meditate.

"Meditation is a privilege. You are nothing more than an entitled little girl," the entity hissed. It did not seem to be in the room with her, but its voice came through the walls and surrounded her on all sides.

The phrase, *"not separate from God"* repeated in her mind. Then, another thought: *But I don't believe in God.*

Then another, less familiar notion—not *her* thought, but that nudge again, perhaps from Rhea:

"You don't have to believe in God for God to exist. God is everything. God is Nature. You are not separate from nature, are you?"

Bray had never considered the notion that she was part of nature, a part of something bigger. *"Something better,"* Emily had called it. Maybe she did need to let go of semantics to see what was so obviously being revealed to her.

Bray recalled the few times she had spent in nature. How, after she and Elliott got past the Colorado border, wild horses had saved them when she called on them for help. How free and open she felt while in the expanse of the Wyoming terrain, experiencing the fresh air and the stars at night. How she'd come to feel most herself, most alive, most *connected,* in those moments she sat outdoors in Meeteetse, close to earth, letting all thought go while in meditation. How, in some of those moments, she felt herself fade away, become mute, as if non-existent, as if she were one with nature.

"You are not nature. You are not deserving of it. Nature cares nothing of

you, child, and would destroy you with its magnitude without consideration. Keep ignoring me, and I will do the same," the entity's voice rose to an echoing boom.

She knew the entity was blowing smoke, to use Kage's expression. It was taunting her, trying to pull her from her focus. What she realized in that moment was that her gift of connecting with animals meant she *was* connected with nature. What else explained her ability to link with the animals, and now with Bertan, a human?

"That's it!" she whispered.

Bray's eyes slowly opened. She stared ahead at the white spaces. The longer she gazed, the more she watched the whiteness become endless. It was endless because there was no time. Being inside this limbo proved that there were other things happening beyond her own reality. There were multiple versions of realities, all perceived by individuals.

No. That wasn't quite right. Through the whiteness ahead of her, she saw that there *was* no separation. . .at all. She reached her arm out toward the whiteness and felt nothing. She got up and walked, to see how far she could go, and the walking was ceaseless. There were no walls. Which meant there was no ceiling. There was no end. She was separate from nothing.

Which meant she was also a part of the entity, or it was a part of her.

"*Preposterous!*" the entity yelled. The yell came at her from behind and hit her in the head, causing a vibrating pain in the back of her neck and along her spine.

"The only way you could exist is if you are some part of me," Bray refuted, turning to the source of the yell. "You are a part of Bertan, which is how you're able to help him, if that's what you want to call it."

There was no response.

"And the only way I could be stuck in this limbo," she continued, the realization becoming more and more clear, "is by you and I being connected."

With that, a smile grew on Bray's face. She may not have solved the problem of getting out of this place, this limbo, but at least now she saw no reason to be afraid. The entity was not to be denied or resisted. Just as Emily had taught her to embrace and feel her most difficult and uncomfortable emotions-such as guilt and shame-so, too, was Bray tasked with accepting this entity as a part of her. The same part of her that wanted to avoid fear and to not be vulnerable. The part, she now sensed, that Bertan wished to turn away from. And so he had, with the help of this entity. It was the dark side that existed in all humans, that perhaps, she thought, led to them doing such cruel things to animals, to each other, and to themselves.

The pain she experienced telepathically had been so real for her because when she linked with animals, she was linking to the truth: that everything was connected. Which explained why she could link with Bertan. Did this mean she could link with other humans? Perhaps humans were the missing link all along.

It explained so much.

Then, suddenly, the entity began to laugh. The laughing grew louder, more pervasive and harsh. Like the bray of an animal, which she found incredibly ironic. Bray stood there, arms down, eyes open, and did nothing to stop it.

The laughing rose into a high-pitched yelping, like that of a dog. She felt discomfort from the off-putting sound, and let the feeling come in and then go.

Breathing deeply. Allowing.

"Just stay with it," she told herself.

She began to feel the yelp enter her mind. The yelp extended out into long, violent screams. Her eyes watered. From above, a liquid the colors of cobalt blue and shiny black crawled into the space and consumed the whiteness. It rolled above her like slow-drifting clouds. It gave off a putrid smell. Bray held her position, arms out, palms up in a receiving pose.

The liquid came for her feet. She stood still, experiencing all the feelings inside contracting and squeezing into her heart space, as if the entity was trying to kill her.

As much as a part of her screamed to run, she did not. She had to see this through, to see where it would go.

The liquid grabbed her feet, covered them, and rose up her legs. It felt simultaneously hot and freezing. Her body shivered uncontrollably while sweat developed along her brow.

This was it.

The liquid gathered along her arms, her torso, and approached her throat. Her heart went still as her throat closed up. She felt an alarming sense of ease. She had died once before. She could do it again, if that was what it took.

The liquid edged up to her mouth, crawled inside of it, and immersed her completely. She was nowhere, a complete, absent, void.

Part Three:

The March to Freedom

Chapter One

Bray

"That's the thing. . .her mother was insistent on moving her to a high-security psych hospital. . ."

A familiar male voice drifted in and out of Bray's consciousness.

"But I looked into it. Those places are for violent offenders and people who are too mentally ill for prison. Not appropriate for Bray. At least here, I can keep an eye on her. . ."

Bray woke suddenly, gasping for air as if she had nearly drowned. Catching her breath, she glanced around the room.

Coming slowly into view was the bed on which she was lying. A bed with white sheets. . .*warm* sheets. An IV tube ran from her arm up to a hanging bag full of clear liquid. A monitor beeped beside her. She recognized the partitions that separated her bed from the beds of other prisoners. She could hear one of them snoring.

She was back in the Health Services Department.

A nurse entered her space. He was tall and slender, with a handlebar mustache, head covered with a blue cap.

"You're awake," the nurse said, smiling. "Let's check your vitals."

He approached Bray's side, checked the beeping monitor.

"Can you tell me your name?" he asked.

"Bray Hoffman," she replied. She found it hurt to speak.

"Birth date?"

"February eighth, 2023." She rubbed her forehead. "My head hurts."

"Lie down," the nurse replied, pressing into Bray's chest and gently pushing her back down on the bed.

Jacob appeared from around the corner. He came and sat in a chair beside her bed.

"How you feeling?" he asked, clasping his hands as his elbows rested on his thighs.

"Like I've been run over." She considered for a moment whether she'd had a bad nightmare, but given that she ended up in Health Services, she must've gone unconscious. Which meant her experience with the entity had been every bit real.

The nurse disappeared behind the desk and returned a few moments later with two cups. He handed one of them to Bray. Inside were two Ibuprofen. She wasn't much for taking pills, but for this headache, she appreciated the help. Bray dropped the pills into her mouth, then took the second cup from the nurse-a small amount of water-and drank it.

"Do you remember what happened?" Jacob asked, looking over at her with eyes that were free of judgment or disdain.

Bray thought. She remembered her attempt to reach Bertan. She was sitting on the bed in her cell, last she remembered. But she couldn't tell Jacob the truth. It would only confirm his belief that she was mentally ill.

"Bray?" Jacob prompted.

"Give her a minute, she's just been in a coma," the nurse said.

Bray's eyebrows lifted.

Coma?

"How long was I out?" she asked.

"A couple of days."

Her face went flush. It was a surprise, but maybe it shouldn't have been.

"Two days," she whispered, her eyes staring down at the bed.

"I. . .don't remember what happened," she lied.

"Well, we need to get you eating again before we can send you back to your cell," he said, reaching over and placing his hand softly on her wrist.

"Bring me some vegan food and I'll be happy to eat," she replied. She hoped he would leave. As soon as the headache cleared, she would reach out to Bertan, see if he was okay.

"We don't have that here," a voice came from the far doors. Bray and Jacob turned in unison. It was a guard.

Jacob shot a look at the guard.

"Surely you can bring her something. A banana. . .some plain toast and applesauce. No butter on that toast," Jacob said firmly.

That was the first time Bray had ever had someone in a medical facility-and a doctor, at that-defend her.

The guard rolled his eyes, turned, and left through the double doors. Bray smiled.

"Now, how can we get you to eat? You can't live on fruit and bread alone," Jacob said, turning back to her.

The nurse had moved on to other patients. Bray could hear him striking up conversation as he checked vitals. Her eyes turned to the concrete wall across from her in this room with no windows. As she blinked, she got a sudden glimpse of the concrete walls inside a factory farm, the one Alice had been confined in.

"Either get me out of prison, or bring

me vegan food," she said, shrugging.
"Beans. Rice. Peanut butter sandwiches.
Can't be that hard."

Jacob exhaled, as if frustrated. He
stood up.

"I'll see what I can do." He started
for the doors.

Bray's body felt heavy and weighed down
as if someone were sitting on it. She was
tired. Despite just coming out of a coma,
she did not feel one bit rested. She closed
her eyes. She needed to reach out to
Bertan. Just as she began to try, something
else took the place of that intention.

"*I hope she's okay,*" the voice said. It
was female, young.

Bray knew that voice.

"Tori?" she immediately called out with
her thoughts.

"*Oh my God. . .Bray! Wait. . .is that
you? Am I hearing things?*"

"You're not hearing things," Bray said
reassuringly, in her mind. "It's me. Turns
out my ability to communicate with animals
extends to humans, too."

"*Well, we're animals too, so I get it,*"
Tori said. "*Are you okay?*"

"I fell into a coma, apparently." Bray
realized her headache had begun to ease
off.

"*Where are you?*"

"Health Services."

"*I was afraid they'd put you in
solitary.*"

"No," Bray replied, though to some
degree she certainly had been in solitary,
if only in her own mind.

The double doors opened. She froze,
closing her eyes to feign sleep. A set of
footsteps approached. She heard the sound
of something being set on the table beside
her. She felt someone, she assumed it was

the guard, come close to her ear.

"Not sure if you can hear me," the guard whispered. "But if you don't want to eat, maybe I'll make sure you end up down in the hole. . .give you some more time to think about it."

Bray held her breath. She listened for the guard to leave, and then exhaled.

Tori's voice returned. *"We've all been very worried about you."*

"We?" Bray replied, turning in the bed and glancing up at the table. There she saw a plate of toast, a very ripe banana more black than yellow, and a bowl of applesauce.

But she was not hungry.

She paused for a moment. She thought of what that guard said about sending her to the "hole." How Tori and some of the other activists had gone on a hunger strike and ended up there. She thought about Ethan, Emily, Trevor, Dennis, Virgil, how they'd spent so many years in hiding, standing by while the world was ending without them. How Ethan was gone now, and what did he have to show for it? A pain struck her heart. She felt regret for Ethan's murder. He should not have gone out that way. How many more activists were sitting in this prison, tucked away from society by a system that worked to silence them, rendering them unable to fight for what they believed in?

And then there was her newfound connection with Bertan, a man she never would have thought she'd sympathize with, given his history. Now she realized he, too, deserved nothing less than a noble life, not the pain he was experiencing.

"I need to get some sleep," Bray finally said to Tori. "I'll be back soon."

"Rest well, my friend."

With that, Bray turned her attention to Bertan. Eyes closed, deeply breathing, listening to the beep of the monitor beside her. She honed in on his energy.

It took some effort, but finally she sensed the hard yet fragile energy she'd begun to associate with the man.

"Bertan?" she called.

Nothing.

She could tell he was listening.

"Bertan. . .are you okay?"

"*I-I don't know,*" he replied. "*I feel so far away from everything.*"

"Can you take some deep breaths? That usually helps me." She paused. "Like this: take a deep inhale. . .hold your breath for a moment. Then exhale."

Bray began to mimic the breathing while she encouraged him. She breathed in, felt him breathing in, and then breathed out. She felt an odd sensation of air within and without, as though she were so linked to Bertan she felt they were breathing together, almost as one.

Chapter Two

Bertan

Bertan didn't know where he was. His eyes were open and he saw a ceiling above him. He felt a coarse blanket beneath, on a mattress. He knew this place was supposed to be familiar, but he did not know why. He breathed deeply, his eyes gently closed, following the suggestion he heard, or sensed. He didn't know which.

A memory came to him.

He was sitting in a small office, across from an older man. The man appeared to be of Mexican decent. He was teaching Bertan some breathing exercises. As Bertan continued to breathe, the name Ruben scrolled through his mind.

His eyes popped open. A wave of calm rolled through his chest, enabling him to sit up and take stock of his surroundings. A cell door. A window. A toilet. Yes, it was coming back to him.

He was in prison. He'd been in prison. He remembered Bray. She could talk to him through his thoughts, and she had tried to help him. Everything had gone black and he'd retreated into himself, just like he used to when things got too intense. But this time was different. He checked his body and didn't see any damage done. No guards or anyone telling him he'd done anything wrong. From the looks of it he'd only been lying here, maybe unconscious.

Suddenly, a deep silence filled the cell. All noises in the hall seemed to wither away. Bertan froze. Turning toward the window, he noticed something very peculiar. The light that streamed in from outside had created a line of dust in its rays. The dust particles were not moving. They remained in mid-air, but hung, motionless.

The walls of the cell felt as though they were *turning*. It wasn't something he witnessed, it was a sensation, disorienting to his mind and stomach. Motion sickness. He felt he might puke.

The dust particles gathered, very slowly. As they did so, they began to twist into a spiral. The spiral grew, turned to one side, facing Bertan. He held his breath, gripped the edge of the mattress. Unsure if he should cry or scream.

Then, the spiral protruded outward until it shaped into the form of a body.

"Not again." Bertan gulped.

He'd been visited by ghosts before. First in the S-Corp slaughterhouse, it was the little girl he'd murdered. She came to him twice. Then a little boy he'd left to die after murdering the boy's parents. Now they reminded him of his capacity for cruelty, and he felt himself drop into an impotent state of fear.

The dust particles gathered tightly, becoming solid. A man stood before him. Hair down to his shoulders. His face developed into the contours of someone Bertan once loved.

His father had returned. Last he saw his father's ghost was the day they brought him to this prison. He'd been outside, walking past the fences toward the prison building when, out of the corner of his eye, he saw a glimpse of his father, there and gone like a beef knocked unconscious. But now he stopped to think a moment. He felt a sense of *déjà vu*, like he'd also been visited while in prison, though he couldn't quite place it.

Maynor, which was his father's name, floated over and sat down beside Bertan. Bertan took a deep breath, releasing his hands from their grip on the mattress. He'd never been this close to a ghost before. The temperature in the room had dropped, and the hairs on his arms rose in anticipation.

"Do not be afraid, my son," Maynor said, placing his transparent hand on Bertan's thigh. His thigh immediately felt warm. The warmth sunk down into his bloodstream, coursed through his veins, and reached into his heart.

"*Don't forget what you promised yourself. . .when you first arrived here.*"

"What's that?" Bertan asked. He honestly could not recall.

"*That being here was a third chance. . .to try and be better.*"

"I don't know how," Bertan admitted.

"*I trust you'll figure it out.*" Maynor smiled at him kindly.

A tear rolled down Bertan's cheek. He had forgotten how much he missed his father.

"I'm sorry, Papá. I've let you down."

"*How so?*"

"I worked for Medina. Killed for them. . .after they murdered you. After you worked so hard to stop them."

Bertan trembled. He felt himself about to cry.

"*Mijo*," Maynor said, placing his hand on Bertan's. A feeling of warmth gathered along Bertan's fingers. His heart felt

full, encased in a cloud of safety, held
for the very first time.

"*The past does not matter. You can make
things different now.*"

Bertan considered all the mistakes he
had made. Following Medina's orders all
those years. The killing. The torture.
Then, the years when he shut himself off to
end the lives of beefs. Distancing himself
from Ruben for his own selfish agenda.

"I'm not sure I can."

"*You have been given a gift, my son.
Use it.*"

Maynor's ghost disolved back into a
spiraling shape of dust particles and then
disappeared into the air.

"What do you mean. . .I have a gift?"
Bertan shouted into the air.

No response.

The warmth left his heart. His whole
body went cold as the room temperature
returned to its normal range. Bertan grew
nauseous. He lay on his side in a fetal
position. He began to sweat. The room spun.
He closed his eyes. One thing ran through
his mind before he passed out:

What gift?

#

Bertan fell into a deep slumber. It was
freezing, and he rolled himself into a
cocoon with his blanket. His body shook and
shivered, ill and feverish, yet he remained
in sleep. Hours passed this way until
nightfall, when he woke and noticed he was
no longer cold or nauseated.

He sat up. His uniform was damp with
sweat. He got up from the mattress,
relieved himself. He removed his pants and
t-shirt, standing in his underwear, and lay
the clothes out on the floor to let them
dry.

Outside, the crisp night sky revealed

layers upon layers of stars. Bertan approached the window and looked up at them, wishing to be home with Carmen, where perhaps they could watch the stars together. He felt hungry and turned away from the window. A tray of food waited for him at the door. He went over and observed his plate: room temperature pasta. Bertan wasn't much for Italian food, but finally he had an appetite, and he ate it all.

He stood and glanced around the room. A guard came by and took the tray, shutting the tray door and moving on. Bertan clearly heard the guard's footsteps outside his cell. Everything was becoming much clearer. The light in his cell was bright against the dingy walls and tile floor. It was as though his eyes were seeing these things for the very first time.

Bertan returned to the window. He leaned against the wall, crossed his arms, and gazed up at the moon. It was full and robust, bright and shining and quiet. There was a calmness out there along the open desert. For once, this did not disturb him. He hadn't felt this peaceful since the days back home in Honduras, raising Gabriella with Carmen. Those were the last memories he had where he experienced a level of sanity. He hadn't realized how much stress he'd been under until now. The stress was gone.

It made him want to cry.

Bertan closed his eyes. He began to think about Carmen. . .and Gabriella. Was this what it was like to feel normal? To not have a million thoughts racing through his head? To not have some anger-driven mission, or some worry that the moment he stood up, someone might shoot him in the back?

Everything that had haunted him, that

had filled him with terror and shame and anger, was gone. He opened his eyes and looked around. Although being in prison was not what he wanted, he felt strangely okay at this moment. His shoulders eased. His chest felt light.

The fugue was gone. The terror was gone with it. His mind. . .blank. And all he wanted was to tell Carmen.

Carmen.

The name echoed in his mind.

He closed his eyes again.

He noticed the scent of cigar smoke and cacao. The sound of voices trickled into his mind, into the space around him. Voices of people speaking. . .in Spanish. In the distance, as if somewhere behind him, a distinct beat came from the bass of a car stereo. Reggaeton, his favorite.

When he felt a hot breeze hold his face-he knew that breeze-Bertan opened his eyes.

He felt sudden tears. Disbelief. His heart jumped into his throat. His heartbeat nearly stopped, he was so aghast by what he saw before him.

He was standing on the corner of a familiar street. It was late afternoon and the sun was pointing him toward a house surrounded by concrete walls. Through an open gate he saw a narrow garden of peppers. He could smell them from here.

In the center of that garden sat a wooden table and two chairs. In one of those chairs was a woman of stout posture, with hair down past her shoulders. She was shucking corn. Beside her, a young girl helped.

"Carmen?!" Bertan yelled. He extended his arms to her.

She turned. Her body froze. Her hands leapt up to cover her mouth.

"Papá!" Gabriella cried. She came running for him.

Bertan ran for his daughter. How could this be real? It made no sense, yet it was happening. Only feet away stood his family, the people he loved. He hadn't seen them in more than a decade.

As Gabriella came closer, he met her halfway. But before they could touch each other's hands, Bertan tripped on something he did not see. His body went airborne. As he fell, his face nearing the ground, the music fell away and the scents shifted into an unpleasant stench.

Gabriella's body faded. He heard her calling for him. When he hit the ground, his chin met concrete floor. His teeth clanked. He'd nearly bitten his tongue.

When he glanced up, he saw that his feet had become tangled in his clothes, which were still lying on the floor. He'd tripped while running for his daughter. But she was nowhere around. The pepper garden, the table of shucked corn, his wife's astonished face-all gone. Bertan was still in prison, alone in his cell.

Bertan sat sullen on the floor, dumbfounded. It had seemed so. . .real. Not like the ghosts that had visited him in the past. He *smelled* Honduras. He *heard* the music, *felt* the humid breeze of his home country. For a brief moment, he had *been* there. This time he knew he wasn't losing his mind. Bertan Duarte hadn't felt more sane in his entire life.

No, this was something else.

"*You have been given a gift*," his father's voice rang between his ears. "*Use it.*"

Chapter Three

Bray

Bray was kept in Health Services overnight and returned to her cell the next morning. She'd missed breakfast, and they brought her a plate of beans and rice—something vegan as requested—before she left Health Services. They'd said she could return to her cell if she kept down food. Bray willingly ate the food, half the plateful, and was cleared to leave Health Services. The nurse had said she was not to return to regular activities, such as work or recreation, for another week.

Bray was fine with that.

Without hesitation, she returned to her bed and folded herself into her meditation pose. She wasn't feeling great, her head still slightly aching and her body feeling weighed down after having been in a coma, but she couldn't stop thinking about Bertan. About her experience with that entity, and the way she had linked with Bertan and learned everything about him in such a brief time. She felt she'd known the man his whole life.

The man had spent ten long years away from his family, working for S-Corp. Living here in the U.S., undocumented. She gathered that his life in Honduras had been much worse. She'd probably never know. She sensed how isolated and alone he felt. A deep pit of sorrow grew in her heart. She *felt* for him, imprisoned with even less rights than she had. The both of them confined because of S-Corp. Had her mother found out about Bertan just as she'd discovered Meeteetse? But how? That was the question she might never get answers to, as long as she remained stuck in prison.

That was when Bray realized: in about two months, they'd give her another injection. It wasn't safe to assume she could overcome the medication again, just because she'd been able to succeed once. A second injection could mean certain ineptitude, no longer being able to access her gift. And with her powers growing stronger now each day, gaining abilities she'd never thought possible, the need to act was becoming increasingly potent.

Not only that, she'd suddenly been able to connect with Tori. Did that mean she could connect with the other prisoners, too? If she tried, what would happen?

She had been given the gift of what she would call "alone time" for the next three hours, so why squander it? Why sit in this prison and do nothing when she could try to do everything? Everything she could possibly do to get herself, the other prisoners, and Bertan to freedom.

"*The success is in the try*," Alice's words sang through Bray's memory.

"Tori?" she called out. She waited.

Tori's reply was immediate. "*Yes, Bray? Where you at?*"

"They returned me to my cell. I'm on bed rest for a week." Bray paused. "I need to ask you something."

"*Shoot*," Tori replied.

"Did you happen to work with. . ." Bray stopped, thought of Lana, then continued, "someone named Lana?"

"*How did you know?*" Tori said, sounding astonished.

"Let me tell you a story, seeing as we've both got the time."

Bray told Tori everything. How Lana had been captured by S-Corp, along with Bray's friend, Kage. How they managed to escape, and how they'd met up with Bray. She told Tori about their home in Wyoming, but left out the exact town, just in case.

"*Hold on now*," Tori said. "*This is. . .a lot.*"

"I know. I'm sorry," Bray replied, holding back.

"*No, it's good you told me. I'm relieved that Lana is okay.*"

"As far as I know," Bray cautioned her.

"*Did your whole team get caught like we did?*" Tori asked.

Bray's eyes began to water. She had confirmed it: this prison, it seemed, housed other animal rights activists.

"I don't know," Bray replied, exhaling. "I hope not. After that whole Embedicare plan went down, S-Corp found our hideout." Again she paused. She almost told Tori about Ethan's murder, but didn't want to overwhelm her. "I gave myself up so they could remain in hiding."

"*And here you are.*" Tori paused. "*This is such bullshit!*"

Bullshit, indeed, Bray thought. She remembered what she'd read about animal activists being imprisoned after President Walker's assassination. Maybe she could get some help from Tori, maybe even some other prisoners, to create some kind of action in this prison.

She knew what she had to do next.

Chapter Four

Cole

Cole spent the entire week on clean-up duty. His office phone and cell phone both rang off the hook, senators, reporters and constituents alike asking for his response to Dianna's claim that he had assisted Bray when she went into hiding in Wyoming after escaping Denver Health. Of course it was true, and it had been the right thing to do. Despite the request from his PR manager to lie low until all of this died down, he gave a press conference. He told the entire nation the truth. That was what they deserved. Meanwhile, S-Corp continued to lie to the public. He knew he could not do the same. He no longer wished to associate himself with the corporation. If he was to regain his daughter's trust, and the trust of his constituents—even if it meant no chance for re-election, or worse—he would have to set himself as far apart from S-Corp as possible.

He'd been completely transparent, explaining to the public that he had tracked Bray down in Wyoming a few months ago, getting there just in time to find Dianna and two S-Corp private guards with guns attempting to force his daughter into a helicopter. Dianna wanted to return Bray to the psych ward. Now, he stated emphatically to the press that he did not believe his daughter was mentally ill.

This, of course, garnered tons of flashing lights and questions. He finished by stating that he did indeed help Bray go into hiding, and, if given the chance, he'd do it again. That he believed in his daughter more than he believed the lies told by Dianna Hoffman and S-Corp. That he would do all in his power to provide accurate information to the public regarding S-Corp as he learned it. Finally, he assured them he would also work to bring any justice necessary to the true parties responsible for the fertilizer disaster.

He may not have increased his popularity by holding the press conference, but he gained back the self-respect he'd lost so long ago. He felt like himself for the first time since he was in his twenties, and no one could take that away from him.

Cole sat in his office chewing away at a salad drenched in hummus and chickpeas. He wasn't going vegan, but he had been eating healthier and was beginning to see results in his lower A1C levels. Replying to emails about his press conference, he clicked over to his spam folder and noticed an unopened email from Kage Zair. It had been sitting there for a week. The subject caught his immediate attention:

SEEKING HELP WITH LAWSUIT AGAINST S-CORP

Cole opened the email immediately.

MR. HOFFMAN-
CAN YOU HELP US FIND A LAWYER? WE HAVE SOME INFORMATION THAT WE BELIEVE IS ENOUGH TO FILE A LAWSUIT.
ANY HELP IS APPRECIATED.
YOU AND I HAVE NOT MET. I AM FRIENDS

WITH KAGE AND ELLIOTT, AND AM STAYING WITH
THEM. I WAS A LAWYER MYSELF, AND I HAVE
BEEN ASSISTING ELLIOTT IN BUILDING A LIST
OF CITIZENS WHO CLAIM THEY LOST A LOVED ONE
IN THE FERTILIZER DISASTER.
REGARDS,

LANA.

"Interesting," Cole whispered.
He sat back for a moment. He picked up
his cell phone from the desk and fiddled
with it, thinking. What information did
they have? Clearly, they must have
something. His assistant had researched
their claims about S-Corp lying to the
public about the fertilizer disaster, and
it seemed they'd been telling the truth. He
knew plenty of lawyers, including himself.
But would any of them want to go up against
S-Corp? By far, S-Corp had the most
powerful legal team in the nation.
He replied:

LANA:
THANK YOU FOR YOUR EMAIL. I'D LIKE TO
DISCUSS FURTHER-FIND OUT HOW I CAN ASSIST.
I THINK IT'S BEST WE MEET. CAN I COME TO
YOU? OR PICK A NEUTRAL SPOT. YOU'LL HAVE TO
TRUST ME.
BEST,
COLE.

Cole hit *Send*. He picked up his cell
phone to check its screen. Full of messages
and notifications. He scrolled through
them, looking for anything from his friend
Thom, anything that might indicate his team
had discovered Bray's location. He'd been
so consumed with fielding questions in the
last week that he'd barely had time to put
attention toward finding his daughter.

"Mr. Hoffman!" Cassie called into his office from the lobby.

Cole went to her at once.

Cassie peered up at him from behind her laptop. Her mouth was ajar, and she had an expression of awe on her face.

"What is it?" he asked.

"I think I found something."

Cole raised his eyebrows, waited.

"I did some digging on animal activists. . .from that manuscript Kage posted on their website."

"Okay," he said, waiting. He wasn't sure what he was expecting. That she'd say it was all a farce? A piece of fiction? Or that this was even more evidence against S-Corp?

"The book claims that these activists were all charged with eco-terrorism and were held in a prison in Arizona. I was able to find court records showing the charges, and the names of the activists. It all adds up."

Cole's skin crawled. He wondered if this was the same prison his daughter was locked away in.

"You think that's where Bray is?" Cassie asked.

"It's worth looking into." Cole felt an edge of hope rising over his heart.

He rushed back into his office. With a fervor he hadn't felt in a long time, he went for his phone.

It was time to call Thom.

Chapter Five

Bray

When lunchtime arrived, Bray was permitted to leave her cell. She walked slowly to the cafeteria, behind all the prisoners in her unit. Her body heavy and sluggish, her stomach empty yet calm, Bray kept her mind focused on an agenda. She grabbed a bowl of salad, lightly dousing it in olive oil and placing it on her tray beside a cup of water.

She sought out Valerie, who was sitting with a group of women Bray did not recognize.

"Val," she whispered, stopping beside the woman's seat. "Can we. . .go talk?"

Valerie stopped eating and looked up. In her face was an edge of concern.

"Sure. It's good to see you back." Valerie smiled and picked up her tray of food. She followed Bray to a lone table in the back of the cafeteria, where the two of them sat side by side. Bray's intent was to tell Valerie about Kage. And then to—

"Don't even think about it—you've been wrong on most things. Don't embarrass yourself." The voice of the entity had returned, interrupting Bray's thoughts. This time, it sounded more feminine, and robotic. A strange sense of confusion came over her, urging her to stay quiet. The source of the confusion was located in her mind, and not in her gut. This was how she knew it was something false, and not her

instinct.

Bray spoke quietly to Valerie. "I need to tell you something."

"Okay, what?" Valerie had picked up her fork, full of baked beans, but held it suspended in air.

"It's Kage," Bray said.

"*Shut up! You're making a mistake!*" The voice pounded at her temples. It felt like someone was in her head, trying to get out. It was disorienting. She wavered, shook her head, and kept on.

"You know something about my son?" Valerie's expression was pure shock.

The pain grew in Bray's head, made it hard to focus. She winced, tried to push through.

"He's. . .he's. . ." Bray formed the words, and then the pain pushed back. More powerful each time, inching into her brain, with the intent to take it over. She closed her eyes, the pain was so massive.

"What's the matter?" Valerie asked. She dropped the fork and turned and placed her hand on Bray's back.

"Okay," Bray said. "He's okay. . .and Trevor, too."

The pain mounted. It stabbed her behind the eyes.

"*Ah!*" she screamed out. The whole room went silent. Bray convulsed. Her body began falling backward, toward the floor.

Caught in someone's arms, she felt herself brought carefully down to the ground.

"Bray?" Valerie called. Her voice sounded far away. Bray opened her eyes. She *thought* she had opened her eyes.

But everything was black. Shadows moved around in the darkness. She felt herself held up in a sitting position. Completely powerless, she reached and grasped for help, for some understanding as to what was happening to her. Her heart raced up into her throat. Her chest tightened.

"I'll go get a guard," Valerie said.

"No!" Bray shouted. When she did, the shout shot back at her head, causing more pain. It felt like a knife slowly pushing its way into the side of her brain. She clenched her teeth.

The pain grew so immense tears poured from her eyes.

"We have to get you help," Valerie insisted, her voice now close to Bray's ear.

The darkness overcame her.

"*You will succumb to me*," the entity commanded.

A sharp pain hit right in the center of her brain. Bray shut her mouth, trying with all her strength not to scream.

"Please. . .listen. . ." Bray said, still trying to talk to Valerie. She reached out, felt the body beside her. She touched along the shirt until she felt the collar, and she grabbed onto it and would not let go.

"This place will end me," she whispered. "Help me get out of here. . .we all need. . .we all need to get out of here." Bray released her grip, losing control of herself, feeling herself fade, so much like that time she experienced Alice's death, yet so much more. . .painful. Excruciating.

"How?" Valerie asked.

"For now. . .just. . .get me. . .to. . .my cell." Bray was no longer able to fight. Nothing left. Fading. Losing. More voices, but she could no longer make them out. Being lifted. Stumbling. Trying to walk. Dragged. Picking up her feet.

"*I will end you.*" the voice whispered into the last, tiny pinprick of a spot within her *self*, the only place where she still remained, still recognized she had a self.

She forced herself to walk. Her head dropped. Too heavy to hold it up. Hands held tight to her arms. A bell sounded, and then it sounded more like a drum. A turn here. A turn there.

And everything stopped.

Chapter Six

Bertan

Bertan wondered what had happened to Bray. He hadn't heard from her since yesterday, a brief moment in which she had reminded him to breathe. In the next moment, he found himself lying in his cell, remembering nothing of the in between. Remembering nothing but a blank space of time where he knew time was lost but he could not find an explanation, only that Bray had been there, and she had gone in to help him. Into his mind.

Now here he was, alert, awake, and able to focus. He thought clearly of what his father said, about how he had a gift. He pondered what had happened when he thought about Carmen and then he saw her. He was there, for a moment. She saw him. Gabriella saw him, too.

Sitting in this cell for weeks on end would destroy his mind for good, if he allowed it. But something had happened through his connection to Bray, something that led him to feel *better*. He felt a little less hopeless. He couldn't explain it. He also couldn't explain how he'd seen his wife last night, as if she were right there beside him. There was nothing else to do but to try it again, to see if maybe he could somehow reach Carmen, the way Bray was able to reach him. As outlandish and ridiculous as it seemed, it was the only thing that made sense.

Bertan closed his eyes.

He thought about San Pedro Sula, where Carmen and Gabriella were staying with Carmen's cousin. He thought about Carmen, imagined her face. Her oval, dark eyes. Her long, wide nose. Her smile like a bended flower. The honey-brown of her skin, the scent of her neck. He called out for her.

The darkness transitioned into a night on the streets. The orange glow of street lamps shone dully on a corner in Barrio Morazan. Bertan recognized the place. He felt the warmth of night, heard people nearby, laughing.

He opened his eyes. Above him a sky of indigo covered the land with a cloak of deep, dark purple.

Bertan sat up.

He found himself on a bench beside a bus stop. Across the street, a *pupuseria* sat beneath an overhead, concrete structure. Picnic tables dotted its concrete floors. The sound of cumbia music drifted out into the street. Bertan felt pulled to it. Without question, he stood up and walked toward the tables.

Inside, fluorescent lights exposed a mostly empty space, a walk-up window at the far end where customers ordered *pupusas* filled with beans, hot sauce and cheese. The aroma made his mouth water.

At a table in the center of the room sat three people. Carmen had her back to Bertan. She was laughing and talking to her cousin Alex, who sat across from her. Beside him was Gabriella, taller and almost unrecognizable to Bertan.

"Carmen!" he yelled, and once again, he ran to her. He could not hold back. If this was not real, he would join in regardless. There was nothing to lose.

Carmen stopped eating. She turned quickly. Her mouth dropped open, eyes wide. Some of the food she'd been chewing fell out of her mouth and onto the floor. She spit the rest out, stood up, and walked toward Bertan, arms stretched out, eyes in shock, mouth agape.

Bertan began to cry. He grabbed for her arms, *felt* the thickness of them, just as he'd remembered. He pulled her in. She lost it, cried into his chest.

"How-how did you get here?" she asked in between tears. Her hands gripped tightly at his back.

Bertan felt the whole earth move.

Then, a set of small, cool hands touched along his waist.

"Papá? Is it really you? Are you really here?" Gabriella asked.

Heat and tears and crying and laughter spun around them like the earth revolving around the sun, the way his whole life revolved around his family. The way everything he had done up to this moment was for them. He could feel the years of loss and distance and regret dropping away in the tears and sweat that fell from his body. His ears thrilled to hear the sounds of his wife and child, who, in this moment, held him so tightly he thought he might like to die just like this.

"You can really see me?" Bertan asked, shaking with disbelief.

"Yes, *amor*. Of course. How did you get here?" Carmen pulled away, looked him over.

"I can't explain it." He was confused, afraid he'd lose this moment with them. An element of him knew this was not real, that his body was back inside that prison, miles and miles from here. And as those thoughts loomed in his mind, the atmosphere shifted. The vision of his family wavered.

"No!" he shouted.

"What-what's happening? Bertan?" Carmen cried, but her voice was drifting away.

Suddenly Bertan felt he was falling, backwards rather than down. Back, back. Farther away from Carmen. . .her arms outstretched, a look of horror on her face. Gabriella was crying.

And then, it was over.

Chapter Seven

Bray

Her mind had been hijacked.

It was the entity, of course. She knew it. Yet knowing that didn't help Bray much. She was lying on a cold, hard floor. No movement around her. Air stiff. Stale. It felt as though everything was spinning, but only on the inside. Twisting like a tornado.

Once, when she was younger, she saw a story on the news about unusual twisters out west. Something unheard of until then, newscasters had said. That would've been. . .the year 2033. What came to her mind now was a vivid scene of dry earth and storm, clouds dropping so close to the land they touched one another. It was striking, how bleak the clouds appeared. The storm was nowhere near her home in Denver. It was somewhere over in Nevada. Its lightning hit nearby rocks. Thunder rolled through so hard it shook the camera filming it.

When the twister formed in the sky, and kissed the earth, it picked up what it could to sustain itself: sand, rock. There had been no water. Sand hit the camera so hard it cracked the screen.

That was how her head felt now.

Someone knocked.

"Bray? You okay?" It was Tori.

Bray wanted to respond but couldn't find where words were located. Everything was fragmented.

"*I can help you.*" This time, though, it wasn't Tori. The voice had returned, the entity. "*Like I helped Bertan.*"

What could Bray do? When she opened her eyes, her vision improved only slightly. Everything was gray now instead of black. She felt so detached from herself.

"*We want to help,*" said Tori. "*Valerie told me what you said. . .we need to get out of here.*"

A desperate urge awoke in Bray's heart. She had to speak with Tori! Yet she couldn't say anything. There was a block.

The entity.

She closed her eyes. Taking a deep breath, as insane as it seemed, she knew nothing else to do than to succumb. Allow. Let it come in, see what it would do.

Bray released herself to its grip.

"*Here we go,*" the entity spoke, loud and penetrating.

The spinning ceased. Her brain fell back together, like a sensation of a jacket being zipped up. The pain dissipated.

Bray felt her body sit up. She became an observer, watching from somewhere else, as the entity lifted her to standing.

Her eyes popped open.

Her vision gradually expanded outward. The cell came into view. Bray knew it well, but that wasn't what the entity wanted her to see. It lifted her head to look directly at the cell door. Bray considered this a time to be frightened, but she was determined to keep her wits about her. Somehow she sensed the entity did not know she was watching from afar.

It was then that Bray's psychic awareness leapt up and out of herself, just above herself. This was familiar. She had done this in the past when she linked with

Rhea to find out the exact location of the testing facility in which Rhea and the other cows had been confined. Astral projection. She'd read about it online.

Bray also recalled something from the meditation book she'd read: how transcendence was all about detaching, watching thoughts. Experiencing feelings until they passed. That when one did this, they would become masters of themselves. And in that awareness, by allowing what was happening, one could then, hypothetically, work with the present moment in such a way as to *change* reality. Bend it into something that made sense. Something that brought eternal calm.

Wait.

No.

That wasn't in the meditation book. These musings were. . .*hers*. Something Bray suddenly realized she had come to believe on her own. To believe that by allowing the entity in and embracing it. . .she could *transcend* the entity's reality, bend it into something of her own choosing, something she could work with.

Bray watched as the entity caused her body to bang her fist into the cell door.

"Hey!" her body shouted.

Meanwhile, as Bray's true awareness remained suspended above her body and not *of* her body, she called out to Tori.

"Gather everyone you can," Bray whispered quietly in her mind. She hoped the entity would not hear. Besides, the thing was distracted, busy banging on the cell door, and Bray could feel a pile of fear building in its chest.

Its fear transitioned into anger.

"*What for?*" Tori replied.

Bray recalled what Tori had told her about how the activists had attempted a hunger strike and ended up in solitary confinement.

"How many cells are there in solitary?" Bray asked her.

A guard opened the cell door. Bray watched herself plead with the guard, the sound of her voice one decibel lower than usual.

"Please," her voice begged the guard. "I'm so hungry. Can you bring me some food?"

It was beyond odd to watch herself move and speak when she wasn't the one in control.

"*Fifty or so, I'm sure*," Tori replied.

"Can you get support from twice that many. . .in prisoners, I mean?" Bray asked Tori.

"*For what?*"

The guard laughed, looking down at Bray's body.

"Now you want food? Well, you'll have to wait till dinner like everyone else."

The entity was not going to like that answer.

Bray felt an urge to act fast. But for what? She would go along with the entity. . .until the time was right. Let it be. Let it do what it was going to do. Accept it. Make peace with it. It was too powerful otherwise.

"Ask them," Bray said to Tori, a slow ache rising from her stomach into her throat, "to hunger strike with me. We'll need everyone. In solidarity with me. To send a message."

"*What message, Bray?*"

The guard turned his back to exit the cell. Bray witnessed her entire body turn. She moved unnaturally fast. Grabbing the child-size desk chair from her cell, she swung it into the back of the guard's knees. The guard's legs toppled as he reached the cell door. She dropped the chair. Taking the side of the door in both hands, she pushed it toward the guard, acting too quickly for him to respond. On his face was a look of shock as she used the weight of her small frame to slam the door into his body. She slammed and slammed and slammed, the door hitting him repeatedly.

"*Bray?*" Tori asked again. "*What message?*"

A moment later, the door was pushed open. Bray's body slipped and fell to the floor. An instant of pain registered somewhere, but pain was more a word to her than a physical sensation, making this an incredibly eerie experience. It was similar to the way she'd experienced the pain of someone with whom she was linked, such as Alice that time she was stabbed with an electric prod. This gave Bray proof that she was linked with the entity, or it was a part of her.

Another guard entered the cell. He stood towering over her. She let out a laugh. Then, she spat at him. Her spittle landed on his thigh. He wiped it off with his hand.

With ease, the guard pressed his boot into her arm, sticking it to the floor so she could not move.

"You're lucky you're under age," the guard said. "Otherwise, I'd have your arm broken in three places right about now."

"Fuck you," a voice spat out of her mouth.

Bray wanted to look away, it was so painful to watch. She cringed, watching from above, and allowed it to continue.

The two guards hoisted Bray's body to standing. Bray watched them yank her out into the hallway. Her heart tightened. She knew exactly where they were taking her. As she watched herself pulled down the hall, terror filled her brain. This was what the entity wanted.

"Tell them," Bray said to Tori finally, pushing the words out of her consciousness, for they would not flow on their own. Her one final thought before collapsing from exhaustion, before giving up, was how awful this must have been for Bertan, had this also been his experience.

"Tell them. . .we cease all activity. . .until all beings are free."

And then her body was thrown into a six-foot by eight-foot cell. The cell door slammed. All sense of herself fell to the floor.

Chapter Eight

Elisha

Cincinnati, OH

Elisha Andrews made the fifty-minute drive from Cincinnati up to Yellow Springs, Ohio. It was mid-morning on a Saturday. The sun had made itself well known by penetrating the miles and miles of dry Ohio fields with unforgiving light, killing off any remaining grass that might otherwise still have been alive. The soy and corn crops were dying. Everything was dying.

The nation's terrorist alert had been reduced to a yellow threat level. She knew there was no threat. Connecting with Trevor only confirmed: there were more animal activists out there, and she needed to tell Emerson.

Elisha's relationship with Emerson was. . .confusing. It dated back to 2034, when she'd met him at Integrated Health of Cincinnati, known as IHC. They'd dated off and on. Anytime she got too close, Emerson would pull away. He had his reasons, she supposed. Five years ago, the two of them discovered that Emerson had been given an unknown, genetic treatment that cured him of Angelman Syndrome when he was a baby. As it turned out, it was his father, a scientist who'd worked for S-Corp, who developed this treatment for his son, using animal DNA. The result: Emerson began exhibiting animalistic behaviors and took on some of their physical traits, such as cat eyes. Emerson discovered this one year after he and Elisha had met. Since then, nothing had been the same.

After Emerson's father was murdered by S-Corp, an act carried out by some terrible man by the name of Carl Florez-Emerson went into hiding. Elisha didn't blame him. The FBI and S-Corp were after him for some past animal rescues he'd attempted. Plus, Emerson had explained to her, Florez seemed to be interested in his genetic disposition. He had a gift for using his animal-like features to assist him in rescues. Features such as jumping extraordinary heights, running fast and long distances without tiring. A gift Florez seemed to want to exploit for his own science project.

Elisha pulled into the driveway. Before her, a brief hill of yellow, fading grass led up to a single-story, brick house with an empty front porch. The home was owned by two former animal activists, Steph and Dek. Emerson had been living here with them, hiding away from the threat of S-Corp.

As Elisha sat and looked at the house, slowly turning off the car engine, she recalled the time she assisted Emerson, Steph and Dek in their attempt to stop S-Corp. It was five years ago. Emerson had seemed ready to stand up to the corporation after the loss of his father. They'd managed to rescue a number of farm animals, and then Emerson went right back into hiding again. Elisha had secretly hoped he would move through his grief and fear enough to come out of hiding and continue his crusade, but just as with their tattered relationship, she surmised that once again he'd gotten too close, then turned away.

Elisha got out of the car. She shut the door and glanced up at the property. A black barn stood back away from the house. From it, a pair of fully-grown pigs came running. She smiled and started for the barn.

Stepping around the corner of the house, she saw Steph's head pop up from a lounge chair. The chair was facing outward toward the hills and valleys beyond the property, where oak and pine trees stood gallantly and without restraint.

Steph stood up to greet her. On her head was a round sun hat. Her eyes were covered by a pair of sunglasses, which she promptly removed. She leaned down, her six-foot stature towering over Elisha, and hugged her with such strength it nearly pushed Elisha backwards.

"Good to see you," Steph said in her tranquil voice. She released her grip from Elisha's shoulders. She adjusted her hat, which had flopped sideways when she hugged Elisha. Steph carried herself with an air of modesty that Elisha admired. The woman had tact.

"Where is he?" Elisha asked, thinking of Emerson.

"Back here." Steph pointed past the deck at a half-tilled back yard.

Elisha followed Steph past bright-blue chrysanthemums that had been planted in a space where two baby piglets were buried. Elisha knew this because she helped with the burial. These were piglets that Emerson had attempted to rescue from an S-Corp facility, but they did not survive. Elisha took a deep breath, nodded toward the ground as if to wish the piglets well, and stopped beside Steph.

"Before you go over there," Steph said,

placing her hand on Elisha's shoulder, "Dek and I want you to know we're here to help in any way we can."

"Thanks," Elisha replied, touching Steph's hand with hers.

Steph smiled, let go, and returned to her lounge chair.

Elisha continued toward the back of the yard where Emerson was pulling weeds from a section of marigolds. He had his back to her. Black, baggy pants hid his legs, but just below his back end was an open square slit where a six-inch tail waved in the breeze. The shirt he was wearing had sleeves that hung down over his arms, designed like a poncho, which provided space for his ever-expanding wings.

Elisha took a deep breath, preparing herself for the changes she was about to see in him. Five years was a long time, and although Steph kept her abreast of Emerson's changes, it didn't mean she could know how she would feel when seeing them in person. She didn't want Emerson to notice any look of shock or disapproval on her face, lest it cause him to retreat further.

"Hey there," she said, hesitant.

Emerson froze. He stood up slowly, a pair of cat-like ears jutting out from the sides of his head. His hair hung down to his lower back in a tie. The color had changed to a much lighter brown, almost golden. It was thick like a horse's mane. It was quite stunning and. . .she was surprised. . .quite beautiful.

When he turned to face her, Elisha's eyes lit up in awe. Her brain could not compute what she was seeing. There was so much to take in. Her heart, however, saw Emerson, the young, passionate man with whom she had once fallen in love.

Without question, she walked over and

wrapped her arms around him.

"Emerson!" she cried.

"Yes," he replied, his hands resting softly on her sides. "What are you doing here?"

Elisha pulled back. She looked at his eyes. Blue as ever, yet taking on even more of a cat's eye shape.

"Nice to see you, too," she said, grinning and releasing him from her grip.

"Sorry. I just wasn't expecting you."

"I know. And you can trust I came out of great importance."

"Is everything okay? Your family. . ." he asked, his voice trailing off.

"Yes." Elisha paused. Her mother, Stacie, had been working for a genetic corporation, GeneUS.com for several years, and, unfortunately for Elisha, she had been working with Carl Florez of S-Corp on more genetic testing and experiments.

"Then what is it?" he asked, wiping his hands as dirt and soil fell away from them.

As Emerson turned, she got a good look at the whiskers protruding from his upper lip and sides of his mouth. He'd grown a distinguished, pure white goatee. On either side of his mouth, thin, white, hairs grew in single strands, all the way down to his chest. Yet he had the same thin nose, giving him a look both young and old, and it did not frighten her. If anything, when Elisha looked at Emerson, no matter how much he had changed, she saw the same guy she met six years ago, the man on the inside who tried and who cared. Who once wished to stand up for what was right in a world where few people would. Yep, she still loved him, and she wasn't sure she'd ever tell him that.

Suddenly Elisha realized she'd been staring off into space. She blinked, bringing herself back, avoiding tears. Emerson evidently hadn't noticed. He was already a few steps away, walking toward the house.

"You coming?" he called back.

Elisha caught up with him, being careful not to bump his tail as she followed him up onto the deck. He sat down at a round table. She sat across from him, facing out into the back yard.

"I assume you heard about the Embedicare takeover?" she asked.

"Is that what they're calling it?"

Elisha nodded. She felt surprised that he seemed so. . .composed. A part of her hoped he'd jump at the topic, that it would make him want to act again.

"Steph told me about it," he continued. "It sounds incredible, if it's true."

"What do you mean, if it's true?"

"What if they weren't activists at all? What if it was just some set-up by S-Corp, or what if it really was terrorists?"

"Really? That's what you think?" Elisha was shocked.

Emerson shrugged, looked at her and smirked.

Elisha pressed on. "It's why I'm here, actually. They need help. I've signed up to be a representative for Cincinnati."

"What does that mean?"

"Helping communicate plans and information from the activists to people in our area."

"What kind of plans?"

"Well, they have plenty of proof against S-Corp. The fertilizer disaster. . .and they just released a video showing a garden they had grown out west, but S-Corp destroyed it, along with their home." Elisha paused. "They're planning a march. March for freedom, they're calling it."

"That's good." Emerson nodded. His eyes trailed off into the distance, somewhere past Elisha where she could not follow, and wouldn't. She'd come here to persuade him to get back in the game.

"Will you help us?" she asked.

"No way," Emerson replied at once. "We have no idea who these people really are."

Elisha tensed. She hated it when people doubted her.

"They could say the same about you, Emerson," she replied, feeling tested. "You're the one who's the activist. At least, you used to be. It was you who convinced me to get involved. Is it so crazy to think there are others like us out there. . .who want S-Corp stopped?"

"I guess not," Emerson replied in a low tone. He appeared to shrink into himself just then.

Elisha took a deep breath and tried to calm herself down. She missed her friend, and she didn't feel she could say that to him.

"I've changed a lot," he admitted. "More than what you can see. I get tired more easily than I used to. All these genetic changes have me feeling. . .old. You don't know how hard it is for me to get through a day."

"You won't let me," she refuted.

"I know. I realize I haven't been a good friend. That I've backed off and I've been isolating. It just seems to be my nature these days. I don't think I have any energy to give to such a cause, as much as I'm truly in awe of what's happened. I hope they succeed, whoever they are. I'd just rather they do it without me."

Elisha looked him in the eye, noticing she didn't see the same drive she used to

see there. Maybe it wasn't fair of her to
show up here and expect he'd want to help.
Maybe their relationship really had dried
up, much like the climate.

Maybe some things were impossible to
save.

"Well," she finally spoke. "It was nice
to see you."

Emerson sat up. He reached over and
took her hand. She let him, but she held on
loosely.

"I'm sorry. I wish this thing had never
happened to me, so I could be normal. So I
could go back to the times I used to see
you every day." He smiled.

Elisha began to tear up.

"Those were good times," he said. His
eyes glazed over.

"They were." She paused. "And if
memories of those times are all we've got
left between us, then so be it."

Elisha released herself from Emerson's
hand. She stood up. Wiping her tears away,
she started for the steps.

"Wait."

Elisha stopped.

"A hug before you go?" he asked.

At the sound of his request, Elisha's
eyes closed. A hug would do her in, but
maybe they both needed it, if this really
was goodbye.

Elisha turned and he approached, taking
her head into his shoulder. He smelled of
dirt and wood chips. She felt his arms
reach around, his wings creating a kind of
blanket against her back. She breathed him
in, had a brief cry, then disengaged.

"You haven't changed that much. Not
really," she said, and then walked down the
steps, through the yard, passing Steph
silently and getting into her car.

Elisha drove back to Cincinnati alone.

It was Emerson who inspired her to become the activist she was today. She was sad he would not be marching alongside her.

Chapter Nine

Bray

Bray remained in suspension above herself as her body rocked back and forth inside the cell. That body was laughing. It was becoming increasingly more difficult for her consciousness to feel her own physicality.

"*There will be nothing left. . .when I am finished with you,*" the entity's voice echoed all around her. She was not afraid. Admitting there was nothing she could do for herself, she thought to rise above the prison, see if she could get a glimpse into the lives of the other prisoners.

Her consciousness rose. It was like watching a film, only she was the camera. Lifting beyond the prison's thick, concrete ceiling, her view stopped just at the top floor, where she and the other prisoners were held.

It must have been lunch time, as every cell was empty. She shifted her view through the hallways, where guards sat and scrolled through their phones, until she arrived at the cafeteria doors. With ease, the expansive room and all its tables were revealed to her.

There, a group of twenty prisoners stood in line for food. They must've chosen not to participate in the hunger strike. The remaining twenty kept to their seats. A sense of tension hung above them. They all looked around the room at one another. As the line dwindled, no one else stood to get in line. The guards began pacing up and down the floor between the tables. The room was quiet except for the voices of the prisoners standing at the food buffet.

"*Where are you, Bray?*" Tori's voice etched into her mind.

"I'm here. You can't see me," Bray replied through her thoughts.

"*How?*"

"No time to explain. They've placed me in solitary."

"*It won't be long before the rest of us join you.*"

"What's happening?" Bray asked.

"Get in line!" one of the guards yelled. He stood against the wall beneath the windows, where Bray noticed the light coming in from outside.

The twenty prisoners remained seated. Those who had gotten in line were now carrying their meals and sitting at the empty tables in the back of the cafeteria.

"We don't eat until Bray is freed," Tori said in a firm voice.

"Until all animals are free," added Valerie.

"No more talking!" the guard yelled. He pulled a walkie talkie from the side of his belt, requesting backup.

"Get in line, now!" the second guard yelled as he paced rapidly between tables, staring at the prisoners.

Not one prisoner moved.

"Fine!" the guard spat. "No one eats. Back to your cells."

The bell rang. The prisoners stood in unison. Those who had chosen not to participate and had received meals hadn't had time to finish. As everyone stood in line facing the cafeteria doors, waiting to exit, Bray began to feel fragmented.

The cafeteria doors opened. The prisoners walked calmly back in the direction of their cells. Bray attempted to follow, still not in physical form but as consciousness, removed yet able to observe, but she was stopped. The view in front of her was being erased, as if someone were using a black marker to color over everything.

"No!" she yelled, the hallways of the prison quickly disappearing.

She let out a wail.

Everything went black.

Chapter Ten

Cole

Cole met Kage and Lana the next day. Elliott had emailed him exact coordinates. He hoped to see Elliott, a friend of Bray's since Bray was a child. He thought it might help him feel closer to Bray. Not knowing if he would ever find his daughter was beginning to weigh on him. Thom had yet to reply to his text asking if S-Corp was holding activists in the prison in Arizona.

It was mid-afternoon. It had taken him four hours to drive up to Shoshone National Forest, where the northern Rocky Mountains roamed the distant horizon. The sun hung over him and gazed down on his face as he stood leaning against his car. He closed his eyes a moment, felt the fresh air, and a tear rolled out. He wiped it away. How he'd missed being out here. He'd been cooped up in Denver and Washington, D.C., for too long.

A black truck came into view. He recognized it immediately as belonging to his friend Rick, a retired rancher. Rick had answered his call a few months ago and had assisted Bray in Wyoming after she freed the sows from the transport truck on their way to slaughter. Cole was amused that Bray's friends held on to the truck, not that Rick would have minded.

The truck rolled to a stop facing his BMW, fifty feet away. Cole peered inside.

Two passengers, neither one Elliott. One got out of the driver's seat, appeared to be a female. Cole's height, blonde hair, long on top and the sides shaven close to her head. As she neared Cole, he hesitated, trying to figure her out. She was dressed in jeans and a button-down shirt. As she approached him, he began to wonder if he'd misgendered her.

The second woman, petite, attractive, dark-haired, of Asian background perhaps, walked up to him with her arm outstretched.

"Cole?" she called, stepping up to him.

"You must be Lana," he said, shaking her hand.

"You guessed it," Lana replied. "This is Kage."

"Ah, yes. Of course." He nodded. Kage made no effort to shake Cole's hand, but she/he/they. . .whatever their pronouns were. . .smiled and waved.

"Nice to meet you, Mr. Hoffman," Kage said, their voice sounding neutral, increasing Cole's curiosity.

"May I ask your pronouns?" Cole asked.

Kage shot a glance at Lana, who glanced back at him. They were standing side by side, facing Cole. It was evident the two were good friends.

"He/him," Kage replied. "Thanks for asking."

"Great," Cole said, exhaling. He realized Kage must've been transgender. It was the only thing that made sense. Cole had worked with a number of transgender people while he was in law school. Even as a very loyal Republican politician, he was never one to take up personal issues like body rights and reproductive rights. He had always been more of a moderate, fiscal Republican, which nowadays he was reconsidering.

"You said you might be able to help us with the lawsuit?" Lana asked.

Cole raised his eyebrows. He supposed there was no point in wasting time out here, given these two had removed themselves from their hideout to come meet with him, and he, at least, had a four-hour trek to get back home before dark.

He had already given Lana's request some thought, based on Elliott's email. He'd even contacted a number of lawyer friends, but, as he'd suspected, no one wanted to take on S-Corp. Not even after the revelations of the Embedicare takeover. Cole had spent all of last night mulling it over. Instinctually he felt it was the right thing to sue S-Corp for all the losses those families must've endured due to the fertilizer disaster. Not just financially. It wasn't about the money. These types of lawsuits, they were about principle. Or so Cole believed. The principle at stake here was one Cole could easily stand by, and at the end of all things, believed he *had* to: the principle of family. That family was more important than corporate greed. He had to be sure. . . if he were going to take this case, it couldn't be about Dianna. It had to be *for* his daughter, and for all those families.

"Yes," Cole finally replied. "I'll take it on myself."

He saw Kage's eyes light up.

Then Lana's.

"For real?" Kage asked, his voice audibly louder.

"My concern is. . .it could be seen as a conflict of interest. Because Dianna is my ex-wife." The divorce was so fresh that the term still sounded odd.

"Right." Lana nodded, seemed to agree.

"So I'll need to hire a second lawyer to work on the case, to balance things out. And I have no idea who that person would be right now."

"I may be able to do it," Lana replied. "Depends on what kind of expertise you need."

Cole looked at Lana. He had no idea her background, but it was worth considering. She had, after all, been working on this issue with Elliott.

"How many people have said they'd be willing to testify?" Cole asked. Without families actually willing to stand up in court against S-Corp, there would be no case.

"So far. . .about twenty," Lana replied.

Cole raised his eyebrows. If that was true, the number was significant. But Cole knew enough about these types of cases to assume that, when push came to shove, many of those families might start backing away.

"I'll need to speak with them. We need them to provide as much evidence as possible."

Lana opened her mouth to talk, when Kage quickly jumped in.

"With all due respect, Mr. Hoffman, we just. . .have a hard time trusting anyone associated with the government."

"Correction," Lana added. "*Some of us* do."

"You mean there's more of you?" Cole asked, intrigued.

"We've said enough," Kage replied bluntly.

"That's okay. I don't need to know." Cole lifted his hands in a surrender motion. Kage's hesitation was valid. Events of the past, decisions by government, had led people like Kage to distrust the system. It had been this way for decades, and Cole remembered back to when he was Elliott's age, just beginning law school, how much he thought he could change things. How he once believed he could become a politician and mend the government's relationship with its people. Instead, as a senator, he became part of the problem.

Maybe it wasn't too late to change.

"I won't keep you two any longer." Cole looked to Lana. "Email me and we'll keep talking."

Lana nodded.

"And I just want you to know," he said, shifting his attention to Kage. "I don't expect you to trust me. I get it. If I were you, I wouldn't trust me, either. I divorced Dianna because I couldn't go along with her anymore, couldn't condone what she's doing at S-Corp. And also because we couldn't agree on decisions about the best way to help Bray."

He stopped for a moment, looking into Kage's eyes. The sun had hit them in a way that lightened them to a soft copper. Cole saw a youth in them that made him feel warm, remembering his own youth and how he'd never had the guts to do anything like these two were doing right now, standing up against the entire system. It wasn't that he wanted the same things they wanted, necessarily, but he did want people to have access to the truth. And he wanted his daughter safe, which was something they could all stand behind.

"Bray is my number one priority now. I'm sorry for all that's happened to get us where we have to be standing here today. I hope we can all be on the same team. I am with you in that we need to stop S-Corp. What they've done is abhorrent."

"Have you heard anything from Bray?"

Kage asked. "Anything about where she is?"

Cole took a deep breath.

"I have reason to believe she's being held in a facility in Arizona," he replied.

"That's the same prison my dad talked about-in his manuscript," Kage said, suddenly shifting his position to face Cole.

"Yes," Cole said. "My assistant has been reading the manuscript. We've been fact-checking it. So far, it's accurate."

Kage's chest rose and fell. A slightly warm smile formed on his face as he looked at Cole.

"Your father seems to have been a brave man," Cole commented. *Much braver than I,* he wanted to say, but held back.

Kage's eyes welled up.

Lana stepped over and put her arm around Kage's waist. Kage smiled down at her, cleared his throat, and gently pulled her arm away, taking her hand in his.

Cole smiled. Watching the two of them gave him hope.

"I do have to be careful," Cole continued. "If I contact the prison, they'll notify Dianna. We don't want that. So I have to find a way to confirm she's there."

"Then what?" asked Kage.

"Then I'll see about getting her out."

With that, the three of them exchanged goodbyes. Cole stood and watched as Kage and Lana got into the truck and returned north. He waited until they were out of sight before he returned to his BMW.

Sliding into the driver's seat, he sat for a moment. It was so peaceful, so silent out here. He used to hike and get out in nature when he was young. Why did he ever stop? Why did he allow his connection with his daughter to wither for so long? And how was he going to find her?

He closed his eyes. In the quiet of the lone afternoon, out here beyond distraction, beyond the mundane tasks of his everyday life, he thought of Bray. She'd reached out to him when she needed him, during the Embedicare takeover. She'd wanted him to experience the slaughter of a cow, and he still wasn't sure why. Or how she'd done it. But he had *heard* her.

Maybe it could go both ways. It was certainly worth a try.

"Bray," he thought. "If you can hear me. . .please tell me where you are. Are you in Arizona? If so, I will come find you. Please. Help me find you."

His mind went quiet. Slow tears slipped out of the corners of his eyes and traveled downward, dropping onto his pants. Out here in nature, alone, he could breathe.

Opening his eyes, Cole looked out at the mountains. He felt an odd sense of peace. He could only trust that, somehow, he would find his daughter and bring her home.

Chapter Eleven

Bertan

Bertan paced the cell floor. It was early evening. His mind raced. How was it that he had been able to find his family like that? He had felt and sensed he was in Honduras. He had smelled familiar smells and *felt* Carmen and Gabriella against his skin. It *had* to have been real. His only worry was that he might've been doing his family more harm than good by appearing briefly and then disappearing, since he had no control over the duration. All he knew was that the image of his wife and daughter was disrupted the moment he felt fear. The moment he no longer believed. How could he control that? He worried that Carmen might've started to believe he was deceased and that it was his ghost who was visiting her.

So he stopped.

Instead, he began to consider what was happening to him. Somehow, beyond his understanding, when he thought of his wife, called her name and imagined her face, he could project himself into her reality—more than a thousand miles away.

Maybe his father was right.

He had a gift.

But where had it come from? Why now?

No time for that. There was one person who had been on his mind since he'd arrived here. One person he needed to know about. His good friend, Ruben. Maybe he could reach out, find the man who'd helped him in the past. Maybe it was his turn to help Ruben now.

Bertan sat on his bed. He closed his eyes. Just as he had done with Carmen, he thought about Ruben. A Mexican man in his fifties. He had curly, black hair and a full beard with aged gray mixed in. Scars hid beneath the fibers of his beard, and Bertan wondered what those scars were from.

"Ruben?" his mind called out, no different than times he'd reached for Bray.

There was no response.

Eyes forced closed, feeling on edge, he tried again.

"Ruben! Please, can you hear me? Where are you?"

Bertan waited, breath held. Nothing but darkness behind his eyes, silence between his ears. The occasional clink of keys and clapping of feet outside his cell.

But no Ruben.

Exhaling in frustration, Bertan opened his eyes and glanced at the wall. He remembered the last time he had seen Ruben, his face bloodied and unrecognizable. He was lying in a utility closet in the S-Corp facility in Idaho. Unconscious. Tape over his mouth. He'd been caught. They must've sent him somewhere. Surely there would be a record of it. And who had records? The warden?

Bertan shifted his attention. He remembered the warden from the conversation they'd had upon his arrival at the prison. The warden wanted him to spill the names and whereabouts of the activists. Even now he felt frustrated by it. Shaking off the emotion, he imagined the hallway that led to the warden's office. The off-white walls, the high ceiling. He tried picturing the doors leading to the warden's office.

    His mind went blank.
                    #
    Hours must have passed. Darkness fell
outside his window. Bertan had been sitting
on the bed, staring out at nothing. What
was he to do?
    Again he recalled the experience of
visiting his wife and daughter. It seemed
so far-fetched, out of a book he might read
or some sci-fi movie, for him to be able to
do that.
    "What did I even do?" he asked aloud.
    The thought came to him clearly: *I
traveled. With my mind, I traveled home.*
    So why couldn't he simply travel up one
floor to the warden's office? It was much
closer in proximity than Honduras. He'd
been to the office before, so he knew what
to imagine. Maybe there he could find out
something about Ruben.
    Bertan tried again.
    This time, he lay down in bed, hoping
this would help him feel more at ease. He
closed his eyes. Thoughts of Carmen and
Gabriella filled his mind. What were they
thinking? Did they fear him dead? He'd been
so far removed from them for so long that
not seeing them had become normal. They had
become this loose term in his mind: family.
But when he got a taste of it, and felt the
skin of his wife, actually *breathed her in*,
it all came barreling back to him, the
memories. Family was real.
    It became hard to focus.
    "Come on, Bertan," he whispered to
himself. His heart tightened. He was
growing more frustrated by the moment.
    Bertan shook off thoughts of his family.
He tried the breathing exercises Ruben had
taught him, which brought his mind back to
Ruben. The times he had spent in Ruben's
office at the S-Corp facility. Their talks.

As he thought about his friend, he dropped down into his breathing, playing a kind of game where he thought of Ruben's name on the inhale, and exhale.

Inhale: "Ru-u-u. . ."
Exhale: "Be-e-n."

He went on like this for a while.

Eventually, he imagined his cell. He imagined the ceiling, and the hallways outside his cell. He imagined the stairwell leading up to the warden's office. That placard drilled into the wall outside the office that read: WARDEN.

Bertan imagined himself standing in that hallway. He imagined he was there, and he looked around, saw a guard pacing the far end where a set of barred windows behind him looked out into the night. Bertan turned and looked at the doors, which were closed. With it being night, the Warden would not be inside. At first this discouraged him. Then he saw this was his chance to practice. He could practice until morning. Until he got it right.

Bertan stepped up to the double doors. When he touched the steel handle, he felt nothing but air. His shoulders slumped. He passed his hand along the door to get a feel for the coldness and hardness of it, but again, he felt nothing.

Frustrated, he lifted his fists and began punching at it. Punching and punching, his head turning hot. Punching at air, feeling a hardness beneath his body. Hearing the bed move because he was punching in midair at nothing.

Bertan opened his eyes, saw he was lying in his bed. He grabbed his prison slip-on shoes from beneath the bed and threw them at the cell door.

"Mother fucker!" he shouted.

This was going to be a long night.

#

Feeling defeated, when morning arrived Bertan got up and walked over to the cell door. He dropped his head against the surface of it, feeling the cold steel against his forehead. Exhausted from having tried all night to get inside the warden's office, he figured this was never going to work. He was stuck here, and he would never know the truth about Ruben. He would never see his family again.

The thought of never seeing his family became too painful. Visceral, as if he'd just been stunned by his own knock gun and was about to be cut into pieces and served to the world because the world did not care about him. This was how he felt, and as he felt it, a brief whimper came out. His shoulders shook.

"Come on, Ruben, help me," he whispered, wiping tears away. "Help me find you."

He grasped at the thought that if he could manage getting into the warden's office to learn about Ruben, then maybe, by some long shot, he could do something about his own situation.

Bertan remained there, with his eyes closed. He felt his chest tighten. He breathed deeply. His arms dropped to his sides, and eventually he felt a pressure release in his neck. He fell into a rhythmic breath. The darkness in his mind extended outward, and the hallway came back into view.

Slowly, his vision rose. He looked down and realized he could see himself standing in his cell. This was different. It was incredibly disorienting, and he wanted to open his eyes.

No.

He knew that if he did that, he'd lose

his focus.

His vision continued to rise one level, above his cell. He saw a pair of guards walking down a dim hallway littered with empty chairs. Bertan followed the guards. They turned a corner and started down another hallway. There were the off-white walls he remembered. Offices passed by on either side, some doors open, many closed. Bertan detached from the guards, felt himself hanging in mid-air, in the center of the hallway. He hoped no one could see him the way Carmen had. He searched the doors until he came upon the steel double doors. On the wall outside the doors, he saw the nameplate: WARDEN.

Bertan immediately passed through the doors, as if he were a ghost. This both amused and startled him. He was still aware of the hardness of his body as it stood in his cell, while also feeling like he was in constant motion, dizzy and floating and slightly aching.

Inside the office, the warden sat at his desk, typing behind a laptop. He did not stop or look up when Bertan entered the room. That was good. He must not have noticed the Honduran inmate suddenly standing beside the chairs across from him.

Bertan felt a wave of motion sickness came over him. He could not lose focus. He had to keep going, find out what had happened to Ruben if he could.

He carried himself around the warden's desk, facing the man's back. From here, he could see the warden's laptop screen. The scent of decaying apple and turkey hung above a trashcan beside the desk. On the laptop screen was an email the warden had been reading.

"What happened to Ruben Sanchez?" Bertan asked, his voice sounding hollow,

bouncing around in his consciousness like a
ball.

The warden did not move. In fact, he
went still. His hands were on the laptop,
his fingers hanging over the keyboard
letters, but they had stopped moving.
Bertan's mouth watered. All he wanted was
for those fingers to move, to type in
Ruben's name.

Suddenly the man stood up. He stepped
around the desk, began pacing the floor.

Bertan's shoulders slumped. This wasn't
going to be as easy as he'd hoped.

#

When Bertan had visited Carmen, he
could *feel* her body. She seemed to be able
to feel his as well, which meant that
somehow, he had been able to take on some
physical presence. He could touch things.

Bertan shuffled down into the warden's
seat. Glancing up at the man, who was
whispering to himself about how he swore he
heard a strange voice in his head, Bertan
was grateful the man could not see him.

Reaching for the keyboard, he touched
the letters, felt the rising buttons
against his skin. He pressed down on one
while looking at the screen.

The cursor did not move.

"Damn it!" he cursed, standing up.

The warden paused.

"What was that?" he asked, looking
around and then down at the floor.

Bertan didn't feel he had much time.
The longer he delayed, the more likely he'd
lose his connection and be sent hurling
back into his cell.

The warden hurried over to the desk.
Bertan stood aside, his back against the
wall where the warden's framed photos hung.
The warden pulled open the top desk drawer
and grabbed a prescription bottle. Twisting

it open, he dumped two pills into his palm
and opened his mouth, dropping the pills in
and gulping.

The warden sat back down. Bertan heard
him exhale and resume typing.

What now?

As the warden worked, Bertan stepped
around the desk and sat across from the man
in the very same spot he'd occupied when
the warden had offered him a chance at
freedom in exchange for information on the
activists he helped during the Embedicare
takeover. Now, his eyes meandered up to
that photo of the warden in Honduras.

Bertan closed his eyes. He held onto an
image of that photo, the warden standing
beneath sunlight, oil palm trees in the
distance. Bertan asked, "Have you always
been this way?"

He heard the typing stop, but did not
dare open his eyes.

"Has there ever been a time you cared
for others?"

"*What?*" a voice responded, but not in
the room. It replied in Bertan's mind.
Bertan leaned forward, held his eyes
closed, kept his attention on the warden.
He heard the man speak to himself.

"The meds are supposed to work faster
than this-"

Bertan considered making himself
visible to the man. But after thinking it
through, he knew that wasn't the move.
Apparently the warden had some kind of
mental health issue, perhaps akin to his
own. And it wasn't long ago that Bertan
allowed himself to listen to a "fugue" that
wasn't real. A time when he'd allowed it to
dictate his life.

How could he get the warden to do the
same?

Bertan briefly opened his eyes, which

landed immediately on the photo of the warden in Honduras. He closed his eyes again.

"You remember that time in Honduras?" Bertan said, this time in his mind.

"This can't be happening," the warden said aloud, dropping his head into his hands.

Bertan opened his eyes to see what the warden was doing. When he saw the man in dismay, he stood up and returned to the warden's side. He lifted his hand toward the man, hesitated, and then gently placed his hand on the man's shoulder. It wasn't that he felt any sympathy for the man, because he didn't. But he did understand the turmoil, and he remembered that in his own darkest moments, all he needed was to not feel so alone.

Bertan took a deep breath. He imagined a warmth exuding from his hand and onto the warden's back. He felt the warden's back tighten and his shoulders relax. The warden began to cry. As he did, Bertan, with his hand still on the man's shoulder, looked over at the photo on the warden's desk. He saw a woman and a young man standing together, smiling dimly at the camera. Was that his family?

The warden ceased his crying. He sat up and took the framed photo into his hand.

"I do care," he whispered, staring at the image and running his fingers along the glass.

Bertan removed his hand from the warden's shoulder. Leaning over, he whispered:

"Then please do this one thing. . .look up Ruben Sanchez."

The warden glanced at the laptop screen for a moment. The tears on his face began to dry. Inside, Bertan felt a calmness he had rarely ever felt, a stillness.

"But why?" the warden asked.

"Trust me, and do it. It's the right thing," Bertan whispered slowly.

The warden set the framed photo back on the desk. He turned and reached for the keyboard. He moved his finger along the laptop's mouse. The screen switched from email to a database search. The warden typed something. Bertan watched as the man entered Ruben's name into the search bar. His heart stopped. He silently prayed for an answer, just not the one he feared most.

A black screen popped up. On it, a photo of Ruben. The tape had been removed from his mouth. His face was bruised. His eyes were barely open, revealing a man who appeared disoriented. Below his birth date, in bold, capital letters, were these words:

DECEASED.

DIED IN CAPTIVITY.

"No!" Bertan yelled.

The warden leapt from his seat. He looked around the room.

"Who's there?" he yelled, reaching down and opening a desk drawer to reveal a pistol.

Bertan's vision crumbled. He fell, a fast retreat downward, shrinking and tumbling. It about made him sick. Suddenly everything went still. He opened his eyes. He was standing. Lifting his head, he saw his cell door before him. He kicked and punched the door. Coming down onto his knees, he tried as hard as he could not to scream. Not only had they taken his only friend, they'd treated him so poorly he'd died in their custody.

Bertan lay on his side on the floor and cried an angry, painful cry. The remainder of the day was lost to him, spent in deep mourning.

Chapter Twelve

Bray

Bray wished more than anything she could rid herself of this entity. She wished she could end it, end the way it was taunting her. But as she lay on the floor, completely returned to her body after an episode of watching the other prisoners from afar, she was exhausted. Her body felt heavy and weighed down by the power of the entity within. If it were possible for a mind to ache, hers most certainly did. There was an emptiness in her stomach and in her chest. Her heart rate slowed. Staring up at the ceiling, she contemplated what to do.

The cell door clicked open. Bray willed herself to sit up, but her body remained held down with force.

"*I call the shots*," the entity said.

Bray had no energy to disagree.

Above her stood Jacob, holding a file folder in his hand. He looked down at Bray with pity.

A guard entered the room, shut the door. He walked over and stood in the corner.

"I wanted to come check in on you," Jacob said. He knelt down beside Bray. "Can we talk?"

"About what?" Bray asked, her mouth dry.

"Can you tell me how you've been

feeling?"

How she was feeling? That was a loaded question. A question with no right answers. A question that, no matter how she answered, would land her in trouble.

"*It's a trap*," the entity said.

It was then she feared she couldn't trust her own thoughts. How much of this was her? How much was the entity?

"May I sit?" Jacob asked.

Bray made eye contact with Jacob. He had always been nice to her. Approachable, non-defensive. Gentle.

Jacob twisted himself into a seated position, his legs crossed in front of him. The guard came near, started for Bray's hands.

"No," Jacob said to the guard, his eyes fixed on Bray's face while waving his hand toward the guard. The guard shook his head.

"She's dangerous, sir," he commented.

"Let me determine that."

The guard backed off, returned to his corner.

"*Fucking guard*," the entity's voice blurted out of Bray's mouth. She attempted to move, but she felt trapped in her own body. As though she was tied up in several feet of rope.

"I want to help you, but I can't do that if you don't tell me what's wrong."

"*What's wrong. . .*" the voice spat out. Harsh, dark. It sounded like her voice, but deeper, a growl, as though possessed. "*What's wrong is you, you dick.*"

Jacob froze. His eyes narrowed as his chest visibly rose and fell. Bray's eyes shifted to watch Jacob's expression. He seemed to compose himself immediately.

"There's clearly something wrong," Jacob said, but he was speaking to the guard. His hands folded in his lap, he continued. "We need to get her back upstairs to medical. Leaving her down here alone. . .will make things worse."

Jacob worked his way up to standing.

"Bring her up to me. We'll get a bed ready. Strap her in, if you have to, but I think she needs an adjustment to her medication, to say the least."

The guard nodded. He approached and stood beside Jacob. They both looked down at Bray. Bray's eyes developed tears. She wanted to say something, but when she opened her mouth, only laughter spilled out.

Jacob crossed his arms. He watched without emotion as the laughter grew louder. Bray's body shook.

"I'm going to need some more time with this one." Jacob was speaking as if to himself, or to some colleague. "We'll give her a sedative, relax her. Then go from there."

He exited, followed by the guard.

The moment the cell door shut, leaving Bray alone inside, the laughter stopped.

"You got what you wanted, didn't you?" she asked the entity. She remained on the floor, her back on the concrete, her eyes getting an uncomfortable view of the blinding, fluorescent lights that stared down on her in such an uncompromising way, she felt she might finally go insane.

"*I always get what I want*," the entity responded. With its words, Bray felt a vibration in her head.

If she did not come up with a plan soon, she feared her chances of getting out of this prison would elude her forever. Escape was always a wish in her heart, never a reality. Being sedated was not going to help matters. Plus, an "adjustment" to her medication would only dull her senses, not that she felt in control of them anyway.

There was something else Jacob had said. . .something about needing "more time" with her. What did that mean, she wondered. Did that mean he wanted time to get to know her. . .to gain her trust? Bray knew that was how they got patients to take meds. It had worked well in the psych ward— at least, it had worked for everyone except her, because she knew she wasn't mentally ill.

How many psychiatrists had she sat with throughout her times in psychiatric wards? They would begin by discussing the things Bray enjoyed: writing, books, animals. At some point, the doctor would broach the subject of medication. It seemed a manipulation, though she knew they meant well. For people who needed medications, it made sense. It just never could make sense for her, given she had a gift they didn't understand, and they refused to see it that way.

"They were trying to use you for their own—"

Bray flipped the script, interrupting the entity.

"For their own what?" she asked it. Maybe it was time she used their techniques, as if the entity were the patient and she the doctor. Or better yet, maybe it was time to use the technique Emily had taught her.

"Get to know your feelings," Emily had said. *"Like friends. Sit with them, let them tell you what they need."*

This had been a foreign concept to Bray. What had Emily meant? How did one befriend feelings when feelings were nebulous? They weren't *people*, or *animals*.

They were to be felt, sure. But befriended? How?

It dawned on her: she wasn't supposed to take it literally. It meant. . .get to know them, ask questions. Be curious rather than afraid of those feelings.

"*For their own devices. Don't you see? To further their own agenda*," the entity replied.

"What agenda is that?"

"*To hurt us.*"

"I see." Bray was beginning to understand where all of this was coming from. She took some deep breaths, tried to relax herself.

"I have a question," she continued.

"*What's that, child?*"

"What do you want from me?"

"*Ha!*" the entity laughed. "*What kind of question is that? I AM you!*"

"You are?" Bray asked innocently. Her body gradually felt softer, relaxing. She found that she could blink her eyes, wiggle her fingers and toes. The rest of her body still felt weighted down.

"*I am more you than you want to admit.*"

"Who are you? Help me understand."

The entity went quiet.

There was a pressure in Bray's head she did not realize was there until the entity silenced itself. Her mind's fogginess was slowly beginning to clear, as if morning had come and the day was beginning to reveal itself.

Suddenly her body shot up to sitting. Then, coming to stand, she felt the entity controlling it, moving her form across the floor, to the back wall.

"Did I say something to upset you?" she asked, suddenly rattled and confused.

She faced the wall. A surge of fear jolted through her bones, but the fear did not seem to be hers. It was like when she'd connected with animals in the past and could experience their emotions. She'd had to learn to discern her own emotions from theirs. She'd have to do the same here.

"It's okay," she said deliberately. "However you're feeling. Whatever you think you need to do."

"*I could kill you this instant*," the entity replied.

"I'm sure you could," Bray said, choosing her words carefully. She got the icky sensation that the entity was planning to bash her head into the wall-as many times as it took to end her life. "But then. . .what would come of you?"

The pressure that had come into her head now dropped into her neck. It began to tighten. She felt fear, felt her throat squeezing shut. Panic.

"I was only asking. . .," she continued, but she struggled to get words into a cohesive sentence. The squeezing was creating a choking sensation. She tried to raise her hands to her throat, but they would not move. Her eyes watered. Her head lightened and went hot. She shut her eyes, cringed. The only thing she knew, the only thing she had control over, was surrender. She'd have to let go, and trust herself.

"Asking. . .because. . .if you kill. . .me. . .won't. . .you. . .die, too?"

Breathing became too much effort. She felt herself grasping, in her mind, in her heart, for life. The squeezing around her throat went tighter, face hotter, eyes feeling as though they would bulge out of their sockets.

Then all at once, nothing.

\#

Bray felt a release. She fell to the

floor. Grabbing at her throat, she coughed, expelling little drops of blood onto the floor. Her lungs pumped air back up to her brain. She cried, lying in a fetal position, shaking.

After a while, she managed to calm herself. Her body felt lighter, no longer weighted down. She lay back, looked up at the ceiling. Tears rolled out from the sides of her eyes and down onto the floor. Her throat throbbed. Her head cleared. Never in her life had she felt as grateful as she felt in this very moment. . . Relieved. She was *ALIVE*. She laughed, even though it hurt her throat to laugh. This time, it was her who did the laughing. Nothing else was controlling her now.

This realization made her stop and wonder.

"Hello?" she called out in her mind. "Are you still there?"

In the very back corner of her brain, she sensed a faint pulse. No response, just a slight nudge. The entity was letting her know it was still there. And in that moment, she realized: the entity had never been a foreign object. It was a *part of* her, and it was a part of Bertan.

"A part of us all?" she asked herself quietly.

Bray sat up, amazed at how easy it was to have control over her own body. To experience the quiet in her mind. The weightlessness of having let go.

That was when clarity edged into her mind, followed by a voice:

"*Bray. . .if you can hear me. . .please tell me where you are.*"

It was her father.

"*Are you in Arizona? I will come and find you. Please. Help me find you.*"

A glimmer of hope! Her father had

reached out to her! Never in this lifetime would she believe him to do such a thing.

"Yes!" she replied, in her mind, with astonishing ease. "Please, Dad. I hear you. I'm in prison in Arizona."

No sooner did that hope rise than it quickly fell. The cell door opened. The guards had come to return her to Health Services.

Chapter Thirteen

Bertan

Bertan did not hesitate. There was no reason to wait, no point in spending one more day, one more moment, in this prison.

Not if he could get himself out.

And now he believed he could. He would.

He had projected himself into the warden's office a second time. It was morning and the windows across from the warden's desk blinked out between open curtains, revealing more of the desert landscape. Bertan looked to the horizon briefly, thought about his family, and turned to the warden, who was sitting at his desk eating a doughnut.

Once again, Bertan manipulated the warden's mind into opening Ruben's file. He wanted to find an address. He knew Ruben had a sister in Mexico. It was only right for her to know what had happened to her brother.

There on the screen, Bertan leaned in and saw the name of Ruben's emergency contact:

ELENA GEORGINA BARRERA SANCHEZ

"Mexico City," Bertan whispered to himself.

Had the prison contacted her? He imagined not. This he felt was the sadness of the world: humans didn't consider other humans enough to do something as civil as ensuring someone didn't die in police custody. That it happened all the time didn't make it right. He'd made plenty of similar mistakes, had held the lives of too many people in his hands and blown out their lights.

No more of that, he whispered. *Now I make it better.*

Bertan committed the woman's address to memory.

Convincing the warden to exit out of Ruben's file, he turned the focus on himself.

"Bertan Duarte," he whispered.

But the warden stopped. He dropped the doughnut onto a napkin beside the keyboard.

"Not again," he whispered. "I just took my meds. Why am I hearing things?"

Reaching over, the warden pulled up the sleeve of his shirt to reveal his forearm. Bertan hadn't had many chances to see those Embedicare implants in action. Most of the S-Corp workers he'd known either did not have one or, if they did, rarely used them.

The warden stared at his forearm for the longest time. Bertan assumed the man was about to send some text message, but the warden forcefully pulled his sleeve back down to hide his arm and turned away. He closed his eyes and rubbed his forehead. Bertan sensed tension in the room. There was no way he was going to get out of prison if he couldn't convince the warden to open his file in the computer.

He remembered the way the fugue had held *power* over him. How he had given it his power. How Bray had somehow removed the fugue from him. Now he was about to try something similar to get the warden to do what he wanted.

It suddenly felt wrong.

Bertan stepped away. As he watched the warden trembling in his chair, Bertan realized he was at a crossroads. Either he would use his gift to manipulate the warden, which felt like the old dirty work he was trying to quit, or he would have to give up. Let them keep him in prison until. . .when? The rest of his life? He didn't know. Was he to risk never seeing his family again, in order to be a more honorable man? Were there times in life when one had to choose the lesser of two evils? Was there a time to commit such acts for some greater good? What was the cost? For the warden. . .the cost would be a temporary concern that he was experiencing symptoms of some mental illness. For Bertan, a loss of family, a potential loss of life. And for his family, more loss.

Bertan could not fathom that.

He remembered back to the times his father used to teach him about leaders like Che Guevara, philosophers such as Socrates and Plato. How some would argue that it was morally unjust to commit wrongdoing even for a "greater good." Hadn't Bertan already committed a "wrongdoing" by assisting Bray with the Embedicare takeover? Did he regret that? No.

Bertan grinned. He had his answer.

"I am no Socrates," he whispered.

"I am Bertan Duarte. . .and if you ask me, right and wrong are always subject to opinion."

Bertan moved for the warden.

Standing beside the man, as gently as possible, Bertan placed his hand on the warden's upper back. He thought about warmth. He thought about Carmen. Gabriella. About freedom.

The warden stopped rubbing his forehead. His shoulders eased. Tears fell from his eyes and landed on the desk. Swiveling in Bertan's direction, he closed his eyes. Bertan released his hand from the warden's back and stood and faced the man. He knelt down and placed his hand atop the warden's. He didn't quite understand why he was doing this, but he just went along with what felt right in that moment.

All Bertan wanted was to lift the man's hand, place it on the keyboard, and use it to type in his name.

But the warden's hand did not move.

He sensed that communicating with the warden wasn't going to work this time. There had to be some other way.

Bertan glanced at the phone on the desk. He imagined it ringing, and someone on the other line instructing the warden to set Bertan free.

The phone remained silent.

Bertan considered an email, but the warden was unresponsive. He thought about someone entering the room, but the doors remained closed. As he glared at the warden, he noticed the man seemed in some kind of trance. Not fully awake, and not fallen to sleep.

As he looked into the man's face, for an instant he thought he saw himself. At least, the way the man sat there, as if waiting for something, made Bertan wonder if this was what he looked like when the fugue took over.

He reminded himself that he was not here in his physical form. His body was still back in his cell. He stood in the warden's office not as a ghost, but as a form of his own consciousness. He suddenly realized what had to be done.

Bertan turned and sat down in the chair, landing *in* the warden's body.

Suddenly, Bertan was thrusted back

through time and space, hit with a myriad of memories that were not his own. The warden's childhood, bleak and sadder than his own. The time he met his wife and got married. The family they created together. His absence from their lives due to his own mental illness.

Bertan was floored.

But he had work to do. He could not be sidetracked.

He turned. The chair turned with him. He was looking through the warden's eyes at the laptop screen. He felt a sense of freedom mixed with awe. He watched as he willed the warden's arms to lift as if they were his own. Disorienting as shit, but it also felt *good*.

On the screen was the prison database, which had remained open with a blank search bar where the cursor blinked. Bertan typed in his name.

Bertan's file opened on the screen.

The photo was one Bertan did not remember being taken. He was wearing his prison-issued t-shirt and a wiry smile that he almost didn't recognize. It was him, but not quite him.

Glancing over the file, Bertan noticed a court date in the lower right corner: October 2040. That was months from now.

Bertan wanted to get angry, but he couldn't allow it. He had learned that intense emotion, such as fear, only pulled him out of these psychic projections. He had to remain neutral, no different than all the times he'd dissociated when he killed a man. Or a beef.

"I need a release date," Bertan whispered.

He paused for a moment. What reason could he put into the file, so there would be no questioning from guards or anyone else that might impede his release.

"For severe mental illness," Bertan whispered. "Incurable, debilitating mental illness. . .not suited for a prison setting."

Bertan scrolled down the screen and found a Notes section. He typed:

PRISONER GIVEN COMPASSIONATE RELEASE DUE TO SIGNIFICANT MENTAL ILLNESS.

Bertan paused and reviewed his work. He smiled, took a deep breath. But he wasn't out of the woods yet. Next he had to actually get them to *release* him. And how did the warden go about that? What was the protocol?

Bertan sat back in the chair. He scrolled through the warden's mind, searching for the answer.

"Ah-ha!" he said.

With the warden's hand, Bertan reached for the phone beside the laptop, picked up the receiver.

"Get in here, please," he said, then hung up. He was jarred by the sound of the warden's voice, midwestern, without an accent like his own.

A guard, six-foot-four with thick arms and legs and a commanding presence, entered the room. Nervous that the guard might find out a prisoner had projected himself into the body of the warden, Bertan's hands shook. He slipped them under the desk, gulped, and cleared his voice.

"We're going to release one of the prisoners early," Bertan said.

"Who?" the guard asked, frowning.

"Bertan Duarte."

"May I ask why, sir?"

It was working. The guard looked down at him but did not seem alarmed by the man he was looking at.

"Pretty severe mental illness," Bertan replied, reminding himself he was acting as the warden. "I want him out of here."

"Where do you want him transferred?" the guard asked.

Bertan didn't want to be transferred. Bertan wanted to go home.

The warden took a deep breath and glanced up at the guard.

"Just give him some money and put him on a bus," Bertan replied, pausing. He thought about Ruben's sister, Elena. "Send him down to Mexico. He can be their problem."

Without argument, the guard left the office. Bertan fell back into the chair and let out a sigh. It was over. He had done it. Feeling the warden's eyes tearing up, as if he himself were crying, Bertan shook himself back to the task at hand.

He didn't want to be in this man's body any longer.

Bertan turned in the chair and stepped back out. He felt woozy, light, like a balloon full of helium. Suddenly he lost his footing. The room began to dissipate into dots of color gradually overcome by darkness. Before long, he was back inside himself again, crying with relief on the cell floor.

Chapter Fourteen

Bray

Later that day when the guards had come to get her, Bray had allowed them to cuff her hands behind her back and carry her up to Health Services. There was no fighting. The entity, though still present, had subsided. This gave her the clear mind to reach back out to Tori, to find out what was going on.

"*They've placed us in solitary*," Tori had said.

Solitary cells were at capacity, Tori told her. Twenty prisoners had not only chosen to go on hunger strike, they had simply refused to move. This led to the guards battering and injuring the prisoners, many of whom had ended up in Health Services. The guards who had beaten prisoners were relieved of their duties and sent home.

As Bray was led through the halls toward the elevator, she'd heard the faint whisperings of her counterparts: "*until all beings are free*."

She couldn't discern if the voices were in her mind, or if the prisoners were actually whispering.

"I'm being taken to Health Services, too," Bray had replied to Tori. The guards led her into the elevator. One of them was clasping her tightly by the arm. "They're going to try some new treatment on me. . .which means I may not be able to communicate for much longer."

And that was all.

Bray was now lying in one of the last open beds in the clinic, her wrists strapped down to the bed with brown leather straps. She'd been in here enough times to recognize some of the regulars, who'd sat up in their beds and watched her arrival quietly. The room was bustling with nurses trying to get the patients to eat food with their medications. But the patients were not cooperating. Two extra guards walked the floor, eyeing the prisoners, radios in hand. Bray could feel the tension in the room. Only the sound of beeping monitors cut through it; otherwise the air was thick with it. It felt as though one of the guards might lose control at any moment and hurl himself at one of the prisoners.

In a moment of desperation, Bray closed her eyes and imagined Jacob. If anyone could get her out of here, it was him. Perhaps if she communicated telepathically with him, he would believe her. He would understand then that she had a gift. And maybe then he would stop forcing medication on her.

"Jacob. . .please," Bray pleaded in her mind. "This is Bray Hoffman. I am not what you think me to be. I have a gift. If you can hear me, please, listen. Do your job and let me out of here."

It was the last thing she could do before a nurse approached her bed, revealed a syringe full of clear liquid, and injected it into Bray's upper arm.

Chapter Fifteen

Bertan

Bertan sat at the edge of his bed, waiting. The uniform hung close to his skin, scratching at it. He couldn't wait to take the damn thing off, get some real clothes.

The cell door opened. In walked two guards, one holding a bag, which he tossed on the floor.

"Get dressed," the guard mumbled. It was the same six-foot, hulking guard he had seen in the warden's office the day before.

Bertan grabbed the bag and opened it. Inside, he saw the teal shirt and tan pants he had arrived in, clothing he'd taken from the garment rack in Ruben's office back at the S-Corp facility. Before he had been detained. His breath stopped. He'd completely forgotten about stealing the clothes that day. The memory sent a sudden pain from his eyes downward into his chest. It stuck there like a hard, unmoving darkness. If only Ruben could be leaving with him.

Bertan dropped the prison-issued pants, let them fall to the floor. He kicked off the shoes they'd given him and quickly slid on the tan trousers, feeling a sense of power as he did so. The t-shirt he yanked up and over his head, tossing it on top of the discarded pants. His chest opened and a sense of relief overcame him. Buttoning up the teal shirt, he felt a weight lift.

The bag now empty of clothes, he noticed his ID and. . .a necklace. He pulled both out, slid the ID into his pants pocket. The chain and pendant he held up before his eyes, watching as his daughter's clay thumbprint dangled before him like a carrot. Bertan smiled and clipped it on around his neck.

"You're coming with us," the guard said.

Bertan knew what was coming. It felt surreal. A part of him feared they were just playing some joke and weren't going to take the release seriously.

The second guard walked out into the hall. Bertan stepped to the cell door where the husky guard stood without expression.

"You're being released today."

It had worked! Had it? Was it that simple? Maybe it was best not to get his hopes up, not just yet. He'd been tricked before. Good things like this didn't happen to men like him.

The guards led him through the halls to an elevator. They pushed him inside. One got in with him, the hulky one. The other remained where he was, watching Bertan absently as the doors closed. Bertan felt the elevator rise. He began to shake with anticipation. When the doors opened again, the guard led him out, where a line of offices led to the metal detectors and an increasing number of windows. Bertan winced at the light they let in.

It took about an hour for a worker to process the paperwork for Bertan's release. The worker asked him if he had family to come pick him up. No, he said. His family was in Honduras. All he wanted was to get back to Honduras and never leave. The hulky guard bent down and whispered something into the worker's ear. The worker rolled his eyes. After a few clicks of his mouse, a shuffling and stamping of papers, the worker made a call. He ordered a taxi for Bertan and gave him two hundred dollars for the taxi and a bus ticket. The taxi would drive him to the nearest city, Houston, and drop him off at a bus station. From there, he was instructed to take the bus into Mexico so he could be "Mexico's problem," as the worker put it.

Bertan spent a half hour sitting, cuffed, in a chair, until the hulky guard came and got him. The guard walked beside him as he crossed the lobby, exited the main doors, and stepped into the outside world. Bertan felt electricity surge through his bloodstream, as if he were being awakened and jolted back to life.

The doors closed behind him. One step forward. Another. A few more. On either side of him, the chain-link fences watched in resignation as he passed. The ground beneath his feet was hard, but alive, not as unforgiving as the place he'd just been. And the air, it was warm and stale and he breathed it deeply, tears releasing from his eyes.

As he picked up his pace, Bertan felt his heart tremble. This was *it*. This was *real*.

One hundred feet ahead, the gate awaited him. One guard on either side, rifles strapped to their backs. Bertan turned his gaze to the fence, thought about his father, wondered if the man would visit him again.

He stepped up to the gate. Closed his eyes. Waited. The beat of his heart paused as he strained for his escort to unclasp his cuffs. A click here. A rattle, keys jingling. His wrists released. His arms fell to his sides. The guards shut themselves back inside the fenced-in perimeter of the prison. They were in, he was out.

A taxi waited for him.

Bertan could hardly believe it. Was he projecting? Was he still somehow inside his cell, imagining all of this? He walked up to the taxi, grazed the side of the driver's door with his fingers. He *felt* it. He bent down and glanced inside. The driver was a young Hispanic man with long, black hair down to his shoulders.

"Houston, yes?" the driver asked.

Bertan nodded and got into the car. His chest tightened. The driver put the car into drive and hurried south along an expanse of road that, for miles and miles, seemed to lead to nothing. It would be another hour before he saw the city of Houston.

Chapter Sixteen

Kage

A plan had been set in motion. It was what Kage thought of as mass in motion, something Dennis had taught him when he was being homeschooled back in Meeteetse. How momentum was directly proportionate to an object's mass and velocity. Something like that. Since the Embedicare takeover and the exposure of S-Corp's dirtiest secrets, Kage and Trevor had cultivated a small following of citizens, and over time, that following had grown. Now they had representatives in almost every one of the twenty-nine remaining cities in the country, ready to act.

The momentum would lead to one defining moment: they were planning a series of marches throughout the nation, all on the same day, to call for Bray's freedom and the freedom of the billions of farmed animals being held captive by the industry. The marches were a bold move, but the momentum had necessitated them.

Kage looked around at the group now sitting in Elliott's apartment. Elliott, leaning back in his office chair, squeezed his prized T-rex toy so tightly Kage thought its head might pop off. Lana sat on the floor beside Kage. Outside it was mid-morning and the sun was hiding behind thick cloud cover. Kage was supposed to be at work, but he'd made Chad aware of their

plans to march. Chad, of course, wanted
nothing to do with any marching, but
because his son had died as a result of the
fertilizer disaster, he wasn't going to
stop them.

Emily, Dennis and Virgil were sitting
together on the couch. Trevor was sitting
in a chair beside the couch, opposite of
where Kage had been standing. Kage couldn't
remain still. He was too excited about this
march.

"I want to give a speech," Kage
announced, his eyes shooting over to
Trevor.

"Good idea," Lana agreed from her place
on the floor. "Talk about your
parents. . .how they went missing after
they saved some farmed animals and began
documenting the disappearances of other
animal activists."

Trevor said nothing. He merely smiled
at Kage, as if in awe.

Virgil cleared his throat. Everyone
looked over at him.

"Listen," he said. "Dennis and I have
been talking. We've decided to sit this one
out. We both like it here in Red Lodge, and
our time as activists. . .it's over. It's
time for kids like Kage, and Elliott, to
take up the lead and do the work."

Kage glanced over at Virgil, feeling
deep respect for the man.

"We are very proud of you, Kage,"
Virgil continued. "And we think you'll do
the right thing."

Kage observed the people around him,
some he'd known since he was a teenager.
How close they had all become, camaraderie
that comes with a shared loss. How they'd
all been through so much. How loss could
either bring people together or tear them
apart. These people had become his family.

For better or for worse. He had slowly been coming to terms with the reality that he'd never see his parents again. The friendships and bonds he developed with this group of people had, recently, eased the pain of such realization. He was beginning to feel that never seeing his parents again was something he could live with.

This was what he had to march for, no matter the outcome. For his parents. For Bray. For family.

"For the future," he said aloud. "For the animals."

Everyone nodded in unison.

"We'll make signs!" Elliott's voice rose. He jumped up from his chair, started for the door.

"Where are you going?" Kage asked, turning to him in amusement.

"To get supplies. We've got work to do."

Chapter Seventeen

Bray

A heaviness hung over her. Bray lost track of space and time. No way of knowing how long before they'd give her another injection, or if they'd already done it. She found she had little agency to care. Everything was so still. She lay there in the medical unit, listening to her heart beat slowly through her chest. A muffled sound. . .thu-ump. . .thu-ump. . .ump. . .ump. . .quieter and quieter. If she lifted her head, it only came tumbling back onto the pillow.

When she opened her eyes, blurred vision. Scrambles of color. . .blues mixing with white, brown, beige. Movement along the periphery, no idea what. Took too much energy to care. To be concerned. Sounds didn't register. A click here. A mumble there. No ability to translate or interpret.

In the very back recesses of her mind, behind her memory, in the corner of her consciousness, came a string of voices:

"*She's not responding.*" Bray recognized this voice but could not pull up a name to go with it.

"*They've sedated her, I bet.*"

A scent of bleach and cleaning products burned her nostrils.

"*We must keep going. They're losing control.*" This voice was very masculine.

"*So many of us have gotten injured,*

though."

"*Don't fight them. It's painful, I
know. I am so tired and weak from hunger,
yet Bray has been on strike longer than us.
We do this for her. For the animals.*"

"*For the animals!*" voices called in
unison.

"Ow!" Bray whispered, reaching for her
head. Her arm was so heavy it fell back
before it could get there. The voices had
caused a shiver in her brain, an odd
feeling of a quake between her ears that
made her feel nauseous for a moment.

Or was it the sedative?

Who knew what was what anymore. Bray,
completely despondent, had no more ability
to respond. She couldn't put words together
in her mind. Wishing she could reply to the
voices, just alert enough to know that it
was the prisoners who were communicating,
she formulated what she thought was a full
sentence:

"Thank you for what you're doing."

But what came out instead was a bunch
of gloopity-gloop.

"*What was that, Bray?*"

"*She's trying to speak.*"

Bray's mind went quiet, as if she'd
been given the floor.

Then, another voice entered. Firm. At
the forefront of her mind rather than in
the corner. As if in the room with her.

"*Bray.*"

The voice came from *outside*, not from
within the prison. This was the only thing
she could tell for sure. And it was male,
familiar.

"*I know where you are. I'm on my way.*"

Bray's eyes closed. Tears rolled out of
them as she released a sizable exhale.

Please. She wanted to say. *Stop them
from medicating me.*

She wanted to say more. The sedative was too strong. Gradually, she sunk down into a deep slumber.

Chapter Eighteen

Cole

As the jetliner cut through thick cloud cover, turbulence pushed Cole back in his seat. He gripped the armrests, clenched his teeth. Outside the windows the clouds puffed in dark-gray plumes. The other passengers on the commercial flight were asleep. How they could sleep through this kind of turbulence, he did not know.

Cole sat leaning forward, on edge. He'd received a message from Bray the day prior. It was all in his head, of course, and he preferred to believe he wasn't losing his mind. He couldn't afford to assume he was imagining voices. He had to believe he was hearing his daughter's voice. It sounded like her. And so he caught a flight immediately.

As they came within twenty miles of Phoenix, the plane broke free of a rainstorm. Blue sky revealed itself, as if it had not just been raining at all. Cole released his grip on the armrests and glanced outside. The earth below was brown and abandoned, save the city-which, as they neared it, popped up like an eyesore. There was no transition from suburb to city. No suburbs anymore. These days, when he flew, he watched miles and miles of unfettered land crawl toward the nearest city, then stop abruptly. Massive skyscrapers and apartment buildings now ravaged the land. The approach felt like coming upon a forest of tall, silver trees after seeing nothing but dead earth.

After landing, Cole hurried to the taxis waiting at passenger pickup. He hadn't checked a bag. He'd brought nothing with him but a jacket for the flight.

The taxi drove him seven minutes north to Arizona State Correctional, an elongated, two-level building larger than the Pentagon, but not looking much different. Cole was grateful the drive took only a few minutes, for the streets outside his taxi window were littered with tents, people sleeping on sidewalks and in sleeping bags. It made him shudder, how much of this country he had forgotten about or ignored due to the ease of living inside his own bubble.

"Is this really it?" he wondered as they pulled up to the front gates of the prison. Cole stared at the ominous fences, at the sign confirming he was in the right place. He couldn't believe they'd been hiding all those animal activists, and his daughter, in such clear sight. Right outside the city of Phoenix.

A guard from the front doors approached the gate. Cole stepped up to the fence and glanced in at the man's eyes, which he could hardly see beneath his face covering.

"Cole Hoffman," Cole said. "I've got a meeting with Warden Fisher."

"ID," the guard said plainly.

Cole pulled out his wallet, showed the man his driver's license through the fence.

With a set of keys, the guard began unlocking the gate. He walked a few feet away, hit a button on a tall utility pole, and the gate rolled open.

As Cole entered the building, he felt the constriction immediately. Narrow hallways. No windows. Metal detectors where he was instructed to take off his belt, his shoes, and remove everything from pockets before walking through. On the other side, he hurried to put his shoes on and buckle his belt. Anxious, heart trembling, he followed the guard down the hallway to a row of offices. Nowhere did Cole see any prisoners. He figured that was intentional.

The guard stopped at an office, where a steel door was propped open with a doorstop. Cole peered inside. An older man stood behind a pristine, white, adjustable-height desk.

"Come in, Mr. Hoffman," the man called. "Have a seat."

Cole cleared his throat. He entered the office, stood before two red chairs. The warden was exceptionally tall. He approached Cole, shook his hand.

"You arrive here okay?" asked Warden Andrew Fisher, his breath smelling of vinegar and cigarettes. As pleasantries went, this seemed inane to Cole. He was here, wasn't he?

"Yes," Cole replied. "Now about my daughter."

"Yes." The warden nodded. He returned behind the desk, pressed a button causing it to lower. He sat down in the desk chair and looked at Cole.

"You see, Mr. Hoffman. . .we can't simply release your daughter."

"I understand that. But I'm here to ask if you'd make an exception, on account of her mental illness."

"She committed a federal crime. . .computer hacking and abuse, the file says. She hasn't even been given a trial date."

"She's a minor," Cole argued.

"True," Andrew said, pausing. "Does Mrs. Hoffman know about this? Does she know you're here?"

"No." Cole shuffled in his chair. It was stiff, rigid. "We're. . .divorced."

"I see. What is it you expect from me? To release your daughter?"

"That would be ideal, yes." Cole grew annoyed, took a deep breath. This wasn't going to be easy. "Can I at least see her?"

"You want to visit Bray?"

"Of course. She is my daughter."

"She's in Health Services right now." The warden tapped at a keyboard, his eyes shifting back and forth between Cole and his laptop screen.

"Why? And how come no one informed me?" Cole leaned forward. His hands clenched into tight balls.

"Take that up with your ex-wife."

"Listen, I just want to see her. If she's in medical, then I want to know she's okay."

The warden came around to lean his backside against the front of his desk, a few feet from Cole.

"She's sedated," he replied.

"What?" Cole stood up.

"From what I understand, she's not responding to the medication our psychiatrist administered."

"What medication?" Cole asked, but he knew what the warden was going to say.

"We gave her an injection to treat the schizophrenia."

"She's not schizophrenic," Cole interrupted firmly.

"What are you. . .a politician *and* a psychiatrist?" Andrew smirked.

"No."

"Then let us do our work."

They both went quiet. Andrew locked eyes with Cole, and his were stern, judging. The man looked Cole over, exhaled, and spoke.

"We'll have her moved to one of our private clinic rooms. You can have five minutes with her."

"I appreciate that," Cole said, pushing his hands down into his pockets.

The warden turned back to the desk, lifted the receiver from a desk phone, made a call.

"I'll have the guard take you over," he said, returning behind the desk.

Cole nodded, started for the door.

"One more thing, Mr. Hoffman."

Cole paused, waited.

"You get us the location of the other eco-terrorists. . .the ones responsible for this Embedicare takeover, then we can discuss the release of your daughter."

Chills ran up Cole's back. Who did this man work for, the state prison system, or S-Corp? He knew the answer. Cole shivered, tried not to let it show. He wouldn't even look back at the warden.

The door opened. There stood the guard, motioning Cole into the hallway. Cole obliged, wanting to get out of the warden's office as fast as he could.

Chapter Nineteen

Bertan

The bus to Nuevo Loredo left Houston late that afternoon. Bertan kept to himself, catching up on sleep in a chair inside the bus station, until it was time to board the bus. He had nothing on him, save his identification and the money the prison had provided, which after this bus fare would only be twenty-five dollars.

It would take six hours to get to Mexico. From Nuevo Loredo, he would change buses again and travel further south into Mexico City. He had one stop to make before finding his way home to Honduras. He had no idea, at this moment, while boarding the bus and taking a seat in the middle section, how he would get home. But if he could get himself into the U.S. in the first place, surely he could get himself home now.

An old woman came and sat beside Bertan. She had coffee-colored skin, wrinkled and aged. She smiled at him. She was missing her teeth. He smiled back and turned to the window. Outside, the heat was rising, and beyond the bus station he saw the high-rise buildings that made up the city of Houston. The sight of so much concrete made him anxious. He wanted to get away from Americans, lest someone somehow recognize him, call the police, have him thrown back in prison.

The bus jolted to a start, moving down a side street, twisting and turning its way onto the highway. Bertan's shoulders had been tight and squeezed up near his neck. As the bus traveled farther south, away from the city, he allowed himself to relax.

He closed his eyes. The image of the cell where he'd been confined popped into his head. He didn't want to see it, but the image seemed imprinted on his mind, as if this time he'd spent in prison would never leave him. Always it would be a part of his fabric, the isolation that made him cringe now when he was around people.

Shaking his head, he turned his thoughts to that girl. Bray. Had it not been for her, he didn't think he could have gotten himself out of prison. It seemed supernatural, and hard to believe, but it had happened. He had to tell her. . .to find out if she thought maybe her abilities or strange voodoo gift, whatever the hell it was, had *rubbed off* on him. Was that what she meant when she said they were "linked"?

"Bray," he thought, trying to *send* her the thought. He didn't know her last name. He concentrated on Bray, what he remembered her looking like. Long, brown hair hovering over a young girl's short, heavy frame. Puffy cheeks, large, brown eyes. He thought about Arizona, where she'd said she was imprisoned.

"Bray?" he called from inside his mind.

There was no response for a while. Then, he sensed a slight moan. Then, silence.

Gradually, Bertan felt pulled out of his body. It was a strange sensation, one moment in a bouncing seat on a bus, the next into air, like flying. Within seconds, his vision was floating through hallways

that reminded him all too much of the
prison he'd just left.

But he could not find Bray. He couldn't
reach her. Her mind was cut off, not
available to him. Did she no longer want to
talk to him? He wouldn't have blamed her.

"Bray. I am here to help you," he said.

Another moan. It seemed she was trying
but couldn't speak.

Switching gears, Bertan searched the
prison for administrative offices. For the
warden. He floated past a pair of offices,
doors closed, people talking inside. At the
third door, he felt a strong sensation in
his chest, like the stinging of a bee. He
paused. On the outside wall he saw a metal
name plate:

Andrew Fisher
WARDEN

"Ah, ha!" he whispered.

With ease, Bertan floated into the
office, seemingly through the walls. He was
beginning to get used to the disorienting
feeling.

The warden's office was empty. Bertan's
powers were of little use to him if he
could not find another human to link up
with, as he began to think of it.

Removing himself from the room, he
dropped down through layers of concrete and
steel, into a unit of cells that he
recognized right away. Solitary
confinement. It was completely full with
prisoners. He heard them calling out,
mumbling, whimpering. It made him sick to
his stomach to hear so much of it and to
feel as if it were a part of him. He
wondered if this was what Bray felt, too.

He pulled away.

Bertan searched. Bray was nowhere to be

found, at least not in solitary confinement or any of the individual prison cells.

Had they released her?

Suddenly he felt a hard nudge. Something pushing at his back.

Someone was trying to get his attention.

Bertan opened his eyes, felt dizzy from the sudden shift back down into his physical body.

"Identification," a man said.

The bus had stopped. A man was standing over him wearing Homeland Security emblems and black police gear. The old woman who'd been sitting beside him was gone. Bertan blinked his eyes, looked out the window. They had arrived at the border. Six hours had passed within minutes. How could that happen? Had he fallen back into a fugue again? Was he starting to lose track of time? Ruben had warned him it could get worse.

"Sir," the officer pressed. "Do you speak English?"

"Yes," Bertan replied. He hurried to pull his identification out of his pocket. He lifted it up to the officer.

The patrol officer took his license, turned it over in his hand, looking at it closely. The officer shifted his sight to his forearm, where Bertan imagined the man was doing a search under Bertan's name. Bertan sat still, his mouth all the sudden very dry. Sweat gathered along his back, the back of his neck, his forehead. He'd forgotten how hot it was down south.

"Headed back home, are we?"

"Yes, sir," Bertan replied.

The officer handed back his identification. Bertan let out an exhale.

The officer looked him over, held his gaze. Bertan refrained from saying anything.

Finally, the officer continued on down the aisle, checking the remaining passengers in the back of the bus. Bertan waited for the officer to clear out and the bus to continue into Mexico. Soon, he'd reach Mexico City, where he'd try to track down Ruben's sister.

First, he had to find Bray. There was no reason he couldn't find a way to get her out, the way he had done so for himself. It was the least he could do.

Chapter Twenty

Bray

    Rising above herself, Bray witnessed the prison lockdown. Prisoners shouted, louder and louder, not violent, and in unison. Bray felt herself a part of it, realizing she could rise above because she was a part of something bigger, something greater, than herself, than her physical body. This uprising, the prisoners coming together to be heard, was part of the grand symphony, the consciousness that held all things together, that Bray now felt herself a part of, but only along with everyone else. Only could she be in this space because of everyone else—Alice, Rhea, Kage, Tori, Valerie, the other prisoners. She had a quick vision of people she didn't recognize and had never met. . .and she knew they were the ones whose voices she'd heard when she first entered this prison, prior to medication. They had returned. Elisha, Tim, Mateo. . .together, all linked to one common goal, united, somehow "carrying" Bray, and Bray carrying them. A kind of God, if you will—not Bray alone, but everyone, together, like pieces of a puzzle finally finding their way back to one another to create the whole.

    Exhausted, Bray sank back down into her body. Each time she tried to rise above, connect or project herself, it lasted but a few moments and then became too much for her sedated mind. She'd run out of steam.

Bray turned her head to one side, facing away from the entrance to Health Services. When she opened her eyes, her vision remained blurred. It was as though she were under water with her eyes open, seeing only vague shapes, some still, some moving.

There, among all the abstract, cloudy shapes, something began to unfold. Or come together. Bray blinked her eyes, trying to clear her vision. She was still awake, she *thought*.

Slowly, an image appeared. It was clear as day. Not foggy. Not confusing. Not like the abstract shapes around it. Bray tried lifting her head, feeling complete curiosity, but she had no energy to lift the weight of her head off the pillow. She let it drop, her gaze remaining on the figure as it neared her.

A man. Short stature. Wearing beige slacks. A teal dress shirt. When he approached the bed, she recognized his eyes.

"Bertan?" she said. She thought she'd said it, but she'd only spoken his name in her mind.

"*Yes, it is me*," he replied, but his mouth did not move. It only smiled down on her, then turned into a subtle frown. His eyes narrowed. A crease developed between them. He looked. . .upset.

"*What have they done to you?*" he asked.

"I'm. . .sedated," she responded, struggling to form words.

Bertan placed his hand on hers as it lay there strapped to the bedrails. She could feel a very soft warmth. She had a question for him.

"How are you here? Are you. . ."

"*I'm not dead, if that's what you're*

thinking."

A sudden shock passed through her mind and left.

"*When you entered my mind, when you said we were linked*," he said, looking down to her, "*something happened, and now I have this gift*."

"Gift?"

"*I can come and see you, with my mind. I was able to visit my family in Honduras, too*."

Bray's eyes lifted.

"*I can even change things*."

"What do you mean?" Bray found the words were coming a little easier.

"*I got myself out of prison*."

"How?"

Bertan turned his head. He was looking at something. Bray shifted her eyes in the same direction but saw only shapes coming toward her bed. Her eyes watered as she noticed the very concrete, well-defined image of Bertan standing beside her bed as if he were in the room. His body stood out to her like an image superimposed atop a blurred background.

"*Oh, no*," he whispered.

"What?"

Two shapes, one the color of forest green, the other white, came to stand by her bed. Bertan pulled his hand away from her, looked at the shapes, then down at her arm.

"What's happening?" she asked, growing frightened because she could hardly see the shapes standing over her.

Bertan did not respond. Instead, he turned and faced one of the shapes. He whispered something. Bray couldn't hear. Her heart went still.

The shapes stood there for ages. It felt as though everything in the room had stopped.

Bertan whispered again.

Eventually, the shapes went away. Gone.

Bray watched as Bertan turned back to her.

"What was that?" she asked.

"*They were about to inject you with something.*"

The medication! she thought instantly. Had Bertan convinced them not to medicate her? Had they been able to see him?

"*We don't have much time,*" he continued. The image of Bertan began to fade. "*I'm going to get—ou—owe—t—of—ere.*"

She could barely make out what he'd said before his image disappeared completely. It sounded as though he said he was going to get out. Or he was going to get *her* out.

Chapter Twenty-One

Cole

Cole sat waiting in an office not much different from any doctor's office. Where an examination bed would be, the space was empty. No computer or laptop. Only the chair he sat in, a desk beside him, and a desk chair that was bolted into the floor.

He gulped.

A steel door across from him pushed open. Cole stood up. A guard entered and stood to the side. Behind him appeared the foot of a bed. Two nurses pushed the bed into the room, set it in that empty space, and retreated into the hallway.

Lying there, strapped to the bed, was his daughter. He could not tell if she was conscious.

"Are the restraints necessary?" Cole demanded.

The guard adjusted her bed, placing it perpendicular to where Cole stood. The guard did not answer him. He checked her restraints, stepped back, and remained in the corner, unmoving.

"Can I be alone with my daughter, please?"

The guard cleared his throat. He met eyes with Cole. Cole saw no expression in the two black dots that stared back at him.

Cole rolled his eyes, then approached the bed. He didn't want to see his daughter this way, unable to move her arms. A part of him wanted to avert his eyes, look at the wall. Bending toward her, he intently watched her chest rise and fall. He placed his hand gently on her belly. He stared closely at her, forcing himself to not look away. He always believed his daughter was beautiful. It was only the restraints, her hair wet with sweat, the prison uniform, that made him nearly crumble at the sight of her.

"Bray, it's your dad," he spoke softly.

Bray's eyes rolled over and up. For a moment he thought she might be looking at him, but she was looking past him. He wanted to cry.

"Just nod if you understand me," he said.

Bray's eyes closed. Slowly, her head moved. Up. Down.

Cole smiled. He rubbed the wetness in his eyes, looked up at the guard.

"Can I see the doctor?" he asked. "Or whomever is in charge of the clinic?"

The guard, not moving his eyes from their place fixed on Bray's bed, reached up and pressed a handheld radio attached to his chest, hidden beneath some kind of protective gear. Cole wondered if the guard really needed that protection in a place like this, a prison Cole understood only held non-violent offenders.

Cole stood beside Bray's bed, holding her hand. Because of the sedation, there wasn't much communicating with her.

Eventually, a man in civilian clothing entered the room. He nodded at the guard and let the door close behind him. He appeared to match Cole in age, and was slightly shorter, with a significant shadow of facial hair, a thick, black goatee and glasses.

"Mr. Hoffman," the man greeted him,

walking over with hand outstretched. "My name is Jacob Stalzky. I'm the psychiatrist treating Bray."

Cole shook hands with the man, watching intently as Jacob walked over and sat in the desk chair.

"Have a seat," Jacob began, nodding at the chair Cole had been sitting in until a moment ago.

Cole did so.

"About my daughter," he began, wanting to get the first word in.

"The warden and I have spoken," Jacob replied firmly. He set a blue folder down on the desk, opened it and looked through it.

"How can you justify keeping a minor in a prison like this?" Cole asked.

"It was at the direction of Mrs. Hoffman. I assumed that was your wife."

"Ex-wife," he corrected.

"Whatever the case may be." Jacob went on speaking, but Cole stopped listening. He was distracted by a disruption in the room, although the psychiatrist seemed not to notice it. Behind the doctor, an image appeared, startling Cole. It was a man, Hispanic, short, with green eyes.

Cole had never actually seen a ghost before, but the only sense he could make of this apparition was that the place must be haunted. *Was this real?*

"Uh. . ." Cole started to speak.

The ghost lifted a finger to its mouth, encouraging Cole to remain quiet. Cole's eyes widened in surprise.

"Mr. Hoffman, are you okay?" Jacob seemed to have noticed his reaction.

Cole turned to the guard. The guard's eyes were locked on Bray's bed. They had not moved. Was he the only one who could see this ghost? Was he losing his mind?

Cole began to raise his arm to point toward the ghost.

"*Don't*," came a man's voice. The ghost's mouth had not moved. The voice had entered Cole's mind directly, not through his ears.

Cole shook. His stomach tightened in knots. What kind of place was this?

"*Bray's father, I'm a friend of Bray's. My name is Bertan. I'm here to get her out. But you need to stay quiet.*"

Cole raised his eyes again. He didn't know whether to scream or freeze.

"Mr. Hoffman," Jacob said. He stood up. The ghost approached Jacob's side. It whispered something into his ear. The doctor froze. Cole watched something register on his face, as the doctor seemed to understand what had been said. A lightbulb went on, perhaps.

Cole elected to keep his mouth shut, despite how wrong it felt to do so. If he gave the psychiatrist an inkling that he might also be mentally ill, he would never get his daughter out of here.

Jacob sat back down. He flipped through the file, then closed it. He sat for the longest time, staring into space.

Meanwhile, the ghost stepped back. It remained standing beside the wall. Cole looked to Jacob, then back up at the ghost. Its eyes had moved over to Bray's bed. Its head slightly downturned, a smile gradually appeared on its face. Faint, but oddly warm.

"Mr. Hoffman," Jacob spoke finally. "I don't know why. . .but I am going to go ahead and approve the release of your daughter."

Cole and the guard simultaneously shifted in the doctor's direction. Without looking over at the guard, Cole could hear the sound of his body armor moving.

"What?" Cole asked. He wasn't sure he'd heard the man right.

"She *is* a minor, that is true. And she is clearly suffering in this prison," Jacob said, his body still, as if frozen in place, while he spoke.

Cole, eyes watering in disbelief, glanced up at the ghost.

"We'll let you take her home, tomorrow. Give it overnight for the sedation to wear off," Jacob explained, whispering to himself, "I can't believe I'm saying this."

"You're doing the right thing," Cole assured him, a deep sense of relief rushing through his body, into his chest. It took effort to remain composed.

"You can pick her up in the morning."

That was it. Cole was out of the prison before he could completely grasp what had happened back there in that room. That ghost. He was the only one who had seen it. Had it been it real? He couldn't be so sure, but he had a feeling the prison was haunted. He would return in the morning, but he had to reduce his expectations, not get his hopes up that they'd release his daughter with such ease.

Chapter Twenty-Two

Bertan

Bertan was riding in the back of a Mexican taxi cab when he projected himself into the Arizona prison and found Bray in that medical room. He assumed the man in there with her-the one with similar brown eyes-was her father.

Bertan had managed to allow her father the ability to see him, while simultaneously blocking the guard and the psychiatrist from viewing him. He had attempted to enter the psychiatrist's consciousness the way he had with the warden, but he was blocked. He hoped that what he had done was enough to set Bray free.

His taxi rolled to a stop outside a house in Colonia del Valle, a middle-class neighborhood with two-story apartment buildings and businesses lining the streets. It reminded him of the more affluent neighborhoods of Tegucigalpa, in Honduras. The house outside the taxi windows was tri-leveled, stacked like boxes on top of one another. Beige brick, windows on every floor, and a balcony resting atop the second floor. Two concrete walls lined the sidewalk, separating the driveway and the house from the street. Between them, a tall, white, steel structure with a cut-out door stood blocking entrance to the home.

Bertan handed the taxi driver the last

of his funds and got out, letting the car door shut softly. The taxi sped off. Bertan found a buzzer outside the door, hesitated, and pressed in on it.

A dog barked. Scratching sounds came at the door on the other side. Bertan stepped back, startled. Someone, a woman, came out into the hidden courtyard between the house and the sidewalk and yelled for the dog to stop. The scratching ceased. Bertan stood beneath a blinding sun, feeling increasingly exhausted. He was relieved to be out of prison, and he was also completely spent.

The door cracked open. The woman, seemingly close to Ruben's age, with long, curly black hair, peered at him.

"*Sí?*"

"My name is Bertan Duarte," he spoke. "I am a friend of your brother. . .Ruben Sanchez."

The woman closed the door. It made a clanking sound, followed by something sliding. The door opened wider, revealing the woman in full. She was slightly taller than Bertan, with a prominent nose and beady yet warm dark eyes.

"Come in," she said, stepping aside while holding the door open.

Bertan walked in and the woman closed the door. A driveway revealed a black Honda with tinted windows. The dog had gone inside but was standing at the open door, staring at Bertan. It did not look particularly friendly, yet it did not growl or come at him.

"My name is Elena. Ruben is my younger brother." She looked at Bertan curiously. "Can I get you a *café*?"

"*Sí.*"

The woman led Bertan inside, where the dog turned and hurried off through the kitchen and into the living room, jumping up onto a leather couch and lying on a green blanket.

Bertan took a seat at a folding table set off to the side of the kitchen. The far walls were lined with cabinets and countertop. So much space for cooking. Something Carmen would have loved.

Elena walked over to a fancy machine on the counter a few feet away from the sink. Bertan had never seen such a thing. She placed a carafe into the top of it, and an empty coffee cup in the bottom. Moments later, a stream of hot liquid poured out into the cup.

How long had it been since Bertan had a cup of authentic coffee? The question alone made him feel things he hadn't felt in quite some time. Things he wouldn't allow himself to feel. A kind of nostalgia. Every day he was coming nearer and nearer to his home, and it was beginning to make him *feel* again.

"How is my brother?" Elena asked, her back to Bertan while she started the process for a second cup of coffee.

This part Bertan had feared most. Telling someone who'd never met him that their family member was dead.

"That's why I'm here," he replied, hesitating.

Elena brought a cup full of coffee and set it in front of him. From the refrigerator she grabbed creamer, then set it down on the table. When her cup was ready, she pulled it out carefully, walked it over and sat down across from him.

He took a sip of the coffee while he had the chance, tasting a pleasant hint of cayenne pepper, and something sweet and heavy, like cacao. It was delicious, and warm. It awakened in him his own memory of life back home.

"Is he all right?"

Elena leaned forward. She released her hands from her cup.

"No. I'm afraid not."

"What's happened?" she asked. She began turning the rings on her fingers.

"I'm sorry to tell you. . .he died."

Bertan could hardly believe it was true. Ruben had been there for him and now he was gone, just like that. A connection severed so swiftly it didn't seem real.

Elena sat there, looked past Bertan. Composed. Unshaken. Yet her face contorted into a frown. Her eyes glossed over.

"I was afraid of this," she said. She stared down at the table. "He'd been in the U.S. for too long. I know plenty of how that country treats our people. . ."

Her voice trailed off.

Bertan didn't know what to say. When was it the right time to tell her it was his fault Ruben had been killed? He couldn't leave here without telling her the truth.

"I don't know if it was the country itself," Bertan admitted.

"How did you know him?"

"We worked together. He was my plant manager."

"And what happened?"

Bertan looked at the woman. He hadn't touched the coffee again. He wasn't sure he could.

"It's a long story. He was working undercover. . .as an animal rights activist," he began.

Elena shuffled in her seat. She turned slightly, and crossed her legs. She too, had stopped drinking her coffee.

"He was always helping undocumented immigrants here in Mexico. Always the bleeding heart, that man."

"He was a good man. I could tell you everything, if you want." Bertan paused. He feared that if he told her about the plan they'd helped with to bring S-Corp down, she might call the police on him. She may have already heard about it on the news. She struck him as an intellectual. But he couldn't lie to her.

Elena nodded, as if waiting for an answer.

Bertan told her everything. How Ruben was an undercover animal activist who'd been working for S-Corp. Why Bertan wanted S-Corp destroyed. How he'd worked with Ruben and some other activists to inform the U.S. public about S-Corp's secrets. He wasn't sure how to tell her about the girl, Bray, so he omitted that piece.

"He got caught. Doing animal rights work," Bertan finished. "We both did. I was taken away and I never saw him again."

Elena nodded. . .then frowned. A crease developed between her eyebrows. *Had she known he was an animal activist*, Bertan wondered.

"I knew it," she said, smiling for the first time. "The Embedicare takeover, right? I saw it on the news. Is that what you're telling me? He was in on it?"

Bertan's face went flush.

"Yes."

"My kid brother. . .little Ruben. He didn't know how not to help people. Even as a kid, he was rescuing animals off the streets, giving homeless people money he found lying around the house."

Bertan took a deep breath, feeling the sorrow of this loss.

"He helped me a lot, your brother. I would not be here, if not for him. He saved my family's life. And my own. Many times over."

They met eyes. The world stopped. Everything went quiet. Right there, the two of them were connected by one man. A man whose life mattered for an instant and then was gone. A man the rest of the world would never come to know.

Heat filled Bertan's back. He reached his arms out to the woman, wondering maybe if he felt her, he could feel Ruben, too. She took his hand, squeezed it.

"You have family?" she asked, pulling away to take a sip of coffee.

"Yes ma'am. In Honduras. I'm on my way there now."

"How long has it been?"

He understood what she was asking.

"Ten years, at least."

"How the world tears us apart, yes?"

"And brings us back together," he replied, though the words did not feel as though they were his own. The moment felt ethereal. Fluid. Unreal.

"It's us who brings things together, wouldn't you say?" she asked. Her smile grew broad, encompassing multitudes. The gravity of the situation heightening Bertan's senses. He could smell the scent of the coffee in the room, hear the dog sleeping on the couch, and when Elena touched him, he could feel her heartbeat through his veins. He trembled a moment, near tears.

"I suppose you are right."

They went quiet again. Elena released his hand, sat back with her cup. She held it close to her chest.

"Where is he? His body?"

"I don't know," Bertan said. "But I think we can find out."

"How?"

"He died in custody. What they did to

him. . .was wrong."

"My husband, he's a government official. I bet we could find out."

"Do you have a piece of paper? Pen?" he asked.

Elena set down the cup, went to a kitchen drawer, opened it. Bertan leaned over to peek into the living room. The television was on, but muted. The program looked to be a *tellanovella*. Two men were talking. One of them went at the other, grabbed him around the neck. The camera shifted to something off in the distance. . .darkness. . .and then the barrel of a gun. A shot went off. Bertan startled and turned away.

Elena returned and set down a notepad and pencil. Bertan wrote the name of the prison and the name of the S-Corp facility where Ruben had worked.

"Here," he said, sliding the notepad over to her. "That was where we both worked. And the prison I was taken to. Maybe that will help you find him."

"You were in prison?"

"For the illegal immigration," he said, lying. Some truths were best not told. "I was just released."

"Stay for dinner," she said. "You can get cleaned up, before you head home."

At that, Bertan's eyes filled with tears.

"I could not impose."

"You wouldn't be." Elena smiled. "You're as good as family now."

"Thank you," he said.

"Thank you. For coming here, to tell me."

"You deserved to know. Like I said, Ruben was a good man. Far better than me. I owe him everything."

"How did you even find me?" she asked,

standing beside the table.

"I had a lot of time on my hands. . .in prison. And the internet," he replied, smiling.

Elena nodded. She lifted her arm, glanced at her watch.

"My husband will be home soon. Then we'll eat. You can wash up, if you wish."

"How can I repay?"

"You want to repay me?" she asked, laughing. "Friends don't repay."

Funny. Ruben would have said the same.

Elena smirked. She returned to the chair across from him and leaned forward. Her eyes glimmered with a mixture of sorrow and peace.

"Here's what you can do: go be with your family. Be with them every day. Don't waste another moment. Make your job loving them. That's how you can repay."

The woman's words vibrated through his bones, down into his heart.

"Yes ma'am. I fully intend to do so."

"Great. Now come help me cook. Tonight we dine on Mexican mole!"

Bertan forced a smile. He was grateful, and he was also extremely worn and torn with the heaviness of Ruben's absence. Being in this house brought him so close to Ruben that he began to grow homesick for the man. What a shame, to only learn about a friend's life after he was dead.

Chapter Twenty-Three

Bray

The sedation gradually wore off. Throughout the night Bray tossed and turned, her sleep mixed with a few hours of rest, but mostly mired in constant, changing dreams. Some were unsettling: images of the prisoners slowly dying in their cells; animals tortured in confinement. Others were more neutral: her standing in the aisle of an empty airplane as it flew silently through the sky. By morning, Bray was not rested, but she was beginning to feel more alert.

A nurse came by, checked her vitals, removed her IV drip, and left. Then came two guards. One handcuffed her to the bed while the other unstrapped her restraints. Her wrists were sweaty and raw.

She assumed she was being taken back to her cell. If they had medicated her, she couldn't tell.

The nurse returned with a banana and a piece of toast. Bray wasn't going to eat, but she did drink down a glass of water.

"Once you eat, we'll have you get dressed," the nurse said.

"What?" Bray handed the empty cup back.

"You're being released," the nurse replied, gently taking the cup.

"They're releasing me. . ." she said, but not to anyone in the room. It was for Tori.

Her head went quiet. It felt foggy,

while also light. No headache. No pain.
    "*Are you serious?*" Tori replied.
"*That's great news!*"
    "I'm not leaving without the rest of
you," Bray replied. "Until all beings are
free, remember?"
    "No! Absolutely not," Tori insisted.
"You get out of here as fast as you can."
    "But what about everyone else?"
    "Eat," the nurse said, pointing at the
banana.
    Bray considered it, then grabbed the
banana and peeled it. As she took a bite,
her mouth came to life. She couldn't recall
the last time she'd *tasted* food. Bray
chewed the banana slowly. Her appetite was
minimal. Her stomach felt the size of a
pea.
    "What will you all do?" Bray asked
Tori, uncomfortable about leaving the other
prisoners behind. Guilty, in fact.
    "Don't worry about us," Tori replied.
"Get out. Get strong. You can help us much
better from out there."
    Bray finished the banana and the toast.
    She'd been given a private bathroom
where she could change, putting on her old
sweatpants that made her legs feel at home
again and an oversized t-shirt Kage had
given her back in Meeteetse—which, in this
moment, felt like an entirely other
lifetime. She wondered where Kage, Trevor
and Emily were now. Oh, how she deeply
missed Emily. A pain grew in her heart. She
didn't know who she felt like anymore, but
she didn't feel herself. At least not the
self that had entered this prison.
    Bray did not see a single prisoner once
she left the Health Services unit. As they
walked her out in handcuffs, she looked
back and saw Jacob standing beside her now-
empty bed. His hands were in his pockets.

His face, expressionless.

"I hope you believe me now," Bray said in her mind, aiming the thought backward at Jacob.

His eyes widened. His mouth opened as if he were going to speak, but before she could see him moving for the door, it closed behind her. They passed through the hall and turned a corner, starting for the stairwell. Jacob did not follow, but she sensed he had heard her.

As Bray was marched onward, up the stairs and down the halls, leaving the unit in which she'd met Tori and Valerie, her heart sinking with every step, the walls became distant and surreal. The sun invaded the front of the building through large windows. Outside she could see the fences and, beyond them, a waiting vehicle.

Within her mind came a gradual chanting.

"*If you can be freed, there's hope for us yet.*"

"*Finish what you started.*"

"*We'll hold down the fort,*" Tori said. "*Until all beings are free.*"

The voices were solemn and tired, coming from people who had refused food and had done this because Bray had asked them to.

She'd have to find a way to get them out.

#

As the prison disappeared below them, a heavy cloud cover hung over the city of Phoenix. The plane ride north was bumpy, turbulence causing the food in her stomach to drop and tumble.

Bray was shocked to discover her father had followed through and come to get her. But what of her mother? How long before she found out and intervened? Could Bray ever enjoy an amount of freedom?

"How are you feeling?" her father reached over and asked. He was sitting in the seat beside her. Across the aisle, another window revealed nothing but white atmosphere. Bray looked over at her father. His face was more attentive than she remembered. He seemed. . .unusually present. And thinner.

Bray did not answer his question.

"How did you get me out?" she asked instead.

"I don't really know. It's all. . .very confusing."

Bray glanced up at his eyes. They were full and teary.

"What do you mean?"

"Did you know anyone by the name of. . .Bertan?"

"Yes. He's my friend."

Bertan. Standing at her bedside, while she was in the clinic. She thought it had been a dream. It felt like that. Her entering his mind, the entity controlling her, all of it. Nothing seemed real anymore.

"Was he. . .Hispanic? Really green eyes?"

"He *is* Honduran," she replied, placing an emphasis on the word *is*.

"So you think he's still alive?" Cole asked. His eyes trailed out the window beside her.

Bray frowned. "Why are you asking me that?"

"Strangest thing happened." Cole's eyes turned downward to the seat in front of him. "I was visiting with you in the clinic, while you were sedated. The psychiatrist was there." He paused. "I said something about how you were a minor, and I asked him how they could justify having you in that prison."

Bray leaned over, waiting for him to get to what he was going to say, as if she already knew. Only she couldn't understand how she knew.

"He was there in the room. That man. . .Bertan. A ghost. I was the only one who could see him. He whispered something in the psychiatrist's ear. Then he spoke to me-in my mind." He paused. "During the Embedicare takeover, I heard your voice. Was that you, calling out to me telepathically?"

"Yes," Bray replied. She was candid with him. "I told you I had a gift. That I communicate with animals. You're an animal, too."

She found she didn't care now if he believed her. It didn't make the gift any less real.

"And Bertan, he has this gift, too?"

Bray sat back. She looked out the window again. The plane was bouncing through thick clouds, their goofy, cauliflower-like shapes rounding into themselves in such stillness it left Bray disarmed.

"I don't know. He's not dead, that's for sure." Bray paused. "He has some kind of gift," she said, trailing off. Something passed through her, like a breeze through the branches of a tree. Some knowing that didn't belong to her but was given just the same.

"I don't understand," Cole admitted.

"Some things in life aren't meant to be understood," Bray said, realizing this as she spoke. She took a deep breath. "He got me out, didn't he?"

"I-I don't know. I guess what matters is that you're safe now."

"Where are you taking me?" she asked,

her mind clearing as she looked over at
him.

"Some place in Montana."

"Red Lodge?"

"Yes."

Bray searched herself for a sense of
excitement. Relief. Something. All she
sensed within her chest, where once she
carried anxiety and fear, was nothing more
than a blank, open sky.

"You've spoken with Elliott, then?" she
asked. She wanted reassurance that her
friends had made it out of Meeteetse
safely.

"And Kage. They're in hiding."

So my plan worked, Bray thought,
smiling. The whole reason she'd surrendered
to her mother and those S-Corp thugs, the
reason she'd risked being locked up, had
been to give the others a chance to escape.

"What about Emily? Trevor?"

"I don't know everyone's names. I was
lucky enough they told me their location.
Your friends agreed to let me bring you
there myself, but only if I stay and don't
leave, not until all of this is over."

"All of what?"

"Wait until we get there. Let them be
the ones to tell you."

Bray considered what he'd said, hinting
at events to come. She felt no particular
way about it. There was so much happening
outside of her, yet inside there was a
stillness. A set-right way of being. A
presence and a resolve she had never felt
before.

"I just want to say," Cole added, "I'm
sorry I allowed your mom to dictate our
family decisions. I could've done more to
stand up for you, and I chose not to. I
messed up."

Bray looked at him. His eyes softened.

Chicken-talon wrinkles spread out from the corners of his eyes. He had more wrinkles now. Bray took his hand in hers.

It was never too late to make things right.

Chapter Twenty-Four

Dianna

Dianna was standing aimlessly in the kitchen when her implant buzzed. She flipped her arm over to see the screen. A message from Dan at S-Corp Security. This was her first contact with anyone at S-Corp since she'd been asked to leave. No one had reached out. Not her assistant. Not Carl. A stark reminder that she hadn't made any friends in the ten years she'd worked there.

DAN: DID YOU SEE THE EMAIL?

"What email?" she said aloud.

Picking up her phone from the kitchen counter, she opened her work email.
She saw one email from corporate with the subject heading:

MIDWEST PRESIDENT CARL FLOREZ ACCEPTS NEW ROLE.

Dianna opened the email. Her eyes widened in shock. Her heart went still, then dropped. For the longest time she stood there, alone in the kitchen, reading the email over and over again.
They'd handed her position to Carl. His

new role: S-CORP PRESIDENT: WEST.

Carl would still be overseeing S-Corp facilities in his territories of Nebraska, Oklahoma and the Midwest, but also her territories: the Dakotas, Wyoming, Colorado, Montana and so on, clear to the Pacific Ocean. They'd taken her territories away and handed them over to someone she had thought, *believed*, cared for her.

"Smart man," she said, in disbelief. And to think she'd had sex with Carl. How naive.

Dianna tossed the phone into a kitchen drawer, slamming it shut. She couldn't deal with this. She didn't want to deal with any of it. She sauntered into the living room, wavered, and sat down on the couch. Her body remained there for the longest time, while in her mind, it all piled up-the years of time put in at S-Corp, the years of exhausting work trying to get help for a daughter who had turned out to be a terrorist.

Where on earth had she gone wrong?

Chapter Twenty-Five

Bray

As the afternoon with her dad led Bray back to her friends, she remained aware of her inner world. She noticed disbelief that the things going on around her were real. What she could see and touch now seemed surreal. Ungrounded. All the while, she felt anchored by a consistent calm, unwavering center.

This awareness began when the plane landed in Cheyenne. Cole had arranged for his friend Rick to pick them up and drive them to Red Lodge. Bray remembered the man, vaguely, as one who'd helped Alice and the remaining sows Bray rescued from the transport truck. Now she sat in back of his SUV, staring out the window, while he and Cole caught up. An aching sunlight on her face left her body desperate for sleep, and she succumbed. She did not wake until their arrival six hours later.

#

At some point, Bray noticed the SUV had stopped moving. She woke, her eyes heavy and her mind disoriented. She heard one of the front car doors shut. That was her father, stepping out and facing a two-story apartment building. She had no idea where she was.

She heard a knock on the back window. Bray looked over and saw Cole waving her out. She opened the door, gathered her bearings, and stepped out into a temperate evening. The sun was quickly falling behind foothills in the distance. She followed Cole into the building. Rick drove off. She hadn't even noticed he was still inside the car.

Bray wasn't quite ready to encounter all of her friends. She wanted to see them, but the unexpected transition was of such shock to her, everything shifting so smoothly, that her mind struggled to believe this was happening. Was she walking into a trap? When Cole opened that door he'd placed his hand upon, would her mother be on the other side?

The apartment door opened. Bray heard an array of voices. Entering slowly, she held her breath. First, she saw Virgil, Dennis and Emily, sitting on the couch. They turned toward the door. As soon as Emily saw her, she jumped to her feet and covered her mouth. From Bray's position she could see Emily's tears.

Cole closed the door behind them. Elliott and Kage had been standing just inside it. They were both smiling, and they came at her like two large bears, pulling her in for a massive hug she was not at all prepared for. But she allowed it, because she knew how much they'd missed her, perhaps fearing for her life. A scent of sandalwood deodorant came from Elliott's arms. Bray knew that scent.

Kage released himself and stepped back as Bray remained in Elliott's embrace. She would allow him to hold her until he was ready to release. He was her best friend, after all. Being held felt foreign. She also felt unmistakably needed. Her chest opened and she felt tears rolling down her face.

"Thank God," Elliott said.

Trevor walked over from the kitchen and waited. When she looked up at him, he smiled.

Elliott finally released her, his face wet and his eyes red.

"Good to have you back," Trevor said warmly.

"Is it?" she asked sincerely. Last she remembered, Kage's uncle was not at all supportive of her plan to expose S-Corp. If anything, he would've sent her to the psych ward himself, given the chance.

"Yes. It really is." He smiled and placed his hand on her shoulder.

"Bray!" Lana yelled. Bray could see her in the kitchen where she'd been cutting up fruit. She left her place, setting down the knife. Trevor stepped back. Bray and Lana embraced.

Bray let go, turning to the living room. Their reception was overwhelming. Almost suffocating. A mixture of feelings and calmness. Like she could finally breathe, while, in the back of her mind, she still felt a deep sense of loss and even guilt. There were others who still were not free.

Emily walked over to Bray.

"How are you feeling?" Emily asked, putting her arms around Bray. She smelled like a forest. Not much had changed.

"I don't know," Bray admitted.

"What do you need? We don't want to overwhelm you."

Bray tried to think. Her mind was empty. Open. Vast.

"Are you hungry?" Lana asked.

Bray shook her head. She felt everyone watching her. She saw that Elliott was introducing her dad to the others. *Thank you*, she wanted to tell them both.

"I just need some time," she said.

"How about a hot bath?" Emily asked.

"Thank you," Bray replied, nodding.

While Emily disappeared down the hall into the bathroom, Virgil waved her over to the couch. She went and sat down beside him. He took her hand in his. It was warm, coarse. He sat with her, saying nothing. Perhaps he knew what it was she needed.

#

After the hot bath, Bray fell asleep in Elliott's bed. When she woke, she had no idea how she got there, only saw that the door was closed and a blanket lay atop her body. She heard Elliott's voice outside, laughing.

She sat up. Her body felt loose. Slowly, taking her time, she walked out into the living room.

"Come have breakfast," Lana called from her seat at the kitchen table, as radiant as ever. Beside her sat Emily. Taking up a corner seat, Virgil. Beside Virgil, Trevor. Beside Trevor, an empty seat waited.

Bray sat down, yawned.

"You look more yourself today," Emily said.

Bray smiled. Emily took her hand beneath the table, squeezed it and let go. Bray felt the embrace in her chest, warming like the sun that had already risen outside. Its rays shone in through the window and hit Trevor against his back. Through the window, Bray could see other apartment buildings like this one, and a few people walking by.

At the table, platters of fresh fruit, a large bowl of hot quinoa with raisins, and a casserole dish with mashed sweet potatoes opened Bray's senses. Her mouth watered. She nearly cried, it all smelled so fresh. Finally, she could eat again.

Bray ate and enjoyed the company of her friends, though in the back of her mind remained the burden of Tori, Valerie, the other prisoners. She turned to watch Kage, who was eating breakfast on the couch beside her dad and Elliott. Dennis was missing.

"How did you all get away from S-Corp?" Bray asked, finally ready to hear what had happened after her mother had taken her from the hideout in Meeteetse.

Virgil and Emily exchanged glances.

"We waited," Emily said, "for them to leave. If it wasn't for Elliott's gadgets, I'm not sure we would have made it out."

Bray looked to Elliott. Her dear friend. It was then she noticed that Kage's grin had reduced down to a frown.

"What?" Bray asked Kage.

"Meeteetse." Kage paused. He set down his plate, stood up. He came over to her. "The house and garden. They set it all on fire. House is half-standing."

Bray didn't know what to say. She looked down at her empty plate. The best food she'd ever tasted had been from that garden. She had learned to meditate in that garden. It was in that house Bray had come to realize what was possible in this world, that life could still flourish despite the damage her mother and S-Corp had done to the earth, to the country.

"And Ethan. . .his body?" Bray asked. The memories of that time came rushing back to her, Ethan killed by S-Corp security, their home under siege, Bray surrendering to give the rest of her friends a chance to escape.

"We buried him in the cellar," Kage replied. "Lana and I went back a few days ago, made a video there. So at least the whole world knows what happened."

Bray nodded, her mind processing the information.

"And what's happened. . .since I've been gone?" she asked, not sure she was ready to know.

"I'll let Trevor explain," Kage said, grabbing his plate and returning to the couch.

Bray turned her attention to Trevor. She wondered if maybe he had changed. He had been so adamant about not wanting to fight S-Corp. Seeing her father now in her periphery, quietly eating breakfast on the couch, she was reminded that people could change.

Trevor caught her up on everything. All the emails they'd received, how many people wanted to help. The videos they had made and posted. The lawsuit that Elliott, Lana and Cole were working on.

"Dad?" Bray asked, surprised.

Cole looked over at her.

"I know, shocking, isn't it?" he replied. "But the truth is the truth, and I've gone too long not seeing it. These families have lost everything because of S-Corp's actions. It's the least I can do."

Trevor continued, all the while Bray sat there looking at her dad, dumbfounded.

Trevor went on to mention the representatives in each city, their communication tree that he'd created.

"You left out the best part," Kage chimed in. They all turned to him in unison. He'd forced one last bite of sweet potato into his mouth and quickly swallowed, smiling and wild-eyed.

"Maybe we should hold off on that," Lana interrupted. "Give Bray time to breathe."

"It's okay," Bray said. She went over and sat down on the floor across from Kage. "Tell me."

"We're going to march," Kage said, suddenly enthusiastic. He bent down and sat on the floor beside her.

"March?"

"Day after tomorrow. All of us, from César Chávez Park to the S-Corp facility in Lakeside."

"In Denver?" Bray asked, glancing up at Cole. "You mean where mom works?"

"Yep. I'm preparing a speech," Kage said.

As Kage spoke, his voice drifted away from her. Bray's mind ventured to images of hundreds of people in the streets, from here to New York. A nation up in arms. It did not shock her. She had experienced first-hand the horror and outrage in the minds of citizens across the country during the chaos of the Embedicare takeover, the media's name for her experiment. It had come to this. It was destiny. Her only question: what would be her part in it now?

"You can join us, of course," Kage finished.

Bray glanced over at him. His eyes were alive, the brightest she had seen them in the few months she and Kage had known each other. While she was imprisoned, the man had become a leader. He was the better one for it.

"No," she said at once. She spoke, but it was not her speaking. It was a transmission she was receiving. "I need to stay back."

"You want one of us to stay with you?" Elliott asked.

Bray shook her head.

It was coming together. Yes, it was.

"No. It's best I be here alone," she

replied. Something was coalescing in her mind. Gathering. Developing. Taking flight. "I've got some unfinished business."

Bray felt everyone's eyes upon her. Gazing. Quiet. Expecting.

"This is in two days, you said?" Bray asked.

Kage nodded.

"Then I'll need some time. . .to prepare."

"Prepare? For what?"

"When I have the answer, I'll let you know," Bray replied. She stood up. "If you'll excuse me, I've got to go be alone. There's some sorting out to do."

Bray went down the hall and closed herself in Elliott's room. She made up a comfortable spot on the floor, using a blanket and a pillow to sit on. Pressing her back up against the wall, she got into position, closed her eyes, and waited.

Chapter Twenty-Six

Bertan

In thirty-two hours, Bertan would arrive in San Pedro Sula. Elena had graciously offered to purchase his bus tickets from Mexico City to San Pedro, by way of Guatemala City. She paid for them with a credit card, something Bertan had never been able to do. He hoped one day his life could be simple enough to allow such things. As he sat on the bus and waited for it to fill, quietly glancing out at the street, at the people beneath his window carrying bags and backpacks, he hoped he'd never need another train or bus in his life.

The bus filled to capacity. It reeked of body odor and fried foods. The heat rose. The door clamped shut. The bus rolled forward, jolting bodies in their seats. Bertan peered out the window, ignoring a baby crying in the back seat, as the bus station disappeared behind them. It was really happening. He squeezed his hands together. If there had ever been a time to pray to some God he wasn't sure existed, it would be in this moment, when there remained hours of time between here and home when something could go wrong.

Bertan closed his eyes. He pictured the argument he'd had with Carmen that led him to leaving for the United States, more than ten years ago. How he'd nearly hit her, he had become so angry and unhinged from his work with Medina, and she'd said she was going to leave him. And he believed her. So he did the only thing he could. He left. He came to the United States feeling a mixture of fear and hope. His family was supposed to follow him to the United States. It was supposed to be a place where they could get away from Medina and start over. But years of work in the S-Corp slaughterhouse did not bring him the proper funds to get his family across the border. Not in any way that was safe. And in a blink of an eye, the world passed him up while he worked in hidden places for a corrupt corporation. Little did he know he'd fallen back into Medina's hands, so to speak. Because, he realized, listening to the baby cry and the mother trying to settle it, Medina was *everywhere*. Medina was a *concept*. A thing people did when they chose greed and money over family and love. He knew because he had been one of them. He'd been lost for a long time, lost in pride, stubbornness and anger.

When he met Ruben, things gradually began to change. Finally he'd found someone he could talk to. Ruben was his one good friend in life, aside from Carmen herself. And it was Bertan's short-sightedness, his unwillingness to recognize his mental anguish, his stubborn idea that he could handle everything on his own, that led, ultimately, to his own fall and to Ruben's death. One day, he would have to forgive himself all of this. It was what Ruben would have wanted, he knew.

The bus slowed. Outside people were shouting. Bertan opened his eyes. He turned and held his breath, watching as people on the street held signs and protested. These were indigenous people, it appeared, fighting for land rights-something Bertan knew all too much about. Medina had stolen land from indigenous people, and, working for Medina, he had done some dirty, dirty things. Attempting to help Bray end S-Corp was his way of trying to redeem himself, because he'd come to learn that S-Corp had ties with Medina.

His thoughts turned to Bray. He should check in on her.

"Bray," he whispered in his mind.

"*Good morning, Bertan.*" Her reply was immediate, as if she had been expecting him.

"Please tell me you got out."

"*Yes, thanks to you.*"

Bertan smiled.

"*Where are you?*" she asked.

"I'm on a bus. Headed home."

A softness approached his heart. It was Bray, he felt. She was happy for him.

"*To be with your family.*"

"*Sí,*" he replied, pausing and taking a deep breath. "I need to tell you, so you can inform your friends: Ruben. . .he died."

A drop into sadness, then silence.

"*How?*"

"He died in custody. That's all I know."

"*I'm sorry. I know he was your friend.*"

Bertan nodded silently.

"I wanted to make sure you were okay, before I go home," he said.

"*I am.*"

There was a pause. Bertan sensed a quandary, or something missing.

"What's the matter?" he asked.

"*Your gift has made you very perceptive.*"

"Is it the same with you?"

"*Yes.*"

"Are you going to tell me?" he asked.

"There is something I have to do. Something. . .unmeasurable. My friends are going off to march, against S-Corp."

"I don't understand-unmeasurable?"

"You ever had a time in your life when you knew you had to go through with something, even if it meant doing it alone?"

Bertan thought of all the sacrifices he had made. All the lives he had to take so his would remain intact. Leaving his family to cross the border into the U.S. Living without his family for ten years. Every day in that country was met with sacrifice.

"Yes," he replied.

"It's like that."

"I see." Bertan felt the bus jut forward. Escaping the crowd of protestors, the bus turned down narrow, cobblestone streets, past Spanish-influenced houses. "What's this march you speak of?"

"After the Embedicare takeover, hundreds of people reached out to us, wanting to help. People are angry about S-Corp. They have marches organized all over the country. Maybe it will create some change."

"You're not sure it will?" Bertan sensed doubt.

"There is too much uncertainty, too many variables in life, to be sure of anything."

Bertan nodded again. He knew exactly what she meant.

"I have to go," she said. *"Take care of yourself, out there in the world."*

"You do the same."

That was it. Bray was gone. A rush of gooseflesh ran up his arms. Something about that conversation was too cryptic and left him feeling on edge. He opened his eyes. Outside, the bus cleared the state of

Chiapas and rolled onto a highway, headed further south. Bertan closed his eyes again, thought a bit longer on what Bray had said, then trailed off to sleep.

Chapter Twenty-Seven

Bray

Bray knew what she needed to do. What was strange and equally comforting was that. . .it didn't shock her. It was her *destiny*. Something she was meant to do.

She woke to the sounds of others in the apartment. Walking gracefully, as if in a dream, she entered the living room. To see her father, Elliott, Kage and all these people in the same room, eating, gathering supplies and packing equipment into bags, was beyond anything she would have or could have imagined, only three months prior. Three months. . .and her entire life had changed. As a matter of fact, all of the lives in this room, she realized, had changed because of her. They were together in this room, in this town, because of something she had done.

Bray ate breakfast and mingled with her friends. It was important for her to be in the preciousness of these moments, for she could not guarantee there would be another. Two times in the past, when she had taken great risk, her life had been spared. She could not expect a third.

After breakfast, she pulled Kage and Lana into Elliott's bedroom alone and shut the door. She sat them both down on the bed beside one another.

"What's going on?" Kage asked, his voice chipper.

"I've got some things to tell you both.

I don't think it can wait."

"Okay. . ." Lana frowned. A crease developed between her eyebrows.

"Ruben passed away," Bray said right off.

Lana's shoulders sank.

"How did you find out?" she asked.

"It was Bertan, believe it or not."

"Is he okay?" Kage asked, leaning forward.

"Yes," Bray replied. "He's on his way home."

"How do you know?" Lana asked.

"Long story. I just needed to make sure you knew about Ruben, that he died in custody."

"Damn," Kage said. He slapped his hand against his knee. Then, he turned to Lana. "You okay?" Lana and Ruben had worked together as activists, and Ruben had been undercover at S-Corp when Kage, Bray and Elliott met with Ruben and Bertan to plan the takeover.

"I'm disappointed," Lana said. Bray saw that her composure had fallen into a slump, like a tree having gone weeks without water.

Kage put his arm around Lana. Bray would have smiled, seeing them get close, but there was still too much to tell.

"There's more," she continued. She told them about Tori. That she'd been imprisoned with Tori, that she'd developed the ability to communicate with humans and had sometimes communicated with Tori that way.

Lana's head dropped between her knees.

"They're alive." Her voice was muffled.

Kage rubbed her back.

There was a knock at the door. Bray walked over and opened it. Trevor leaned in, whispering.

"We've got to go-about five minutes,"

he said.

Bray nodded, shut the door. She turned back to Kage.

"I'm sorry we don't have more time, but there's one more thing."

"What?" Kage asked.

Lana sat up. Her face was flush and growing warmer by the second.

Bray stepped over and knelt down before Kage. She took his hand.

"Why are you acting so weird?" he asked.

"Your mom," Bray started.

"What about her? Come out with it already!"

She could feel him grow stiff.

"She's. . .alive."

Kage's eyes welled up with tears.

"You're sure?" he asked, remaining still.

Lana exchanged glances with him. She took his other hand.

"Valerie. I've spoken with her," Bray confirmed with a nod. "There's so much I wish I had the time to tell you, but you have to leave now."

"She's okay?" he asked. He was crying. "And my dad?"

Bray shook her head. "I don't know."

Another knock at the door. Trevor poked his head in.

Bray got up and backed away. Kage rubbed his eyes, then, as he started for the door, turned and hugged Bray. He squeezed hard, cried, held the back of her head with his hand. She pressed herself into his chest. His body was warm. She could tell he'd already begun sweating.

"Thank you, friend," he whispered, and pulled away.

"You sure you don't want to join us?" Lana asked, standing up.

"My place is here," Bray replied.

"See you later," Kage said, walking out into the hall.

"Take care. There's plenty of food in there. . .to get caught up on," Lana teased, touching Bray's face.

Bray smiled as she watched them leave. She stood back, remaining in the bedroom. The door was open, and from where she stood she could see into the living room. Trevor opened the front door, disappeared through it with Emily. Lana and Kage followed.

Cole came to her. He reached out and gripped her shoulder.

"You sure you'll be okay here?" he asked.

"Yes Dad, thank you," she replied, touching his hand.

He pulled her into his chest, squeezed her tight, and let go. When he returned to the living room and started out the door, he glanced back at her and winked. She quietly watched him leave.

Elliott was the last to go. Carrying a black backpack over one shoulder, he stopped at the door for a moment. He looked back to Bray. Bray waved, feigned a smile. For the longest time he stood there and watched her. She recalled that three months ago he had almost left Denver without saying goodbye, and she just happened to show up at his apartment the day he was leaving. Had she not gotten out of that psych ward, had she not found him before he left town, would she have made it this far? She didn't think so. She owed everything to Elliott, to her friends. Truth was, Bray was here because of *them*. Because of Elliott, Emily, Kage. Alice and Rhea. Bertan, Ruben. All the ones that came before her. It was because of her friends, Bray realized, smiling tenderly at Elliott, that she had been able to accomplish anything. In that moment, as Elliott readied himself to leave, she came to know what she'd needed to know: it was friendship that bound the world together, and it was friendship she would go down fighting for.

Elliott nodded to her and left, shutting the door behind him.

Chapter Twenty-Eight

Kage

It took nearly nine hours to roll into Denver, where they stayed with a supporter, a widower by the name of Stanley Everton. It was night when they arrived, and Kage was spent. He'd considered telling Trevor the news Bray shared about his mother, but his mind was shot. He wasn't sure. Was this the time to tell his uncle, the night before the march? There was a chance Trevor would not believe him, or not believe Bray, until he *saw* his sister-in-law alive and well. And Kage did not yet know how-or if-that would come to be. At Stanley's dining room table, where they all sat around and ate while Stanley talked about his wife, who had died as a result of the fertilizer disaster, Kage thought it probable that he might not ever see his mom. A new ache arose in his heart, one that reminded him of the years he pined for his parents. He had just begun to let them go, to give up hope, when Bray gave him this news.

Kage glanced over and saw Trevor sitting alone on the couch, staring at Elliott's laptop. No, this was not the time. The news would have to wait until all of this was over and they had a better understanding of whether these marches would do anything to topple S-Corp.

Instead, Kage decided he would depart to the second bedroom, where Stanley had left out an air mattress. He went in, shut the door, and began prepping the mattress. Thoughts of tomorrow filled him with uncertainty as much as hope. He had no idea what to expect. He was nervous about giving a speech in public, where anyone would be free to come after him.

For the first time in his adult life, he was about to expose himself to the world. Although he knew it was the right thing to do, that everyone was okay with him taking the lead, the fear of doing this crippled him down into the mattress, where he lay looking at the wall, trying to calm himself down so rest would come.

#

Kage knew of Cézar Chávez. Ethan had taught him about the activist who fought for the rights of farm workers. How appropriate it was that he had chosen Cézar Chávez Park for the place where they could meet with representatives and marchers. In researching Denver locations, he had selected it in honor of those who came before him.

Standing before an outdoor seating area, Kage was shocked by the number of people who had gathered. He stood atop a circular, concrete structure that faced four rows of concrete walls, each two feet tall. In between them, artificial grass hid beneath the feet of dozens of people. The steps, which climbed up a slight hill, were full of people. Beyond the steps, the sun was rising. He watched the sky for drones. It wouldn't be long before Marshals were alerted about their gathering.

Beside him, Elliott had set up a speaker and a microphone that he rummaged together in Red Lodge. Kage picked up the mic, looked it over. He'd never used one before. The people were looking at him,

many talking amongst themselves, holding
their protest signs, waiting.

Lana ran over to him from the side,
where Trevor, Elliott, Cole and Emily were
also waiting.

"You ready?" she asked him.

Kage glanced at her. His heart was
beating out of his chest. He was sweating
through his jeans and jacket. Despite the
heat out west, he had never been one to
reveal his chalky legs. The more hidden
they were, especially given his femininity,
the better. His social anxiety in front of
others was a reminder that he never had the
chance to transition, and so he stood
there, looking out at the crowd, feeling
the tension in their energy, hoping they
didn't think they were looking at a woman.
He felt outside himself. Like he was both
present and somewhere else.

"So many people," he whispered to Lana.

"You got this," she replied, patting
his shoulder.

This was his chance. His one and only
chance. There would not be another time
like this, in all his life, to get across a
message to this many people, all at once.

Out of the corner of his eye, Elliott
gave him a thumbs up. He was being recorded
live, for the world to see. The amount of
clothing he wore to hide his skin did not
help the nakedness he felt. He closed his
eyes, breathed. The crowd silenced.

Lana stepped away, returned to
Elliott's side.

"Good morning," Kage began. His voice
echoed out into the park. He felt so
uncomfortable, the sound of his voice
so. . .foreign to who he truly was. A voice
so high when he wished for depth. His skin
crawled at the sound.

"Thank you everyone for coming out

today," he started again, wiping sweat from his brow. "It won't be long before Marshals arrive. When they do, do not engage. This is a peaceful protest."

A sudden shuffle appeared to the right and up two levels of steps. Kage paused. He spotted two men standing close together, equal in height. Sunglasses hid their eyes. Kage would normally think nothing of it, given the intensity of the sunrise. But the way they stood, the way their arms, side-by-side, seemed to be hiding something, so still it was unnatural, made Kage hesitate. He gulped and continued with his speech.

"They may arrest us-"

He was interrupted by a shriek. The people surrounding the two men ducked. In that moment, seconds slowed into minutes. Kage's eyes widened. When he saw it, his mind could not register the reality. . .that someone would actually do such a thing. But, of course they would. There was no forgetting that a majority of the country was either indifferent to or against their cause. So when the barrel of a handgun rose into the air, pointing at Kage from afar, it was no wonder it took him a moment to realize what he saw and to react accordingly.

It was hard to determine which happened first: Kage alerting himself to *fucking move!* or the gunshot.

Chapter Twenty-Nine

Bray

Bray needed nature. No more hard floors for her feet to stand on. No more concrete floors, concrete walls without windows. No more ceilings to block the sky. No more artificial noises. She needed the wind, the sun, the grass and the birds.

Out in the living room, she slid on her shoes. She had no other clothes than the sweatpants and t-shirt on her body, and they would do just fine.

Once outside, she began walking. Other people were out walking the sidewalks, nodding to her as they passed by. A few blocks down, she encountered the General Store where she and Kage stopped when they first came to Red Lodge looking for Elliott. She stopped and stared at its reflective glass, gazing at the image of herself. Her hair sat on her shoulders, hiding her neck. Her face was thinner, changed from last she saw it, and she could not remember how long ago that had been. Her eyes were heavy and full. Her mouth sat in line, no smile. It was the face of a young, stoic woman fully aware of what was about to happen.

Outside the town, she came upon a grove of pine trees beside the road. Bray deserted the road and turned for the trees, crunching through dry grass, and found a spot beneath a tree where shade covered her from the sun. It was early, yet the temperature had already risen fast. Here Bray could smell the strength of the pine trees, the sweetness of them bringing a temporary smile to her face. She got into meditation pose, closed her eyes. Deep breathing led her into a round of chakra cleansing, as Emily had taught her. Her mind quieted. She waited. Breathing. Only breathing.

"Do your will," came a whisper from her mouth. She didn't know why she said it, but this was no time to doubt.

Her attention dropped down into her belly. The breath shallow, ever-present. In. . .out. . .in. . .out. Rhythm. Thought fading into background. Feeling herself fade. Realizing no-self. Stepping aside. Allowing.

The focus drifted down into bone. Further down into cell, into the stuff of life. The stuff that *gave* life. That was life.

It floated through her body, rested along her forearm. A warmth permeated there. Vibrated. Hummed. A vision flashed onto the black screen of her mind.

She saw a park with a semi-circle lined with short concrete walls, artificial grass in between. Hundreds of people. Bray floated above them like a bird, observing. She saw Elliott, her father, Trevor, Emily, Lana, standing off to one side. Kage was standing on a concrete structure, speaking to the crowd. A man raised a gun. Bray wished to stop it. A thought came to her that maybe she could.

"*No*," came a whisper. It was the entity.

The gun went off. Kage leapt to safety. The crowd began to scatter. A group of protestors rushed two men, taking control of the gun. They began fighting.

Bray fell down into Kage.

"Stop!" she yelled. It was disorienting to hear her voice come out of Kage's mouth, to sound like his voice. "Please, do not fight!"

The crowd paused. They all looked to Kage. He stumbled to his feet, grabbing the mic, which had fallen down beside him.

"We've come to be in peace, not to fight! Please. . .our message is on reducing harm, not adding to it."

Bray was yanked out of the vision. Everything went dark. She felt hot with nausea from the sudden change in time and space. A breeze brushed through the valley where she sat and rustled the trees, providing temporary relief. Her nausea passed.

In the dark space she felt herself rising. Up, up, as if being pulled into the sky. It was both exhilarating and frightening, for she could not see.

The entity had returned. It was not finished with her yet.

Chapter Thirty

Bray

Bray sensed a fascinating dichotomy within her. On the one side, a deep, inner knowing. What she was tasked with next. On the other, persistent doubt. These doubts took shape, coalesced into a dark figure. It rose up to take space inside.

The entity.

It remained there because Bray had allowed it. There was no end to it.

"*You know you can't do it*," the entity began.

"I can do it, and I will," Bray replied adamantly.

"*But you don't believe.*"

Bray could not deny this. Somehow, the entity knew things. Bray had already experienced a lifetime, however brief, of disbelief. Not in her abilities, but in the capacity of others to *believe* in her. She had been let down by her parents, repeatedly, from the beginning. Every psychiatrist in every psych ward disregarded her explanations, her telepathic abilities. Only recently had she found people who would believe her, but that didn't mean she could expect the nation to do the same.

"That's true," she admitted.

"*You know, deep down inside, that try as you may, the people will not follow.*"

The entity's words yanked at her as though an anchor had been tied to her ankle and was pulling her downward.

"I want to believe," she said, and this time she wasn't responding to the entity. She was speaking to herself while not quite able to determine where her self had gone.

"*We could force them.*" Both voices—Bray and the entity-spoke these words in unison.

Bray's head began to pound. Pressure built up in her sinus cavity. A fog spread through the darkness, gray, thick as the walls of prison, heavy enough to block her concentration.

She was lost.

Bray took the form of herself, her seventeen-year-old *perceived* self, within her mind. Was that where she was? Was she somewhere else? That would be ridiculous. Where she was felt like a whole other reality. Another dimension.

Bray had been lost before, when she and Elliott were out in the Wyoming landscape, heading north, and were found by a Marshal. A pack of rabid dogs had run at them, killing the Marshal. A dog attacked Elliott and bit him in the arm, injuring him badly. Bray and Elliott had roamed the open prairies, seeking refuge. They were completely lost. Bray had stopped and listened to herself. Her instinct eventually guided them to a house in Casper, Wyoming, where she was able to save Elliott's arm. The trick was in believing *enough*, and being willing to follow.

"*You cannot follow what you do not feel*," the entity said.

It was not wrong.

She could not feel what she wanted to believe because the entity was too strong.

"*I wish you'd stop calling me that!*" the entity shouted. Its words hit Bray like the sharp, hard pelting of hail.

"What do I call you?"

"*I cannot be named. Try to define me and you have already lost.*"

"How so?" She was genuinely curious, unthreatened.

"*Once something is given a name, it is judged.*"

Bray felt something closing in on her. It was massive, and too dark to see.

"*You humans define an entity as some distinct thing, a construct, separate from yourselves,*" it continued. "*I am no thing.*"

"Then what are you?" Bray was trying to remain patient.

"*In an effort to understand, you miss the truth.*"

Bray began to worry that she was running out of time, and that this thing was intentionally distracting her.

"*Ha!*" the entity laughed. "*I am your final lesson, dear child. We sit here in limbo until you learn. Or, perhaps, just let me help. Let me be the one to help you force them into seeing, just like you did with the implant. It's right there, at your disposal. . .*"

Its voice trailed off.

Bray's forearm buzzed. A heat exuded from it, pulsing into a strange pain. Was she supposed to do something? She didn't know. She picked up and ran. She ran to one end of her mind where she could go no further, hitting up against a wall. Turning, she ran again. The entity came into view at the far end, opposite the place where she stood. It gelled into chrome, then took the shape of a body whose skin was nothing but mirror.

"*The mind is the greatest prison, is it not?*"

Bray stopped in her tracks.

It was then she realized *there was no escaping.*

Bray sat down right where she was. The sensation beneath her was both hard and in movement, like sitting on water. Black, cold and the texture of jelly. Bray shivered. A putrid scent overpowered the pine trees that were now far, far, away from wherever this was.

Closing her eyes, she exhaled. There was nothing else to do. No. . .thing.

Is that what it meant, when it said it was no thing?

"*You're getting warmer, my child.*"

"If you're my final lesson, then how come you're not trying to stop me?" she asked.

The entity snickered.

"*You are doing enough of the stopping for the both of us. You don't see, my child. I don't even have to try.*"

A natural inclination to understand arose, but she realized that wasn't the point. For some reason, there was no answer and she didn't need to understand. This confused her. She felt the confusion like a pulsing in her head. The confusion dissipated into a muted pink color, became like soft dust, and evaporated.

Bray returned to where she began. The self-doubt. The disbelief. She admitted she didn't believe that her plan would work, the plan her instinct had tasked her with today. She'd doubted herself many times, but not like this. When she had come up with the idea to connect citizens through Embedicare implants, she'd believed. But this time, there was a block. She wanted to believe.

Bray opened her eyes. She looked around for the entity, and she did not have to search for long. Within seconds, it appeared before her, inches away. It mimicked her position, sitting. It faced her, a head without a face, without hair. Nothing but mirror.

A moment later, the entity transitioned into a circular, spiraling form. It did not lose its mirror-like exterior, and Bray could watch herself watching it. She saw herself bending into its shape. A warmth exuded from it. Reaching out her hands, she found there was nothing to touch as the warmth ran up her arms and stopped at her shoulders. Pulling back, she gazed at herself in the mirror.

"I am no thing," she whispered. "I. . .am. . .no. . ."

Once when Bray was sitting in the yard with Emily in Meeteetse, Emily taught her about the concept of obscurity. How sometimes there are no answers. That sitting with the gray areas of life, the *unknowns*, is the truest form of peace. The not knowing. The awareness that life is a mystery, and ought to remain that way. That we are not to know all things, or to be certain of everything. Bray had asked her how that applied to being vegan, since she believed, as did Emily, that using animals for food was wrong.

Emily had replied simply, "I don't know."

Suddenly, it came to her:

I am nothing, therefore I am everything. To find the light we must embrace the dark. There is light because there is dark. One could not be had without the other. Therefore, both are necessary, and neither can be determined as right or wrong.

"I am nothing," she said absolutely.

Suddenly the darkness around her made a dramatic shift into sky and earth. Faster than the blink of an eye, she felt suspended. In air, above all of earth, all

of universe. Bray. . .nowhere to be found.
Bray becoming *part* of the sky. . .her
essence blending into it as if a cloud.
Feeling herself a part of everything.
Having let go of the self she thought she
was, Bray found the great paradox: that in
life there were no clear answers. All
beings were deserving of feeling the
freedom of no-self. The freedom to be
authentic and true.

And with this realization, she
understood what it was she had come here to
do. And she believed.

Chapter Thirty-One

Bray

Bray's vision expanded outward like a wide screen-spanning from Washington, D.C., to Denver, Colorado. She saw citizens in every major city crowding the streets and preparing to march. The numbers rose into the thousands. Standing idle, waiting to move. A massive wave of electric feeling pulsed through Bray's being.

"I am nothing," she whispered.

The whisper formed into a chant.

Tears rolled from her eyes. She was releasing energy. Releasing all bondage to the desires within herself, bondage to fear and doubt. No longer was there a *need* for anything. A formidable calm grew within, like a sky free of clouds; only, she found she *was* the sky. No body. No arms, legs or feeling of heaviness. Only floating, above the land, watching everything below.

The sun, her neighbor, stood beside her, a friend along on the journey. The destination, she did not know and did not need to know. In the past, that would have scared her, not knowing where she was or where she'd end up. She discovered trust. She felt willing to be led. No longer did she need to be in control. This too, had happened before.

Just prior to the Embedicare takeover, right as Bray had begun to tap in to the force that would power it, a similar thing had happened. She stood aside, so to speak, and something else had taken over.

What was that something else?

"*Try to understand and you lose the truth.*"

Bray traveled across sky and plains. Simultaneously, she felt herself to be part of an infinite stillness. At times, the constant breeze sifted through her hair, gently pulling strands away from her face.

Miles above herself, she looked down, saw the tree she was sitting beside. She experienced a sensation of leaping upward, and a flip in mid-air. She'd never dived before, but if she had, she imagined it would feel like this.

Joy.

Her awareness turned, flipped, faced the earth. She began to fall. First, the earth hurtling toward her, her heart leaping up into her throat. The wind, too fast. She could hardly breathe. The hot air smacked the flush of her face. Diving down through pine tree foliage, she passed between branches, untouched, unscathed. Falling toward her body. Feeling awareness dwindle, not in scope but in size, becoming as precise and thin as a needle. Watching as the awareness neared her forearm. Arriving on skin. The hairs on her arms. Entrance not visible to the naked eye. Dropping in as if into a pool of water. Not water, but blood. Awareness was pulled along through the current of her blood cells, then stopped by a chip.

The implant.

As awareness entered the implant, time stopped. Space and time pausing. A sensation of heat warming her forearm, followed by vibration.

With a sudden shift in her perspective, drifting through space, a satellite came into view. Bray's vision neared its two solar arrays, nearly blinding her from the intense light of the sun. Without force, she felt pulled into the light. Gliding back down to earth, over the countryside, from city to city, awareness finding every last Embedicare tower, Bray felt herself connected to all of them. Through awareness she was able to split in several directions all at once, like rivers cutting away from the ocean and running for miles and miles through the broad country.

Soaring again, she traced dizzying circles, spinning out and across vast plains, mountains and wilderness unencumbered. Rising farther, high into New England and as far south as Florida. Expanding over into Texas, throughout the Midwest and back again. Simultaneously everywhere, and here, all at once. . .

Chapter Thirty-Two

Bray

Bray felt multitudes inside, multitudes of beings, human and animal alike. Multitudes folding in on themselves and becoming one. Feeling as though she had the attention of the nation, Bray knew what was coming.

Her final mission.

Any doubts that came, she welcomed and folded into her beliefs. For there could not be one without the other.

"The fate of one. . .*linked* to the fate of another," she whispered.

Bray's awareness traveled into thousands of spaces all at once. Hundreds of closed-in, hot, S-Corp facilities built of concrete and steel. Not a sound of breeze, of waving tree branch, nor bird could be heard. No scent of fresh grass. No sunlight.

Gradually, Bray came to stand in each facility, split into hundreds of pieces of awareness, her mind aching and feeling spliced by knives. Humans in smocks continued on with their work, dismantling animals, part by part, unable to see Bray's presence.

Her mind had fragmented into so many places that she'd lost count, all held together by what felt like a string as strong as the silk of a spider.

She thought for sure she would die after this.

The awareness bore witness to countless locked pens, cages, gestation crates throughout the nation. In each one, the animals mooed, clucked, grunted. They *saw* her, and they called out for help in unison so powerfully it could not be understood by human language. It could only be felt, in Bray's body, as pure desperation.

Bray shifted her attention to the workers. She thought about Bertan. It could've been possible to convince the workers to free the animals, the way Bertan had convinced the warden to set him free. But the workers had to be spared. There could be no proof of any worker involvement in the freeing of the animals.

Why? Bray thought of the worry stone her grandfather had given her lifetimes ago. On it was inscribed: *Love ALL beings, equally.* She saw those words roll through her mind. As a child, she thought "all beings" meant animals. Now she realized that loving ALL beings couldn't stop at animals. If she was to succeed, she had to extend that love to humans.

If any of this was to work, there could be no harm to humans or animals.

Therefore, the work here had to be purely supernatural, and for once she believed she could make it so. She believed she had the power to release these animals, from hundreds of facilities throughout the nation, and set them free.

Bray closed her eyes.

Suspended.

Floating.

She linked with the pain and the experience of animals held captive, of the workers in these places held captive in their own right. Within this deep feeling, Bray traveled beyond boundary and thought, into one coalescing space. Into the vast

open fields of her mind. She pulled in with
her the emotions of exponentially more
beings than she had reached during the
takeover, and watched them gel and take
form. What appeared shook her to her core.
Shook all attempts at understanding. *Try to
understand. . .you lose the truth.*

The mass of thick, slick substance,
unmeasurable, formless, became a perfect
mirror. Bray looked into it and saw an
image of herself, younger, less frayed,
hair free and shining. A great pain and
confusion grew in her heart. The fear made
her want to understand what was happening.

Inside her there was a breaking, a
splitting of mind from truth. What *was*
truth? How could she know? How could anyone
know?

Crying, she looked upon herself in that
mirror. Staring into her own eyes, she saw
within herself the fear from which she
wished to run. A fear that, deep down
inside, she was incapable of saving anyone.
That this, in truth, was not the final
task. Not at all. In her eyes she witnessed
both multitudes and nothingness. She was
not important.

"I am nothing," she said to herself.

Reaching forward, her hand rising up
toward the mirror, Bray felt the deep urge
to reach herself. Her fingers grazed the
mirror. It was freezing. Her fingers stuck
to the substance.

Her hand reached in, breaking through
the surface. The mirror bent to her, and
her image smiled. She smiled back. A
vacuum-like suction slowly pulled her in.
The mirror, the substance of the mirror,
and Bray came together; it molded over her,
and within it she saw the deep love she had
for herself. She saw and felt the vast
running and flying and spinning thrust of

life and incredible beauty, crying,
flowing, water. Complex color into no
color.

Bray became it and, from there, she
acted.

Her arms lifted into the air. Workers
kept on prodding animals into chutes, into
shackles, into knock boxes. She waved her
hands around the facilities, collectively,
all of the facilities, her attention first
focused on the chutes, which suddenly
closed off and allowed no more animals in.
Workers began to shout as they saw their
machinery no longer operational. Bray spun
around and pushed energy out toward the
prods in workers' hands. The prods dropped
to the concrete floor, breaking apart. More
screaming. She flipped back around, reached
in the direction of a knock gun attached to
a wall, and, with a pulling sensation, she
watched as it was yanked from its place,
thrown across the room, shattered against a
wall. Workers began running out of the
rooms they were in. Buzzers went off.

Bray turned toward a garage-like door
that was closed over a wide entrance where
animals were forced inside from transport
trucks. She focused her mind on the
electronic pulley above the door and
squeezed her eyes shut. It took almost-
insurmountable effort. Her head began to
ache. Her eyes watered. She focused on the
image of that door in her mind, of not just
one but all doors at loading docks across
all such facilities throughout the nation,
prying them open with her mind.

It was unclear how she did it, how a
young girl with the power to communicate
telepathically with animals and humans had
advanced to moving objects and overriding
machinery to open heavy doors, but it
happened. The doors unleashed themselves

and rolled open, the kill floor of each facility now empty of humans, all having run out into their parking lots to watch helplessly. There was nothing any of them could do, and Bray, upon lifting the doors, corralled the animals out into the open.

Suddenly her awareness shifted. She was no longer inside the facilities but had risen above them. The pain in her head ceased, replaced with dizziness. She was floating again, watching the span of the nation.

Bray looked upon the animals, from Colorado to the Carolinas, and she felt herself expand outward, spread like a cloud across the sky, gazing down at clusters of humans preparing to march in cities, and at animals wobbling, walking and making their way out of factory farms. Thousands of animals. Bray looked upon them not as herself, but as something greater, something god-like. She looked down upon them as a mother gazing on her children, and she smiled.

"Let us march," she said.

Bray's physical body stood up from her place beneath the pine trees. The breeze brushed through her hair and along her bare skin. Feeling a slight nudge from behind, her eyes closed, she allowed herself to be guided slowly away from the tree.

All the while, her implant had been activated.

It was time for everything to be made equal.

Chapter Thirty-Three

Tim

Washington, D.C.

When the nation went into lockdown after the Embedicare takeover, Tim Saffi had gone right to the internet. He found the truthaboutscorp.com website and he read everything there. It confirmed what he'd suspected deep down inside about S-Corp. . .that a corporation that massive and in control of the nation's food and water systems could only get there one way, through corruption and lies.

This was the move he'd been waiting for. He sent a message through the website's contact link, and he waited. Gradually the lockdown ended. The terror threat levels decreased nationally from red to orange. He returned to work, although what he really felt fired up to do was to quit everything and become a climate advocate. But the money wasn't there, not yet. He had been on his way to a job interview when the Embedicare takeover occurred, and, of course, he had yet to hear back as to whether he'd get a second chance to interview.

Tim was sitting at his desk at a dead-end IT job, an entry-level position he acquired post-graduate-which, for an IT job, did not pay what he really needed to live on his own-when he got a *ding* and a vibration from his implant.

Someone by the name of Trevor had sent him an email. He was one of the animal activists, or "eco-terrorists," as the media and government had labeled them, calling for representatives from each city to assist with the dissemination of information.

Bingo! Tim thought, and he signed up right away.

Time passed and the threat level decreased to yellow. He set up a Discord server, seeking DC residents who wanted to stop S-Corp, and he built an online following. It would take weeks, but with his experience in IT, he managed to create an encrypted chat room so he could pass along information from Trevor, who said he was a social worker and had worked on President Walker's campaign in the twenty-tens. *Good company*, he thought.

When they called for marches throughout the nation, a "march for freedom," they said, Tim needed no convincing. He was no animal activist, but he was a wannabe. His greatest fear was the gradual destruction of the climate, the worsening of his every-day life by the increase in drought, storms, flooding and the like. It was difficult watching his parents struggle with their housing in North Carolina, pounded by hurricanes, the magnitude of which worsened every year.

And now he was standing in Folger Park, ready to march, watching as the crowd grew. He'd expected one hundred. But this was closer to three. The grass and sidewalks were covered with protestors. People carried signs reading, "FREE BRAY" or "FREEDOM FOR ALL" and "NO MORE S-CORP" and so on.

Tim stood on a picnic table with his megaphone, eyes scrolling over the crowd, listening to the cacophony of voices. It was 9:50 a.m. He'd been instructed to start the march at 10:00 a.m., to be in sync the rest of the nation. Denver, where Trevor would be marching with other activists, would start promptly at 8:00 a.m. Mountain Time. It would all go off like a steam truck barreling down the highway, unstoppable, unavoidable, powered with the frustrations and fears of a people made complacent by misinformation they had believed for years.

Clouds had gathered above, closing off the sun and casting a grayness over the park. Tim noticed a few people in the crowd pointing at something behind him. He heard a dull mumbling, followed by an echo of booing.

Tim turned. Coming around the corner of Second and D Streets was another kind of crowd. A crowd of Marshals, lined up to span the street, in full riot gear, coming toward the park.

Tim bent down and picked up the megaphone. He waved his free arm up in the air to get the attention of the people.

"Everyone. . .please," he spoke. The crowd hushed. "We knew this would happen. The Marshals would come. They'd try and stop us. But we cannot let them. We must march, peacefully. No fighting back. We march only for the freedom of others and for our own. Here's to the end of S-Corp."

"Here, here!"

"Fuck yeah!"

Tim climbed down off the picnic table. He glanced at his forearm, saw that it was 10:00 a.m. on the dot. He turned in the direction of the Capitol, four blocks away. The top of the White House looked out at him as if it had nothing to say. It had been silent for too long, as had he.

Megaphone in hand, Tim guided the crowd away from the Marshals, in the direction of the White House.

The march had begun.

Chapter Thirty-Four

Mateo

Houston, Texas

The march began slowly in Houston. Gradually. Mateo Perez walked hand in hand with his girlfriend, Mandi. The Embedicare takeover had led them here. Mateo had previously been a voracious meat-eater. It wasn't something he'd been ready to change, but he'd sensed some internal juggling going on. How could there not have been? Only weeks ago he received a transmission, by way of his implant, of the slaughter of a cow. Not only that, he'd *experienced* it, as though he *were* the cow. It was disturbing, and he hadn't been able to get much sleep since. He was resentful of the "activists" who had done this to him, but he could not ignore the reality they'd forced him to see. He couldn't unsee it. And after he and Mandi had researched the activists' website, all that stuff about S-Corp, there was no turning back. Besides, Mandi had already been the tree hugger between the two of them, and he was doing this largely for her. Mandi was a bulldog when it came to decisions. Once she latched on to one, there was no letting go. She'd decided to join up and be a representative for the activists, to lead people on a march through Houston's Central Business District. Now, sky-high office buildings, including S-Corp's Houston office, stood staring down at them blankly and with a stupid resignation.

They were at the head of the crowd, a number likely nearing two hundred, when Mateo and Mandi saw the Marshals. The protestors were marching down Lamar Street directly toward a barricade of Marshals at the far end, a line of black, like a thin-lipped, expressionless mouth closed shut. They had no chance of getting through. Mateo could not tell from this distance, more than five hundred feet away, but he thought he saw riot gear. Shields over the Marshals' heads glimmered in the sun, its reflection bouncing off of them and hitting the crowd.

They had been expecting opposition.

Mateo looked to Mandi. He squeezed her hand. She smiled at him.

"You ready?" he asked.

Mandi nodded.

"Anytime it gets scary, we can stop," he said.

"I'm not stopping. Those animals didn't get to stop."

When she was right, she was right.

"Return to your homes!" called a Marshal from behind a megaphone. "You will be arrested if you do not turn back."

The crowd continued forward, picking up speed. The Marshals stood their ground. They were getting closer. One hundred feet away. Mateo's heart began to pitter-patter like the shuffling of the crowd, feet against concrete. This was getting real, real fast.

Mateo's implant vibrated. He and Mandi eyed one another. She must've felt it, too. A warmth drifted through his bloodstream, both alarming and calming.

"*Do not fear*," came a feminine voice.

Mateo heard it and turned and glanced around for the source.

"Did you hear it, too?" Mandi yelled over to him.

He nodded.

The voice returned: "*This is Bray Hoffman*."

Mateo's chest tightened. He remembered that name. That was the girl who started this whole thing. If she was about to expose them to another one of her slaughter experiences, this whole thing would be over for him.

"*I am only here to urge you forward. In a moment, you will experience something. . .quite beautiful*."

"The girl. . .from that video!" Mandi called over. She glanced down at her forearm.

Suddenly, the crowd picked up their pace. Mateo wondered if they'd all received the same message. They came within twenty-five feet of the Marshals. Close enough for Mateo to notice billy clubs in their hands. He gulped. Was he ready for this? Would he be able to resist fighting back?

The Marshals began to shuffle in place. Several of them looked to their forearms, and they froze. Time seemed to slow to a stop. Mateo's vision narrowed, focused on the Marshals. One Marshal continued yelling into a megaphone, but Mateo was not listening. Within his bloodstream he felt a smooth, warm and vibrant tickle. The source: his implant.

Chapter Thirty-Five

Elisha

Cincinnati, Ohio

It was impossible to count how many people had shown up for the march. A sea of them stretched from Fountain Square, down Fifth Street, along Vine Street, awaiting the signal to begin. Elisha stood beneath the Tyler Davidson fountain, a 43-foot-tall bronze structure with a statue of a woman, the "Genius of Water," they called it, hovering over the crowd. Elisha listened as water trickled from the statue's hands, thinking the symbol of water was quite ironic in a time when she felt she had been fighting alone to find ways to save the climate from S-Corp.

But she wasn't alone anymore. This Cincinnati crowd was breathtaking. Patrons and servers gathered outside restaurants. Office workers came to their windows, looking down from tall buildings.

Marshals lined the far sidewalk in riot gear. Elisha did not feel intimidated by them. She knew that was their goal, intimidation and eventually arrest. She only hoped they'd keep it civil, and that the march didn't break out into a mob of violence. The heat of the morning air carried with it a stuck kind of tension. At any moment it might snap in two.

A hundred feet above where the Marshals stood, a fifty-by-twenty-foot video board hung atop the Foundry building. Elisha did not pay much attention to the scrolling advertisements for upcoming films, city events and restaurants. She was waiting to begin marching. As a representative for local activists, she knew the route from Fountain Square to the Federal Building a mile away. It would be a slow, deliberate march. People were mingling and holding their signs close. The Marshals stood their ground but did not do much else.

Not until other people began glancing down at their arms did Elisha notice something off. First one, then another, then a group of ten. Elisha stood up on a nearby chair, scanning the crowd, where a significant number of people had gone silent and were staring at their arms.

She was one of the few without an implant. She'd had hers removed the moment she realized what S-Corp was capable of, after the Embedicare takeover. She hadn't wanted to be tracked when she visited Emerson, since he remained in hiding. She watched, curious, as the crowd went quiet. The Marshals had also noticed, for they had turned to one another and were speaking amongst themselves. That was when Elisha looked up at the massive screen and realized it had gone dark.

Suddenly, the screen lit up with an image of the sky. The point of view was moving toward something. Elisha stood there looking up in awe, watching.

The crowd looked up in unison. Everyone watched as the image on the screen transitioned from sky to earth, to the Midwest and the western prairies and desert, to the places where drought had not

yet reached, such as Wyoming and along the
Dakotas. Hundreds upon hundreds of farmed
animals were running like wild, toward some
objective, it seemed, with their hooves
pounding dirt away from the ground, the
very earth seeming to bow beneath them.

Chapter Thirty-Six

Bray

The sensation of walking did not feel to Bray like walking at all. More like a drifting, as if she were walking along clouds in the sky. She was being led by something, that "something better," on a journey toward something. . .or someone.

All the while, animals freed from factory farm captivity were on the move. Cows walking or running alongside pigs. Chickens, their weight massive, an unnatural burden, struggled the most. Many could not walk. They lay stuck in fields of long-gone soy and corn crops, watching helplessly as the cows and pigs moved on without them.

Bray could see it all.

She lifted her hands into the air, reaching up above her head. As she did, the chickens rose with her gesture, away from earth. Their wings broke loose from years of entrapment. Feathers fell away. Shaky at first, they began to take flight, their weight seemingly no longer an obstacle.

From all directions, as far east as Nebraska, as far south as the U.S. border, and coming from the Dakotas, animals were on the move in numbers Bray could not count.

Bray's journey continued farther south. As she crossed the border from Montana into Wyoming, a murder of ravens hovered along above her, and the sun bore down on her body and the trees went still.

Chapter Thirty-Seven

Dianna

Dianna was forced to resign. Her boss
had called her a few days ago, telling her
she could either resign immediately with a
hefty severance package or be let go
without one. She didn't fight it. Typing up
the resignation letter was the most surreal
thing she'd ever experienced. All her years
dedicated to S-Corp, and it had come to
this? And that damn Carl. She had a
suspicion he was in on it. He hadn't
reached out to her. The way he wasn't even
acknowledging her made her feel she was
non-existent. A feeling of loss hung in her
body, heavy with disappointment.
Disappointment in herself, mostly.

Sitting at the dining room table, where
the walls—now free of photos and art—echoed
every last sound she made, Dianna signed
the letter on her touchscreen laptop and
sent it off to Dr. Brisbon. She slapped the
laptop shut and leaned back in her chair.
She felt some weight fall from her
shoulders and cascade down her back to the
floor. At least she no longer faced the
challenge of trying to salvage her career.
She'd lost everything. She began to cry.

When the tears slowed, she rubbed her
face with her sleeve. She got up and paced
the room. Out in the foyer, all of the
boxes had been cleared out, placed in
storage. Just walking into the living room

brought chills to her spine. She had sold the living room furniture, and the room sat waiting for someone new to come along. Dianna had put the house up for sale, and now she stared out the window at the sign in the yard.

Dianna noticed a bike in the neighbor's yard, lying on its side. The front wheel turned slightly, slowed, then stopped. When Bray was a child, she'd never expressed much interest in bikes. Dianna had gotten her one with training wheels when she was five, but she seldom tried it. All she seemed to want was to sit in the yard and watch the animals or play in the grass.

Suddenly, her implant vibrated. She glanced down at the screen and saw a broadcast of protestors marching and scenes of similar marches throughout the country. One group in particular, right here in Denver, was marching toward the S-Corp building.

The implant screen went black. Dianna, wanting to see more, started for her laptop, which was sitting on one of the last pieces of furniture in the house.

"*Mom.*"

Bray's voice popped into her consciousness.

Dianna whipped her head around, looking upstairs.

"*You won't find me here,*" Bray said.

"Bray!" Dianna yelled. She started for the stairs but stopped when she heard no response.

Dianna frowned.

"*Would you please stop and listen to me?*" Bray asked. The voice echoed clearly in Dianna's mind, yet Bray was nowhere to be found.

"What the hell?" Dianna whispered.

"*You'll never believe I can communicate

*with animals. I accept this. All I ask is
for you to listen.*"

"Okay, fine. I'm listening!" Dianna
shouted, throwing her hands up in dramatic
surrender.

This was madness. Talking to herself!
She had just lost her job. The stress was
getting to her.

Suddenly, she froze. Her body stuck in
place, one foot on the bottom stair, the
other on the foyer floor. She tried lifting
an arm, but it remained on the banister.
She began to shake with fear.

Before her, an image spiraled into
view. Dianna wanted to scream and run but
could do neither. As a result, she began to
panic. Her chest constricted. Her heart
raced.

At the top of the stairs appeared a
smokey image of Bray. She was wearing
sweatpants and a t-shirt Dianna had never
seen. Her hair hung down past her shoulders
and it waved slightly, as if a breeze had
just brushed through it. Bray was looking
down at Dianna, and she was smiling.

Her daughter was dead, was that it? Was
she being visited by her child from beyond
the grave? Dianna didn't believe in life
after death, but it was the only thing that
made sense now.

"*Mom.*" Bray laughed. "*I am not dead.
Take a look.*"

Dianna found she could now move her
left arm. When she tried to run, her legs
were still stuck to the floor. She raised
her arm and looked at the screen.

There on her forearm was an image of
her daughter walking outside. The area
looked familiar. Open plains dotted with
sage brush. Yes, Dianna had been in a place
like this before. It looked like Wyoming,
where she had taken a helicopter in an

attempt to retrieve Bray after Bray escaped the psych ward.

"What in the world?"

"*That's me. . .in Wyoming*," Bray said.

"But. . .you're in prison." Dianna was so confused.

"*Dad helped get me out.*" Bray paused. "*What you did was wrong, putting me in there. Yet, had you not. . .*"

Bray's ghost appeared to be walking in place.

"*If you hadn't put me in that place, I wouldn't have met all the activists S-Corp locked away, like Kage's mother. I wouldn't have learned to do this,*" she added, waving along her body.

"So you're telling me Cole got you out and now you're roaming around alone in Wyoming, while also somehow visiting me here?" Dianna asked, dropping her arm.

"*Look again.*"

Dianna's arm rose, this time without her effort. On the screen, hundreds of farmed animals were running or walking free along state routes. The screen flipped from an image of cows in Nebraska to another of pigs in Idaho, and so many more. Dianna was speechless.

"*They've been freed.*"

"This is absurd-"

Bray waved her hand in the air. Dianna went quiet.

"*I know S-Corp let you go.*" Bray was changing the subject. "*I know you were manipulated by Carl.*"

"How. . ." Dianna went pale. "This has to be a ghost, or some very bad dream."

"*You don't have to believe me. I only came here to make peace. You've made your mistakes. They've caught up with you.*"

Dianna attempted to move away from the stairs, to get to her cell phone. Her body fell backward. Finally she had agency over her body. She turned and ran into the kitchen, her chest heaving as she grabbed her phone, eyes watering, frantic.

"*There is no one to call, Mom.*"

Bray's ghost approached her and smiled. Dianna turned, saw the ghost up close, and froze. The phone slid out of her hand and onto the floor. She felt she might cry. Or that her heart might stop.

"*The thing I learned about mistakes,*" Bray said, "*is that the greatest of them can lead to the greatest gifts. When you left me in prison, I learned what I was capable of.*"

The ghost shifted a few steps back, as if it knew Dianna was panicking. A warmth exuded from it and fell over Dianna as though she'd been inside a sauna. Her muscles relaxed. The ghost of her daughter stood across from her, smiling. A calm breeze touched Dianna's shoulders and they dropped. She began to feel at ease, yet her thoughts continued to race. Why was this happening? How was this happening? She'd spent too long cooped up inside this house.

"*You will never listen to your own daughter, will you? Something prevents you from opening up. I hope you find a way to let the world in. I feel for you. I'm sorry that all your choices have left you here alone. If you ever change your mind, I will be here. Just. . .reach out,*" Bray finished, tapping her finger against her head.

She disappeared.

Trembling, Dianna came down to the floor. She wrapped her arms around her legs, pulled her knees into her chest. She started to feel a deep sorrow, certain her daughter had died in prison. She would never be able to forgive herself for that.

Dianna reached over and picked up her phone. She took a deep breath and called Arizona Correctional. She was dispatched through to the warden.

"This is Dianna Hoffman," she spoke hurriedly. "Is my daughter okay?"

She held her breath.

"Mrs. Hoffman. I'm sorry I did not call. Our prison has been experiencing some. . .upheaval," the warden replied.

"Will you just tell me what's going on with Bray?!"

"I assumed Mr. Hoffman would have informed you. Your daughter was released a few days ago."

Staring off into space, Dianna ended the call. The phone fell to the floor. She lay down beside it, her eyes searching the ceiling for some answer. How on earth Cole had gotten Bray out. How Bray had visited her. She glanced at her forearm. Once again, she saw Bray walking, silently, along the Wyoming terrain.

Chapter Thirty-Eight

Bray

It hadn't felt, physically, as though Bray had walked a day, but on the soles of her feet, blisters began to form, and her calves burned. Yet she continued on, moved forward by an unstoppable force.

In that time, she'd utilized Bertan's gift of astral projection to check in on her mother. She couldn't explain it, but she'd been aware of the news of her mother's resignation from S-Corp, something Bray never saw coming. What she did see coming was her mother's reaction to her arrival. Her consistent unwillingness to see Bray for who she really was. Unwilling to *believe* in her, just once. Bray knew there was no convincing her mother. Her mother would have to decide on her own, and in her own time. She felt for the woman. Truly, she did.

As she continued walking southward in the direction of her destiny, she knew ultimately her mother would not be along with her on her journey. The tie had been severed, but at least Bray had tried to connect one last time, to show the woman the compassion she'd never given herself.

As she walked, her vision reached miles and miles in all directions, where the farmed animals continued their trek toward a similar destination. The chickens had

found full flight, their excess weight
dwindling away as they flapped their wings.
The cows had fallen into a comfortable,
steady gallop. The pigs and turkeys, ducks,
baby calves half-starved were now running
in a line through vast prairies, across
plains. Lines of them formed like rivers
flowing. . .all in the direction of one,
single source.

Bray's vision pulled away from the
distance beyond horizons and returned to
what body she could still feel. Nearing
ever closer to her inner knowing, Bray
released herself and projected herself
backwards in time, back to the day before,
into spaces both east and west, north and
south. She flew through city streets and
paused, hovering above the twenty-nine U.S.
cities where protests were taking place.

Chapter Thirty-Nine

Bray

What Bray did next was quite simple. With it all laid out before her, everything made sense. The purpose of her gift. Her reason for being alive. She felt it picking up steam, rolling toward a certain outcome. All of the pieces of her life and the lives of others fit into one intricate puzzle that came together to create two dichotomies: consciousness and the lack thereof.

As her body continued its walk south, her pace began to slow. Pain gathered in her lower back. Her legs shook and grew increasingly weak. She did not know where she was supposed to end up, but she sensed it was not here. That somehow she had to keep going. The way the animals had kept going despite the pain they felt, the pain-theirs-that she felt in her own bones and in her soul.

Bray witnessed crowds of protestors edging closer to phalanxes of Marshals. In Houston. In Denver. New York, Cincinnati, Washington, D.C., and beyond. Meanwhile, Marshals had begun to close in on the migrating masses of farmed animals. Transport trucks followed. Bray's vision expanded out miles from the animals, all of them nearing the state of Utah. They were coming together, hundreds upon hundreds, barreling forward, shaking the hardened and dying earth.

Out beyond them, along highways in all directions, came Marshal vehicles. Drones circled the sky like vultures.

"Move yourselves!" Bray called to the packs of animals. "Toward the mountains!"

The farmed animals advancing from the east and south entered the state of Colorado, converging as they reached the Rocky Mountain Range. They now moved as one unit, galloping and flying toward the north. Verdant foothills covered in pine trees stood watch alongside them, shifting and rolling into higher elevations, progressing north into Wyoming. The mountains seemed from Bray's vantage point to open and welcome their presence.

The drones dropped away. The Marshal vehicles slowed, unable to follow. The transport trucks coming from the south had stopped along the highway.

Twenty more Marshal vehicles and trucks approached from the north, followed by five helicopters. Bray felt the helicopter blades thumping in her chest, but that could have been the thumping of a thousand hearts beating within her, linked through her implant.

Bray, somehow, had linked, not to one human, but to hundreds. Not to one animal, but to all.

This linking allowed Bray to shift her awareness back to Kage, Mateo, Tim and the protest groups throughout the nation. She hung above them all, gazing down with a consciousness as wide as the world, and she watched without concern as Marshals and citizens collided, as Marshals brought force down upon the people, with billy clubs and tear gas and gripping hands. Bray watched and waited. At any moment, the timing would align, and she would act.

#

Bray had been walking for hours. Hovering outside her body, she could feel the physical sensation of pain while remaining detached from it. As much as she felt the sun burning her skin, the wind scratching at her face and her legs trembling beneath her body, none of it mattered.

The unit of farmed animals that had crossed into Wyoming from the south converged with yet another band of animals coming from the Dakotas, Montana and Idaho. Now numbering into the thousands, the animals traveled alongside the Wyoming range. Helicopters were upon them, within shooting range. A new series of Marshal vehicles sped down Wyoming 120-East, the highway clear of civilian vehicles.

It was time.

Bray shifted her attention downward to the city marches, the protestors and the Marshals there. She dropped down, down, down. As she did, a pain surfaced in her head space, as if she were diving into water and sinking while holding her breath. Her consciousness flew down into the streets, and the shakiness of it made her stomach flip. Her body was failing, but she needed it in order to do what she had to do. Practicing some deep breathing, she pushed her breath outward, pushed it into the spaces of her body that experienced pain.

The animals began to slow. Their bodies, too, were wearing thin.

Bray felt them falter. Her feet stumbled. She caught herself, corrected, and continued walking. She rubbed her hands together fiercely, creating heat, and pushed her hands outward in the direction of the animals. The heat traveled and wrapped itself around the animals, passing through their skin and into their blood, healing and giving them the strength to carry on.

Bray was growing increasingly exhausted. The dizziness caused her to lose her footing again. Because she was walking on flat ground, she was able to catch herself again. She wanted to stop, to rest. But if she did, everything else that was happening might stop as well.

The Marshals were fifty miles from the animals, thirsty for blood. Transport trucks barreled along the highway. Marshals in copters with rifles loaded and ready to shoot awaited the moment when the animals would come into view.

#

In this moment, when Bray felt she might have nothing left, unsure she could push through, but knowing that she *had* to, she summoned that last bit of strength and came down to earth, beginning at the farthest stretches of the nation, in Washington, D.C.

Her body still stumbled along the terrain of Wyoming. Her awareness, in D.C., latched onto a random citizen with an implant. His name was Tim Saffi, and she knew him because she'd heard his voice in prison, before they injected her with medication.

He was a young, attractive man with short, blonde hair and large, brown eyes. He had stopped in the street as the marching crowd approached a line of Marshals blocking their procession to the White House. Bray sensed the tension in the air, and, before it could escalate, she dropped into Tim's consciousness by way of his implant. She received an instant download of his memories. They flooded into

her like water from a cold shower. Harsh
and refreshing. Bray focused her attention
him, and he remained in place.

She held Tim's consciousness in the
palm of one hand while she used the other
to reach into the nearest Marshal. When she
felt the energy of the two of them within
her palms, she brought her hands together,
and in this way, she *linked* them.

From afar, she sensed the urgency of
the farm animals running alongside the
mountains, aware that at any moment, the
Marshals hovering in the helicopter above
them would shoot. Bray lifted her hands
into the air. Connecting with one of the
cows leading the pack, she melded the cow's
consciousness with Tim and the Marshal in
D.C.

Bray's head began to pound. The linking
became so powerful that her body struggled
to contain it. In that instant, she lost
her eyesight.

Chapter Forty

Tim

Washington, D.C.

Tim stood, frozen. He watched as the Marshals blocked the road, their bodies hiding behind tall riot shields. This show of force was ridiculous, but he was not surprised. What surprised him was that he could not move. Oddly enough, it felt as though he'd been hijacked. It reminded him of what he'd heard some people had experienced during the Embedicare takeover. Those with 4D implants had, for a few minutes, been frozen in place, experiencing the slaughter of cows. He had witnessed it happen to someone on the subway. He thought they'd been having a stroke.

And now it was happening to him.

A smooth, warm sensation coursed through his blood. It felt. . .*good*. It felt like the warmth of tea in winter. His eyes were open and everything around him went black. Not as if the sun had gone out, but as if his eyes were closed. Against a dark screen like the back of his eyelids, he watched the life of a man he did not recognize. A man by the name of Steve who'd grown up in Woodland and had watched his mother overdose on drugs as a small child.

Tim was confused. How was he seeing this? Like watching a film of someone else's life. Suddenly, the comfort coursing

through his bloodstream rose to his brain.
His consciousness shifted, and no longer
was he Tim Saffi, but now he was some guy
named Steve, and he was no longer standing
across from the Marshals. He was standing
across from the protestors.

He was standing. . .across from
himself??

He was experiencing the Marshal's life,
and it was not pleasant.

He made eye contact with himself.

No, wait—with this guy Tim, the one
standing across from him. His head felt
split and his stomach turned. If this was
another Embedicare takeover, he was going
to—

Suddenly, as Steve, he saw into the
life of Tim, a young man scared to death of
climate change. Scared to death his parents
would die as a result of it. Steve was Tim
and Tim was Steve. Gradually their beings
melded together so finely it was hard to
separate.

The shared consciousness of Tim and
Steve shifted to a view of stunning
mountains and a broad range of open land.
Miles and miles of clouded sky with a sun
that dropped brilliant, milky light onto
the earth. A sensation of running and
pounding feet. A sensation of sore muscles,
back pain and stinging body sores. Three
hundred pounds of weight, running like
they'd never run before.

Looking up, they saw a Marshal in a
helicopter, and he was pointing a rifle in
their direction. They turned to see cows
running beside them. They realized they
were, as with the Embedicare takeover,
experiencing the sensations of the cows.
They felt no sorrow. No pain or suffering.
The Marshal shot a cow beside them, and its
body fell backward, trampled by a number of

cows behind it.

     But they kept going. A beating in their heart kept them moving forward, not only for themselves but for the hundreds of animals that followed. They were carried by a feeling of pure aliveness unlike what any of them had felt before. Not Tim, not Steve, not the cows. Feelings of ecstasy and deep vulnerability. The sense that, at any moment, the pure beauty of it might break them into pieces, for this level of joy was not something they had ever experienced and they did not know how to feel.

Chapter Forty-One

Bray

In these final moments, Bray lost all sense of her own reality. Any perception of her "self," that she had a self, was gone, replaced by the single consciousness of everyone everywhere-finally sensing the pure knowledge that separation did not exist. That separateness was an illusion.

"I am nothing. . .". With her body's eyesight gone and the vision behind her eyes seeing only a vastness and mystery that could not possibly be explained, she began again. Losing sense of her feet, which had stumbled up a hill, the consciousness that was Bray combed through the nation, linking one citizen with another, in city after city, Marshals with protestors, humans with animals.

Her nose had begun to bleed. Her hearing went. The body that was hers began to sway, stumbling this way and that, until it rolled down the hill it had just climbed, hitting rock and stone and tumbling into sagebrush.

When her body reached level ground, she hit a boulder and lay there.

"Send. . .help," she called, and went unconscious.

Chapter Forty-Two

Mateo

Houston, Texas

What Mateo experienced, and what his girlfriend Mandi equally experienced, as she would describe to him after it was over, was a sensation of running from prison. Mateo had never been locked up, but his brother had, many times, and this felt like what his brother described as a genuine gratitude for something as simple and as sacred as freedom. A freedom, his brother had said, most everyone took for granted.

Instead of prison, Mateo realized after the fact, what he experienced through his Embedicare implant was the escape of an animal from a factory farm. A sow, to be exact. Age four, nearing slaughter, the sow had explained to him. She had no name, but as she was running along the prairie of Wyoming, advancing toward her freedom and witnessing the open sky for the first time, she told him of her life. What she wanted Mateo to understand, more than anything, was that she'd never known the feeling of grass or the scent of fresh air. That, before this, in all her four years, she hadn't known what it was to be able to walk, much less run.

Through the sow's experiences, Mateo began to feel as if he were the sow, a

feeling similar to when he first met Mandi.
It was a feeling of elation. Of finding
love and getting to experience it every
day. Mateo understood then that he had this
freedom on the simple basis that he was
born human.

He understood that, being human, he'd
had something others did not have. And that
this was unequal, and unfair. That when it
came down to it, in those brief moments
when he'd experienced the feelings and the
life of a pig-of all things, a goddamn pig-
he'd come to know himself in her. He'd come
to know that all feelings were the same.

Chapter Forty-Three

Elisha

Cincinnati, Ohio

Elisha's mouth began to water with desire. What she longed for was what she was seeing on that screen. Not having an implant, she could not feel what was happening, but she could see it, and what she saw was a mass exodus the likes of which her mind simply could not fathom. Overwhelmed by the magnitude of it, she began to cry.

Something squeezed her left shoulder. She jumped. Turning quickly, she faced an old friend. Wearing a sun hat, an ankle-length, flowered skirt and a retro Animal Rights Movement t-shirt, was Steph. Beside her, Dek was staring up at the screen, grinning like a child.

"Can you believe this?" Steph cried. Her voice was loud over the hush of the hundreds of people in the streets. The Marshals lining the sidewalk hadn't even made a move.

Elisha looked around at the citizens, many of them as still as the statue behind her, others staring up at the screen, and she realized it was happening again. This must've been what the Embedicare takeover was like, but without violence or slaughter.

"Elisha," Steph whispered into her ear.

Elisha glanced over at her and then past her. Behind Steph, in a black hoodie and baggie pants, was Emerson. *Emerson!*

Elisha's face lit up. Tears filled her eyes. She went to him and they hugged. She knew what it must've taken for him to come here, to come out of hiding, reveal himself, and be open to the world around him.

Finally, everything was coming together.

Chapter Forty-Four

Kage

One of the only things Kage wanted in life, before his parents had disappeared, was to transition into the man he knew he was. Having never had the chance to start hormone therapy, to have gender-affirming surgeries, was a kind of prison for him. And so, as he grew into his twenties, a vegan all of his life, he deeply sympathized with animals confined in factory farms. He often wondered if what they felt might be similar to his own entrapment. His sense of disconnection from himself. The inability for him to live his life authentically because his body was not in alignment with his identity. The freedom he had wanted for himself was what he also wanted for all animals.

Now he marched among three hundred strangers who, the longer they walked, had become like extensions of himself. By the time they arrived at the Denver S-Corp offices, Kage felt a strong kinship with these people, most whose names he would never come to know.

The S-Corp building looked the same as it had when he'd last seen it, only a few months back when he'd come looking for Dianna Hoffman. What a mistake that had ended up being.

Today, instead of facing a glass structure in a barren parking lot, the mass of marchers stopped before a line of

Marshals in riot gear. Kage was immediately angered by this, even though he'd expected it.

Cole, leading the pack, stopped them one hundred feet from the Marshals, who were blocking the entrance of the building, holding billy clubs and riot shields. Kage felt he was going to war.

Cole turned and faced the marchers. Standing several rows back, Kage could only see the top of Cole's head above the crowd. Emily, Elliott and Lana were scattered throughout the crowd, Trevor right beside him.

Cole's voice lifted above the crowd through a megaphone.

"We are here to demand answers from S-Corp!" he began.

The crowd jeered in response.

"We are here to demand the release of all animal and environmental activists from Arizona Correctional!"

"Here, here!"

"We are here to demand answers to the loss of Ruben Sanchez, who died in custody. And to demand a return to sustainability for our climate, for our people!"

More jeering.

Kage's chest lifted. He turned and looked at Trevor. Trevor winked at him. Kage smiled. There was a feeling of raw power exuding from the crowd, a feeling that entered into Kage's bloodstream and made him feel more alive.

Suddenly, people around him froze and fell silent. Something was wrong, he could tell by the way a couple of people to his right had dropped their signs, the cardboard landing hard on the ground, as they stared down at their forearms.

"What's going on?" Lana whispered. She had come up behind Kage. He could feel her breath on his neck.

Cole had stopped speaking. Kage stood on tiptoe, but he could not see Cole.

"I'm going to check," Kage replied, and he pushed himself through to the front of the crowd. People around him began whispering and talking to each other, seemingly distracted. Most of them were looking at their forearms. Kage knew enough about the Embedicare implants to realize that they were looking at the screen on their arms.

Kage didn't have an implant.

By the time he reached Cole, the megaphone was on the ground. Behind Cole, the Marshals, too, were all distracted by whatever it was they were seeing on their forearms. Under any other circumstance, this would have been the time to storm the S-Corp facility and demand what they'd come for.

But something was not right. He wished he had an implant, just to see what was going on.

Kage hurried up to Cole, whose head was bent downward, his eyes watching something in complete awe, his mouth agape, eyes unblinking.

"Cole, are you okay?"

"Shh," Cole replied, raising a finger at Kage.

Kage did not move. He waited. . .for what? Half the people behind him were confused and bickering. The others, in complete silence. In that moment he remembered that Bray had chosen to remain behind. She had said something vague about having something of her own to attend to.

Was this it? Had she found some other way to connect to people, something that didn't require Elliott there to help her?

No. . .that made no sense. She would

have told him. *Wouldn't she?*

Suddenly, Cole went down to his knees. Worried, Kage dropped down before him, placing his hand on Cole's shoulder.

"What's wrong?" he asked.

Cole gave no response. Instead, his eyes remained transfixed on his arm, where all Kage could see was white skin. Kage looked into the man's face and saw that he was crying. But he did not appear sad. His lips formed into a pure smile. He seemed. . .happy.

The Marshals began to scuffle in their places. Kage glanced up and watched as they began to disperse, some of them sitting on the ground, no longer paying attention to the gathering they had come to confront.

Kage turned and searched the crowd for Trevor, Lana, some recognizable face. He wasn't sure whether to panic. Confusion seemed to be the dominant expression among those without implants, many of whom were looking to Kage for some kind of answer.

Kage grabbed the megaphone and pressed the button.

"Everyone, it's going to be okay," he said. "I don't know what's happening, but-"

"Over here!" someone yelled from the left. "Come see!"

Kage set the megaphone down beside Cole and ran in the direction of the voice. Lana met up with him, along with Trevor, and they started toward a young man who was waving them over.

The man, no older than Kage, was sitting on the ground, facing a laptop. Kage bent down beside him. Lana did the same. Trevor remained standing behind the young man, who lifted the laptop screen so everyone around could see.

The screen displayed a video of farmed animals running through prairies.

"What is this?" Kage asked the young man.

"Bray Hoffman," he replied, smiling. "She's doing it!"

"Doing what?" Trevor asked, his arms crossed.

"She, she set them free. Somehow these animals got free from factory farms. They're migrating, they're headed west!"

"Would you look at that!" Lana said quietly, her eyes wide, taking in the images on the screen.

Kage couldn't believe it. How had all those animals just. . . gotten free? No S-Corp facility would have allowed this.

Suddenly Kage heard the sound of people wailing. He glanced up past Cole, past the Marshals, where the doors of the S-Corp building were now open and people were coming out, falling to their knees in the parking lot, crying, sobbing.

"What in the world?" Kage whispered.

"She's doing it," Lana said.

"Doing what?" Kage was befuddled.

As Kage watched the images on the laptop screen, animals running freely along the prairies, and he looked at the people around him who had implants and seemed to be feeling that same burst of freedom and joy and absolute expansion, he began to feel it, too. Through pure osmosis, Kage felt an electric surge run through his bloodstream. The feeling became so strong that he sat himself down on the concrete, no longer able to look at the powerful images on the screen, and he felt tears coming to his eyes. He couldn't understand how this was happening, but he knew somehow Bray was responsible, like she had unleashed a force, an energy powered with freedom and love that was shared among protesters, S-Corp workers and Marshals alike, and it was magical. Even Trevor had come to sit beside him, and he was watching the screen in a daze. Lana was laughing. In the distance, Kage met eyes with Emily. She was standing beside a pregnant woman, helping hold the woman up so she would not fall down. Emily smiled at Kage in a way that made him shake. He felt so open, like his insides were being revealed to the entire world and the world accepted them completely, accepted *him*, completely.

In those moments he got a brief taste of what it was to be free.

#

Kage and the others returned to the Red Lodge apartment the next day. He pushed through the front door with exuberance and exhaustion. He had to see Bray. His heart racing for concern and awe for his friend, he called out for her, fully expecting her to be in Elliott's bedroom where they'd left her.

"Bray?" Kage yelled. He was standing in the living room, pulling off his boots and letting them drop hard to the floor.

Cole, Emily and Trevor entered behind him, talking and quickly taking respite at the kitchen table and on the living room couch.

Elliott and Lana entered last, the door shutting behind them.

Kage hadn't heard any response from Bray. Her shoes were missing.

"Bray?" he called again.

Walking down the hallway, he saw the bathroom door was open, the room empty. He approached the bedroom, its door opening to an empty, made bed.

Kage entered and stood there, still. Lana came up behind him and stopped.

"Where is she?" Lana asked.

Kage's eyes widened.

"It was real, wasn't it?" Kage asked under his breath. His eyes remained stuck on the empty bed. He'd thought for sure Bray would be resting there.

"What?" Lana asked.

"That migration of animals. My mind wasn't making that up."

"No," Lana said, smiling broadly. "That was Bray."

Kage turned, hurried past Lana back to the living room.

"Bray's missing," he said at once.

Everyone had been talking, Trevor prepping food in the kitchen. He stopped and looked up at Kage. Cole stood up from his place on the couch.

Kage ran over and grabbed his boots.

"You're not going back out there?" Trevor asked.

"What else am I supposed to do? We have to find Bray," Kage responded, both panicked and annoyed.

"I'll come with you," Cole said, stepping over to the door.

"I'm coming," Elliott added. "But where would she have gone?"

The three of them started for the door.

"Wait!" Emily called out. "Stop!"

Kage stopped. He turned back and looked at her. Emily had been sitting at the kitchen table. Her eyes were closed.

"What is it?" Kage asked. He didn't feel like he could wait.

"Quiet," Emily replied, raising her forefinger in the air.

Kage stood there by the door, hand on the door handle, sore feet aching in his boots. He wanted her to hurry. He worried for his friend.

"I'm getting something. . .Bray's trying to tell me. . .s. . ." Emily's voice trailed off. "*Send. . .help.*"

"Send help?" Cole asked, walking over to Emily. "Can you ask her where she is?"

Emily raised her finger into the air again, commanding the room to silence. Kage watched her while his head boiled with fear. Why had Bray left? Why couldn't she have done what she needed to do from the safety of this place? He knew from experience what happened when Bray linked herself to animals. It depleted her. She hadn't even recovered from being in prison and practically starving herself there. What he'd seen on that screen yesterday surpassed anything she had done before, even the Embedicare takeover. What must it have done to her to bring marchers and Marshals and S-Corp workers for god's sake- into some kind of shared energy and compassion for each other and for the animals running free?

"No," Emily replied. Her hand dropped to her lap. "She's unconscious."

"Oh, no. Not again," Elliott groaned.

"But I see something," Emily added. Her eyebrows rose. Her lips parted and her mouth formed into a gape. "Oh my. . .she's, she's just outside Meeteetse."

"What!" Kage blurted. "How is that possible?"

"Are you sure?" Cole asked.

Emily's eyes opened. She looked to Kage and shrugged.

"I saw what was left of the house. The garden," Emily replied, with sorrow. "You're right, Kage. Our home was destroyed." Emily paused. "Bray fell down, only a mile from the house."

Kage realized in that moment that he was never going to understand how Bray did what she could do, this gift of hers. His chest lifted. What he did understand was that something had happened to him, something *changed* him, because of knowing Bray. Like the hundreds of farmed animals he'd seen running free on that laptop screen yesterday, he had come to feel a sense of peace unlike anything he'd felt before. Because of Bray. Bray had become his family.

He hurried out the door with Cole, Elliott and Lana. When he stepped up into the driver's seat in the truck and shut the door, the silence in the cab was palpable, and in the best way possible. It was as though they had all felt the world change, and they had Bray to thank.

And thank her, he would.

Chapter Forty-Five

Bray

Tha-dump. . .Tha-dump. . .tha-dump. . .
Tha-da-da-da-dump. . .Tha-da-da-da-dump. . .

The ground shook. Dry earth of summer, bending beneath hooves. Muscles churning. Wild manes of gold and ebony and sand-brown whipping through the Wyoming air. Heavy breathing. Running at forty miles an hour, out toward the Wyoming range.

There, a band of wild horses split off, twenty of them running with power toward the migrating animals. Two horses broke away, eastern bound, in the direction of Casper.

The band of horses surrounded the farmed animals. Gradually, they guided the animals away from the mountains, their hooves digging hard into the ground, kicking up dirt and rock in their wake.

The farmed animals followed, tired, consumed with hunger and thirst. The energy of the horses pushing in and around them gave them fresh life. The horses steered them, turning, turning, bending toward the east.

The two horses that had split off from the band raced along the hillsides, across Wyoming 120 East, and came to a slow trot. There lay Bray, her breath weak, eyes open and blank. Unconscious.

One horse came down onto its knees. The

other used its snout to push Bray's body up and onto the other horse's back. She lay there, stomach against mane, as her arms and legs hung over either side of the horse's torso.

"*Hold on*," a voice coaxed.

Her hands clenched the horse's mane in response.

The horse rose.

Together, the two horses hurried southwest, toward the migrating farm animals. Along the horizon, the band of horses approached, hundreds of farmed animals following. Bray still lay across one of the horse's backs, barely holding on. The sun approached the land as day fell toward night. The color of its rays, brilliant yellow mixed with subtle gold, cast upon the earth a glow of power and magic.

In a field below hills, the horses and farm animals gathered. The farmed animals were made to lie down and rest, the chickens landing softly in the grass, pecking and chirping. Bray was laid to rest beside the cows. The two horses that had found her remained lying beside her, close enough that the heat emanating from their bodies radiated toward Bray, keeping her warm.

Meanwhile, a group of wild horses set off north along the highway. A cavalcade of Marshal vehicles was approaching. The screens inside their vehicles had gone blank, and the Marshals' implants vibrated an alert instructing them to pull back.

Some things were beyond explanation.

As the horses raced toward the vehicles, the remaining light of the sun gleamed on their fur from the south, its rays warming them with the last bit of daylight. The sky, free of clouds, gave the

sun one last chance to display itself. The
sun gave its all, as if a dying mother
holding on for her final breath in time to
say goodbye to her child. Its rays flew at
the windshields of the Marshal vehicles,
temporarily blinding the drivers.
Simultaneously, the Marshals hit their
brakes, screeching to a stop, dust hurtling
up behind them. Sitting in their cars,
astonished and awe-struck, the Marshals
watched as the horses blocked the highway,
barricading the way south.

From her place between human
consciousness and the heavens, between wake
and sleep, between worlds, Bray watched.
She knew what was happening, because she
had become the source of it.

She had become the catalyst.

Chapter Forty-Six

Bertan

Bertan stood staring at the gate for the longest time. It was late afternoon. The sun twinkled behind the branches of a mango tree in Alex's backyard. Alex, Carmen's cousin. It had taken Bertan thirty-two hours by bus from Mexico City, with an overnight stay in Guatemala City's bus terminal. The trip had been more effortless than he could ever have imagined. Now, he hesitated, waiting for something to change or for someone to come get him and remind him this was a dream, that he was still in prison. The life he had lived in the U.S. seemed a far cry from where he was today. Not just physically, but mentally. Emotionally. *Spiritually*. Ten years of being lost. He closed his eyes. The sounds of his home. . .the slow song of the thrush, the distant bass from someone's car, and the unmistakable sound of freedom. Of life.

Bertan began to tear up. Strangely, he did not feel afraid. For ten years he had believed that if he returned to Honduras, Medina would be after him in a heartbeat. But now, he could see how wrong that was. How much he had lived in fear while doing that horrific job for S-Corp. He couldn't see it then, the way the job knocking beefs had pounded into him the nasty, cruel ways of this world, reminding him every day of

the horrible things he had done for Medina.
For years he had allowed this to happen.
Now it was time to start over.

"God. . .let this be real," he
whispered.

Walking up to the gate, he pushed the
buzzer.

Alex stepped out through a door on the
side of the house and saw him. Ten years
older than when Bertan had last seen him,
Alex was a stout, heavy-set man in his late
twenties, with cheeks that always looked
full with food, which charmed Bertan
because Alex loved food. He had soft, hazel
eyes that lit up beneath a head of thick,
black, cropped hair. Bertan's eyes wavered
and he began to tremble.

Alex stood there, his mouth opening
slowly.

"Bertan?" Alex said under his breath.

Bertan approached the gate. He grabbed
one of the steel rungs and held onto it.

"*Sí*, cousin. It's me."

Alex dashed inside, disappearing from
view. The sun popped through the mango
tree, leaving a shadow of the tree's
branches on the concrete. Bertan's eyes
followed the shadow over to the door, his
heart pounding through his rib cage, like
the sun through the leaves, awaiting
Carmen.

He felt himself beginning to
hyperventilate.

"Deep breaths," he said to himself, his
heart stinging at the memory of Ruben.
Those had been Ruben's words.

And then, through the side door, Carmen
appeared. She was holding a dish towel.
When she saw him, the towel fell to the
ground. The gate rolled open. Bertan walked
toward her. She shook, trembled, began to
wail.

Bertan ran over and took her up into his arms. Carmen cried, squeezed him around his torso. He felt her trembling and, in response, let himself cry.

"I thought you were dead," she said, her head close to his heart.

"No, *mi amor*. I am here."

"*Papá?!*"

"Gabriella?" Bertan yelled, hearing her voice coming from inside the house.

Her feet clapped against tile floor. A moment later, he glanced up from Carmen and saw his daughter standing still, her hands holding onto the doorframe. She had grown so much. As tall as Bertan. Her hair was longer, cascading over her shoulders.

Bertan waved her over. She let go of the doorframe and in a few steps was at Bertan's side, grasping him and Carmen together. Bertan cried harder than he knew he could.

#

Bertan spent the remaining day holding his family. Carmen sat on one side, Gabriella curled up against him on the other. Alex's couch seemed to hold them together as if they'd never been apart. The warmth exuding from their embrace shook Bertan. He cried and hugged and squeezed them and laughed.

"You look so old, *Papá*," Gabriella said.

"And you look so beautiful," he replied, his smile so wide it hurt his face.

Bertan glanced around the room. The concrete, white walls held framed photos of Alex's family, one of them a photo of Carmen holding Gabriella as a baby. Bertan thought back. How many years, lifetimes and sufferings had come and gone since his child was born? He noticed the age on

Carmen's face, added wrinkles and a narrow scar jutting down from beneath her earlobe to the start of her neck—something he hadn't noticed before but was not going to ask about. Not in this moment, when all that mattered was rekindling what he'd lost by leaving his family so long ago.

In the kitchen, Alex prepared a meal of rice, tortillas and fried *platanos*. The scent of their sweetness carried into the living room, and Bertan's mouth watered. The simple smell of Honduran food, the scents of home, added to his tears.

"Did you do what you needed to do?" Carmen asked him.

Bertan looked down into Carmen's eyes. He thought about the times they had talked on the phone and he told her there was something he had to do before he could come home, he had to end S-Corp, which could also end Medina because they were the same. He felt the heaviness of Gabriella's head resting on his shoulder. He thought about Bray and the gift she had given him. Something caught his eye from the hallway opposite the living room. A shadow of the mango tree dancing against the walls, peering in through a side window. The shadow took the shape of a hand, as if waving. This made him think about the time his father had visited him, had told him to end Medina. As he sat here with his family, one thing kept coming to mind:

He *had* ended them.

He ended his *fear* of them. Their *power over* him. What grew in the place of this fear was the love he had for his family, which he suddenly realized had always been there, only hidden beneath the depths of fear and anger and self-degradation. That love was stronger than any fear he'd experienced in the United States, and

stronger than the fear that had made him
flee Honduras in the first place. Medina
could not touch him, not today, not ever.

"I did," he replied. "I came home."

The best revolution for him, after all,
was to choose to live a life of peace, and
to love his family while he could.

Chapter Forty-Seven

Bray

Dusk fell over the land, covering the farmed animals and horses in a faint dusting of cool lavender and indigo. The sun touched the horizon with white, golden light, providing one last moment of luminosity before the moon and the stars took stage.

The horses lay in a circle around the farmed animals. Bray lay motionless on her back. Inside, a faint beat approached her chest, subtle, rhythmic, constant. She became aware of a rise and a fall in her belly. Her toes moved. Her fingers wiggled.

Her eyes opened. At least, she felt the physical sensation of her eyelids blinking and opening. What she saw was not what she'd expected, and yet she was not surprised. It was dark. Above, and from the corners of her eyes, she saw nothing but darkness. Her ears picked up the sounds of animals grazing on grass, of hooves pressing into earth. The clucking of chickens. Bodies rolling around in dirt, probably the pigs.

Bray carefully brought herself up to sitting. Looking around, her eyes picked up vague colors of deep blue mixed with black. Where there were horses or other animals, she saw only outlines of steel gray in clumps and in groups.

Bray had gone blind. She was too tired, weak and frankly unconcerned with her body to care that she couldn't see. The only thing that mattered involved sitting here and being with these animals.

Against her back she felt a sudden, hard pressure. She felt a rise and a fall of a heavy body. One of the horses had rolled onto its side behind her.

"*Rest, child*," she said.

Bray leaned back, allowed herself to use the horse's body for support.

She closed her eyes and listened. Around her she heard insects that came out only at night, their vibrations dancing near and far in distance. She could hear her heart beat softly and without restraint or concern. When she focused her attention on the animals, she could hear some of them sleeping.

In that moment, knowing the animals felt secure enough to fall to slumber beneath the stars, tears rolled down from her eyes. She allowed her emotions to run free, unrestricted and without resistance. She cried and cried, and laughed and smiled.

Eventually, she passed back into sleep.

#

Dawn arrived with a nudge to Bray's side. She'd been sleeping on her back, her mouth open and body in deep rest unlike any she'd ever known. The nudge came a second time. Bray turned toward it. She slowly opened her eyes and saw there a movement of subtle alabaster light against darkness. Something wet nudged her neck. There was a grunt and a brush of hot air against her cheek. Bray lifted her hand and felt the muzzle of a horse, its hair equally coarse and soft.

Bray sensed a group of horses come to surround her, their bodies radiating a warm energy like a bubble around her body in the cold, early morning.

"*If you are well, we must carry on,*"
was the message that traveled from the
horses' awareness into hers.

"Then carry on, you shall." She smiled
in response.

Bray listened as the horses picked up
their hooves, running off like pounding
drums. The drumming sound faded gradually,
until it was gone. Bray took a deep breath.
Something had departed from her, but in a
way that nothing was lost.

Coming onto her hands and knees, Bray
crawled over to a group of animals, their
bodies revealed as alabaster against the
darkness, similar to the horses. Their
bodies were still. When she neared one, an
adult sow that had been lying on its side,
she reached out and felt its belly. She sat
and rubbed it, smiling as she thought of
Alice.

The sound of a vehicle approached in
the distance. Bray closed her eyes and
listened more intently. The engine did not
sound heavy and mechanic like a truck.
There were no sirens. She had nowhere to
run, and she wasn't going to leave the
animals, so she hoped it was a passerby.

Suddenly she heard wheels crunching in
earth. The engine stopped, which meant the
vehicle had stopped. Her heart went as
still as her body. A warmth hit her side,
indicating the sun was beginning to rise.
If this was a Marshal, there was not much
she could do about it. But something told
her she was safe, that drones had not
followed her here.

"Bray!" came a yell, masculine,
distinct.

Bray's heart lifted at the sound. She
smiled, let out a moan. She opened her eyes
with the hope that maybe she'd be able to

see, that she wasn't actually blind. But what she saw was a deep indigo and subtle, dark shapes growing larger in front of her.

"Bray," Elliott called. "Are you okay?"

She heard him come close. His feet against the ground. The feel of his racing breath against her arm. She reached out for him and a hand grabbed hers, coarse and warm.

A series of footsteps followed. They stopped. Bray felt the energy of others around her. Not the animals, who had been sleeping and seemed to have woken in the commotion. She heard familiar voices, all four of them she could name. Kage, Lana, Elliott and her father, who took Bray into his arms.

"Oh my God," he said. "You're safe."

Cole began to shake and cry. He squeezed her into his chest. Bray took it in, allowed herself to be held by her father. For once, she felt his love, and it felt like the closest thing to a home she'd come to know, like those days on the land in Meeteetse where she could wake in the mornings and hear the whistling of trees outside. Where it was so quiet and peaceful she could sit all day staring at the sky.

"What the hell are you doing all the way out here?" That voice was Kage. Bray sensed him standing above her, perhaps looking down.

None of them seemed to notice she could not see. At least, not yet.

Bray pulled away from Cole. She looked up in the direction of Kage's voice.

"I did what I came to do," Bray replied simply. She knew that none of what had happened could ever be explained. It wasn't to be spoken of, for it was hers and not hers. It was the will of something *bigger*. Something better.

"Did you walk all the way here?" asked Cole, who placed his hand on her leg. When he did, she felt a slight pain and remembered that yes, she had walked all the way here, wherever here was.

"I don't know where here is, but yes."

There was a silence, followed by Lana's voice.

"Bray," she said. "We're just outside Meeteetse. It would take an entire day to walk here from Red Lodge."

Bray listened, and again, could not explain. She sat there, feeling the air, feeling the sun rising slowly. She wanted to see her friends' faces, but at least she had them committed to memory. The shapes and dim colors of bodies surrounding her- human and animal alike-only solidified the truth she had recently come to know: that everyone was the same stuff, that there was no separation. That all the suffering she had come to witness, animal and human alike, was because people saw too much separation, too much difference, not looking closely enough at likeness of all being.

"I know it doesn't make sense," she replied. "But why is that important? Look at all the animals that were set free." Bray pointed toward the nearest sound of cows chewing grass.

"It's extraordinary," Lana replied, her breath falling out with her words. Bray listened as feet moved in the direction of the grazing cows.

"How on earth?" Kage asked, his voice trailing off.

"I was able to connect with everyone through the implants." Bray reached for Cole's hand and held onto it for support. She came up onto her knees. She spoke freely. "But that's not all. It was like

I. . .became a part of something bigger. Like maybe there is some higher power or source we are all a part of, and that because we think we're separate from one another, we cause each other all this pain and suffering. I felt myself rise above all of that, and what came together was some *power*, some *ability* to free these animals and to make citizens feel what that freedom was like. So maybe they'd want it for themselves."

Elliott stood up. He remained beside her. She could feel his energy. And she sensed what he was feeling: confused, baffled, unsure.

"You don't have to believe me for it to be true."

"I believe you," Cole said.

Bray smiled widely. Her heart expanded. The indigo color she saw began to lighten, perhaps with the coming of the day. Everything was still cloudy. She suspected that the experience with the implants had made her permanently blind, and she found that it did not sadden her. It was what was happening, and she found herself complete in it.

Then, ever so gradually, in her periphery, a clouded image took the form of a sow she had once called her friend. It was the only thing Bray could see, and she could see it because it was not real. It was the ghost of old Alice, her eyes aged and full and her ears raised to the sky.

"*Now you can go be free, my child*," Alice's voice echoed through Bray's mind. When she heard it, a tear rolled from her eye. She felt its salty, warm drop tickle her cheek. She giggled.

"What is it?" Cole asked, sitting beside her.

Alice's image transitioned. Gradually,

the round shape of her body elongated. The
vivid color of pink softened to white
splotched with black. Her snout changed.
Her ears lengthened and flopped to either
side of her head as she took the shape of a
cow.

It was Rhea, sitting not far from a
cluster of dark gray blotches, which Bray
gathered were other cows.

"Rhea!" Bray whispered.

Transfixed by the image, Bray laughed.

"Who?" Cole asked.

"Nothing, just a passing thought," she
said.

"I think we need to get you back, to
get checked out," Cole commented, his hand
rubbing her back. "Something
seems. . .off."

"Cole," Elliott whispered. "Can you
come over here a moment?"

The two of them stepped away. As they
did, Rhea looked deeply at Bray, her eyes
wide and full. She said nothing, only sat
in complete peace. Bray looked upon her for
as long as she could, grateful she could
see her friend. That she could *see*
something.

She heard Elliott whisper to Cole about
how she might be blind. That it didn't seem
like she could see them. Bray let it be.
She kept her focus on Rhea.

A moment later, Elliott and Cole
returned, followed by Kage and Lana. Bray
felt the four of them kneel down beside
her.

Bray's attention was focused on the
image before her, but it began to fade. As
it did, two images took its place and then
took shape as humans. Gradually, they
presented as people she had known. Ethan,
tall, a full white beard, that tattoo on
his head. She could only make out his head

and face. The rest was clouded blue against indigo. Beside him, shorter and with the same blue body, the face of Ruben smiled at Bray.

Simultaneously, Ethan and Ruben nodded to her. She nodded back, crying fully. Her heart felt like it might implode inside her body, it had grown to a capacity she could barely manage. Her heart was full, encompassing all that had happened.

She waved in their direction, and they were gone.

Everything around her had fallen into a cobalt color, which reminded her of the color of Trevor's eyes.

"Is everyone else okay?" she asked her friends.

"Yep," Kage replied. "They're waiting for you, back in Red Lodge."

Bray smiled. She readied herself to lean against her father, to see if she could come to stand up. As she reached for him, she saw yet another image out of the corner of her eye. She turned in its direction. A white, beautiful, hazy ball of light spun toward her and came to pause beside the group of grazing cows. She could not see the cows, but she could smell them and hear them and feel their presence.

The light flipped instantly to become a clear image of a brown-skinned man wearing plain jeans and a t-shirt. He knelt down and reached his arm out, his hand resting on what Bray assumed was the stomach of one of the cows. It was Bertan, his eyes green as ever, smiling with ease. He lifted his free hand and waved to Bray.

A tear rolled slowly down her face. She smiled back.

"So," Cole broke into her concentration. "What now?"

Bray watched as Bertan nodded and then

stood up. He looked down upon her, silently.

"Are you. . .going to be with Ruben?" Bray asked him in her mind. She wasn't sure she was ready to hear that he had died, but she wanted to know what had become of this man she'd come to know so intimately.

"*No*." His voice echoed in the chambers of her mind. "*I am in Honduras with my family now.*"

And isn't that just it? she thought as she watched him fade away. He was with his family. She was here, with hers. With the animals and with her closest friends.

There was no better purpose to be had in life.

Bray finally replied to her father.

"That's for us all to decide, together."

THE END

Epilogue

One month after Bray's release from prison, the president granted more than three hundred pardons to animal activists who'd been imprisoned in Arizona Correctional. These individuals had been incarcerated, some for as long as twenty years, without court dates or plea bargains, with no access to communication with family or friends—who, like Kage Zair, had come to believe them deceased.

It was Kage and Lana who went to the airport to gather Kage's mother and, as he was shocked to find, Kage's father, Todd. With them, Lana's team members Tori, Ben, Sarah and Alex. Kage, seeing his mother and father for the first time in twelve years, broke away from Lana's hand he'd been holding and ran at them, embracing them fiercely. His parents, now thinner and aged more than he ever could've imagined, could not stop crying at the sight of their adult son.

Kage introduced his parents to Lana, affectionately referring to her as his girlfriend. Together, along with Lana's team, they returned to Meeteetse, where volunteers had traveled down from Red Lodge to assist in rebuilding the home and the lost gardens. Chad had donated the materials and extra workers to help rebuild the house, something Kage knew would have given Ethan much pride, to say the least.

Often in the mornings when Kage went out to sit with his mother and father in the yard, or when he worked alongside them to replant vegetables and marigolds, he would glance over at the hidden entrance to the cellar, and he would smile. He thought about Ethan. If only Ethan could see the

way citizens had come together after their
marches and to this day continued to work
on organizing grassroots actions for
animals, for sustainability, for the
removal of corporate control of the food
system.

Yes, Ethan would have been proud. He
would have seen Kage come into his own and
get what he had always wanted: the
reunification of family.

#

Cole Hoffman did not run for re-
election. He no longer wanted to be a
senator. The job he wanted was to be a
father to Bray. She had become legally
blind. He thought he would feel more
saddened by this, but his sadness was
lessened by her acceptance and embracing of
it. He'd never seen his daughter more at
peace. They spent hours together each day
in Meeteetse. He made sure she had all the
tools to learn Braille, as well as free
access to audiobooks, audiobook and music
players, and a specialized laptop so she
could easily communicate with her friends
and others throughout the nation.

Once she was all set up, Cole felt
freed to step away, temporarily, to pursue
a lawsuit against S-Corp. Although he
worked tirelessly with Lana and traveled to
prepare arguments and testimonies from more
than one hundred families impacted by the
fertilizer disaster over ten years ago, he
always made time for Bray.

It was clear to him that his
relationship with Bray ought to have been
his number one priority from the beginning.
It was Bray who had taught him the
importance of relationships, after all.

#

And what of the thousands of farmed
animals freed by Bray Hoffman? More than

half of them passed away in the days and weeks proceeding the march. The months and years spent in captivity were too much on their bodies. Those that survived were petitioned by U.S. citizens—from Elisha Andrews in Cincinnati to Mateo Perez in Houston, Texas—to receive amnesty and protection by the government. What was more, members of Lana's family returned to the mainland from Hawaii to organize volunteers to assist with the animals. Hundreds of thousands of dollars were raised, and eventually, the open and untapped land of southern Wyoming was designated as a farm sanctuary for hundreds of chickens, pigs and cows that had finally come to know freedom.

#

Bray Hoffman sat at a desk facing a window that looked out over the new garden. Although blind, she liked feeling the sunlight when it entered the room in the afternoons, how it felt when it grazed her arms as she sat and wrote. It reminded her she was still alive, and well. She could not see what others could. What she saw was far greater. Not colors or shapes alone, but what was *beyond*. . .the feelings and emotions and energies of people that could not be viewed by the mechanics of physical sight. On a moment by moment basis, she could feel and communicate with the farmed animals that had survived the march. And what she felt was a deep sense of expansion that often left her in tears.

Trevor and Cole had worked together to remodel the front room of the house in Meeteetse as a bedroom so Bray could remain safely on one floor. A second bathroom was erected just off the side of the kitchen, complete with an accessible shower and toilet. It had taken months to finish, and

Bray was grateful for the people who'd become such strong family for her. People who cared enough to do such things for her.

As she sat there, quietly thinking, a blank screen staring back at her, waiting for her to type, the voices of Emily and Kage bounced into the room through the open window. The air was fresh, and it grew warm as summer drew to a close.

She took a deep breath, typed the below letter, and sent it out into the ether:

An Open Letter to the Citizens of the United States:

I don't have the answers. I searched for them. I found only more confusion. My own insecurity, my own shame in being human. Knowing that because I am a part of this human race, and I see how we harm the planet and we continue to harm animals, I am a part of that. I am, quite frankly, complicit. Guilty by association.

We all are.

And so I had to learn to forgive myself. I had to forgive that I live in a world where cruelty exists. Forgiving myself led me to realize this truth: we are all the same. I had to forgive that, too. I had to come to terms with the fact that I, alone, am not gifted enough to stop every human from harming animals. And even more, that I shouldn't. . .stop people. It's not my right. I gave you the information. I showed you what goes on with these animals. I showed you what life could be like if they could be free. But then I had to let it go. This is the divine paradox: to both live in and love a world like ours. To know that some of you might decide to continue to harm animals. To not shame or judge you for it, and especially, to love you just the same.

And. . .I do.

How sad it is to be human; to know that because we are human and we have free will, there may always be suffering in this world. And maybe that's the point: can we forgive ourselves? Can we forgive the reality that we will inevitably cause harm, and can we be with ourselves anyway?

I am here, if ever you wish to talk. I'd love to connect.

Best wishes,

Bray.

ACKNOWLEDGEMENTS

We have come to the end of an eleven year journey—one filled with constant rewrites, unexpected detours, and moments of doubt, but also deep joy, connection, and purpose. It wouldn't exist without the incredible people who have walked beside me, lifted me up, and reminded me why stories matter.

First, I have to thank the Muse—God, the Universe, or whatever force it is that has given me the time, the energy, and the will to sit down in the chair, day after day, year after year, and write. That has gifted me these stories, these characters, and the creativity to see the vision through to the end. I am not much without the Muse—just a conduit producing what she sets forth. And I thank her.

To my family and friends—your unwavering belief in me, even when I struggled to believe in myself, has been a guiding light. Thank you for your patience, encouragement, and love.

To my beta readers—your keen insights, thoughtful feedback, and enthusiasm helped shape this story into what it was meant to be. You saw the heart of it even in its roughest drafts, and for that, I'm forever grateful.

To my friends Belinda Gullette for your knowledge on law, and Sharon Penko for your expertise in Transcendental Meditation, I thank you both for your time.

To my writing coach Robin and Editor, Susan—your wisdom, honesty, and expertise made this book stronger. Thank you for pushing me to dig deeper, refine my words, and trust my voice.

To the incredible supporters of my crowdfunding campaigns—this book is as much yours as it is mine. Your generosity and belief in this story made its publication possible. Thank you for standing with me, for being part of this journey, and for proving that storytelling is a collective act.

And finally, to the activists, visionaries, and everyday people working toward a more just, compassionate world— your courage and kindness inspire me endlessly. Don't give up. The world needs you.

With gratitude,

Jay.

ABOUT THE AUTHOR

Jay VanLandingham's writing explores the transformative power of empathy. Through meaningful connection, empathy can flourish, opening us to the freedom of all beings—ourselves, animals, and nature alike.

Above all things, Jay wishes for peace and serenity in his life, as well as the lives of all beings.

Jay holds a Master's degree in Social Work as well as a Bachelor in English. He is also a certified Mindfulness Meditation Teacher. In his spare time if he's not outdoors spending time in nature, he's enjoying time with friends, family, and his one-eyed cat Lucky.

Jay is based in Cincinnati, Ohio.

You Made It! Now, One Last Thing...

If you've reached this page, that means you've finished *Sentient Being*. Thank you for spending time with this story! I hope it resonated with you.

If you enjoyed the book (or even if you just have thoughts to share), **please consider leaving a review on Amazon.** Reviews help self-published authors like me **reach more readers**, **gain visibility**, and **keep telling stories that matter**.

How to Leave a Review on Amazon

1. **Go to** Amazon.com and sign in.

2. **Search for** *Sentient Being* **by Jay VanLandingham** (or find it in your order history).

3. **Scroll down to the "Customer Reviews" section** and click "Write a customer review."

4. **Give it a star rating** (5 stars makes my day, but be honest!).

5. **Write a few words** about what stood out to you — no need for anything fancy!

Even a short review, like *"Loved the characters and*

themes!" or *"This book made me think!"* goes a long way in helping others discover *Sentient Being*.

Thank you for being part of this journey. Your support means everything.